Hearts **racing**.
Blood **pumping**.
Pulses **accelerating**.

**Falling in love can be a blur...
especially at 180 mph!**

So if you crave the thrill of the chase—on and off the track—you'll love

LEGENDS AND LIES
by Katherine Garbera

"Your brother doesn't like the fact that we're dating."

"He wouldn't accuse Tucker of something just because he doesn't like you," Annie said.

"I'm not so sure about it."

"I am. I know that Dave can be overprotective when it comes to me, but the rest of the guys on his team don't care about who I date."

"You have a point," Jared said. "But I don't think that this is going to be an isolated incident. Tucker is going to be scrutinizing everything your brother does, and vice versa."

"So, where do we go from here?" she asked.

"We stick together. At the track we'll do our jobs, but in our free time...we'll be together, right?"

"Yes," she said. She'd taken a huge leap of faith by coming here today and Jared...well, Jared had proven he was worth the risk.

Dear Reader,

My son was born on February 20. Do you know what that means? If you are a race fan, you do. There was the possibility that he'd be born on a Sunday when the race in Daytona was running. And can you imagine the dilemma this presents each year when I try to plan his birthday party? Now that he's older (he's ten!) it's a little easier to pick a birthday-party venue where there will be a television tuned in to the race!

My uncle Pat used to camp in the infield every year at Daytona, and I'd be envious of him. He's a great storyteller, and when he'd return from the race he'd have the best tales of his time there...of the excitement of being so close to the race and listening to the roar of the engines.

In fact, I can't remember a time when I didn't know about NASCAR, although back then we simply called it stock-car racing. I'm so excited to be a part of Harlequin's officially licensed NASCAR series.

Check out www.katherinegarbera.com for some exciting behind-the-scenes stuff on the creation of *Legends and Lies,* as well as some research photos from the Speedway in Texas.

Happy reading!

Katherine Garbera

NASCAR

LEGENDS AND LIES

Katherine Garbera

HARLEQUIN®

TORONTO • NEW YORK • LONDON
AMSTERDAM • PARIS • SYDNEY • HAMBURG
STOCKHOLM • ATHENS • TOKYO • MILAN • MADRID
PRAGUE • WARSAW • BUDAPEST • AUCKLAND

ISBN-13: 978-0-373-21778-6
ISBN-10:   0-373-21778-1

LEGENDS AND LIES

KATHERINE GARBERA

is the award-winning, bestselling author of more than thirty-five books. She's a native Floridian whose earliest memories are of walking in front of the television set while NASCAR Sunday races played in the background. Her uncles used to race on Friday nights on tracks in the small rural towns where she once lived. Racing has always been a part of her life.

This book is for my dad, Dave Smith. I always assume that everyone has the kind of loving and caring parents I do and am shocked when I realize that they don't. I feel so blessed and fortunate to have my parents in my life. I love you, Dad.

This book is also for my sister, who is a huge race fan, and her husband—Donna and Brian Sutermeister and my five-year-old niece Emily, who likes Junior, too!

Also for the other huge NASCAR fans in my life: my grandfather Robert Wilkinson and my uncles Pat and Charles Nappi, and Dave Kane, my good friend.

CHAPTER ONE

ANNIE JENNER tried not to think about where she was or how long it had been since she'd been here. *Daytona*. Since she was a little girl it had been the start of the year for her family. Everyone else celebrated the New Year in January but for NASCAR racing fans it really started in Daytona in February.

The daughter of legendary driver Brandon Jenner and the sister of up-and-coming driver Dave Jenner, she knew the tracks better than she knew the towns that surrounded them. She'd grown up in this world and after three long years away when she'd followed her faithless husband through Europe, she was glad to be home.

She'd made a name for herself as a professional sports photographer. Her reputation had netted her a permanent job with *Sports Illustrated* but she'd taken a leave of absence to chronicle her brother this year for a book that the NASCAR publishing division was doing—*The Jenner Legend*—as well as any extra photos of NASCAR wanted. She was flattered that they asked her to take the pictures of her brother and his team.

The flag dropped. The race was on. Annie stared through the lens of her Nikon watching for the stock cars to come speeding by. She took pictures quickly, not thinking too much about the shots, confident that she knew how to get the best angle with the cars traveling at speeds of 180 miles an hour.

Suddenly, she heard a roar from the crowd. People were shouting. It was then she became aware that they were responding to a crash. She had been so busy shooting, she wasn't focusing on the reality of the action.

The crash reverberated around turn four. Shooting the event through the lens of her Nikon Annie didn't notice the car numbers at first. She was focused on the refraction of light and the crushed car body. She watched the cars spin sideways, bouncing off one another. Annie captured it all in a stop motion, her shutter clicking and her finger moving minutely.

When the cars stopped and the ones behind them had all maneuvered through the wreckage, she lifted her head and finally the number sank in. *Number 153.* Dave's car. Her brother had been involved in the crash.

Annie couldn't breathe as she waited for the medics to arrive. She'd always believed even as a little girl that nothing bad could happen to the men she loved while she watched them on the track. She felt that there would be some kind of warning signal, something deep in her gut that would let her know if her twin brother was mortally wounded.

Her hands were trembling as she dropped her camera and let the strap around her neck hold it up. Her eyes burned and she shook her head, determined not to cry. It was crisp and cool on this February Sunday. Though the sun was warm a chill moved over her.

She refused to take her eyes off his car, as if her watching him would make everything okay. The entire race track had gone quiet. Everything was blurring and she struggled to remember to breathe.

The ambulance arrived. Voices of the paramedics and firemen carried on the wind. The smell of oil and burning rubber filled the air.

There was no fire, but the firefighters all stood there just the same, ready for anything that might happen.

What was with all this waiting?

It felt as if time had slowed and each second was an hour. Her breath froze in her lungs until she saw the medics arrive at his car. Dave lifted his arms and she was close enough to the track to hear his voice. It was raised and he was cursing—but using words that wouldn't get him fined.

She felt faint as relief starting flowing through her. Dave was alive and that's what mattered. She swayed a little and couldn't catch her breath. It sawed in and out as if she was having an asthma attack, except she knew she didn't have asthma.

Oh, God, she was hyperventilating.

She felt a strong hand grip her shoulder, pushing her head down toward her knees.

"Breathe," the voice said.

She did as he directed and stayed there for a minute before standing up. She glanced over her shoulder into eyes that were darker than midnight. He had thick lashes and a strong face. Not really classically handsome. Not like her ex-husband's, but this face was memorable.

Annie shook her head to clear it. "Thanks."

"No problem. You know the driver?"

"Dave's my brother."

She really looked at the man and realized he was dressed in a pair of casual slacks that easily cost more than her entire outfit—she just wasn't a clotheshorse. He had on hand-sewn Italian leather shoes and a thick fleece jacket with the collar turned up. There was a discretely embroidered logo on the pocket—JM's Coffee House.

Immediately she knew who he was. Jared MacNeil—founder and owner of JM's Coffee House, a national coffee chain, as well as owner of the Number 186 car driven by Tucker Aldridge. She'd seen him, Jared, on one of the sports channels. He was intelligent and well-spoken when she'd seen him on television, but right now none of that really mattered.

She turned her attention back to her brother. Glancing at the wreck, she let out her breath as Dave started walking off the track. One of the medics had an arm around his shoulder and Dave lifted his hand toward the bleachers, waving to the crowd. There was a roar of approval from the fans as her brother limped away from the track.

She scarcely paid attention to anything else. Instead she focused on one thing. Getting to her brother and seeing for herself that he was okay. She wanted to hug him tightly.

Dave looked over at the other car and Annie realized that Tucker Aldridge had been the second driver in the crash. Jared stared at the track and it was hard to tell if he were only concerned because the car he owned was involved or if he was worried about Tucker's health.

As soon as Tucker pulled himself out of the car and stood next to it, Jared exhaled a deep breath.

"I'm glad they're both okay," she said.

"Or at least seem to be," he replied. "Do you still feel dizzy?"

She shook her head, a little embarrassed by her reaction to Dave's accident. "No, I'm fine."

He nodded at her and walked toward the fence. As a tow truck arrived to remove Dave's car from the track, Annie turned away and started running toward the media center. She wasn't just the sister of a driver today. She was being paid to photograph the event. They'd need to get someone else up on Turn Four because she wasn't going to be able to shoot anything worth printing until she talked to Dave.

She raced through the crowds, with their pit and garage passes, to the media center and found her contact. The photography coordinator understood that she couldn't continue until she knew her brother was okay. Annie made her way across the infield to the care center, keeping an eye out for her parents, who were probably making their way from the VIP suite that her father always rented.

Her father had been a NASCAR NEXTEL Cup champion back in the '80s and everyone—fans, drivers and crews alike—still adored him. Dave got a lot of press about being the son of a legend, but her brother was building his own legend. Last year he'd come in second in points for the Chase for the NASCAR NEXTEL Cup Series and this year, he was determined to win the NASCAR NEXTEL Cup Championship. Hence her chronicling his year.

Dave's job offer had given her an excuse to return to the world she'd once been so much a part of. She noted a few media types outside the care center. From past experience Annie knew that the care center was one of the few places in the infield with extremely limited access.

The waiting room was packed with people. The room was sterile with white walls and uncomfortable chairs. The floor was hospital-grade tile. Someone had tried to warm the place up by placing two framed photos on the wall. The first was an aerial shot of Daytona on race day. The stands were packed and a blur of cars was visible on the track. The second was a shot of Daytona Beach just after sunrise. The sun reflecting off of the water and the beach empty of everything save a pair of footprints left in the sand.

Jared MacNeil was there along with Donovan Allen, who worked for her father on the Jenner Racing team. She tried to push her way into the back but they weren't letting anyone in until the track doctor had a chance to examine the drivers.

"Have a seat, Ms. Jenner. We'll let you know when you can go back there," the attendant told her.

Her cell phone rang and she pulled it out, checking the caller ID screen. It was her mom. She hesitated before answering the call, knowing that if her mom was upset and started crying so would she. And she was in the waiting room with two men who didn't look like they were going to be emotional at all.

She turned away from the others in the room, facing the vending machine.

"Hi, mom."

"Where are you, baby?"

"I'm in the waiting room. Where are you and dad?"

"We're in the tunnel on our golf cart. We'll be there in a minute. Have you seen him yet?"

"No, no one is allowed in. They are still examining both drivers." She heard her own voice waver.

"We've got a problem back here," she heard some-one say behind her.

"Mom, I've got to go."

Annie hung up the phone and moved toward the doorway leading back to the examination rooms. Jared and Donovan were both on her heels. She rounded the corner and heard voices raised—using the kind of words that would get you a big fine from the NASCAR folks.

TUCKER and DAVE were in each other's faces and Jared had the feeling that they were seconds from coming to blows. If the wreck had been with anyone else, Jared knew Tucker would have let it go. But for some reason these two men always rubbed each other the wrong way.

Jared grabbed Tucker's arm and spun him away from Dave Jenner. To be honest "Gentleman Dave," as he was known around the track, didn't appear to be too gentlemanly. But Annie placed herself in front of her brother and put her hand on his shoulder.

"Dave, chill out."

"Dammit, Annie."

Donovan stood in the doorway leading to the waiting room talking loudly to another man. Jared knew he should get his butt over there and help provide a distrac-tion in case any media reps had arrived and somehow managed to get into the waiting room. But he was more interested in watching the byplay between brother and sister.

As the only son of older parents, he'd never experienced anything like the relationship he saw now—though his parents and he had been very close. Dave calmed down and walked over to the corner with Annie.

"What are you staring at?" Tucker asked.

"Nothing," he said, turning back to Tucker. Tucker had taken off his uniform and had on a pair of baggy pants and a T-shirt. "You okay?"

"I'm fine. How's the car look?" Tucker asked.

"Not too bad. Billy said most of the damage is superficial. They'll have it back in the rotation in no time. What happened?" Jared asked, trying to figure out how Tucker, who had a reputation for avoiding most accidents, had been involved in one less than five laps into the first big race of the season.

"I was trying to get Jenner loose so I could get around him," Tucker said.

Getting close to the end of Tucker's car like that would have taken the air off the spoiler and made the rear tires lose traction. Usually the other driver just moved out of the way and let the second driver pass. But sometimes, like today, accidents occurred.

"What can I say, someone forgot his manners," Tucker announced.

"Someone should go back to the dirt tracks," Dave Jenner responded loudly.

Tucker had started out racing on dirt tracks illegally when he was only sixteen. Jared counted Tucker as one of his best friends. They'd met in college when a ballsy Tucker had approached Jared about buying him a stock car. Most of his fraternity brothers were more subtle about asking him for money than Tucker had been. But there had been something in Tucker's eyes that had told Jared that his money wouldn't go to waste. And it hadn't.

Investing in Tucker had turned out to be a solid decision. And when Tucker had started racing in the NASCAR NEXTEL Cup Series, Jared, whose fledgling coffeehouse had started taking off regionally, had gone with him as his car owner.

"Both of you should stop acting like boys and start behaving like the men you are," Annie said, crossing the aisle between Dave's curtained cubicle and Tucker's.

"Are you okay, Tucker?" she asked once she was standing next to Tucker.

"Fine," he said, turning away from Annie and sinking back down on the hospital bed that had been assigned to him.

"You okay?" Jared asked her. She still looked a little flushed. Her pale skin made her light eyes seem even bluer.

"Yes. Did I say thanks for your help earlier?" she asked.

"You did. I don't think we've been introduced. I'm Jared MacNeil, by the way," he said, offering his hand.

She took it. Her hand was small and cold, and her

nails were painted a pretty deep red. "I know who you are. I'm Annie Jenner."

"Everyone knows the Jenner family."

"That's right, everyone knows us and yet no one really does," she said.

She blushed, putting her hand over her mouth and glancing around to see if anyone had heard her comment. No one appeared to have noticed the two of them but he drew her away from the crowd, liking the feel of her soft skin under his grasp.

"Please ignore that last part. I'm not myself today," she said, a worried frown on her brow.

"I think that's expected. You and Dave are close?"

"We're twins. I know, not every set of twins are close, but we are. We've always been like a unit. When we were little we'd follow my dad through the garage tooling around the cars together."

"You'd think someone who'd been around tracks all his life would know when to move over," Tucker said, raising his voice so that Dave could hear it.

Annie glanced over at the other man. "Let it go, Tucker."

"I can't," he said.

She shook her head and walked back over to her brother, leaving Jared alone with Tucker. Jared wanted to tell Tucker to cool down and stop acting like an ass. But he understood how important this year was to Tucker and to their race team.

"Where's the doctor? I'm ready to get out of here," Tucker said.

"I'll see what I can find out. Try to stay away from Dave. The media will be outside as soon as they can get across the infield."

Tucker shrugged. But Jared knew his friend was listening and hoped that he'd refrain from engaging Dave in any more arguments. He was fairly certain that Tucker wouldn't do anything in front of the media but Jared never knew what to expect from him. His friend had been born fighting and had never really stopped.

Dave's parents walked into the infield care center and went to their son. Jared stared across the aisle as Dave Jenner's little cubicle area filled with people. Annie's mom put an arm around her daughter's waist and the two women leaned together.

Jared went to find the doctor. Five minutes later he accompanied the doctor back to Tucker's cubicle where, after evaluating his condition, he signed Tucker's release.

Jared led the way out the door. But when they reached the waiting room the media was there. They had questions for both drivers and Jared stepped to the back, out of the spotlight for the minute.

He heard the whir of a camera and glanced to his right to see Annie Jenner taking photos of everyone in the area. She'd stepped out of the crowd and was moving around capturing all the action on film.

He watched her for a little while until she turned her lens toward him. She took a few shots of him and then lowered the camera and walked over.

"Why are you staring at me?"

"You're a very pretty woman."

"Ah, I bet you say that to all the girls."

He shook his head. "I do find most women attractive."

"I'm not surprised."

"Really? Why not?"

"You strike me as a man who likes most people," she said.

He wasn't sure what she meant by that but he let it go. "I do. Are you free for dinner?"

CHAPTER TWO

"SURE, BUT IT'LL HAVE to be late. I'm working until nine."

"Where shall I pick you up?"

"I'm staying at a condo on the beach. I can meet you somewhere."

"You could, but my mother raised me to pick up my dates."

"What else did she raise you to do?" Annie asked, wanting to know more about the man behind the image.

"To be a gentleman," he said.

Time would tell. "And are you?"

"You'll have to be the judge of that."

The press conference was winding down. "Until later."

She walked away from him, quickly. Her brother was staring at her as she approached. Annie gave him a narrowed glance, silently asking, "What's up?"

He tipped his head at Jared, who'd moved back to Tucker's side. She shook her head at her brother. The last thing she wanted to do was discuss this with Dave.

"Hold up, Annie. Walk with me to my motor home."

She glanced back and remembered that minute when she'd been uncertain if he'd walk away from the crash. She rushed back to his side and wrapped her arms around his chest, holding him tightly to her.

"I'm okay," he said, his words just a whisper.

"I know. I'm just glad."

He grinned at her, for the first time looking like the carefree brother she knew. There was a lot of pressure for Dave to perform and perform well during race season.

"Good," Dave said.

He kept his arm over her shoulder and she felt that natural rhythm that had always flowed between them. That twin thing that she could always sense when they were together.

Dave dropped his arm from around her as they approached the entrance to the garages. There were a flock of fans with cold pit and garage passes lined up waiting to see the drivers when the garage would be "cold" again. Annie pulled her credentials out of her pocket and flashed her hot pass at the official at the gate. She waited just inside the gates until Dave finished signing hats and T-shirts and joined her.

"Shouldn't you go talk to Vinnie?"

"We're meeting in fifteen—he's still with the team trying to assess all the damage done to the body of the car."

They reached his motor home and he opened the door, waiting for her to go inside. She did, taking a seat on one of the plush leather captain's chairs.

"What do you need to talk to me about?" she asked, leaning back on the padded seat. She could tell their mom had been by here at some point during the day because there was a bottle of citrus juice with a sticky note on it just like the one her mom had given her this morning.

"I see mom is doing her best to keep you healthy."

He flushed a little. "Did you get one, too?"

"Yes. I think it makes her happy to take care of us."

"That's what dad is always telling me," Dave said. Then he leaned forward, bracing his elbows on his knees. "I want to talk to you about Jared MacNeil."

"What about him?" she asked.

"What were you and he talking about before?" Dave asked, doing his protective older brother routine.

"Nothing," she said.

"You looked pretty close for nothing."

"Dave, I'm twenty-eight."

"I'm aware of how old you are. I just want to know what's up with you and that man."

"We're having dinner. That's all. End of story."

Dave cursed under his breath and she didn't have to guess at why. Her brother had been completely snowed by Malcolm, her ex-husband. The entire family had bought in to his easygoing charm and it had taken them a long time to come around to listening to her when she'd said he was rotten to the core.

"I don't want to see you get in over your head," Dave said.

"Ah, Dave, you're a sweetie for worrying, but this isn't any big thing. Just dinner."

Dave ran his hand over his jaw and cracked his neck. "I just don't want to see you make another mistake."

Her, either. This was another reason why she'd busied herself with her job at *Sports Illustrated*. Here in the world she'd grown up in she was surrounded by family and friends that wanted to put her in some kind of protective bubble wrap. "I'll be okay. Have you heard anything bad about him?"

Dave shrugged and then pushed to his feet. "He's good friends with Tucker Aldridge. That says it all as far as I'm concerned."

"You are rivals on the track—that doesn't make either man a bad one off the track," she pointed out, knowing that Dave normally got along with everyone. His reputation wasn't a false one. He was a gentleman, even to those ladies he ran through like the high-speed driver he was.

"Why him?" Dave asked.

She glanced at her brother, trying to really see if this was a sticking point for him, if he was really upset that she was going on a date with someone from another racing team.

But in his eyes she saw only that brotherly concern.

She shrugged. "I don't know. I kind of like Jared. I don't know Tucker, what's he like?"

"He needles me. I can't put my finger on why exactly," Dave said.

"Tucker is a good driver," she said, stating something that her brother could respect.

"I know. Some say better than me."

She gave him a smile. "Better than a Jenner—no way."

He reached out and tugged on her hair, something he'd started doing when they were teenagers and his friends had needled him for hugging her. She knew the gesture meant *I love you*. She reached out and rubbed his neck as her return gesture.

"I'm still not sure about Jared. He's not like us. He grew up in a family of socialites. I think he knows the Hilton sisters."

"That's not a crime, you know."

"Yes, I know. All I know is that he seems to keep people at a distance. You need someone who'll—"

"Don't, Dave. Don't try to tell me what I need. Because I'm not sure that either of us really knows."

ANNIE LEFT the after-race party well before it was over. She wandered around the empty condo with time to spare before her date with Jared. She didn't want to think about him or their date.

Grabbing her Nikon she took out the memory stick and downloaded the photos she'd taken at the track today. As the images flashed on her computer she tried to stay detached. Tried to be a photographer dispassionately viewing her subjects, but she couldn't be.

The crash looked even worse in still-frame. It was amazing to her that both drivers had walked away. She changed her view from single-photo to proof-sheet and started marking notes on which pictures she wanted to submit for the book on Dave's year.

She enlarged a photo she'd snapped of her parents and noticed for the first time how tired her father looked. She leaned closer to the screen but knew that photos didn't lie. They showed the unvarnished truth about a subject and the viewers had to decide if they were going to believe it or not.

She'd always just seen the masculine beauty of Malcolm and had fooled herself into missing the vacuous expression in his eyes.

The doorbell rang. She left her laptop on the breakfast-bar counter and walked through the open room to the front door. The condo was typical of Florida. Open spaces with large windows that overlooked the ocean and clean white walls. This condo was owned by one of her relatives and had photos of the ocean on the wall that Annie had taken over the years.

She opened the door to find Jared standing there. He hadn't changed, but then he'd looked good before.

His eyes slid over her body. She fought the urge to suck in her stomach or fiddle with her hair. She heard her cell phone ringing in the background.

"Go ahead and get that. I'll wait here," he suggested.

"Come in," she said, stepping back so he could enter.

She hurried to the counter where she'd left her cell phone.

"Hello, Mom."

"Hey, sweetie, where did you disappear to?"

"I wanted to get a look at the photos I took today and that party really isn't my scene," she replied. She didn't want a bunch of questions, especially in front of Jared. Her family would be like Dave, warning her about dating another man in the racing world. Especially one they didn't know. She appreciated that they were protective of her, but at the same time she wanted to just be a girl going out with a boy. Not a Jenner going out with the team owner of a rival race car.

"We're all heading over to Uncle Steve's place. Do you want to join us?"

"Umm…not tonight. Tell everyone I said hello," she said, hanging up with her mother.

Jared had come into the main room of the condo and stood on the threshold of the kitchen, staring at the images on her computer screen.

"You're good at what you do," he said.

"Thanks. Sorry about the call."

"No problem. I have to take calls all the time."

She'd bet his calls were about business, not from overprotective relatives. "Does your mom phone you all the time, too? It's like she still thinks I'm twelve."

He shook his head. "My mom's deceased."

Great, Annie. Nice way to start the date. "I'm sorry."

"You didn't know. And it's been a long time."

"Were you close?"

"Yes, we were. I'm an only child so my parents doted on me."

"Ah, so you were the typical spoiled only child?" she asked, wanting to know more about him. Maybe the appeal of Jared was that she knew so little of him.

"Not typical," he said. "What about you? Spoiled princess or tom girl?"

"A bit of both actually. When Dave and I were little we'd tag around after my dad when he was in the garage before races. But at home I was definitely a princess. My family can still be kind of protective."

She led the way to the front door and locked up when they were both outside. Her condo was on the ground floor and the smell of hibiscus filled the air.

"I think I like that about them," he said.

He put his hand on the small of her back and directed her toward the parking area. The night breeze was cool and she was glad she had on her leather coat.

"You wouldn't if you were the one being protected."

"I don't know about that. I've never had anyone try to protect me."

She tipped her head to the side, stared up at his profile and realized just how much he'd revealed to her. "Not even your parents?"

"They did hire a bodyguard for me when I was seven," he said.

The comment was so off-handed that she knew there had to be more to the story. "Why a bodyguard?"

"My father had annoyed some people and they threatened me."

She knew so little about Jared. "Who is your father?"

"Benjamin MacNeil," he said. "Captain of industry and CEO of one of the largest banks in the world. My father had been born into money and then proceeded to make more of it before his death. My mother had been an actress/model from another wealthy family."

She couldn't imagine what it had been like growing up in the MacNeil family. But she was curious. Her family had money and were well-connected, but they'd never traveled in the kind of circles the MacNeils had.

"My car's over there," he said, pointing to a silver Aston Martin. Everyone she knew drove American cars. Her brother was a Chevy driver, so they all drove Chevys except for her dad, who'd driven a Buick back in his racing days and still had one in his garage.

"You've got to take a lot of flack for this car."

"It's worth it. Drives like a dream."

He opened the door for her and seated her in the car, then walked around to slide inside. The smell of his aftershave lingered in the air. She glanced over at him and felt the weight of his stare on her.

Their eyes met and held. She tried to tell herself this was just a dinner date, one like every other one she'd been on before, but there was something different about

Jared. Something that made her wish…that she still believed in fairy-tale love and happily-ever-after because he definitely looked and acted like Prince Charming.

CHAPTER THREE

THERE WAS SOMETHING different about Annie from the women he'd dated in the past. Since his parents' deaths he'd kept a barrier between himself and other people—and she tempted him to drop it. "Fasten your seat belt."

He was beginning to believe that asking her out was going to be one of the biggest risks he'd taken since he'd started sponsoring Tucker. She was breathtakingly beautiful in the bright lights of the parking lot, with her curly, black hair falling in smooth waves past her shoulders.

But it was more than physical beauty that drew him. She fastened her seat belt and put her hands in her lap, fingers laced tightly together.

He couldn't explain why she was affecting him so deeply. Maybe it was seeing Tucker crash today. He realized that they were both mortal and no longer college frat boys with more guts than brains and a long lifetime ahead of them.

"Where are we going for dinner?" she asked.

"It's a surprise." He'd arranged a private dinner for

them at a restaurant in Cocoa Beach. It was a forty-minute drive from Daytona.

"I don't like surprises," she said.

"You'll like this one." He hoped she liked it, and he wanted some privacy for their first date together. He wanted them away from the press that followed the drivers, team owners and their families. And getting out of Daytona seemed the best way to do that.

"You are cocky and arrogant."

He laughed, feeling good to be alive. It was one of the rare moments in a life filled with monotony. "Hey, I thought you didn't know me."

"Traits like those can't stay hidden," she replied.

"I was hoping you wouldn't notice," he said.

"I'm very observant."

"Is that why you are a photographer?"

She shrugged. "Partly."

He thought she was pausing to gather her thoughts, but as the minutes passed and she said nothing else he realized she was going to leave it at that.

He started the car and put down the convertible top. "Do you mind?"

"No. I like the fresh breeze."

"What else do you like?"

"Hot pretzels, Stevie Wonder and watching my brother win."

He backed out of the parking lot. "So what about arrogant men? You must like them, too."

"Not like so much as learn to put up with them."

"Who do you put up with?"

"Dave and my dad—they both think they know what's best for everyone."

He glanced over at her and sensed there was more to her comment than she was saying. He wondered if knowing her down to the bone was going to be a good thing. But he knew himself well enough to know that he wasn't going to be satisfied until he'd uncovered all of her secrets—every last one of them.

And he couldn't do that without revealing parts of himself that he normally didn't like to share.

"I'm a rank amateur compared to them. I only know what I like and what I want."

"So you'll like this surprise dinner and think I will, too."

"Something like that," he said.

He headed south out of Daytona with the top down on the Aston. The cold Florida breeze filled the car as did the scents of the ocean. He saw Annie start to shiver so he turned on the heater, pumping the hot air from the vents.

"Word around the track is that this is your first race in a few years."

"That's right," she said, wrapping one arm around her waist.

"What have you been doing?"

"I've been working for *Sports Illustrated* and other sports magazines."

"What do you cover?"

"Mainly racing," she said. "It's what I know. My dad always says that racing gets in your blood and I have to agree with him. Even though I'm not part of the family racing business anymore, I still wanted to be at the tracks."

"The U.S. racing circuit?"

"No. I've been in Europe for a while.

"The F-1 circuit in Europe?" he asked.

"Not really," she said and pointedly changed the conversation to Lance Maxwell, the driver who'd won the race today. Lance drove for Jenner Racing and was a teammate of Dave's.

He wished this weren't a first date, then he would have been able to push harder and find out what she was hiding. Whatever had taken her to Europe was definitely something she wanted to hide. And that just whetted his curiosity. But he knew better than to push past barriers that people put up in conversations.

He'd learned that lesson the hard way when he'd let a reporter push him into talking about his parents' deaths.

THE MEAL WITH JARED was relaxed and fun. He'd kept the conversation light talking about books and movies that they'd read and seen. He was genial and self-deprecating and he put her immediately at ease.

Annie should have found it comforting, but instead she seemed to be having a delayed reaction to Dave's accident. The images kept playing back in her head exactly as she'd captured it in her camera. The second-by-second still frame in her mind of the cars bumping and spinning. Except this time she knew Dave was the driver of the car.

She felt the impact and jolt as the seat belt held him in place and then felt the car spinning out of control. She started to hyperventilate again, and pushed herself away from the table, mumbling some excuse to Jared.

What was wrong with her? She made it as far as the hallway leading to the bathroom before she sank down on the floor, burying her head in her hands.

She'd forgotten about this. Forgotten in the years she'd been away photographing other drivers that she hated watching the men in her family race. Annie didn't like the worry that seized her whenever Dave got behind the wheel and didn't let go until he was safely out of that car.

It had been the same with her father. For years she'd been able to hide and push those feelings aside, but not anymore.

She felt a hand on the back of her head and glanced up at Jared. "Want to get out of here?"

She nodded as he tugged her to her feet. They left the restaurant, but he didn't direct them to his car. Instead he twined their fingers together and led her down the historic district of old Cocoa Beach. The buildings stood like silent sentinels of time. They'd weathered hurricanes and population booms, and witnessed the birth of the space program.

She wanted to be like that—a witness to the action going on in her life but not affected by it. But she never had been. Not even with the camera around her neck could she keep the distance she craved. And she had a feeling this racing season was going to be a test for her...one she wasn't exactly sure she could pass.

"Want to talk about it?" he asked.

She thought for a moment of playing dumb. Of saying something like "about what?" but she liked Jared and didn't want to play games with him. So she shook her head. "Not really."

"Was it me?"

She glanced over at him, not sure what he meant.

"Some women find me so attractive they have a little trouble breathing."

She gave him a wry glance. His silly conversation distracted her as nothing else could have. "Sorry, it wasn't you."

"A man can hope," he said.

But she knew she hadn't really hurt his ego. The night air was cool, and slowly she felt the panic that had attacked her at the restaurant fade away. "Sorry about that."

"No problem," he said. "It's been a long day."

"Were you worried about Tucker? Dave said the two of you are tight."

"You asked your brother about me?"

He was deflecting her question, but she'd avoided a topic she didn't want to talk about so she let him. But in the back of her thoughts it reminded her that they were both hiding things. "He was warning me about you."

"Really? What did he say?"

"Just that no one really knows that much about you."

"No one knows all that much about you, either."

She took a deep breath. Either this date was going somewhere or it wasn't. At this point she could keep up the silly chatter and never go out with him again or she could push deeper and see if there was anything worth knowing beneath the facade of the charming man.

He said nothing in response and she knew this was a test for him—her way of gauging him to see if he was the kind of man she wanted to spend more time with or not. She liked him. Liked his smile and his laugh.

"I'm not sure you're the right man for me. And—" she took a deep breath "—I'm afraid to trust my instincts when it comes to men."

Jared drew her to a stop, pulling her into the shadow of the storefront and wrapping one of his big hands around her waist. He drew her into his body, putting his other hand on her face and tipping her head back so that their eyes met.

"You're not like the other women I've dated," he said, so softly she almost couldn't hear his words.

She started to speak to apologize for not being what

he wanted, but he put a finger over her lips, then rubbed his thumb back and forth over her lower lip until her mouth tingled and she wanted more.

Adrenaline pumped through her veins and anticipation tightened her skin. She leaned forward, going up on her tiptoes, and met his mouth as he descended toward her. His lips weren't light or tentative, but were firm and forceful as he opened his mouth over hers and kissed her.

She braced her hands on his shoulders and threw herself into the maelstrom that was Jared. She forgot all the warnings from Dave and her own internal fears that she was drawn once again to the wrong man for her. She'd never craved a kiss from a man the way she wanted this kiss from Jared.

She wanted this chance to know this man, who was more than she expected him to be. And as his head came down to hers, she realized he wasn't her proof-she-was-over-Malcolm man. He was a man she wanted just for himself. And that should have scared her more than it did.

JARED HAD NEVER TASTED anything sweeter than Annie. He knew kissing her was a mistake. She brought out things in him that he didn't want to admit were a part of him. And she wasn't going to play it light.

That was why he had been unable to resist her lips. He wanted to see what kissing an honest woman would taste like and it was sweeter than he'd guessed. Annie wasn't pushy in her embrace. She savored the kiss and let him set the tone.

He fought against taking it too far too fast, because a part of him wanted to get to that point where he'd stop thinking and just react to her.

But he didn't want to be on autopilot. He smoothed his hand down her back to her hips, and held her in his arms. He wanted to remember every second of this embrace. Wanted to remember the way the breeze stirred the long strands of her hair, wrapping them around his neck, and the way her body moved against his as she leaned close for support.

She wasn't aggressive, but at the same time wasn't shy, either. She just took her time with the kiss as if they had all night. As if time could stop in this one moment.

He pulled back, dropping soft kisses on her lips, afraid to completely break the contact, but knowing he had to before things got totally out of control and he took this embrace where he wanted to.

He tucked her head against his shoulder and rested his cheek on the top of her head. He tried to breathe deeply to regain his control, but every breath he took was filled with Annie, a mixture of the scent of her shampoo and something more elusive, some essence that was just her.

She wrapped her arms around his waist and held him tightly to her. He heard her say something, but the words were lost in the front of his coat.

"What?"

"I like you, Jared."

She made him feel good inside and he didn't want to examine that. There had been few people in his life who'd liked him just for who he was. Was Annie one of them?

He told himself that it was just the kiss and the hormones talking, but for once he was going to accept the words at face value.

"That's nice," he said, trying for a light tone.

She glanced up at him, feminine knowledge in her eyes and…something else. Something he couldn't name but it made him feel…ah, hell. They needed some space. Some distance. He needed to cool things out and get her out of his head.

Except he liked the way she felt in his arms. He liked…he just plain liked the excitement she brought out in him.

"I'm not good at relationships," he said, wanting to be honest.

"How do you mean?"

"I have a problem with staying power," he said.

"So don't expect too much from you?" she asked.

Hearing those words, the very ones he wanted her to understand from him, on her lips, made something tighten in his stomach. "Yeah…yeah, that's what I was saying…but…"

He couldn't say anything else. He didn't want to

sound like some kind of wuss. God, this was why his dating track record was full of women who were more into serial dating than commitment. Women like Annie came along once in a lifetime and that freaking scared the crap out of him. He'd built his life by always keeping moving, always going forward, and at this point in time he really wasn't ready to slow down.

She took a deep breath. "Thanks for the warning."

"Was that what I was doing? Warning you?"

"I think so. And you should know…"

"What?"

"I'm not good at trusting men," she said.

"Why not?"

She shook her head. "I can't get into that tonight."

"No pressure. This is just our first date."

"First date? Are you planning to ask me out again?"

He let his hands slide away from her body and took her hand in his. He wanted to ask her to go to Tucker's after-party, but had the feeling that wasn't the best idea. He needed a breather.

"Will you be in Fontana next weekend?"

"I will be."

"How will that work with your job?"

"I'm doing a special project."

They reached his car and he unlocked the door and seated her.

"Tell me about your special project," he said, once he had the car in gear and they were headed back to Daytona.

"It's a book about the Jenner family. Dave's going to win the NASCAR NEXTEL Cup Championship this year."

"Some of the other drivers might not agree with that," Jared said, thinking to himself that Tucker had a pretty good shot at winning.

"I think I mentioned that I'm surrounded by arrogant men."

"That you did. I hope you aren't too disappointed if your brother doesn't win."

"I'm pretty sure he will. He was so close last year. And he's made some adjustments to his car and team that will make him unstoppable this year."

"What kind of changes?" Jared asked.

"None that I can share with the competition," she stated.

"I wasn't looking for you to share secrets," he said.

She nodded and changed the subject, but underlying the small talk was the knowledge that they were both a big part of two different teams and they both wanted their driver to win the NASCAR NEXTEL Cup Championship.

CHAPTER FOUR

ANNIE'S CELL PHONE rang as soon as they entered the Daytona city limits, breaking the tension that had sprung between her and Jared. She glanced at the caller ID and saw that it was Dave. She was tempted to ignore it, especially since she knew that her last comments to Jared had reminded them both of the reality of their lives at the track—the fact that they were both affiliated with rival drivers. But Dave wouldn't call unless it was something important.

"I have to take this," she said to Jared. She wanted to pretend she was just Annie and not a Jenner, but she knew that wasn't reality. She was a Jenner and that was going to play a part in any relationship she had. Not just with Jared but with any man she dated.

"No problem," he said, lowering the volume on the radio.

"Hey, Dave, what's up?" she asked, thinking he'd probably had a last-minute media event for the next day that he wanted her to photograph.

"Daddy's having some chest pains. We don't know

what's going on, but Dr. Rivers thinks it might be a heart attack. We're en route to Florida Hospital Oceanside."

She wasn't sure she heard her brother right. She'd seen her father a few hours earlier. He'd been fine. There was nothing the matter with him.

"Annie, did you hear me?"

Her hand was shaking. "Yes. Where did you say you're taking him?"

"Give the phone to Jared. I'll tell him where to meet us."

She did as Dave suggested, and Jared just looked at her, but she couldn't say anything. Didn't want the words *my father's having a heart attack* to come out of her mouth. She didn't want to believe them or think that they might be true. She was vaguely aware of Jared talking to her brother. Vaguely aware of his deep voice saying things, and then there was silence. And all she heard in her mind were Dave's words. They echoed over and over until she wanted to scream.

She tightened her hands into fists, her nails digging into her palms, and the pain was a careful reminder that this wasn't some kind of bizarre dream that she'd drifted into.

She couldn't cry and felt numb from the inside out. But she was breathing heavily again. Too fast. She needed to calm down. She held her breath, hoping that would help, but instead stars danced in front of her eyes and she was very afraid she was going to pass out.

And she didn't want to do that.

Jared put his hand on the back of her neck, urging her head forward as he maneuvered the car off the highway and onto the shoulder. "Breathe."

She forced herself to calm down and breathe. "I'm not normally hysterical."

"You aren't hysterical now. Here's your phone," he said, handing the unit back to her.

She tossed it into her purse without looking at it. She just stared at her lap, kept her head down and breathed. With each inhalation she took in the reassuring scent of Jared.

His hand was on the back of her neck, stroking over her skin. His touch was a soothing rhythm that helped her calm down and allowed her to come back to herself and shake off the panic. There was nothing she could do about what had happened to Daddy, until she got to the hospital and heard what a doctor had to say.

"We'll be with your family in a minute."

Her family, she thought. They were going to be very emotional. Dave's wreck would still be in the forefront of everyone's mind. The way it was in hers. And she was sure the media would get wind of her daddy's heart attack.

And she'd be back in the center of the storm like she'd been at the infield care center.

She wasn't ready for that. But this was life. It didn't follow any carefully ordered plan, no matter how hard she tried to make it. Her life had never been contained inside the nice neat box that she longed for. Her life was never about any quiet moments of normalcy.

Dave always asked her what normal was. But she knew there was a real world where people didn't deal with... She stopped herself.

People dealt with heart attacks every day. This was normal. But she didn't want this normal. She wanted the normal that had always been just outside her grasp. She shook her head, sitting up.

Anger came quickly on the heels of her panic. And she hated that about herself. She hadn't been angry at the track when Dave had crashed, but now she was angry at her father. Daddy's last two physical exams had revealed hardened arteries and the doctors had advised him to change his diet and lifestyle, but the old man hadn't. He refused to let someone else tell him how to live.

He'd survived too many crashes and had some kind of belief that he was invincible. She glanced at Jared, who was watching her in the interior of the car. Only the lights of the dashboard illuminated the both of them.

He raised one eyebrow at her and she realized some of that irrational anger must be visible in her expression. She buried her face in her hands and shook her head. She felt tears stinging the back of her eyes.

"Annie, what can I do?" he asked.

She didn't know. Honestly, she had no idea what

anyone could do. She'd never had a day like this before. Of course, there'd been close calls before. Over the course of her life she'd spent many hours in ICU waiting rooms, hoping and praying that her father or brother would recover. But this was different. This wasn't a crazy crash. This was his body telling him to change.

And her father had never listened to anyone. He was stubborn and bullheaded just like Dave. She lowered her hands and looked at this man she barely knew. This man she wanted to get to know better, but not this way. Not when she was feeling so raw and exposed. She shook her head and he didn't say anything else, he just maneuvered the car back out on the road, driving her to the hospital.

When they arrived she noticed a news van parked in front of the E.R. entrance and could see already that some reporters were inside with their camera crews.

"Can't they leave us alone?" she asked.

"Annie, the Jenner family is big news in Daytona, especially on race day."

She knew that. "Please come in with me?"

"I'll be right beside you, I promise."

JARED WASN'T SURE how he'd be welcomed by the Jenner clan. Her brother had warned her off him and this really wasn't the time to try and make new friends. But Annie was asking him to go with her. And he found that he didn't want to deny her.

He nodded.

He turned the car off and got out. She hesitated in front of the Aston Martin. Just stood there staring at the hospital, saying nothing.

He could clearly remember his own father's heart attack. He'd gotten a call in the early morning hours from his mother. By the time they'd arrived at the hospital his father had passed.

He knew exactly what held Annie in that spot in front of his car. He'd blithely entered the hospital. He had tucked his mother's small hand under his arm, confident that his father was going to be okay. Because his father had always been bigger than life and the MacNeil clan was always unstoppable. In business they were unrivaled and in life his father had always been invincible.

But that early morning Benjamin MacNeil had lost his super powers. And Jared had realized how human his father had been, how unpredictable life could be. He'd started moving on that day. Always staying busy so that he wouldn't have to slow down and feel the grief. He didn't want to feel anything really—he'd watched his mother shatter and knew he'd never wanted to end up that way.

He didn't think that Annie was ready for that lesson. Ready to learn that the legend who was her father, the legend who'd escaped several serious crashes on the track, might be laid low by a heart attack.

Jared came up next to Annie and waited. They weren't

a couple, not really. They'd tentatively agreed to start dating but that still left him unsure of what to do here.

She didn't say anything, didn't move, and he thought that maybe she was frozen in that moment where if you didn't move forward nothing worse could happen.

If she had been his, he'd wrap his arms around her and hold her tight. But she wasn't.

"Let's go in," he said.

In the lobby they walked right by the media, who were all asking questions.

Jared held up his hand, stopping to talk to them while Annie kept going to the information desk.

Carl Winnly approached as Annie disappeared down the hall.

"Why are you here?" the reporter asked.

"To give my support to the Jenner family," Jared replied, hoping that Carl would take his words at face value. NASCAR was a tight community and when something like this happened to one of their own, they would all rally around the Jenner family.

"Will you excuse me, Carl?" Jared needed to call Tucker and let him know he was going to be later to the after-party than he'd originally expected.

"Sure. Do you know who the family spokesperson will be?"

"No. I'll try to find out for you."

Jared stepped back outside into the Florida night. It was turning cold and the air sank through his clothes, chilling him to the bone. There was a glow from the security lights in the parking lot.

He hit the speed dial for Tucker's number.

"Yo, Jared. Where are you, man?" Tucker asked.

"My date is running longer than I expected."

Tucker chuckled. "That's not a bad thing."

"No, it's not," he said. Though he and Tucker were close Jared didn't really like to talk about the women he dated.

"We can catch up tomorrow. I want to talk to you about next week's race."

"Sounds good. I'll be back in the motor home lot tonight if you want to stop by."

"Will you be alone?"

"More than likely," he said. He thought that even if there hadn't been a Jenner family emergency, Annie wasn't the kind of girl to go back to his place on the night of their first date.

He started back to the hospital, wondering if he should stay despite the fact that she wanted him to. He wasn't really good at being a part of something. His parents deaths a mere six months apart had insulated him. He allowed himself to care for Tucker, but even that was filtered through the distance he liked to keep between himself and other people.

Part of it he knew harkened back to those years he'd spent alone at boarding school and the behaviors he'd learned then. But another part of it was simply that life was easier when he didn't form deep bonds with others. And if he stayed…well, he was already more into Annie than he was comfortable with.

He shivered in the cold, feeling like the kind of man his father would have sneered at in disdain. For the first time in his thirty-five years he didn't feel like he was a MacNeil. How had he come to this?

He felt like shallow shell of a man who was more comfortable being charming to strangers than caring for people he knew. And the answer was very clear.

He walked back into the hospital. She'd asked him to stay and he'd said he would. MacNeils honored their promises—he heard his father's words echoing in his mind in his father's deep voice. He'd always been careful about the promises he made. Careful not to make too many or to give them too lightly.

The one he'd made tonight hadn't been given easily or lightly. He wanted to be there for Annie. Be there *with* her. He strode down the hallway to the waiting area. And when he stepped inside he didn't go back to his corner, but met Annie's gaze head-on, and there was something there that he was almost afraid to believe was real. A kind of welcome that had always eluded him before. She held her hand out to him and he went to her side, sitting down next to her and just holding her hand.

Dave glanced over at him, but there was no malice or anger in her brother's gaze. Instead there was the same kind of panic he'd glimpsed in Annie's eyes earlier. Jared had no words to reassure the family but he found them all the same. He started talking about the kinds of breakthroughs that had been made in the past few years.

Drawing on his photographic memory he recited the statistics he'd read recently. Out of habit he read everything he could get his hands on and he was glad of that. As he was able to use facts to reassure the Jenner family.

THE NIGHT SEEMED to go on forever and Jared left shortly after midnight. Uncle Steve and Dave spoke to the doctors twice during the long night.

"Dad's out of surgery and they're moving him to ICU," Dave said as he came hours.

"Did they say anything about his recovery?" Annie asked.

"Yes. They are optimistic that he'll pull through."

"Thank God," Annie said.

"When can we see him?" her mom, Carol, asked.

"The doctors want to talk to you, Mom."

"Right now?"

"Yes," Dave said. "Annie and I will go with you unless you want Uncle Steve to."

"You and Annie."

Dave nodded and the three of them were led to a nice sitting area in a private room. Dave paced around the small room while Annie sat on the couch holding her mom's hand. Finally the doctor came in and explained the surgery he'd done on her father.

The doctor left them a few minutes later.

"What are we going to do about Daddy?"

"Well, as soon as he's recovered I'm going to lay down the law as far as his health is concerned."

She heard the relief in her mom's voice and felt as if her family was going to be okay, like they'd weathered a storm.

"You two okay?" Dave asked.

"Yes," her mother said. "How about you? It's been one crazy day."

"I'm fine, Mom. Annie?"

"I feel strung out. I'm almost afraid to believe the doctor."

Dave rubbed his eyes with the heels of his hands. "Yeah, me too. Listen, I've got to take a break."

Annie stood and walked her brother out into the hall. "Go ahead. I'll stay here with Mom."

There were lines of strain around Dave's eyes and he kept rubbing the back of his neck as if he had a lot of tension there. She worried about her brother. Worried about the stress of the new season, the crash and now this.

"You okay?"

"I'm fine, Annie," he said and walked away.

DAVE WAS STILL RUBBING the back of his neck as he walked outside. He reached in his pocket for the pack of cigarettes that he wasn't supposed to be carrying around anymore. But he needed one. The night had been endless.

He palmed his lighter and lit the cigarette sinking deeper into the shadows, hoping that the nicotine would help him numb out a little, but knowing it wouldn't be enough.

He wished like hell he could do this day over. Go back to the race and win the sucker instead of crashing so quickly. Then he could have won Daytona and maybe his dad wouldn't have been so stressed that he'd had a heart attack.

He took another long drag on the cigarette. He wanted the NASCAR championship more than ever. He wanted it this year so that his dad could see him win. And he needed to get his head in the game. Start thinking about winning instead of letting Tucker Aldridge distract him.

"Can I get a light?" Carl Winnly asked as he approached him.

Dave tossed the lighter to the reporter and leaned back against the cold stone wall of the hospital.

"What a day," Carl said.

"Off the record?"

"Yeah."

"It's been a bitch."

Carl laughed. "A lot of owners and drivers stopped by the waiting room tonight."

Dave knew that. He'd been out to talk with them at

different times. One of the things he liked best about NASCAR was the close-knit community. To be fair it was also one of the things he didn't like about the community—there were no secrets in NASCAR.

"I was surprised to see someone from MacNeil Racing here," Carl said.

Dave knew the reporter was fishing for something he could print. And tonight Dave was tempted to say something he'd live to regret. Instead he shrugged.

"Jared's an okay guy," Dave said, even though he doubted it. God, that man was…hell, he had no idea, he just hoped that his sister knew what she was doing.

He dropped the cigarette on the ground, stubbed it out with the toe of his boot and walked back into the hospital. His relatives were starting to disperse and he hugged everyone and told them he'd call as soon as they heard anything else. Uncle Steve was going home for a few hours' rest and would be back later in the morning. Soon it was just Annie, Mom and him.

He sat down between the two of them, putting his arms around their shoulder.

"Finally, some quiet," Annie said.

The Jenners were a big crowd. His dad was one of four boys. Dave had fifteen first cousins on his dad's side. And since they were in Daytona, his mom's cousins, the Daltrys, had come as well. They lived in Deltona, only an hour away. All totaled Dave thought they'd had close to twenty people in the waiting room.

"It was nice to have them here. To have their support," his mother said.

"Yes, it was," Dave agreed.

Silence fell between them. He could only guess at what was going on in his sister's and mother's heads. His own was filled with endless regrets and possibilities. The things he hadn't said to his father that he wanted to say.

He didn't like the ache that was still near his heart. Couldn't close his eyes and rest despite the fact that Annie did and his mom pretended to.

He wanted his father out of that bed and wrapping all of them in his arms. Brandon Jenner was a legend. Bigger than life and invincible, he thought. And he wanted his dad to wake up and cast that long shadow he always had. The one that Dave knew he was lost in.

But tonight had made all those feelings seem insignificant. He was almost ashamed of how many times he wished that he wasn't his father's son, thinking stupidly that life would somehow be easier.

Tonight he'd realized that life wouldn't be easier without Brandon Jenner as his father. Life would be stark without his father there. And he thought maybe he needed this to happen to make him understand that wanting the NASCAR NEXTEL Cup Championship and needing to be his own legend weren't the same thing.

Annie curled closer to him. And he was so glad that she was there. So glad that she'd finally put Malcolm and the life she'd lived in Europe behind her and returned to the world that she belonged in.

He tipped his head back, feeling the weight he'd been carrying around for too long—the worry for his twin. That anxious fear that she'd never be the smiling girl he'd once known. But tonight with Jared MacNeil, of all men, he'd caught a glimpse of the girl he remembered.

And that was a good thing because he'd almost forgotten the boy he'd been. He'd gotten lost somewhere between his dreams of becoming a NASCAR driver and his quest to get out of his father's shadow.

He didn't like the man he was becoming. He'd always prided himself on being a gentleman, on being the kind of man that would live up to the Jenner name. And in the last few years—hell, last year—he'd started to realize that he wasn't that man anymore. He'd changed and gotten lost somewhere. But sitting here in the waiting room with his father recovering, he found the path back to himself.

CHAPTER FIVE

ANNIE HAD ALWAYS liked Southern California. For the first time since Sunday night she was thinking not about her father and his recovery, but about the race coming up and her job. And there was something about a track lined with palm trees and VIP boxes filled with Hollywood's biggest stars. As a teenager she'd been able to meet some of her favorite Hollywood hunks thanks to her dad's popularity as a driver.

It was nice to be back to work instead of sitting at her parents' house watching her dad looking too pale in bed.

Fontana was a driver favorite. The track was a regular oval and not an odd shape, as some of the others were. The surface of the track was smooth, which made for good driving.

Walking through the infield, Annie told herself she wasn't looking for Jared. He hadn't called her during the week, but she hadn't expected him to. Their date had ended a little strangely.

It was Friday and qualifying would happen later this morning. Her brother and the other drivers were getting ready to run a few test laps. She had her camera in her hands and snapped photos of her brother's team as they worked on the car.

She took a few photos of the other bays and spotted Jared talking to Tucker.

She stopped a few feet away next to Tucker's car, waiting for Jared to acknowledge her. She stroked her hand over the JM's Coffee House logo. Tucker waved her over.

"Hey, Annie," Tucker said. "How's your dad doing?"

"Good. He's home recovering." They were all relieved to have him home. She knew it was silly to think that nothing could happen to him when he was home, but she just felt better knowing he wasn't in the hospital. She suspected her mother did, too.

"Glad to hear that," Tucker said. "I like your dad, wouldn't want anything to happen to him."

"He thinks you're a maverick," Annie said, recalling her father's words about Tucker after last week's race.

"Yeah, well he might be right," Tucker said with a grin. Annie wished she had captured it with her camera. There was a certain reckless joy in Tucker's face.

"He usually is," Annie replied. Why wasn't Jared saying anything? He was quietly standing to the side just looking at her. She tucked a strand of hair behind her ear.

Tucker cleared his throat and she glanced back at him. "Sorry I was an ass last week."

"Apology accepted," she said. Tucker's crew chief,

Billy Toughton, called him over and he left her alone with Jared.

"Your dad is really okay?" Jared asked when they were alone.

"He's doing better. He's recovering. The doctors want him to take it easy for a while, which is hard on him. Thanks for going into the hospital with me."

"No problem."

"You seemed to know a lot about heart attacks," she said, not wanting to pry into his past but curious about it all the same.

"My dad collapsed while jogging. When he got to the hospital they ruled it a heart attack. So I read everything I could get my hands on about it."

"You remember everything you read, too, right?"

"Yes. Did I tell you that?"

She flushed realizing that he hadn't mentioned it. She'd read it on the Internet when she'd done a search on him. "I think you must have."

He arched one eyebrow at her and she felt her face get even hotter.

"I don't think I did. I was trying not to sound arrogant."

"But we'd already established I like arrogant men," she said, hoping to change the subject, but really having no idea what to change it to.

"That's right...we had. Are you sticking to your story?" he asked.

She shook her head. "I guess not. I read an article about you."

"Which one?"

She'd actually read seven articles on him and two on his father.

"A couple. I Googled you and then read the articles on the Internet."

"You Googled me?"

"Yup. You had lots of links."

He shook his head. "What'd you find out?"

"Stuff you already know," she said, embarrassed that she'd told him that. Annie had planned to keep her snooping into his past a secret, although it hadn't felt like snooping. She'd just wanted to know everything she could about him. She'd needed to know more about the man she hadn't been able to stop thinking about.

And Annie liked what she'd found in those articles. The man she'd read about was exactly like the man she'd met.

"Do you still think I'm arrogant?" he asked.

She shook her head. "Why do you care about that?"

"I don't know," he said with a shrug. "I think I want to impress you."

She thought about that for a minute. Who wouldn't be impressed by him? "Well, at the risk of giving you a swelled head…you should know that you're very impressive on paper."

He leaned closer to her, his face inches from hers. "Only on paper?"

She shivered a little as she felt the warmth of his breath against her cheek.

"Maybe."

"What can I do to change your answer?"

"I'm not sure. If you try too hard, I'll see through your actions. And then you'll just be arrogant again."

"I'm going to have to work harder to improve my image."

She glanced around Tucker's garage area as his team moved the car around, getting it ready for the test laps. Their movements were a familiar dance to her. They pushed the car out of the garage and then maneuvered it around to push it back in, nose facing out.

"You can do that later. I have to get back to work," she said.

In a few minutes the crews would start testing the engines and she needed to get back to Dave's garage to take some more photos.

Jared took her elbow and led her out of the garage into the alleyway between the bays and the haulers. There were many people in the area.

"Will you have lunch with me in my owner's suite?"

She didn't even have to think about it, she responded immediately. "Yes."

DAVE SAW HIS SISTER talking to Jared MacNeil and told himself it was none of his damned business who she dated.

"Get your head in the game," Vinnie said, coming up behind him.

He and Vinnie had been together almost from the start of Dave's racing career. He respected his crew chief and together they were damn near unstoppable when they were at the top. "It is in the game."

"I'm not going to argue with you, but glaring at MacNeil isn't what you need to be doing right now."

"What do you know about the guy?"

"Same stuff everyone else does—his team is small but pretty powerful. They win a lot of races with only two drivers."

"I meant personally."

"Not much," Vinnie said.

Dave put his helmet on and got in his car to drive his test laps. When he came in he checked his speed against the other drivers and saw that Aldridge was faster than he was after the first few laps.

"The balance feels a little off, Vinnie."

"Where?"

"The left rear feels like it's sticking to the track," Dave said.

The team made the adjustments to the car. Balance was handled by adding or removing chunks of lead within the frame rails to redistribute weight in the four corners.

When Dave's car was ready again he backed out of the garage just as Aldridge drove past his bay. The other driver gave him a snarky thumbs-up.

Dave knew it wasn't exactly charitable but he wanted a piece of Aldridge. He wanted to beat Aldridge so badly he could taste it. That upstart had pushed his buttons from the very beginning. Always nipping at his heels and trying to…Dave didn't know.

Dave pulled down his driver's netting and saw Annie moving around his car, snapping photos. He didn't like the fact that she was dating someone from Tucker's team, much less the team owner. In the back of his mind was the thought that if he won this weekend maybe she'd lose interest in MacNeil.

"Go get some speed, Dave," Vinnie said though the headphones.

Dave knew he had to let the thing with Tucker go, but he'd never been able to. There were several drivers that he sparred with on the track, but off-track they were buds.

Not Tucker. The man was a loner and he liked to play by his own rules. That was it, Dave thought. He'd been brought up in this world. And he expected the rules of fair play to be observed by everyone.

The next few laps were better. The car was running smoothly and his times were faster. He pulled into the garage. Vinnie and the rest of the team went over the car one more time.

Annie was still moving around the garage snapping photos. Dave climbed out of the car as Vinnie came over to him.

"Great time on that last lap. I think we're good for now. I'm going to tape off the grille," Vinnie said.

"Are you going back out for any more laps?" Annie asked, coming up behind him.

"No, I'm done for now. Why?"

"I wanted to get a few shots of you on Turn One from the other side of the track, but I'll catch you during qualifying."

Annie followed him out of the bay and across the alleyway toward his hauler. Jared MacNeil saw the two of them and waved. Annie waved back and then she blushed a little.

"What's up with you two?"

"You know we went out."

"Yeah, that's why I'm asking. Are you going to go out with him again?"

"Yes."

"Annie—"

"Stop it. I don't want to hear anything else from you about who I date."

"Fine. Stevie Taylor is going to be stopping by later today to check out the car. I think some pictures with him would be good for the book." Stevie was the lead singer of a hard-rock supergroup and over the years he and Dave had become good friends and poker buddies. They often played in high-stakes games in Vegas together. A lot of celebrities attended the race in California since the track was only forty minutes from Los Angeles.

"Dave, I didn't mean to sound rude about Jared. I just don't need you doing the protective brother thing."

He nodded. "I can't help myself, Annie. Something about that guy still rubs me the wrong way."

"What?"

"I wish I could put my finger on it," he said.

THE OWNER'S SUITE high above the track was luxurious and had a great view. Annie stood at the window. The NASCAR Busch Series drivers were qualifying now so the track wasn't quiet, but the skybox was sound-proofed and there was music playing in the room.

Jared had escorted her here and then left to take a call. A table had been set in front of the window. A small present sat in front of the chairs. She felt a little weird thinking that he might have bought her something.

"Sorry about that," Jared said as he entered the room. "Are you ready for lunch?"

She shook her head. She needed a few answers from him. She was almost afraid to ask but she had to. "Why are you going to all this trouble? Is this what you normally do?"

He pushed his hands into the pockets of his pants and leaned back on his heels. "What brought this on?"

"Well, for one thing, my brother isn't too keen on me dating you and I don't want to upset him if this is just some kind of game to you."

"What makes you think this is a game?" he asked.

She gestured to the table. "This feels like a setup."

He arched one eyebrow at her. "How do you mean?"

"Like this is something you've done before."

"It is. A lot of women like to come down to the track and have a private lunch while the NASCAR Busch Series qualifying is going on."

A lot of women, she thought. Well, that told her exactly how he felt about her. She was one of many. Not one of a kind. "I've been in owner's suites before."

"I'm making a mess of this," he said, crossing the room to stand in front of her.

"Yes, you are," she said, unwilling to cut him any slack.

He rubbed the back of his neck. "This is the world you grew up in…I think I wanted to show you that I was part of it."

"Why?" she asked.

"Annie," he said, cupping her face in his hands, "I don't do this for every woman I date."

"Then why me?" she asked.

"I can't explain it. Why are you here with me? I'm not your normal kind of guy."

"How do you know that?" she asked.

"I read a few articles on you, too."

That made her feel so much more his equal. He was into her, she thought. Then his words sunk in and she realized he'd have read about her marriage.

"Uh…that stuff that Malcolm said… Our marriage didn't really end well. We wanted different things."

"What did you want?" he asked.

She hesitated to say it. What she wanted was a little too deeply personal for this early in a relationship, but if she had any chance at something real with Jared then she wasn't going to lie about things that were important to her. She'd compromised herself too often for Malcolm and that had made them both miserable.

"I wanted a family."

"And Malcolm didn't?"

She shrugged. No way was she going to admit to Jared that Malcolm had a very European attitude toward marriage and wives. He'd wanted a family with her, but only if she would look the other way when he had his affairs—something she simply couldn't do.

"When you're ready to tell me about it, we can talk."

"I think I *am* ready for lunch," she said.

"Good. But first I have a little present for you."

He handed her the long slim box.

She took it from him but made no move to open it. "What's this for?"

"To celebrate the start of our relationship," he said and there was a confidence in him that made her want to believe that their relationship would be a good one.

CHAPTER SIX

JARED HAD PURCHASED gifts for women before and had all kinds of reactions to them. But this was the first time anyone had seemed almost embarrassed by the gift. And she hadn't even opened the wrapping yet and seen the distinctive Tiffany blue box.

A part of him knew that it was too early in a relationship for a gift, but he'd been unable to resist the bracelet when he'd seen it in the window of Tiffany's on Rodeo Drive. He had the image of it on her wrist.

She eased the gold foil gift wrap from the box and folded it neatly into a square, hardly even glancing at the box. She had to know it was jewelry but she wasn't grasping at the box or hurrying to open it up.

"You didn't have to get me anything," she said carefully, rubbing her finger over the raised imprint of the Tiffany name. She didn't look down at the box but only stared at him.

"I wanted to. Open it."

She did and just stared into the box without removing

the bracelet. The longer she stared at it the more unsure he became of the gift. He couldn't read her reaction at all.

"Annie?"

"Thank you, Jared," she said at last, lifting her eyes to his. Her pretty brown eyes were wide and her emotions hard to discern. She lifted the bracelet from the box and held it in her long fingers.

"I'll put it on you."

She held the bracelet out to him. Her arm suspended between them as he took the platinum piece from her. He fastened it around her wrist and then bent to leave a small kiss under the clasp.

Her hand turned under his grasp, her long cool fingers brushing over his jaw. He stood back up and met her gaze. She kept her hand on his face. "Thank you, Jared. Really thank you."

Before he could say anything to her, he got a call on his BlackBerry. It was Tucker. Jared decided the call could wait and instead went to the refrigerator, where he'd left a bottle of San Pellegrino chilling.

"Would you like a glass of sparkling water?"

"Yes, please."

"I saw a magazine article about you with the photo of Dave and your father that won the photojournalism award. When did you take the photo?"

"About four years ago. It was the first time Dave made it into the chase for the NASCAR NEXTEL Cup. He was so jazzed standing there in Victory Lane and, well, you can see from the look on my dad's face how proud he was."

"It was easy to see. Tucker's first time in the Chase was like that, too."

"You two are that close?"

"He's like the brother I never had."

His BlackBerry started ringing again.

"I don't mind if you get that," she said.

"I do. I want to enjoy my lunch with you."

He glanced at the caller ID display. Tucker—again. He let it go to voice mail and then heard the phone twitter. He glanced down and saw the text message on the screen.

Call me. Now!

Clearly there was an emergency. He simply couldn't ignore him at this time.

"Will you excuse me? I have to take this call."

"Go ahead. I'm going to sit here and watch the track. I love it from up here."

He exited the suite and called Tucker.

"What so important that it couldn't wait?" he asked without preliminaries.

"Where are you?" Tucker asked. In the background Jared heard Jay-Z being played loudly and guessed that Tucker was in his hauler. He liked to listen to rap music while he got ready to qualify.

"In my suite, why?"

"We've got a problem and I need to talk to you. Can you get down here now?"

"What kind of problem?" Jared asked, starting to get concerned by the tone of Tucker's voice. It was small and tight, which meant that Tucker was ticked off.

"Someone tampered with my car."

"What do you mean *tampered?*" he asked.

"Removed the tape off the front of the car," Tucker said. Though the drivers weren't allowed to use taping during the actual race they were allowed to do it during qualifying. Taping off prevented air flow from cooling the engine and enabled the driver to reach higher speeds.

"Who would do that?"

"Your girlfriend springs to mind."

"Annie? Why would she do that?"

"Qualifying in a top position is important, Jared. Who else would want me to not get the pole?"

"I can think of a number of other drivers."

"Yeah, but they weren't hanging around my garage this morning, were they?"

He rubbed the back of his neck. He didn't know who'd tampered with Tucker's car, but he'd bet all of his money that it wasn't Annie.

"I'll ask her if she did anything to your car."

"Do you honestly think she'll tell you?"

He thought of the way she'd reacted to the bracelet, and in his gut, he knew the truth. Annie wasn't going to lie to him about anything. That wasn't the way she was wired. She reacted to things, good or bad, with honest emotion.

"Yes, I do."

"Hell, you're a fool."

"Maybe you're the one who is."

Tucker hung up and Jared glanced at the closed door to the suite.

ANNIE TRIED TO STOP staring at the bracelet, but since Jared was out of the room she felt like it was okay. She touched the small charm that dangled from the half-inch-thick platinum band. It was a small palm tree with a diamond nestled in the middle of the tree.

Don't read too much in to the gift, she warned herself.

The door opened and she dropped her arm, putting her hands behind her back. But Jared wasn't really paying attention to her hands.

A frown firmly in place on his face, he walked into the room. His shoulders were tense and he wouldn't meet her gaze when she looked at him.

"Is something wrong?"

"I'm not sure," he said, taking a deep breath. "Come and sit down, Annie. I have something I need to ask you."

She crossed the room and sat on the couch next to him.

"Okay, ask me."

He leaned forward, bracing his forearms on his knees. "What were you doing in Tucker's garage bay earlier?"

She frowned. This wasn't what she'd been expecting. "Looking for you."

"How did you know I'd be there?" he asked, his expression carefully neutral and his tone very calm.

He sounded almost too calm and emotionless. Not at all like he had just a few minutes earlier.

"I saw you while I was sitting in Dave's garage bay talking to Vinnie."

"Vinnie, Dave's crew chief ?" Jared asked.

"Yes."

"Did he suggest you come down to find me?"

"What exactly are you getting at here?" she countered, feeling as if she were a suspect in a police interrogation room.

"Someone tampered with Tucker's car."

"What? Is he okay? I didn't see a crash, so it couldn't have been too serious." And the cars were inspected before they went out on the track and when they came off. Tampering wasn't something that was easy to do. She tried to think of things she knew drivers and their teams had tried over the years, but nothing came to mind. She drew a complete blank.

"The tampering would only have slowed him down, not hurt him."

Silence bloomed between them and for the first time it wasn't comfortable. She felt all that he wasn't saying, the accusation that he was trying to tiptoe around.

"Do you think I did something to Tucker's car?" she asked at last.

He shrugged those big shoulders of his and then

leaned back on the couch as if the conversation wasn't that important. But it was to her. She had foolishly thought she was building something with Jared.

"Not really. But I want to hear you say that you didn't," he said.

She pushed to her feet, standing over him. She put her hands on her hips and felt the bracelet move over her skin. Was this the price of his gift? This demand that she prove that she didn't sabotage another driver's car?

Carefully she removed the bracelet and held it out to him. He refused to take it from her. She pivoted on her heel and went back to the table where she'd left the box. She put the bracelet in the box and then looked back at him.

He hadn't moved from the couch and she had the feeling he'd let her walk out the door. Annie couldn't stop herself from walking away. She knew another type of person would have stayed there and forced him to see that she couldn't possibly have done anything to Tucker's car. But she wasn't like that. She didn't like conflict and never had.

Besides, Jared wasn't anything other than a man she knew. They'd only had one date and it was better that she get to know the man he was now. But she still felt as if she'd been betrayed. Damn. He'd seemed so different.

"I didn't tamper with Tucker's car. That's not my style."

She crossed the suite and opened the door, looking back at him and taking a deep breath. "I don't appreciate having to prove myself to you. Tucker, I can understand because he's a hothead. But I thought…I thought you were different, Jared."

She stepped out of the suite and forced herself to walk calmly down the hallway to the elevator that led to the ground floor. A part of her—the romantic part—kept listening for the door to that suite to open. Kept waiting for him to suddenly come after her.

But he didn't.

And that seemed to be the true mark of the man he was. This wasn't a relationship worth having or worth pursuing. She felt sad deep inside, where she'd promised herself she wouldn't let any man hurt her again. She hated that weakness in herself.

As soon as the door closed Jared got up and walked to the window overlooking the track. He couldn't believe that he'd let her walk away, but there had been little left to salvage. She'd been ticked off, and instead of fighting or yelling she'd completely shut down.

And could he blame her? What kind of man accused a woman he wanted a relationship with of tampering with a car?

An idiot, he thought. He pocketed the bracelet and left the suite, hoping he would find her before she was back in the infield.

She was waiting at the elevator. Her fingers were caressing her right wrist, where his bracelet had been a few short minutes ago.

"Annie…" But he didn't know what to say.

"What?" she asked belligerently.

He felt a pang in his chest that he may have really hurt her with his question.

She didn't glance up or turn toward him. And he realized he didn't want to have things end between them right now. And certainly not like this.

"I'm sorry. You're right…I should have asked you differently. Just flat out."

"Why didn't you?"

"I don't know. I'm not used to…"

"The truth?" she asked.

"Yes."

"That's really sad."

He didn't have a response to that. It wasn't that he thought most people lied, but Tucker had raised a few doubts in his mind about Annie. And he knew that he could never compete for her loyalty. He knew that she was a Jenner first.

"Listen, I'll be honest with you. I don't really care if Dave or Tucker wins. I mean, other than the fact that Dave's my brother and I love him. But I figured the best driver at the end of each race will cross the finish line first."

"I—"

She shook her head. "Let me finish."

He nodded.

"My father said that cheating to win isn't winning. My dad is one smart guy and I've always believed what he said. I've never cheated for myself and I won't for my brother.

"I can't be with a man who doesn't trust me. I'm not sure that I trust any man, but being accused…it doesn't work for me. I lived through that with my ex-husband and I can't do it again."

He took a deep shuddering breath, realizing this one moment had stripped them both bare and now she was waiting to see if he was man enough for her. And Jared felt the way he always did when he had to be measured by his own worth. Not his money or business acumen, but his worth as a human.

"What did your ex lie to you about?" he asked.

"Being faithful."

"I'm sorry."

"Don't be. That was my lesson in trusting blindly."

Jared didn't like the way that sounded. Didn't like the fact that she'd been hurt badly by her ex-husband.

"I never believed you had tampered with Tucker's car, but he was insisting and I had to ask."

She nodded. "I understand. If Dave had come to me with the same scenario I would have asked you."

"This was a big screwup on my part. Can we start over?" he asked her.

"I may have overreacted. You pushed a button I didn't realize was so hot for me. I thought…well, it doesn't matter, but I thought I was over that part of my marriage."

"I'm not leaving here until this is right between us."

"It won't be right unless you trust me."

"I do," he said, taking the bracelet out of his pocket and holding it up. "I really want you to have this. Will you take it back?"

She looked at the piece of jewelry with more longing than he'd noticed in her eyes before. "Not now. Ask me again later."

He understood what she wasn't saying. That she wanted to rebuild the relationship they'd started. He pocketed the bracelet and put his hand at the small of her back as the elevator opened.

"Will you have dinner with me?"

"No," she said. "I'm having dinner with a photographer friend of mine."

"How about later?" he asked, trying to come up with some time that would work for him. "After dinner?"

She shook her head.

"Why not?"

"Because I haven't seen Abby in six months and she and I tend to talk all night when we get together."

Well, then that was that. He had the feeling no matter what he suggested she was going to be busy.

"Are you going to forgive me for this?" he asked.

"I'm thinking about it."

"Just thinking?" he asked.

"Yes. I'm not sure I want to let things move beyond this casual stage with you."

"Why not?"

She glanced up at him, her eyes wide and intent. "I just had a glimpse of how complicated our dating is going to be."

"Complicated isn't a bad thing," he said, unwilling to let her go.

"We'll see."

CHAPTER SEVEN

THE ROAR OF THE ENGINES and the bustle of energy in the garage area as the drivers got ready to qualify made for an electric atmosphere. Annie pushed all her thoughts about Jared out of her mind and focused instead on the one world where she was always at home. She lifted her camera to her eye and shot her brother's car in slow motion racing around the track.

The officials had checked over Tucker's car and allowed him to place the tape over his engine again. But he was off as he went out on the track to qualify, posting the fifteenth fastest time.

When it was Dave's turn he blew past Tucker's time—and everyone else who'd qualified—to take the pole.

Annie met him back in the garage with her camera still up. She was capturing life around her, yet keeping herself safely insulated from it.

Through her lens she saw something in her brother's eyes that she'd often noticed in her father's—especially those photos of him when he'd still been driving. It was the glimmer of a winner.

"Great run, Dave."

"Thanks, kiddo. Where were you earlier?"

"Having lunch, why?"

"Stevie was asking about you."

"We're catching up for a drink later at the prerace block festival. I think he's singing."

"Good. You know he's single again."

"Please tell me you are not matchmaking."

Dave shrugged.

"He's not into commitment," she said, pointing out the obvious to her brother. Stevie was on the road fifty-one weeks a year. He liked the rock 'n 'roll lifestyle of traveling and dating a different woman each week. But Stevie was a lot of fun and totally devoted to only one person in his life—his six-year-old daughter.

"You're not looking for commitment, either, are you?" Dave asked, scrubbing his hand over his face where sweat was dripping.

"Maybe," she said, looking for an excuse to escape the garage area and her brother.

"Then why the hell are you dating Jared?"

"Stop it, Dave. He's a nice guy," she said, though she wasn't really sure that Jared was. She thought that he had the potential to be a nice guy if he'd let down his guard…something she wasn't sure he'd ever do around her.

"Hey, cousins," Alan Jenner said, coming up behind her. He wrapped one arm around Annie's waist and dropped a kiss on the top of her head. He was six foot two inches tall and solid muscle. He was also the general manager for Jenner Racing.

"Nice time today, Dave," he said.

"Thanks," Dave answered.

"You two look pretty intense. Is everything okay with your dad?"

"Yes. Dave was just trying to set me up with a friend of his."

"Why? I thought you'd sworn off men," Alan said.

"I was joking when I said that." She needed to get out of here. The last thing she needed was the two of them—

"Who's she dating?"

"Jared MacNeil."

Alan's eyes narrowed. He was two years older than she and Dave and they'd practically grown up together. "We'll see about that."

"That's what I'm talking about," Dave stated.

"Leave it alone, boys."

They didn't say anything else but changed the subject to the prerace events that were planned for later that evening. Annie walked away from them knowing that they wouldn't change their minds because she asked them to.

And she wasn't exactly sure where she was heading with Jared. After their lunch he might have decided that he wasn't going to pursue her, either.

In the alleyway between the garages and the haulers she took a few candid photos of the fans. She got her focus back on the job she had to do and away from the men in her life who were trying to make her crazy. She walked out of the garage area and down pit road.

In the distance she saw Jared and Tucker talking to the folks from one of the television stations. She lifted her camera and zoomed in on Jared's face. She saw the sun lines, evidence of the time he spent outdoors, the hard line of his jaw and the intensity in his eyes.

Jared glanced up and right at her. They were a distance from each other so if she hadn't had the lens zoomed in his expression would have been unclear. Instead she saw the question in his eyes.

Something in his gaze made her realize he might be vulnerable, too. And that reassured her as little else could. She wanted to cut him a little slack on the mistrust thing, but deep inside she knew she wouldn't because she refused to get her heart broken again.

Annie had the feeling that it was too late. No matter how many hoops she made him jump through or how hard she tried to protect her heart, Jared MacNeil was already finding his way into her affection.

THE PRERACE BLOCK PARTY was crowded with race fans, drivers, crew members and celebrities. Jared moved easily through the crowd toward the table where Tucker and D. J. Owens, the other driver on their team, sat.

"Yo, MacNeil, wait up."

Jared could think of only one reason why Alan Jenner would want to talk to him—Annie. Ah, hell.

"What's up?"

"That's what I want to know. What's doing between you and Annie?"

"None of your business."

"Ah, Jared, that's not the answer I wanted to hear."

"Too bad. She's an adult—she can make her own decisions."

"No kidding. Just make sure you remember she's part of the Jenner family and we take care of our own."

"We're dating, Alan. Most people don't get hurt—"

"Annie's not most people."

Jared knew that, but he wasn't going to discuss this any further with Alan. She had warned him her family was protective. It surprised him to some extent because Annie didn't need a man to protect her. She did a good job of it herself with those steel-gray eyes of hers demanding truth from a man.

"Was that all?"

"Don't make light of this, MacNeil."

He nodded at the other man and walked away, working his way behind the table.

"Hey, man, you want to hang for a while?" Tucker asked as he finished signing the last autograph and posed for one last photo.

"Got nothing better to do," Jared said.

"I thought you were dating Jenner's sister."

Everyone wanted to know about his love life, he thought, and right now there wasn't anything to tell. "Yeah, that situation is complicated."

Tucker raised one eyebrow at him. "That's odd. Don't women usually throw themselves at you?"

He punched Tucker in the arm. "She's not like other women."

"No?"

Jared didn't want to talk about Annie with Tucker. Jared rubbed the back of his neck, looking at the man who was probably closer to him than anyone else. They were like brothers.

"No," he finally answered.

"Oh."

"What's that mean?"

"Nothing…it doesn't mean anything."

They stopped in front of the stage where the Jenner Racing team was signing autographs. He scanned the crowd, looking for Annie, and caught a glimpse of her long dark brown hair as she moved through crowd, snapping pictures.

"Yeah, right," Tucker said. "Why are we hanging out in a rival team's crowd, then?"

"We're not hanging out," Jared replied, walking again. He couldn't explain to himself why she was always on his mind. She was like an obsession that he couldn't shake himself of.

Tucker's next event was with a group of Boy Scouts of America. Their top box-car racers were waiting for him. Jared left Tucker with them and moved back through the crowd telling himself he wasn't looking for Annie, but nonetheless he was standing in the shadows of the Number 153 car's fans watching for her. He couldn't spot her and felt like an idiot for hanging out, looking for her.

He walked back through the crowd toward the stage set up at one end of the street. A local band was playing covers of Jimmy Buffett hits.

"Hey, Jared," Annie said, coming up next to him. She had her camera hanging around her neck.

"Hello. Working?"

"No. I've been hanging out with one of the musicians who will be performing later."

"Who?"

"Stevie Taylor."

How did she know him? And why did he care? He tried to come up with something to say but frankly he couldn't. "That's nice."

She arched one eyebrow at him. "He and Dave are poker buddies."

"So why were you hanging out with him?"

"Why do you care? I thought I was just someone you were dating casually."

He thought about that. He'd tried to keep it casual. Their lunch had been anything but casual in the end.

"It's not—listen, I don't know what I feel for you, but I do know I don't want you dating another guy."

She tucked a strand of hair behind her ear and looked up at him. "I'm glad to hear that. I feel the same way."

She smiled up at him. And he knew he was lost. He leaned down and kissed her because he didn't want her to see the emotions in his eyes. He kissed her because it had been too long since he'd had her in his arms and he was only just coming to realize that he wanted her—in his arms and in his life—and he had no idea how he was going to get her to stay there.

Annie pulled back as her cell phone started playing a song. She glanced at the screen and let the call go to voice mail.

"A bunch of us are going to the Beverly Wilshire Hotel for drinks. Want to join me?"

"That sounds great."

AFTER THE BLOCK PARTY Tucker and Jared climbed into the Ford Cobra that Tucker drove when he was off the track.

"I've got a date."

Tucker glanced across the seats and stared at him with that knowing gaze. "I thought Annie shut you down."

Jared didn't respond to that. "Well, you thought wrong."

"Oh. So now you're running to her side."

"Tucker…"

"This isn't like you. I'm going to ask you again—what's this woman got going on that has you so tied in knots?"

"I don't know."

Tucker laughed then, not cruelly, more sympathetically. "Tell her I'm sorry I accused her of tampering with my car."

It turned out that one of the new guys on Tucker's own team had removed the tape after it had been placed. So there was no tampering at all. But Jared wasn't going to bring that subject up unless Annie did. He wanted to get back in her good graces, not remind her that he'd asked her to prove she hadn't done something immoral and illegal.

"Want to come with me? Meet up with her?"

"Ah, no."

Jared glanced at his friend, arching one eyebrow at him.

"Sister of my enemy and all that stuff." Tucker said the words casually, but Jared understood how the other man felt. When they'd first come to NASCAR they hadn't understood all the rules and they'd been branded from the beginning as mavericks—because they'd been so creative with the rules. And Dave Jenner had been one of those labeling them.

"Dave's not really your enemy, is he?"

Tucker shrugged as he raced down the dark highway.

"No, we're just rivals. But something about that guy—actually that whole family—makes my skin itch."

Jared knew exactly what Tucker meant. They were so close and supportive and two loners like Tucker and him…well, all that Jenner family love made him a little itchy, too. The last time he'd let himself really enjoy being a part of a family was way back before his parents had died.

"I know what you mean," Jared said, thinking of Alan's hounding him about Annie earlier.

"I think that's part of the problem. Ya know, I want them to be too good to be true but they aren't. Even Dave—hell, he really is gentlemanly both on and off the track. He has his aggressive stuff like any other driver, but he comes off looking good no matter what he does."

Jared leaned back in the seat, not sure he agreed with Tucker. He didn't want Annie to be too good to be true, but a part of him feared that she was.

He wanted her to be exactly as she seemed. Not a woman who was looking for a red-hot affair. Not a woman like any other he'd ever met.

"What's with all the quiet?"

No way was he going to talk about Annie with Tucker. He just wasn't going there. And in the past he would have. They always talked about the women they dated, but then they both had an endless stream of women who breezed through their lives.

"She's different, Tucker."

Tucker glanced over at him, taking his eyes from the road for a minute.

"Are you serious about her?"

Jared didn't know. But his gut tightened when he thought about those moments in the corporate suite when she'd walked away and he hadn't been too sure he could get her back.

"Yeah."

Tucker didn't say anything else for a while. Finally he said, "I'll come out with you guys."

"What changed?"

"If she's going to be important in your life, then I want to know her better."

He glanced at Tucker, uncertain of how Annie would be important, but not sure how to explain what he didn't understand himself to his friend. But he wanted Tucker to like Annie. To know her well enough that he didn't suspect her of trying to sabotage his car in the future.

"Don't worry, man, I'm not going to blow it for you," Tucker said with his trademark grin.

"I'm not worried about that." Hell, if Annie had a problem with Tucker maybe she wasn't the woman he thought she was. Tucker was like the brother he'd never had.

"Yes, you are." Unfortunately just like blood brothers, Tucker could read him like a book. Luckily it went both ways so he'd always known what was going on with Tucker, too.

"Where are you meeting her?"

"At the Beverly Wilshire Hotel in Beverly Hills."

"Let's go."

Tucker drove down the interstate toward Beverly Hills without saying much more. Green Day blared from the speakers. They valet-parked the car and entered the lobby of the hotel.

Tucker was waylaid by a few fans and Jared stood back to give him room. He hadn't figured on Tucker wanting to meet up with Annie.

A part of him wanted to draw his friend to a stop and take five minutes to finalize the different scenarios running through his head. But Tucker was heading toward Annie, who was sitting at the bar.

Annie smiled at them. And Jared knew he was lost. There were no contingency plans he could make that would help him manage this.

CHAPTER EIGHT

WHEN ANNIE AWOKE the next morning she didn't allow herself to analyze the night before. She'd had fun with Tucker and Jared until her male relatives had arrived and made asses out of themselves. Most of her female relatives had sided with her, and they'd all gone home early.

Annie had agreed to have breakfast with Jared this morning at the track. She'd seen a new side of Jared through Tucker. It was obvious the men had known each other for years, and knew each other well.

She tried to tell herself not to read too much into Jared's interest in her. Not to give the feelings that were developing toward him too much importance. But it was impossible not to.

She made a simple breakfast of fruit salad, cheese and French bread and packed it into the picnic basket. Jared had said he'd bring the coffee, and since that was his business she figured he'd be better at it than she would.

She showered, dressed and headed out the door. She

stepped out into the fresh February morning. The breeze was cool, and dawn was just starting to break over the horizon when she arrived at the track. She reached into the picnic basket for her camera, putting the strap around her neck and lifting the Nikon to her eye.

She waited, holding her breath, as the first pink fingers of the sun stretched up in the sky. Then she started clicking, taking pictures until she'd captured the entire sunrise.

She put down the camera as she heard Jared clear his throat, and she glanced over her shoulder at him. She'd been aware of his arrival but hadn't wanted to lose the sun.

"Good morning," she said.

"Nice sunrise?"

"The best. I was a little jealous yesterday when Abby was talking about her new project. I miss projects like that. Sports photography is fun and I love it, but it's not the same as nature."

He took the picnic basket from her and led her out of the line of RVs toward the grassy area near Turn Two. Since no one was up at this time of the morning, and the infield campers weren't allowed access to that area, they'd be alone.

"How did you get interested in photography?" he asked as they settled into their picnic spot.

"I knew I wasn't going to be a race-car driver when

I was about nine. So I started researching other jobs I could have when I could still travel with my family."

He handed her a travel coffee mug with the JM logo on it, along with a packet of sugar and a small container with half-and-half. "I didn't know how you take it," he explained.

"Just cream," she said, adding it to her coffee. The rich aroma filled the air around them.

"How did you get into the coffee business?"

"It started when I was in college. I always had a lot of extra money, but my father wouldn't let me have control of it until I could prove myself. With my trust fund we purchased a building. My original intent was to make money from the rents, which I did for a while."

She took a sip of her coffee. "What changed?"

"I went to Colombia for the summer on one of those extreme vacations, and broke my ankle doing a high-altitude climb. I spent the rest of the vacation sitting in the main house of a coffee grower. His son was our guide." He shrugged. "I learned a lot from him, and one thing led to another and before I knew it, I'd opened a coffeehouse."

They ate their breakfast and talked about their lives, and Annie realized that the tests she'd thought about last night had disappeared. She wasn't playing games and keeping score anymore. She was just enjoying her time with him.

When the meal was over he helped her clean up the

containers and then repacked them. Then he took her hands in his and drew her around to face him. They sat cross-legged, knees touching. He leaned in, cupping her face in his hands.

He kissed her, a soft, sweet brush of his lips against hers. "Yesterday I meant for our lunch to be the start of our relationship. A real start. But that got botched, so I want to start again."

"Me, too," she said, her voice sounding breathless to her own ears.

He pulled the Tiffany box from a pocket in his jacket and held it out to her. "Will you accept this now?"

She nodded.

He took the bracelet out and fastened it around her wrist. She glanced down at it and noticed that there was a second charm hanging from it this morning.

She smiled and tried not to give the new charm too much importance, but it was a dazzling sun charm. She fingered it carefully and then leaned forward to kiss him.

He pulled her into his arms and leaned back so they were both lying on the blanket.

She closed her eyes and wrapped herself around him. His mouth moved over hers in languid sweeps, making her feel like they were the only people in the world.

JARED TOOK HER MOUTH in his, letting his hands wander over her body. He was still amazed that she'd agreed to give him a second chance. A chance that he was determined not to screw up.

He hadn't slept at all last night. Instead he'd spent the time planning out the next steps he'd take in his courtship of her. Having her accept the bracelet gave him confidence that he was on the right track.

He rolled over so that she was under him. Her legs parted and he settled against her. His arms were braced on either side of her body. Looking down into her serious brown eyes he saw something fragile there, and he knew that she was vulnerable to him.

He caught her head in his hands and brought his mouth down hard on hers. When he finally came up for air he said, "I promise you won't regret this.

He hoped she'd believe him. Jared wasn't the kind of man to make promises lightly. Oh, man, he'd just given her another promise. But with Annie he wanted to make promises he knew he would keep, no matter how hard it was on him.

She turned her head, reaching up with one hand to caress his face. "I promise you won't, either."

He stroked the long line of her cheekbones. Her skin was softer than anything he'd ever touched. Her lashes drifted down as he explored the angles and curves of her face. He traced the lines of her lips as they parted under his touch. He stroked his thumb over her full lower lip, watched the natural pink color of her lips darken.

She tipped her head back and leaned the slightest bit away from him. He knew that despite what she'd said she still wasn't sure that he wouldn't hurt her emotionally. But she'd been willing to meet him here. Seeing the implicit trust she'd just given him by turning to him affected him. He refused to analyze it, happy that she'd let him back into her life.

He leaned down and brushed his lips over hers, meaning for the embrace to be an apology—or perhaps even a thank-you for staying when no one else had. Even though he wasn't sure if this would last.

Jared had never seen anything more beautiful than the woman in his arms. He reached between them, the backs of his fingers brushing her. She shook from the brief contact. She bit her lower lip, and he bent down to lick it.

He leaned back, bracing himself on one elbow so he could run his finger down the center of her body, down her sternum and between her ribs. He lingered over her, caressing her with long sweeps of his hands. She was so responsive to his touch, and he wanted more.

She was the best thing that had happened to him in a life filled with lucky moments. He thought about the story he'd told her earlier about the coffeehouse. He was one of those men who always seemed to be in the right place at the right time when it came to business, but this was the first time he felt like he was in the right place with the right woman.

But he wouldn't say those words out loud. He wanted her, but until this moment he had not realized how fiercely.

She was exquisitely built, soft and feminine. Her breasts were full and her skin flushed. He ran his hands slowly over her torso, almost afraid to believe that after all his hard work, after all his planning, she was really here.

He'd barely explored her before, and he needed to now. He needed to find out how she responded to his every touch. But they were lying on a blanket in the infield, and though it felt like they were in their own private world, he knew they weren't.

"Annie, you go to my head."

She smiled up at him, a sweet, shy smile that made him feel ten feet tall. There was something very fragile inside this ultracompetent woman. He pulled her more fully into his arms, cradling her to his chest with one arm. She closed her eyes and buried her face in his neck. Each exhalation went through him. God, he wanted her.

But he was going to wait. Then he felt the minute touches of her tongue against his neck.

"Isn't this sweet?" a voice suddenly said.

Jared glanced up and bit back a curse. Dave Jenner stood next to their blanket. Annie went totally stiff under him and turned red.

He rolled off Annie and got to his feet, drawing her

up beside him and wrapping his arm around her waist. He refused to act like he'd been caught doing something he shouldn't have.

"What can we do for you?"

"Mom is looking for you, Annie."

"Thanks for passing the message along," Annie said.

Dave stood there, hands on his hips.

"Was there something else?" Annie asked.

"I want to have a few words with Jared here."

"Dave…"

Jared had no problem talking to her relatives, but he could tell she was unsure of whether or not she should leave him with Dave. He tipped her head back and kissed her lingeringly, staking his claim on her in front of her brother. Then he gave her a small nudge in the direction of the RVs. "Go on. We'll catch up with you in a minute."

She shook her head. But she walked away, and he watched her go before turning to her brother.

"How many times are we going to do this?"

"However many it takes until you get the message."

"What message is that?"

"That you're not welcome around here."

"Your sister seems to feel differently."

Dave rubbed the back of his neck. "We'll see about that."

Dave turned to talk away. Jared appreciated the man's sentiments and the fact that he was looking out for Annie, but Annie was his now. And he wished there was an easy way to let the Jenner men know that.

THE NEXT FEW WEEKS flew by. Dave won in Fontana, but Tucker beat him in Las Vegas. Dave had just lost to Tucker last Sunday. And their rivalry was really getting hot. Annie didn't know if it was only because of Jared that she seemed more aware of Tucker, but for the first time she wasn't just paying attention to her brother.

Annie had stayed in one of the hotels on the Vegas strip that was owned by a family friend. She'd had fun at the race, and gambling in Vegas.

She'd gone home for two days to her house on Lake Windemere in Orlando, Florida. The house had seemed too empty and quiet when she was there, probably because she didn't want to be there. Jared had invited her to join him at his home in Atlanta for their days off, but she'd declined. Not for any good reason except that she was afraid to be alone with him. Afraid to take the next logical step in their relationship and sleep with him.

She wanted him. Had fallen to sleep almost every night in recent memory thinking of him, and had woken up to fevered dreams of making love with him. But she still wasn't sure she wanted to take that final step.

Once she did, there'd be no pretending that she wasn't falling for him. She glanced at the bracelet on her wrist—the one that she only took off once a week when Jared added another charm to it. It was a sweet reminder of all the time they'd spent together. And she wondered sometimes if the bracelet would be all she had left at the end of this NASCAR season.

Because no matter how close they were getting there was still a part of Jared that he kept private. The solid inner core of the man that he never allowed anyone to touch.

At first she hadn't noticed the distance, but over time she'd started to observe it. She thought it was only because they were still getting to know each other, but she had observed the distance between him and Tucker as well.

Jared was careful to let people get only so close. With Tucker he did it by joking around with him and always using a kind of masculine bluster to keep from showing emotion. With her he fell back on the physical, to keep her from getting to close. He was always kissing or hugging her when she said something he didn't want to respond to.

Her extended family had taken to arriving early on Thursdays for every race. Every one of her male relatives had at some point over the past few weeks taken Jared aside and spoken to him. She wanted to die of embarrassment but Jared had said only that she should enjoy the fact that they loved her that much.

The women in her family had all sided with Annie and were very supportive of Jared. The tension at Jenner Racing was reaching an all-time high. And if she hadn't been falling for Jared, she would have called things off just to restore the peace.

She'd never thought of her family in that light. But there had been a hint of longing in Jared's voice, which had made her very aware of the fact that not everyone had what she did.

Her father was recovering from his bypass surgery and would be attending the next race. She'd just gotten home from the airport and she wished…wished she'd gone to Atlanta with Jared.

She booted up her computer to download the pictures she'd taken at the race the weekend before. A feeling of sadness swamped her as she realized she was playing at having a relationship with Jared, she thought to herself. She was keeping him carefully in the NASCAR world and not letting him see the other sides of her life.

What bothered her the most was that he let her go. He wasn't pushing to get into those corners she'd carefully kept him out of. It seemed to her that he had his own limitations on them, and her barriers just fit within his.

She put the memory stick from her computer into the flash drive and waited for the photos to download. They started to flash across the screen. She watched the familiar images of cars and tracks come up, and then the pictures she'd had no business taking appeared.

Images of Jared in the garage area watching Tucker's crew work on his car. Even more images of Jared, standing outside Dave's hauler talking to Vinnie. A close-up on Jared's face, the sun and laugh lines apparent around his eyes.

She knew how his skin felt against hers. How his lips felt when he kissed her—when he was smiling, too. She'd traced his mouth as he'd smiled down at her this morning at the airport, saying goodbye.

Their relationship was marked with goodbyes. She knew he was a man with a lot of responsibilities, not just to the cars he sponsored in NASCAR. She'd caught a few glimpses of him in the society pages in the different cities they'd visited. He always had at least one social function outside of the race community that he attended.

Though her family had money, they didn't socialize as much with the moneyed set. Jared had asked her to accompany him to the charity events, but she'd always declined because she was working.

Her phone rang and she ignored it. The last thing she wanted to do was make small talk with anyone right now.

The machine picked up and she listened to her voice telling the caller to leave a message at the tone.

"Annie, it's me," Jared said. "I guess I beat you home this week. I'm going to work out, but I'll be home later if you want to talk."

She reached for the phone. "I'm here."

"Screening your calls? What would your mother say?" he asked, teasing her gently.

"She'd have a fit, as you well know."

"I promise not to tell."

"You make me a lot of promises," she said.

He was quiet for a minute. "I do. And I intend to keep them."

She knew he was referring to the other promise, the one about not hurting her. But she wondered if that was simply out of his control. "It might be hard. My parents are coming to Atlanta this weekend. My mom can crack even the toughest person."

"I'll do my best to withstand whatever pressure she puts on me."

"I know you will," she said. Because she'd seen him carry himself with panache and poise even when being grilled by Dave or Uncle Steve.

"Good. I want to be someone you can count on, Annie."

"You are. Am I someone you can count on?"

"Yes."

"Even though I make you stag it to those society dinners you always have?"

"If I say no, will you go with me this weekend?"

"I'm not sure. Why do you still attend them? You don't seem to enjoy it."

"It was important to my mom that we keep up the MacNeils' position in society."

She liked that about him. "Okay, I'll go with you."

"Really?"

"Yes, really. What will I need to wear? A formal dress, right?"

"Yes. The event is a Cancer Foundation dinner. I can book you a hotel room where the event if being held or…"

"Or?"

"You can stay at my house with me."

"I think I'd like to stay with you," she said.

She heard his quick intake of breath and knew she'd surprised him.

ANNIE FELT MORE glamorous than she ever had before as she entered the ballroom at the hotel on Jared's arm. He looked cool and sophisticated in his tuxedo. The dress he'd picked out for her was a slim-fitting, ankle-length sheath with a simple drop neckline. The dress had a slit on the left side that went to the top of her thigh.

He wrapped one arm around her shoulder, drawing her closer to his side as they entered the crowded room. There was a small jazz combo playing in the far corner, and three bar areas just inside the entrance.

"Do you want a drink?" he asked.

She asked for a glass of wine and stood by herself as he went to get it. She longed for her camera as she glanced around the room. She wished she had the barrier that only having the camera to her eye could provide—though in her mind she knew there wasn't enough light for any natural shots.

As she glanced around the room and saw the high-society people filling it, she started to run through different light settings in her mind, rejecting them until she came up with the right one.

"Here you go," Jared said, handing her a glass.

She took it from him, realizing her nerves had nothing to do with the room full of strangers and everything to do with the man standing next to her.

She lifted her glass toward his and her hand shook, a little bit of wine sloshing onto the back of her hand. Jared raised one eyebrow.

"Everything okay?"

"Sure," she said, taking a fortifying sip of wine before any more spilled.

"Thank you for coming with me tonight."

"You're welcome."

Silence grew between them as all she could think about was the king-sized bed in Jared's bedroom, that lushly decorated room where he'd stowed her suitcase when she'd arrived this afternoon.

She didn't know why she was having a panic attack about it now, why she was thinking about the fact that the last man she'd slept with had made her feel like… she was less than a woman.

Jared never had. And his embraces had left her with the fire of desire coursing through her veins. But at this moment, none of that mattered. At the end of the evening she was going to go home with him and go to bed with him.

And the last thing she wanted was to have him look

at her with disdain or disappointment. She took another swallow of her wine.

Jared's hand came to the small of her back. He led her to a quiet alcove tucked off the ballroom, where they were alone. He took the wineglass from her and bent to set it on the floor alongside his squat whiskey glass.

"What's up?"

She shrugged her shoulders thinking of the all the ways she didn't want to go there. But then he put one hand on her waist and one hand so gently in her hair. He blocked her from the view of anyone who'd pass by, and made her feel safe.

"I'm not sure," she said at last. "I think I'm nervous."

"Don't be. This is a charity event. After the dinner we're going to be entertained by Elton John."

She loved Elton John's music. Who didn't? But tonight not even the thought of listening to him live was enough to distract her from Jared—the press of his large body against hers, the awareness she had of the space between their bodies. When she tipped her head back and met his eyes, she saw knowledge blooming there.

"Annie, honey, nothing has to happen that you don't want to," he said in that deep, sure voice of his, the one that was all confidence and caring.

She felt tears sting the backs of her eyes, and wished she was the woman she'd been before her marriage. The woman who would have enjoyed the heck out of this night and been quivering with anticipation when they returned to his place.

But she wasn't.

"I want…"

He waited.

"…you," she said. And in a rush, before she lost her nerve, she allowed words to spill out of her mouth. She explained about Malcolm and how she'd never been responsive enough for him. How he'd said she left him cold. Lastly she said, "He used to look at me with such disdain in his eyes. I don't want you to ever look at me like that. But I don't know what to do to keep a man happy in bed."

He pulled her fully into his arms, bending to capture her mouth with his. His hands swept down her back and she felt her blood begin to flow a little heavier in her veins. She felt her skin tighten and every nerve ending tingle as he caressed the expanse of skin left bare by the back of her dress.

Then he swiveled his hips, his body brushing against the center of hers, letting her feel the proof of his desire. "You don't have to try to make me happy," he said as he lifted his mouth from hers. "You already do."

CHAPTER NINE

CARS HAD LONG BEEN a passion for Jared and he kept a different one in each of the houses he owned. In Daytona he'd been driving his new Aston Martin, but in Atlanta he kept his classic '67 Jaguar. Tucker had helped him restore the car three years ago.

His house was set back from the road with a winding driveway that led up to the huge mansion. The home had belonged to his maternal grandparents and he always felt like it was still theirs, though they'd been gone for more than twenty years.

His grandfather had let him drive up this circular driveway when he'd been only fourteen. Jared chuckled remembering the experience.

"What are you laughing about?"

"My granddad let me drive his Cadillac when I was fourteen...see that statuary near the stairs?"

"Um...yes."

"She used to have a mate on the other side."

"So your driving skills weren't always that great?"

"No. But my granddad didn't mind."

"Was this his house?"

"Yes. And my mom grew up here. That's why I always attend the Bea and Thom Mellon Foundation Event. My family has supported it for years, and my grandparents were on the board when they were alive."

"I really enjoyed myself tonight."

"I did, too."

He turned off the car and got out. He opened her door and her legs emerged first. The slit in her dress fell open to reveal her shapely thigh. Oh, man, she was killing him.

"You're staring at me," she said, a wry note in her voice.

"Am I?" he asked, stroking his finger down the side of her neck.

She shivered as he rubbed the pad of his finger over her pulse.

"Yes, you are," she said.

"You have gorgeous legs," he said, putting his hand on her back and leading her up the stairs and into his house.

"I can't believe you are just noticing," she said.

"I've noticed before but tonight…in that dress…I just can't take my eyes off of you."

"Then don't," she said.

He drew her down the hall toward the living room. He tossed her wrap and purse over the back of the leather couch. He shrugged out of his jacket and tossed it aside, too. Then he leaned back against the marble-topped wet bar and stared at her.

"What are you doing?" she asked.

"Exactly what you told me I could do," he said.

She shook her head, bringing her hand up to cover her face. "Stop it."

"Now you know how I feel when I catch you with your camera trained on me."

"It shouldn't bother you. You are a very handsome man. I could spent all day photographing you and still not capture that energy you exude in person."

"So you're trying to capture me?"

She raised her eyebrows at him. "Yes, I am."

She closed the gap between them, resting her hands on his chest. "I've had you in my sights for a while now."

"And tonight you're closing in for the kill?"

"Mmm-hmm, but I promise it won't be painful."

"You'd be worth it," he said, drawing her back into his arms.

She flushed. "You flatter me."

"No, it's the truth. Every lush curve of your body makes me want to sink my fingers into it. When we're apart I'm distracted wanting to be with you, wanting to hold you closer in my arms."

She slid her hands around his neck and drew his head down to hers.

"What are you going to do now?" she asked.

"I'm thinking about kissing you."

"Just thinking about it?"

"Yeah, I'm just thinking…wondering if your mouth tastes as good as I remember. I always think that it can't possibly." He whispered the last words against her lips.

She licked her lips. His eyes narrowed as he followed the movement with his gaze.

"Annie?"

"Hmm?"

"Last chance…" he said, brushing his lips over hers. He hoped he could be a gentleman and walk away if that was what she wanted.

She pulled back. He forced himself to let her go. But then she lifted her eyes to his. Taking his hand in hers, she led the way down the hall to his bedroom.

DAVE EXITED the media center. He liked racing in Atlanta, as did most of the other drivers. The track was high-banked, repaved back in '97 and reconfigured into a quad-oval, making it one of the fastest tracks they raced on.

He glanced across at the grandstands where a few die-hard fans were already seated and waiting for the drivers to take their practice runs.

He'd done a couple of media events during the week leading up to arriving in Atlanta and he was tired. He was tired of rehashing his loss last week to Tucker. But he knew it was part and parcel of the life he'd chosen, so he forced a smile to his face as a couple of other drivers who also drove for Jenner Racing waved at him.

His dad's health had been one topic of conversation in the interview. Dave thought it had gone well until that last second when the reporter had asked if he was going to win on Sunday…for his dad.

He'd smiled, said something glib and glanced at Melissa, his assistant, who came over and said the interview was over. He couldn't blame the reporters or anyone else. He was just in a funk.

Part of it was Annie and her relationship with Jared. Another part was Daddy and his health. And his mom's well-meaning calls to update him on his father's slow recovery. He felt the pressure building inside him to not let anyone down. He wanted to be the hero he'd always been to his sister, but she was spending more time in Tucker Aldridge's garage and hauler than his, hanging out with Jared and making friends with the man who rubbed him the wrong way.

Once they were in the garage area he went to the bay he'd been assigned. He'd won this race last year so he was in the first garage bay. Tucker had come in second so his team and car were right next to Dave's.

He glanced over, telling himself he wasn't looking for Annie, but he knew he was. His sister had been in Atlanta since Wednesday and he still hadn't seen her for more than five minutes without Jared by her side.

He had to get his head in the upcoming race and not worry about his family. This was the part that made him feel like a first-class whiner. But there were times—like now—when he hated being a part of dynasty. Hated the fact that more times than not he wasn't just racing against the other drivers on the track. He was racing against his father.

He had to hold up the Jenner family name. Had to ensure the legacy of racing and winning didn't end with him.

"Dave?"

"What?"

"I asked if you had time now to meet with the family here from the wish-granting foundation. Their son, Jon, is your biggest fan."

Kids with terminal diseases and their families. He glanced at the sky thinking that maybe God was sending him a message—one that he needed as a reminder. "Of course, Mel. I can meet him now. I've been looking forward to it. I'll be out in a sec. Did we give him a shirt and hat?"

"Of course. Donovan's been with the family all morning."

Dave continued walking out of the garage into the cluster of fans waiting between the garage and hauler. He signed a few hats and T-shirts. When someone handed him a Jenner shirt, one that had the numbers of his and his father's cars, he signed it but felt like a fraud.

It was as if he was letting down the Jenner family with his failure to win the NASCAR NEXTEL Championship Cup.

ANNIE WAS IN Turn Two photographing the race. The weight of the camera with the large slow-motion lens was heavy, but she was used to it. The race was a close one and she held her breath each time there was a bump or any contact between cars, hoping that Dave wasn't involved. The race was well-run, there were a minimal number of crashes and when it was over she made her way to Victory Lane to photograph Tucker, who'd won.

Dave was talking to a couple of officials as she made her way through the throng to get into position to take pictures. She saw Jared behind Tucker talking with Tucker's crew chief.

Jared smiled in her direction and Annie felt a warm flush cover her body. She knew she was falling for him. Had been falling for him from the first moment they'd met.

Annie wanted to believe he was the kind of man she could count on. The type of man who'd always be there when she needed him. He seemed so rock-steady.

But she couldn't quite believe Jared was all he seemed and she remembered clearly that just over a month ago he'd accused her of doing something illegal.

She tried not to dwell on that. Jared hadn't known her

well enough then to realize she'd never cheat. But he did now. She was slowly relaxing her guard around him, letting him see her as she really was. Not playing at being the kind of woman that would fit into his life perfectly. Not changing herself into what she thought he needed.

She finished her assignment, checked out at the media center and went to find Dave. This loss was going to be hard to take. Not that they all weren't, but he'd mentioned before the race that he'd wanted to win for Daddy, since he was here watching the race today.

The garage was still off-limits so only those with a hot pass were allowed in. Annie was waved through and went to Dave's garage. Vinnie and Dave were both talking to another official.

"What's going on?" Annie asked Dave when Vinnie walked away with the official.

Dave looked tired and pissed off. He still had on his uniform but had unzipped it and she saw he had on her dad's old T-shirt underneath. It was the T-shirt that commemorated their father's first NASCAR NEXTEL Cup Series win. "Aldridge won that race on four tires that hadn't been changed."

"So?" she asked, thinking that Dave was getting a little intense in his rivalry with Tucker. She hadn't seen him so obsessed before.

"So everyone else in the top five had at least two new tires on."

"And fresher tires normally allow you to go faster," she stated.

"Exactly. I should have caught him on that last lap," Dave said.

Her brother was pure brilliance when it came to those last laps of a race.

"We asked the official to check the tires."

"What could Tucker do to his tires?" she asked. All of the drivers used the same tires and they were inspected carefully before they went on the cars.

"We're not sure. I'm thinking he used some kind of synthetic substance that would enable him to use his tires longer than normal."

"Oh. When will you know?"

"Not until tomorrow."

She knew that all the top five cars were always inspected after the races, as well as a group of randomly selected cars from the rest of the pack. That was why the race standings were always unofficial until the following day. If anything out of the ordinary was found on the car the driver could be fined or disqualified.

Dave left to join Vinnie and the officials, and Annie left the garage following her brother and taking pictures of the event.

Everyone was mumbling about the complaint that Jenner Racing had lodged. She tried to catch Jared's eye but he and Tucker were both talking to the officials.

When he did glance up, he gave her a hard look before stalking away.

Annie knew that the fact that they were both a part of rival teams mattered and Jared had just proved that. She found her brother and did her job taking photos of him, finding solace in her work so that she wouldn't have time to think about the look on Jared's face.

CHAPTER TEN

THE INQUIRY THAT Dave had requested didn't turn up anything illegal on Tucker's tires. That had only served to drive a deeper wedge between the two men. Annie felt pulled in two directions.

She'd flown home on Monday morning and there had been no call from Jared. In fact, he'd said nothing to her after Tucker's win. She'd thought about letting this situation with him simmer until he brought it up, but that had been one of the things that had soured her relationship with Malcolm. Instead of confronting him with his infidelity she'd tried to ignore it and keeping it inside had ultimately caused her far too much pain. She wouldn't let that happen with Jared. She needed to see him.

"Um…can you wait for a moment?" she asked the taxi driver when he pulled up to Jared's Atlanta house. The driveway was gated and she didn't want to talk to him through the box with the taxi driver.

"Sure, miss. I'm going to keep the meter running."

"No problem."

She got out of the car at the gate that protected Jared's privacy. A light rain began to fall and she shivered, wishing she'd worn a jacket. But the sun had been shining when she'd left Florida.

She knew he was in residence at this house because she'd called earlier and spoken to his housekeeper, who had told her that Jared wasn't taking calls this morning.

She hit the buzzer.

"Yes."

She took a deep breath. "Hi. This is Annie Jenner. I'm here to see Jared."

"Are you expected?" the woman asked.

"No."

"Just a minute."

She stood there for what seemed like an hour, but in reality was only five minutes. "Come on up."

She went back to the cab and climbed in as the gates opened. The taxi took her to the front of the house. She paid the driver and got out, stopping on the step and re-membering the closeness she'd felt to Jared the last time she'd been here.

The door opened before she rang the bell and Jared stood there in a pair of faded jeans and a faded college T-shirt. His feet were bare and his hair was damp, as if he'd come from the shower. He looked tired.

"Hey," she said, adjusting the strap of her overnight bag on her shoulder.

"What are you doing here?"

"I…things felt unsettled between us," she said.

"It's not us…it's, ah, come on in, Annie."

She followed him into the house. He went to the living room and leaned against the wet bar the way he had the last time she was there. But this time she felt less sure of herself. This was the kind of rift that wasn't going to go away no matter what the two of them decided.

"Tucker and Dave are always going to be rivals," she stated.

"I know. I'm not angry at you or even at Dave," Jared said. "He has the right to lodge a complaint after a race."

"So why do I feel like it has affected us?" she asked, wrapping one arm around her waist.

He shook his head. "I wanted to pretend that Dave and Tucker weren't really a part of what's been going on between us."

"They aren't. That's stuff that happens at the track."

"Yeah, right. Your brother doesn't like the fact that we're dating."

Annie had a sinking feeling in her stomach that she and Jared weren't going to be able to move past this. "He wouldn't accuse Tucker of something just because he doesn't like you."

"I'm not so sure about it."

She took a deep breath. "I am. I know that Dave can be overprotective when it comes to me, but the rest of the guys on his team don't care about who I date."

"You have a point," Jared said. He rubbed the back of his neck. "I haven't slept in thirty-six hours."

"I know it's been rough," she replied. "Let me help you. Relationships are built on moments like this."

"Our relationship...does that mean you still want to do this? I don't think that this is going to be an isolated incident. Tucker is going to be scrutinizing everything your brother does and vice versa."

"I tried to go home and forget about you. It would be easier for my family if I just stopped seeing you, but it wouldn't be easier for me."

"Ah, Annie," he said. He crossed the room and drew her into his arms. He wrapped her in a bear hug that quieted the worries in her head.

"Where do we go from here?" she asked.

"We stick together. At the track we'll do our jobs, but in our free time...we'll be together, right?"

"Yes," she said. She knew that they were facing a rough patch but she felt that he was worth it. She'd taken a huge leap of faith by coming here today and Jared... Well, Jared had proven he was worth the risk.

HER FEELINGS FOR Jared grew deeper each week and they'd spent so much time together, she was starting to not only like the man he was, but see a future where they could be together as she caught glimpses of the man he hid from the world.

Those moments didn't happen often and usually he retreated as soon as he realized he'd let her past his barriers, but she took heart from the fact that he was letting her in.

Her cell phone rang and she glanced at the caller ID.

"Hey, Jared."

"Are your parents there yet?"

"Yes, why?"

"I just want to make sure that everything is perfect tonight."

"Dinner isn't going to change my father's mind about you."

"It could."

"Why is this so important? I thought all the lectures didn't bother you."

"They don't. But I know how close you are to your parents. I don't want to cause a rift."

"What do you mean?"

He took a deep breath and then said, "I know how lonely it can be to lose that closeness with your parents."

"You were close to your parents," she said, knowing from other comments he'd made that he had been.

"Yes. And I'm not going to be responsible for any tension with yours."

"Jared—"

"I've got to go. I'll be there in a few minutes."

He hung up. She fingered the bracelet he'd given her

as she put the finishing touches on her makeup. It was the Friday before the race at Talladega.

Jared had hired a limo to pick them up. She was waiting with her mom and dad outside the track. It was a beautiful spring night in Alabama. And she thought it was a good sign for the evening.

Her father was still leery of her relationship with Jared. A long black limo pulled to a stop where they were waiting. Jared climbed out of the back, flashing Annie a quick grin as he shook her father's hand and gave her mom a friendly hug.

The driver opened the door and her parents got into the back of the stretch limo. "You're early."

"I'm hoping to make a good impression on your parents. Maybe your dad will call off the rest of your male relatives."

"You two coming?" Her dad stuck his head out of the open door. "Or you going to talk all night?"

"We're coming," she said, getting into the car. Jared followed her, sitting next to her in the seat facing the rear of the car. Jared left the door open.

"Aren't we ready to go?"

"No. We're waiting for your brother."

"He didn't mention anything to me about coming," Annie said.

"He'll be here," her father stated.

Annie hoped the evening didn't turn into Dave and Daddy grilling Jared about his intentions.

"Oh, good," her mom stated.

Dave joined them a few minutes later and she found herself sitting on the bench seat between her lover and her brother. Neither man said much to the other but her parents kept the conversation going.

They had a nice meal at the country club where Jared had made arrangements for them to have dinner. When they got back to the track, Dave took her aside while Jared showed her parents the corporate suite he was using for the week.

"Does he think that we're going to forget he's the team owner for Aldridge?" Dave asked.

She frowned at him. "I think he wants to get to know you all better. It's not like we're going to forget about Tucker."

"I'm sure he wants to know us. Most people are envious of the Jenner legacy."

"He's not like that. He has plenty of NASCAR connections. And he has no aspirations to be a driver."

"Don't remind me."

"What's this really about, Dave?"

Her brother shrugged. "Look, maybe I just can't separate MacNeil from Aldridge. They are a team and I'm used to working against them on the track and off."

"Jared's nothing like Tucker."

"No?"

"Tucker's much more gregarious. Jared seems that way but there's a...wall of reserve that he doesn't let

many people see behind. He's trying to open himself
up to the family, Dave."

"You seem to know Tucker pretty well."

"He's Jared's best friend. He's not as bad as you
think he is. But I don't care if you like Tucker or not."

"What are you saying?"

"I'm saying that you should give Jared a chance."

"No, thanks."

"Dave—"

"I'm not interested in discussing this anymore. Tell
Mom and Dad I had to run."

Dave walked away and Annie watched him leave,
feeling a sad ache in her heart. Jared returned a few
minutes later.

"Where's Dave?"

"He had to go. Thanks for taking us to dinner tonight."

"You're welcome. I think your mom and dad
enjoyed themselves. Your dad is even warming up to me
a little. I wouldn't say he actually likes me but we found
some common ground."

"Talking about owning cars and running a team?"
she asked.

Jared shrugged. "It's a start."

THE NEXT WEEKS FLEW BY with more tension than Annie
had experienced in a long time. She couldn't believe it
was May. Annie had always liked coming to Richmond
and this year was no different. Tucker had been careful

to treat her more like Jared's girlfriend than Dave's sister, which she appreciated a lot—especially when Dave was being difficult.

Dave acted as if she'd committed the deepest act of betrayal by continuing to date Jared. In fact they hadn't spoken in the last week because of the fight they'd had in Talladega.

Her respect for Tucker had grown as he'd endured rumors and innuendos about his tires and the resurfacing of the old stories from his rookie year when he'd been a bit of a maverick, always shooting off his mouth and getting creative with the rules.

She'd spent the morning in the garage photographing the crew getting the car ready for the race. Dave wanted to devote a chapter of the book to Vinnie and her father's crew chief, Pete Boscom. But right now Annie was standing outside Dave's hauler waiting for him to get back from the media center so she could make peace with him. She didn't like it when they were fighting.

"Annie, you got a minute?"

She glanced over to see Dave's assistant holding a clipboard. "Sure, Mel, what's up?"

"Um…we got a couple of questions this week about you and team owner Jared MacNeil."

Annie wasn't surprised. She'd been accompanying Jared to a few social events and the media had picked up on it, putting pictures of the two of them together on the society and sports pages.

"What's the problem?"

"Everyone knows that Dave and Tucker are rivals, and with you dating MacNeil…"

"What do you want me to do?" she asked, not sure where Melissa was going with this.

"Well, Dave is not saying much. But Tucker has been saying what a great gal you are and all that stuff."

That explained so much of the argument she and Dave had last week. "Could you ask Tucker to tone it down a little?" Melissa requested.

"I'll see what I can do," Annie said. This was what she'd been expecting from the first. "I was actually hoping to talk to Dave. Will he be back here soon?"

"Yes," Mel answered.

Melissa left a few minutes later and Annie leaned against the hauler waiting for her brother. He showed up about ten minutes later. He stopped when he saw her standing there, then opened the door to the hauler and motioned for her to enter before him.

She rubbed her hands down her arms, climbed up the steps and entered. She sank down on the long bench and tried to think of the right words to apologize for a fight she wasn't sure she'd started.

But Dave just sat down next to her and threw his arm around her shoulder. "I hate it when we fight."

"Me, too," she said. "I'm sorry if I've done anything to complicate your life."

"Are you happy with this guy?"

"This guy? He has a name."

"I know what it is," Dave said, pulling his arm away from her and leaning forward, bracing his forearms on his thighs.

"Yeah, I am happy with him. Mom likes him. Dad is starting to come around."

"He's a charming guy. I'm not surprised the folks like him. He knows how to put everyone at ease."

"Not you."

"I think it has something to do with the fact that I'm your brother and I don't trust him."

Why didn't Dave trust him? She'd never told him that Jared had accused her of tampering with Tucker's car. So what did her twin sense that she was missing?

"Why don't you trust him? I...you know that trusting someone is hard for me. But I've come to see that he can be very trustworthy."

Dave didn't say anything.

"Is it just the Tucker connection?" she asked.

He shrugged and Annie was suddenly mad at him. Mad at the men in her life who endlessly complicated it.

"I think I'm falling for him, Dave. I think he could be the right man for me. So if you know something solid about him, tell me."

"Ah, Annie. Don't fall for him."

"You know love doesn't work like that."

"Yeah, I do. You really like him that much?"

She nodded.

"Straight up, Annie, I don't trust him because I don't know him."

"You haven't exactly been friendly."

"Fair enough, but everyone I've asked about him says the same thing. He's all surface, flash and charm, but no one knows anything solid about the man himself."

She swallowed her own fear that Dave's comments brought to the surface. She knew that Jared could be distant. She'd seen him deflect her with kisses and embraces.

"I think he's afraid to let anyone close," she said.

"Then why are you trying so hard to change that?" Dave asked.

She had no words to explain it that wouldn't leave her feeling exposed and raw. And she didn't want to go there with Dave.

"I'm not trying to bring you down, Annie."

"I know," she said, realizing nothing between Dave and Jared had been resolved. But she did feel as if there was a certain peace between the two of them now.

"I got some good shots of Vinnie and your team this morning."

"You're going to get some great shots later."

"Really? Of what?"

"Me winning."

CHAPTER ELEVEN

DAVE WAS RUNNING LATE to the drivers' meeting. He had qualified in the pole position for Richmond and the last thing he wanted to do was screw up by arriving late to the meeting. All drivers and crew chiefs were required to attend and be on time. Anyone who was late was penalized, usually by having to start last in the pack regardless of qualifying.

When he arrived Dave saw Vinnie was already in the garage bay where the chairs had been set up. He sank down next to his crew chief.

"Late night?"

"Ha, I wish. You?"

"Nah. Darla's here and she likes to 'spend quality time' together."

Dave laughed. Vinnie's wife read a lot of magazines, always had some new relationship improvement in store for him. Though Vinnie groused a bit, Dave knew his friend didn't mind. In fact, Dave kind of envied Vinnie and the solid relationship he had with Darla.

He glanced around at the seats, seeing that they were

almost full. This was the one time each week where all the drivers and crew chiefs were together. It was kind of a last bit of relaxing before the race started in a couple of hours.

The officials were about to go over the rules and ask questions. Though they all drove each week sometimes issues came up. In fact Dave was going to bring up something that had been bothering him.

Nothing illegal had been found on Aldridge's tires the last time they'd been inspected or at any of the five races they'd had since then. Vinnie had been watching the other man's pit stops and noticed that he hadn't taken tires at his last pit in the last four races.

And he intended to bring that up today. Get it out in the open where it could be dealt with.

Aldridge and Billy Toughton, his crew chief, arrived in the midst of an entourage. Dave noticed that Jared was absent and didn't see his sister, either. But other people with garage passes started to line the garage area where the meeting was held.

Aldridge took a seat right behind Dave. During practice he'd been a little aggressive in his passing, almost clipping Dave's car one time, but it wasn't in a reckless way. It had felt like a warning to Dave, as if the other driver was laying down a challenge before the race. It was a challenge Dave had no problem accepting. He wanted to beat Tucker on the track as many times as he could.

Dave got up toward the end of the meeting when concerns were addressed. "I'm still concerned about the tire usage issue we've been discussing for the last few weeks."

Marvin, the official who'd been leading the meeting, nodded. "You know we don't routinely inspect the tires, Dave."

"Yes, sir. That's why I'm bringing it up again. Aldridge has finished in the top five in the last five races *without* changing tires on his last pit."

Lance Maxwell stepped up. "We've noticed the same thing. I'd second the request that you inspect the tires again."

"Give me a break," Tucker said, standing up. "It's not my tires that are winning races, it's my driving. You know the lab analyzed the tires and they came back clean. "

Dave glanced back at the other man. "Your driving hasn't changed all that much from last year."

The official cleared his throat but didn't say anything else. "Take a seat, please. We'll keep an eye on the tire situation during the race."

"Fine with me," Aldridge said. "But if you're going to send *my* tires to the lab, I think you need to check *all* the drivers' tires."

There was a lot of grumbling and the official finally quieted them all down. "I've already said we'd watch the situation."

Dave knew that was the best he was going to get from the officials and honestly couldn't ask for anything more. The meeting moved on. There were a few other concerns that were addressed.

Lance glanced over at Dave toward the end of the meeting and he knew the junior driver on his team was waiting to see if he was going to say anything about Tucker's driving during practice.

"I have one more thing," Dave said at the end, feeling the mantle of his father's legacy on his shoulders. "Just wanted to remind some drivers that the race isn't won by the fastest, it's won by the driver with skill," he said, looking directly at Aldridge.

"I'm pretty sure that'll be me," Tucker said with his trademark arrogant grin.

Dave curled his hand into a fist, glancing back at the other man. "We'll see."

"Boys," Marvin said.

He hated being called a boy and knew the official had done it intentionally to remind them that sportsmanlike behavior was paramount. "We can settle this on the track."

The meeting was adjourned. Vinnie and Dave left together. A few fans approached with T-shirts but Melissa stepped between him and the fans with a promise he'd sign their stuff after the race.

Dave entered his garage area where his team was tearing down the engine while a group of officials watched. Since he'd qualified in the pole position and had broken a track record, the officials wanted to make sure he hadn't done anything illegal to his engine.

"Hey, bro, you ready for today?"

"Yes," he said, hugging his sister with one arm.

"How was the drivers' meeting?"

"Fine."

"Oh, that doesn't sound fine."

But he didn't say anything more. Aldridge needled him and she already knew that. The fact that the man was a maverick on the track wasn't anything new.

"I'm going to stay on pit road for most of today's race and get what pictures I can there."

"You're always welcome." And she was. He loved having her around. She kept him calm.

She nodded at him and moved out of the way as his guys put the engine back together and got his car ready for the race.

ANNIE LOVED THE RACE at Richmond and had since she was a child. To be honest all the nighttime races had always been her favorites. There was something magical about watching a race at night, seeing the darkened track lit up by the lights of the cars and watching the sparks that the cars sometimes threw into the air.

It was a short track, only three-quarters of a mile long, the kind that her brother was really good on. Some drivers were better on the longer tracks but Dave worked the shorter ones like a dream.

This was the race they'd come back to in the fall and it would lock the drivers in to the Chase for the NASCAR NEXTEL Cup. But tonight it was all about this one race. Driving and winning.

It was early May and there was a bit of a chill in the air.

"Hey, girl." Darla Festa was the wife of Dave's crew chief, Vinnie.

"Hey, Darla. I didn't realize you were here."

"Good. I've been trying to get Vinnie to spend a little more one-on-one time with me. So we've been keeping a low profile."

She smiled at the other woman. Darla was tall, almost five-nine and model slim. She had a wealth of strawberry-blond hair that was always perfectly styled and her makeup was flawless. She was easily one of the most beautiful women that Annie had ever seen, but she was also one of the sweetest.

"Did you work things out with Dave?"

"Yes. How did you know…?"

"Vinnie tells me everything."

"Everything?"

"Yes, so I know about that hot guy you're dating."

She flushed. "It's not because he's hot."

Darla threw her arm around Annie's shoulder and hugged her close for a second. "It doesn't matter to me if it is. I'm just happy to see you back at the track and smiling."

"Thanks, Darla. I'm feeling more like my old self."

"It's about time. I missed you the last few years."

"Me, too."

"Was Europe fun?" Darla asked. "Vinnie hates flying but he promised a trip to Italy if they win the championship this year."

The first six months she'd been married to Malcolm Europe had been a lot of fun. They'd traveled every week like the NASCAR racers did and she'd enjoyed seeing some of her favorite cities as well as new ones. "Yeah, it was pretty cool. Kind of the same as this."

"That always amazes me…how similar people are no matter where you go."

Darla had been a model before she married Vinnie and she often said the pressure and the crowds at fashion shows was very similar to race weekends.

"Did you make any good friends over there?" Darla asked.

Annie fiddled with her camera. This was the conversation she'd been dreading since she returned to her NASCAR family. "A few. But it turned out I didn't fit in that well with them."

"Give me a break, you fit in with everyone," Darla said.

"Trust me, D."

"What was so different?"

"Um…they were very open about having affairs with different drivers."

"Oh, hon."

Annie shrugged. "I think it worked out for the best. Instead of hanging out I started to take more freelance photo assignments, which helped me win some awards and get more work."

"It still had to sting."

"It did. Oh, I've got to run," she said, turning away as the announcer got the race started.

Annie moved down the pit road, taking pictures of Dave and his team throughout the evening. There were a few minor wrecks and Lance Maxwell got caught in one of them. But the damage wasn't too bad and his team was able to fix it and get him back on the track. And then Tucker got caught in a little bump but he didn't lose his position.

When Tucker pitted for the last time there was a lot of chatter about what he was doing. Anne turned her camera onto Tucker's crew and snapped a few photos hoping that she'd be able to get something on film that would put Dave's suspicions to rest.

Annie was surprised to see a new guy that she recognized, Rob Mandelay. He'd gone to school with her and Dave. She hadn't seen him in years. She'd have to catch up with him later.

Dave won the race setting a track record and Annie

forgot about Rob and the photos she'd taken of Aldridge's pit as she made her way to Victory Lane.

JARED STOOD ON the fringes of the circle at Victory Lane watching Annie do her job.

"Come to congratulate the winner?" Alan Jenner asked, coming up behind Jared.

"Yes," he said. Dave had run a good race. Jared wasn't surprised since he'd seen the driver twice since he'd arrived in Richmond and Dave had been very focused, as if he wasn't going to let anything stop him from winning. Jared suspected that Dave was trying to prove something to him by beating Tucker on the track.

"Then why are you staring at Annie?" Alan stated.

"Leave it alone," Jared said, getting a little sick of the Jenner men always hounding him. He was willing to cut them a little slack because he cared for Annie, too, but enough was enough.

"Hello, Jared. Wasn't it an exciting race today?" Carol Jenner asked. Annie's mom had on a Jenner Racing jacket and a big smile that reminded him of Annie's.

"Yes, it was, Mrs. Jenner."

"Alan, get up there so Annie can get your picture," she ordered, taking her nephew by the arm and nudging him toward the group from Jenner Racing.

Alan moved to do what he was told.

"I wanted to thank you again for taking us to dinner in Talladega, we really enjoyed ourselves."

"I'm glad to hear it. I enjoyed it, too."

"Brandon and I would like to invite you to be our guest for dinner next week in Darlington."

"Thanks, Mrs. Jenner—"

"Please call me Carol," she said. "I have a feeling you're going to be hanging around our family for a long time."

He felt pressure deep inside at her words but shrugged it off and fell back on the politeness that had been ingrained since birth. "Thank you, Carol."

Carol turned away when another woman Jared didn't know came up behind her and gave her a hug. Jared knew he shouldn't read too much into Carol's support of him.

He made his way through the crowd to Annie's side. She put her camera down and smiled over at him. "What a great race!"

"It was exciting." But more exhilarating was the smile on Annie's face. He could see the joy she had in the moment and he was happy to share it with her. He leaned over to tug her into his arms.

He rubbed his hands down her back, reveling in the feel of her. It had been too long, he thought, too long since he'd let someone be his home. And he wasn't sure that he was going to get used to the feelings swamping him now.

He didn't like them. They made him weak and he'd never been able to abide any kind of weakness in himself.

"When will you be free?"

"Late tonight. I can meet you back at the hotel."

"I'll be around. Text me when you're ready to go and I'll come and find you."

Jared left Annie to find Tucker, who was being interviewed by one of the twenty-four-hour sports channels. Tucker had finished third in the unofficial standings. He was grinning and saying the right things to the reporters who were questioning him, but Jared had known him long enough to see past his smiling facade.

When they were finally alone in Tucker's motor home, Jared asked, "You okay, man?"

"I should have won today."

Tucker always thought he should win. And Jared knew that his friend was going to spend the next few days going over every move he'd made on the track and trying to figure out where he'd lost.

"You ran a good race."

"Yeah. And I changed my damned tires on the last pit so no one would say anything, but I'm not doing it again. I've got to run my races my way."

"I agree. I've already lodged a complaint that Jenner brought up the tire thing again. I think this will be the end of it."

"It better be."

"Or else what?"

"Nothing. I'm just talking trash because I'm pissed off. I hate losing."

"Everyone does."

"True," Tucker said. "You gonna hang at the post-race party or you rushing off to your girl?"

"I'll hang for a while."

"Until she calls you?" Tucker said with a shrewd look.

He shrugged, not willing to cop to what he felt about Annie. He didn't share his feelings with her, so he certainly wasn't going to discuss it with Tucker.

"You've got it bad," Tucker said.

Maybe Tucker was right. The closer Annie got to him the harder he tried to preserve the distance he usually kept between everyone and himself. But she had a way of getting around his barriers.

"It doesn't feel bad," he said, at last.

Tucker stared at him for a minute. "You couldn't pick a girl from our team to fall for?"

Jared wished it were that easy. But he hadn't been looking for a woman. "That would have made life much simpler."

"No kidding."

Tucker went to shower and Jared left to talk to the other members of their team, but in the back of his mind was the fact that Annie had come into his life when he hadn't expected her to.

He tried to keep his mind on racing but instead, as he caught a glimpse of Annie hugging her brother, Jared was filled with a sense of awe that she was his. A sense of rightness…a sense of completeness that he noticed was lacking when she was out of his company.

CHAPTER TWELVE

THE RETURN TO Daytona felt like a milestone to Annie in her relationship with Jared. They'd been together for almost five months.

They'd weathered a few storms, spurred by the fact that they were affiliated with different racing teams, but she thought each one had brought them closer. Or as close as Jared would allow them to be before his cool reserve came back into play.

She didn't know what to believe when it came to Jared, but he held her so close sometimes that she had to believe they were building something lasting.

"Are you sure there's a house out here?" Jared asked as they turned off the main highway onto a smaller, roughly paved road.

This was old Florida at its finest. Scrub pine and swamp grass were on either side of the road.

"Very funny." She smiled over at Jared.

"This is nice," he said.

"Driving?"

"You and me together and away from the track instead of both of us so busy," he answered.

"You're not stressed that your driver is down in the points?"

"Nah. Tucker has come back from worse places before. We've got a plan for this weekend."

"New strategy?" she asked.

"Yes. We're going to surprise everyone this weekend in Daytona."

"Dave's going to be hard to beat. He's really got his groove going now."

"That's true, but I'm confident that Tucker can take him."

"How confident?"

"Pretty damn sure," he said.

Since Richmond, Annie had treaded carefully around her brother and Jared's best friend. Tucker had stopped answering questions about her when the media mentioned her relationship. She and Jared had been keeping a low profile. Mainly, she admitted, because Jared had been working a lot of hours either on the racing team or at the corporate offices for JM's Coffee House.

"Care to make a little wager on the outcome?" she asked, as she made the last turn onto her uncle Steve's property. There was a large wrought-iron gate with a sign that warned trespassers off.

"On the race?"

She nodded.

"Okay. What are the terms?"

"If Dave wins you tell me one thing about your past that you've never shared with anyone else."

"Why?"

"Because I want to be the person who knows you best," she said, putting all her cards on the table.

"I think you are," he said quietly.

"Oh, Jared, I hope not."

"Why do you say that?"

"Because you haven't let me know you at all."

"We're intimate," he said.

She realized that this conversation wasn't the one she'd intended, but now was as good a time as any to have it. "That's physical. You only let me so close."

He rubbed the back of his neck. It was a habit he had when he stalled for time. "I'm trying."

"Good. So if Dave wins, we'll learn something new about each other?"

"Sure. But I'm going to ask about your marriage," he said, warned.

"Deal," she said. And it was.

She reached over for the intercom button.

But Jared stopped her with a hand on her arm. "Will you do something for me?"

"What?" she asked, then realized how that sounded. "You mean in addition to the bet?"

He nodded.

"Yes, I will."

"I'm not ready to ask you right now."

And that seemed to sum up the complex dance that was their relationship. For every inch he gave in the intimacy department, he inserted two more inches of space. She pushed her sunglasses up on the top of her head and leveled a stare across the seat at him.

"When will you be ready?" she asked.

He leaned across the bucket seat and gave her a hard kiss. "Soon."

She tried not to let it bother her, but she felt vulnerable where he was concerned and she wanted, needed, some reassurance.

JARED WAS STARTING to really dislike the men in Annie's family. They were loud and extremely large in numbers and totally shutting him down. Jared told himself it didn't matter to him if the Jenner men liked him, but he knew that was a lie.

Though Annie thought he was keeping her at arm's length, he wasn't. He watched her with her cousins, laughing and talking, and he wanted…wanted to be the one next to her.

Annie moved around the fringes of her family gathering, snapping pictures of every event and every person. She talked and laughed with her family. But it didn't take Jared long to realize that she was avoiding him. The tension that had developed in the car just as they'd arrived hung over them like a storm cloud.

She brought that Nikon up to her eye, shooting pictures of him. He wondered what she saw through the lens of her camera. He tried to relax but was too conscious of the fact that she might not find what she hoped to in his face.

He waved her over to him, crooking one finger at her. The camera dropped and she put her hands on her hips as she approached. "Tell me you didn't just do that."

"Hey, it worked," he said. "What do you see through the lens of your camera?"

"I don't know that I can really explain it," she said. "The camera doesn't lie so I think I'm looking for truth."

Truth, he thought. "What do you see when you photograph me?"

She tipped her head to the side and he caught a glimpse of that vulnerability that she did a good job of hiding. "I'm not sure yet. That's why I keep shooting, hoping I can find some answers."

She leaned forward, resting her cheek against his chest. Her arms snaked around his waist. For a moment it didn't matter what she was searching for when she looked at him. It didn't matter if she didn't find it or if he didn't have it in him to be what she needed.

There was a peace in the moment, and in each other's arms, that he wanted to let envelope them forever.

"Hey, lovebirds, enough of that," Dave said, coming over to them.

They stepped apart.

"So, MacNeil, are you one of those office types who only works out in a gym?"

"No," he said, not sure where Dave was going with this.

"Wanna join the boys for a game of touch football?" Dave asked.

Jared had a really bad feeling about this. But he wasn't one to back down from a challenge. And a challenge had been definitely issued.

"Uh…Dave, we're not really planning to stay that late," Annie said.

"Can't take too much of our family?" Dave asked.

"Not at all," Jared replied. "I'm good for a game. Whose team am I on?"

"You can be on mine," Alan said, as he joined them.

"You don't have to do this," Annie stated, as Dave and Alan moved off to gather more players for their game.

"I think I do."

"Dave and Alan may have said *touch* football but the game always gets rough," Annie said. "I don't want you to get hurt."

"That's sweet but I'm sure I can hold my own unless they are going to cheat."

"They won't cheat but they consider *touch* to include knocking the other player to the ground."

"I'm good, Annie. I played rugby at prep school and in college. I still play a couple of times a year when my schedule allows."

Jared joined the men on the field. The game was as

rough as Annie had promised it would be. Jared took a tackle from Dave and then got one of his own in on the next possession changeover. They played for almost two hours and his team won.

"You're a good player," Alan said, passing him a cold beer.

"You are, too," Jared said, taking a long swallow of the cold beverage.

"If you're serious about Annie—"

"Do you honestly think I'd play a game like that if I wasn't?"

"I guess you have a point. But you better remember that we were playing *touch* out there. You mess with Annie and we'll really kick your butt."

Alan walked away and Jared rubbed the back of his neck. The Jenners didn't make it easy for him. But then he didn't back down from challenges. And he didn't need to be best buds with the men in her family.

"Jared, come on over here and join us." Carol Jenner waved him over to the picnic table, where she sat with a cluster of Annie's female relatives.

He sat next to Carol and Annie joined them a few minutes later, sitting on his other side. When Dave and Alan tried to sit down, the women closed the other men out. It was the second time that Carol had made him feel welcome and he tried not to read too much into it, but it had been a long time since anyone had tried to mother him.

It touched him more deeply than he'd expected and

he had to excuse himself. Had to get away from the welcome that he felt at that picnic table. Annie followed him into the house.

"What's the matter?"

"I just remembered something that I need to do back at the track. Do you mind if I take your car?"

Annie frowned at him. "I'll go with you. Let me say goodbye to my parents."

"I'll wait out front."

He walked out of the house, aware that she was watching him leave, and he knew that if she'd had a camera in her hands she'd capture an image that would show her a man who came up lacking.

ANNIE DIDN'T SAY anything on the drive back to Daytona. She wasn't sure what had happened back at the picnic table, but later, as he parked her car at the condo in Daytona and he still hadn't said anything, she realized he was going to pretend everything was normal. Even though it was clear to her he was disturbed by something. Had her brother finally convinced him that she wasn't worth the effort?

"Did you have fun today?" she asked.

"Yes. Thanks for inviting me," he said.

"You're welcome."

She studied his profile in the setting sun. The play of light would illuminate his skin too much if she took a picture and he would look washed out, but the shadows it created would be interesting. She reached between the bucket seats for her camera bag, thinking that she might be able to capture him half in shadow and half out.

Hidden behind the facade of the man she knew was another man. The one she could never reach.

"No pictures," he said quietly.

"Why not?"

"You hide behind the lens."

She did. Annie knew it and was a little surprised to realize she'd let him see her enough to know it, too. "You're right, but just now I wasn't hiding. I wanted to capture something elusive about you. I can't ever get the exact picture I want."

"I'm not sure that there's anything more to me than what you see."

She heard a note of something in his voice. She couldn't really assign it any emotion because it wasn't like that. But she knew he was trying to tell her something without coming right out and saying the words. "I'm sure there is."

He pinned her with his hard, cold stare. "I don't want you to be disappointed, Annie. I promise not to hurt you."

"And you think if I don't find what I'm looking for, I'll be hurt?"

"You might make the mistake of thinking that because I can't express what I feel for you, you'll assume that I don't feel anything," he said, then cursed under his breath. "Damn, I don't want to have this conversation in the car."

"What conversation?"

"One about our relationship." She felt as if they were getting to the heart of why he wanted to leave Uncle Steve's house so abruptly.

"Let's go inside," she said.

They both went into the condo and Jared paced around the living room.

"What happened there?"

"Nothing important," he said, keeping his eyes on the carpet in front of him.

"Jared, don't shut me out," she said.

JARED WAS TEMPTED to not only shut her out but to walk out of this condo and never stop. To keep moving so that he wouldn't have to admit to the emotions roiling through him. A part of him wondered what she'd do if he laid the truth on the line. If he told her that he'd been alone for too long and that the closest he'd found to a home was in her arms.

But he wasn't ready to be that weak in front of her. To give her power over the relationship and the direction it was taking. This afternoon when he'd watched her with her family he felt a keen longing for something more from this woman.

Normally he was able to keep himself from caring too deeply in a relationship.

"Do you want me to go?" he asked.

"Do you want to?" she asked him.

"No." He searched for the right words, for something to say that would explain what he meant without revealing too much, but he came up empty.

"I'm just not sure where we're heading from here. I'm not good at long-term, but everything about you makes me want to give that a try."

"That doesn't sound bad. I think you know I feel the same way," she said.

He rubbed the back of his neck. "I don't want to hurt you."

"That sounds so lame. You know that, right? It's like a cop-out that you use when you don't want to have to admit that *you* might be the one who gets hurt."

Her words were like a punch in the gut. Not because they were harsh but because they were true.

"I guess you're right. I'm not…hell, I can't do this."

She walked over to him and he was struck again by how beautiful she was. How the emotions in her dark brown eyes never failed to get to him and shake him to his core.

"I'm not going to let this go. A few times we've come close, with both of us admitting more than either of us is comfortable with."

He rubbed his neck again, then realized what he was doing and dropped his hands. He shoved them into his pockets and hoped he looked cool and collected even though inside he was shattering. "Why don't you go first?"

She shook her head and he thought that this was going to be how their relationship ended. Both of them standing next to each other but afraid to reach out and take what they wanted.

And suddenly he was pissed off at himself and at her. At the life he'd always lived that hadn't really prepared him to keep her.

"I want you. But I've never kept a relationship alive."

She exhaled a long breath that sounded like a sigh. "I want you the same way. I've had lots of relationships…my problem is holding on way past the time to let go."

"I haven't noticed that."

"Trust me."

"Your marriage?"

"Yeah. All the signs were there that it was over but I didn't want to admit I'd made a mistake."

"I can understand that. I'm kind of stubborn about things."

"You think?"

"I'm not sure where we are going from here, but I'm willing to try to make this work."

"I'm going to want you to open up more about what you're feeling," she said.

He hated that. What if she realized that he was empty inside?

CHAPTER THIRTEEN

"WANT TO GRAB some lunch?" Jared asked after the stock cars came back in from their test laps. He'd only managed to see Annie for about ten minutes earlier in the day. But she'd had her camera and was heading into Dave's garage.

"Sure. You want to go to the infield cafeteria or drive into Daytona to find something to eat?" she asked.

"Neither. I asked our chef to prepare a special lunch for us that we can enjoy in my motor home."

It was the first time he'd invited her there and he hoped she'd see as him opening up a little more.

"Okay."

All of the team owners and drivers had motor homes in the designated lot for the different race tracks.

She followed him through the rows of motor homes to a cream-colored Prevost Vantare with black-and-gray striping on it. He unlocked the door and held it open for her.

"Welcome to my home away from home," he said.

She climbed up into the recreational vehicle. A large

plasma television dominated the front of the coach. There were a pair of long couches, tables and two large chairs that looked comfortable in the main sitting area.

She took a seat on one of the leather couches. "Where do you consider home, Jared? I know you own a lot of houses and have places all over the country, but do you have one place that you can always relax at?"

He didn't. Places had never been that important to him. His family owned a lot of properties around the world and he'd grown up used to a very transient way of life. Similar, he thought, to Annie's childhood, when she traveled with her dad each weekend as he raced.

"Not really," he said, easily admitting to the emptiness in his life.

"Why not?"

"Most of the houses I own have been in my family for generations and when I go there I…" God, was he really going to tell her?

"What, Jared?" she asked, pushing to her feet and coming over to him.

"I realize how alone I really am. My family isn't large like yours. I have a few third cousins somewhere but we're not close."

"You miss your parents," she said.

More than he wanted her to know. They'd died when he'd been just trying to figure out how to stand on his own, how to get out of the large shadow his dad cast, and their deaths had left a void.

"Yeah, but I didn't invite you to lunch to talk about them."

"Why did you invite me to lunch then?"

"Something you said the other day about building a real relationship…at the track we're both careful to stick to our own drivers' areas, but we can't keep our lives apart."

"NASCAR is a part of both of our lives," she said.

NASCAR was the closest thing he had to a family. Tucker was like a brother to him. "Yes, it is. And your family is a huge part of NASCAR."

"Is that a problem?" she asked.

"Well, it'd be a lot easier on me if the men in your family would back off."

"Don't let them scare you off, Jared."

"I won't."

"Promise?" she asked. "Ah, forget I said that. What's for lunch?"

"I'm not forgetting that. I do promise that your family won't scare me off."

She tipped her head to the side, studying him.

"Why are you looking at me like that?"

She shook her head.

"No more secrets, remember? You want me to bare my soul then you have to step up, too."

She stepped back to the couch. "One of the things that broke up my marriage was that we lived separate lives so far apart from my family. I had no support network…."

"I don't want that for us," he said. "I'm not promising smooth sailing, but I want this lunch today to be the start of something new."

She smiled up at him and all of the emotional confession stuff was worth it. He only hoped that he could keep doing it, because he was sweating and he didn't like the way he felt at this moment. Didn't want to give her the chance to realize how much she was coming to mean to him.

FOR AS LONG AS Annie could remember she'd always been excited about coming to Daytona. She glanced up at the clear blue sky. It was hot today. Sweat dripped down the back of her neck. She swept her hair up, hoping for a cool breeze but there wasn't one.

She was in Turn Two, which was one of her favorite spots. She liked to be in the curve snapping pictures of the race.

Annie thought back to her lunch with Jared. He had admitted to being on his own and wanting a family. And that was one of her fears—being wanted for her family and not for herself. But she didn't see Jared as wanting her for her famous family name...she thought it was more that he wanted her *in spite* of her family.

So she was hiding again, behind the safety of the lens of her Nikon camera. Standing in the middle of the world that both she and Jared were a part of and hoping to be invisible.

She donned her protective earphones and set up her tripod. She adjusted all of her equipment and waited for the race to start. Because it was Florida and the middle of summer, the ever-present afternoon rainstorms had the drivers and their teams watching the sky and listening to weather reports in the hope that the storms would pass over and the race would start on time.

She guessed that Dave and Tucker would both be anxious to get out on the track and beat each other, since the last time they'd been at this track the crash had taken them both out early. Tucker had qualified in the pole position and she'd caught a glimpse of his interview on one of the twenty-four-hour sports television channels earlier where he said he was going to take care of business today.

Tucker was cocky and arrogant but she liked that about him. It reminded her a little of Jared and his attitude toward everything. They hadn't spoken any more about their relationship, but that was okay.

Her cell phone vibrated in her pocket and she pulled back from the camera to answer it. She noticed the number was her mother's. She missed the call but immediately called back.

Even though her father had been fine at the picnic a few days earlier she still worried about his recovery.

"Hey, Mom," she said when her mother answered.

"Hey, baby. Are you available for a late dinner after the race?"

She took a deep breath. Dinner after the race would involve a lot of her family. She wasn't going to bring Jared unless her family welcomed him—all of her family.

"I'll check with Jared, but if we come, Mom, the guys are going to have to back off."

"I'll take care of it," she said.

"Jared might not be available if Tucker wins."

"I always forget that he's tied to another driver." There was a note in her mom's voice that she couldn't read.

"Does that bother you, mom?" she asked. She had been dealing with guilt over Dave but hadn't even thought of the impact her dating Jared might have on her parents. Her dad was a team owner who had three drivers competing against Jared's two teams each week.

"Doesn't it bother you?" her mother said.

"I try not to think about it."

"Annie, that's not realistic," her mom replied.

Like she didn't know that. Like she wasn't totally aware that her attitude wasn't healthy. But it was the only way she could be with Jared and not panic. "I mean he's got this whole other side of his life that takes up as much time as his duties here at the track."

"That's good, but it doesn't change the fact that he is Tucker's team owner."

"I know. Dave and I have yet to make any kind of peace about it and I'm really trying not to let it be too big a deal."

"It's not a big deal to your father and I," her mom said suddenly. "I just worry about you, sweetie."

"Thanks, Mom. I'll check with Jared and call you back about dinner."

She glanced at her watch and then at the laminated card that Jared had given her when they'd arrived at the track on Thursday. It had his schedule along with Tucker's on it. He was giving a tour to a group of potential investors.

Probably not the best time to call him. She text messaged him instead and then went back to fiddling with her camera, getting the last few adjustments made. She was as ready as she could be.

She got a text message from Jared asking her where she was. She told him and wasn't too surprised when he showed up a few minutes later sans his group.

"You didn't have to come and find me," she said.

"I know. I wanted to. I can't do dinner tonight."

"Oh. It's with my family," she said, then thought about how that sounded. Was she trying to bribe him with her relatives?

"Good, then you won't be alone."

"Where will you be?"

"I have an early meeting at the corporate offices in Atlanta."

"Is everything okay?" she asked.

He gave her an odd look. "Yes. Just the usual corporate meetings that I have to deal with a couple of times a year."

"Will I see you again today?" she asked.

He shook his head. "That's why I stopped by."

He didn't say anything else, just pulled her into his arms and kissed her hard before he walked away.

JARED'S BUSINESS kept him away from NASCAR for a month. There'd been a problem with one of the coffee farms in Colombia and he'd had to go down there personally to take care of the workers, who were striking. It was the longest month of his life. He'd been out of reach most of the time. Though he'd tried to keep in touch with Annie they'd spoken only twice. And the last time had been on a bad connection when he'd been in Bogotá.

Tucker had won in Daytona and then again the next weekend in Chicago. But Dave had taken the race in Indianapolis and the one in Pocono.

Watkins Glen was located about eighty miles southwest of Syracuse and not too far from Corning. The city was named for the company that was known today for their bakeware. They also housed a first-class museum of glass photography, and knowing that photography was Annie's life, he'd decided to surprise her with a trip to the museum.

The time apart from Annie had made him realize how entwined their lives had become. He had a glimpse of what his life would be like without Annie in it and he hadn't liked it at all.

He'd asked her to come to New York one day early and invited Tucker to come along as well. Something that Annie had said about being isolated from her family during her marriage had given him the idea to include Tucker. Tucker was the only person he considered family.

And after spending so much time with her clan, he wanted her to see what his family was like.

He waited near the baggage claim at the Syracuse airport. He was a little nervous, which was unlike him, so he forced the feelings aside.

A few minutes later she walked toward him. Annie looked more tanned than he remembered, and skinnier. She paused, a crowd of people hurrying around her. But she just stood there and he understood why. There had been an intensity between them when he'd skipped her family dinner and gone away. They hadn't had time to settle back to normal.

He closed the gap between them, ignoring the people milling around them, and leaned down to kiss her, but she turned her head so that his lips brushed her cheek.

"Hello, Jared."

"Hi, Annie."

Before he could say anything else Tucker came down the hallway with a tall, slender woman. Heidi Miller. "Hey, buddy."

"How was the flight?"

"Smooth sailing. Heidi, you know Jared."

"Hello, Heidi," Jared said, holding his hand out to her.

"Hi, Jared. It's been a while," she said.

"Yeah, what? About a year? It's good to see you again," Jared said.

"Do you mind if we swing by my folks' old ranch in Richfield Springs?" Tucker asked.

Jared thought about the photography exhibit but knew that could wait. Tucker rarely asked him for anything and visiting his parents was something that Tucker felt obligated to do every time NASCAR came to Watkins Glen.

"No problem," he said. Tucker and Heidi went to get drinks from a vending machine while he and Annie went out to the limo.

"Are Tucker's parents like your second mom and dad?" she asked.

"Ah, no. But they are pretty likable."

She tucked her purse next to her hip as Tucker and Heidi approached from behind. "I can't wait to meet them. Will they be at the race this weekend?"

"My parents?" Tucker asked, sliding into the car after Heidi.

"Yes," Annie said.

"No. They don't approve of racing. Think it's given me a swelled head."

"You mean you weren't so sure you were God's gift to the world before you started racing?" Annie asked teasingly.

"Nah, I was sure of it, but that was private and now they

see me on TV and in the papers and they're private people."

Jared knew how much Tucker struggled to get his father's approval, something the other man simply wouldn't give him. Jared didn't understand the relationship there. His own father would have supported him no matter what.

"I've never been to this area before," Annie said as they left Syracuse. "We always just go from the airport to the race track."

"I grew up here," Heidi said.

"So you and Tucker know each other from childhood?"

"We were neighbors. He invited my dad and brothers to come to the race this weekend."

Annie jumped on the conversation about big families and brothers. Jared sat back feeling more of an outsider than ever. Even though he'd arranged this group he wasn't really part of it. He felt himself sliding back, searching for that insulating distance that he always tried to keep between himself and others.

Annie took his hand in hers and turned toward him. "Right, Jared?"

"What?"

"I said that having a big family is a big pain in the butt sometimes," Annie said, wrinkling her brow as she looked at him.

Jared shrugged his shoulder. "I wouldn't know about Heidi's family, but your family…"

"My brothers are the same way," Heidi said. "The first time I brought Tucker home—what was it, seventh grade?"

"Something like that." Tucker was sprawled on the other seat with his arm spread over the back. Heidi sat next to him but didn't lean into the curve of his body.

"They threatened to beat him up."

"Did that stop you?" Annie asked, leaning forward.

"Hell, no."

"What about you, Jared? Any brothers try to warn you off?" Annie asked, keeping him in the conversation when he would have retreated again.

"No, in most circles I'm considered a good catch."

Annie twined their fingers together. "Oh, Jared, I think you're a good catch, too."

He wasn't sure if she was still teasing but her words resonated deep inside him. Though he was afraid to slow down enough to really commit to her, he wanted her to think of him as a good catch. He wanted her to see him as the kind of man he'd always wanted to be.

CHAPTER FOURTEEN

ANNIE ENJOYED MEETING Tucker's parents and Heidi's. Both families had planned a joint barbecue. She saw another side of Jared with the Aldridge family. Mr. Aldridge treated him as an equal, not like one of his son's friends. Annie had overheard Jared giving Mr. Aldridge financial advice.

"Your parents are very nice, Tucker," Annie said, when they were all back in the limo and heading toward Watkins Glen. Heidi was staying with her parents until the race this weekend.

"How'd they end up with an arrogant so-and-so like me, right?" he said.

"I think you're sweeter than you like to let on."

"Well, don't let it get out."

"I won't."

It was just after seven o'clock when they dropped Tucker off at his promotional gig at an auto-parts store. He was meeting up with another driver from their team and would catch a ride back with him.

"Alone at last," Annie said, turning to Jared. "I booked a room at a local hotel."

"I was hoping you'd stay with me."

She'd been afraid to presume that. "I'd like that."

The limo dropped them off at the motor home lot.

"Wait here," he said, when they reached the door. "I want to make sure everything's right."

A few minutes later the door opened again. "Come in."

There was a bottle of champagne chilling in an ice bucket near the kitchen area. And with the click of a button music filled the room—Stevie Wonder singing "Sir Duke." She smiled at him, feeling the weeks they'd been apart drift away. Here was the man she'd been falling for.

His silence had been understandable. But that hadn't stopped doubts from forming in her mind. When he'd left her in Daytona she felt like things were unsettled.

And that last call when she'd barely been able to hear him had been torturous. Her family had made a few remarks on his absence, but then stopped asking when it became clear she had no idea when he'd be back.

She clearly recalled the last time he'd invited her to a private meal like this one. It felt like eons ago. So much had changed between them. Then she'd scarcely known the man behind the image and now…now she knew him better than she'd ever expected to.

"Champagne?"

"Yes, please."

He poured them both a glass and handed her one of the flutes.

"To you," he said, touching the rims of the glasses together.

"To you, too," she said.

While they drank their champagne Jared told her about his trip to Colombia. When they were finished he drew her to her feet and into his arms.

"What are we doing now?"

"Dancing," he said. "I know we should have gone out so we could be around other people…but I want you to myself for a few hours before the race-week events begin."

"I missed you."

"Good."

She pinched his side. "That's not very nice."

"Why not? I was missing you."

"This scares me, Jared. Needing you the way I do."

"We're finding our way. Trust that we will continue to do so."

She bit her lower lip, wanting to believe him but knowing that it wasn't that easy. She'd been unsettled when he'd been gone, which should have been her first clue that she was more than falling for him. She'd worked long hours compiling and editing the photos she'd taken of Dave.

"What, no promises?" she asked.

"I'll only make promises I can keep."

That didn't reassure her. She knew what he was

trying to say and she wasn't ready to make any commitments to him, either, at least not without a guarantee. She wanted him to take all the risks, put himself out in the open with his vulnerabilities so she wouldn't have to take that leap.

Once she knew how he felt about her she'd tell him or show him. But she knew it wasn't fair. "I'm just tired tonight."

"Is that all?"

"Nothing with you is ever easy for me to accept," she said, at last.

"Like what?" he asked. His sincere concern got her every time.

"Everything. Though you try to hide it, you're a really caring man. I can see the life that you have and I'm wondering how I can fit in, with my big family."

"We'll just take it step by step."

He pulled her into his arms, framing her face with his large hands. He brushed his thumb over her lower lip.

Her throat clogged with tears and she could only stare up at him. Then he lowered his head to hers and kissed her. Having been apart from him for four long weeks, she knew exactly what was missing without him in her life.

And his words and this evening told her he'd felt the same way. He hadn't said anything concrete about a future together, but she knew they were building toward one and that frightened her. She wasn't sure she was ready to commit herself to him, but knew she didn't want to live without him.

ANNIE STARED AT HIM so intently he was afraid of what she was trying to see in his expression. Afraid that she might find that he wanted to bind her to him now before she found the thing that had made other women leave him in the past. Jared knew it wasn't something unidentified, like he'd just thought. That thing that drove them away was his coldness, that inner core of himself that he never allowed any of them to breach.

"This is nice," she said, as they danced around his living room.

"I know."

"I'd forgotten how arrogant you can be."

That didn't bother him. He'd always seen arrogance and confidence as sides of the same coin. Success was driven by self-confidence.

"You don't show it all the time, but you did when we first met and you are now. What's up with that?"

There was something almost defensive in her tone. It wasn't the reaction he expected from her. Annie just wasn't good at hiding what she felt and he could tell he'd backed her into a corner.

"You have a way of bringing out that side of me."

"That doesn't sound good," she said.

He rubbed the back of his neck. "I think it only

happens when I'm going to ask you something and I'm not sure of what your answer will be."

"What are you going to ask me?"

He wasn't as sure of himself as he'd been just a few minutes earlier. He was botching this up. He drew her back over to the table and asked her to sit down. He went to the desk where the computer sat and opened the top drawer. Inside was the velvet box he'd put there earlier. He removed the box, and then returned to the table, setting it next to his empty champagne glass.

"Our time apart made me realize exactly how different our relationship is from every other one I've had in the last few years."

"Me, too," she said, taking his hand in both of hers. "Being with you makes me feel good."

"I'm glad," he said, lifting her hand to his mouth to drop a kiss on the back of it.

He pulled his hands back and pushed the velvet jewelry box on the table toward her. He thought of the sapphire choker he'd gotten in Colombia. As soon as he'd seen it in the window he'd been unable to get the image of the necklace around her neck out of his head.

She smiled at him. "For once I have a gift for you, too."

"What?"

She reached into the large bag she carried around with her. "This is for you."

She passed a large square package over to him and he was dumbfounded. He'd received few presents since his parents' deaths more than ten years ago. Most of his gifts had been from business associates.

"Open it," she said.

He reached for the present. The wrapping was colorful, with whimsical penguins on brown craft paper. He ran his finger over the penguins, almost afraid to open it.

He removed the paper and set it aside, opening the box that held a framed picture of the two of them. One that had been snapped at her family's picnic. There was an inscription on the bottom of the frame that read "I see a man of integrity when I look at you."

"Thank you," he said, touched beyond measure that she had gotten him a gift. That she had thought of him and their first meeting after so long apart.

"You're welcome," she said. "I'm not good with words, but it seemed important to underscore what I found in your face when I was looking through my lens."

She couldn't know that he'd always tried to live up to the model of a man his father had been. That integrity had been one of the cornerstones of Benjamin MacNeil.

"Open your gift," he said. He needed to switch the focus off of him and onto her. He wanted to see her reaction to this gift. This time not as a test, but because he liked to see the joy on her face when he gave her things.

She pushed the ribbon off the velvet box. It opened

with a small snick. She held her breath as she looked down at the box. He knew she was seeing six flawless sapphires set with diamonds in between them, strung together in white gold.

"Oh, my God. This is gorgeous. I'm almost afraid to wear it."

Her reaction was priceless. Exactly what he'd hoped for and he knew without a doubt that he was falling for her. That he had already fallen for her. And that scared the crap out of him.

Any kind of emotional weakness was to be avoided. The loss of his parents had left a void in his life. The kind of void he'd carefully managed to prevent himself from falling into again.

But here was Annie making him feel things he didn't want to. He swallowed hard and thought about her and losing her. God, he couldn't do it.

Sooner or later she was going to want something from him that he couldn't buy or arrange. Sooner or later she was going to look up at him with those wide serious eyes and ask him what he felt for her. Sooner or later he was going to disappoint her and she was going to leave.

Unless…

"Move in with me." He said it plainly, forgetting about the words he'd planned and rehearsed. "I know we're both away from home more often than not but I want us to fly home together on Sundays and then leave again on Thursdays. Together."

Annie swallowed hard and he wasn't sure that was a good sign. In fact the more time that passed the tighter his skin felt. She wasn't going to say yes. What the hell had he been thinking to just blurt that out?

When she lowered her eyes, he had his answer and it wasn't a yes.

"Why not?"

She pulled her hands away from the table, wrapping her arm around her waist and watching him with those dark brown eyes filled with tears. He hated to see her cry. He should be the gentleman and let this go, but now that he'd thrown the words out there he was going to seem like he wanted her more than she wanted him.

Jared knew that relationships weren't about competition but when he'd bared his soul—or came as close to it as someone like him could—he wanted her to do the same. She was the one who'd pushed for them to be closer. She was the one who'd said that she wanted to know his secrets and share hers.

"I'm not ready. I'm just getting used to trusting you and being with you."

"What does that mean?"

She seemed to get smaller as she sat in front of him and he knew he should just smile at her and go to Plan B, but to be honest right now he didn't give a damn about his back-up plans.

"I'm not playing around with you. These last few weeks apart made me realize that I'm already falling for you. I mean, I knew it before you left but then I realized how alone I felt without you."

Her words touched a nerve inside of him, echoing what he'd felt as he'd slept apart from her. "That's why we should move in together. Then you won't have to be alone anymore."

"That's not my concern. I can handle being alone. I'm just not sure that I'll be able to pick up the pieces of living by myself again."

"How about giving us a chance to succeed before you break us apart?" He understood her fears. Hell, he was battling them right now. How was he going to walk away from this with his pride intact? He glanced down at the photo she'd given him. The photo captured how they'd been together. He was staring straight into the lens of her camera.

He saw in his eyes that fear that had taken over his gut and made it knot up. That very apprehension that she was going to realize that he wasn't the man she thought he was.

"Is that what I'm doing? I'm trying not to rush into anything the way I did with Malcolm. I don't want to make the same mistake twice."

"It seems like it to me. I'm not your ex-husband, as I hope I've proven to you. If you need more time, I can wait," he said, reaching across the table and taking her hands in his. "I've never asked a woman to live with me."

"I'm flattered."

There were no stars in her eyes and he had a feeling

that those eyes of hers could see straight to his soul. He had the uncomfortable feeling that she knew he was trying to get her in his life in the easiest way.

"But you're not ready?" he asked at last, realizing that he was willing to wait for her to be ready. He'd been doing a good job of keeping her happy. He'd just make it a priority to make her see what she was missing by not living with him.

She tucked a strand of hair behind her ear. He noticed that her nails were trimmed from the last time he'd seen her. "No, I'm not. I don't think you are, either."

"I'm pretty sure of what I want." He'd never wanted anyone or anything as much as he wanted Annie. He was afraid he was pushing too hard and she'd see instead of a man worthy of her time and affection, a man who was desperate. But it wasn't just that he wanted her in his house. He wanted the warmth that she brought into his daily life.

"Why now?"

Jared knew he should just stop the conversation now. He knew that she was going to ask him for something he couldn't give her. And he wasn't ready for that now. But he wasn't above revealing what he'd felt. "These last few weeks apart made me focus on what I really wanted from you. And I wanted you with me."

"I want that, too. Why can't we just continue as we have been until Homestead and then…"

"Then, what?"

"Then ask me again at the end of the season when all the craziness in our lives has died down."

He had a thought that wasn't too nice and he tried to censor it, but it came out before he could. "Will your answer have anything to do with whether your brother wins the championship or not?"

ANNIE WANTED TO WALK away from Jared. His question was offensive. But the truth was, his question hit close to home. And she was done with running. She had made this her year to stop running and start living her life.

And Jared had made her feel more alive than anyone else had in a long time. She reached for him, but he kept the space between them.

"It's not that I care who wins, it's just that it will actually be so much easier for us to move in together when the season is over and we both have less going on."

He refused to look at her. "I'm not going to be any less busy and neither will you. We're both doing our jobs now while we travel with Tucker and Dave. Life isn't going to be any less complicated than it is right now. But fair enough," he said.

His capitulation should have made it easier for her to accept her own decision. Had she made the right choice or was it only her old fears talking?

"I'm sorry," she said, but knew that the words were too little too late.

"It's okay," he said, but she knew it wasn't.

She'd pushed for him to open up to her and when he had…she wasn't shutting him down but she couldn't see really living together.

There was an undertone in his voice that made her realize that he was a little angry over her answer. "Jared, my first marriage was a whirlwind romance. I knew Malcolm less than six weeks before we were married. I don't want to make the same mistake again."

"What mistake?"

She took a deep breath, so tempted to hedge or lie. But in the end she knew she'd only be cheating herself and refused to do that. "Believing that romance and fantasy can survive in real life."

He stared down at her and she could tell that he was listening to her.

"I'm not romancing you," he said.

"I know that. I need to make sure that I'm the right woman for you and you're the right man for me. Does that make sense?"

He cupped her face in both of his hands and kissed her so sweetly she wanted to cry. There was so much in that kiss that it almost scared her.

"I understand. Your family hasn't fully accepted me yet and that's got to weigh on your mind."

"My family will come around, but even if they don't, I'm not going to let them keep me from a man I want. I just need more time."

CHAPTER FIFTEEN

"DAVE, GOT A MINUTE?"

Dave was surprised to see his old friend Rob Mandelay in the garage area on Thursday when he was getting ready to do a few practice laps.

"Hey, man. Good to see you. What's up?" Annie had mentioned she'd seen Rob in Tucker's pit, but he hadn't gone into enemy territory to find him.

"Do you have any openings on your team?"

"Not right now. I'll talk to Vinnie later and see if he knows of anyone who has one. Aren't you happy working with Aldridge and Toughton?"

"They're cool and all, but I'm only the catch can man and I'd like to move up."

"Jenner, we need you," Vinnie yelled from the bay.

"I've got to run, we're getting the car ready for inspections, but I'll find some time for us to chat later."

He waved over his assistant, Melissa. "Mel, this is Rob Mandelay, as old friend of mine. Will you find some time on the schedule for us to chat this weekend."

"Yes, Dave. Your TV interview has been moved

up. They want to do it live from down here, is that okay?"

"Sure."

Dave said goodbye to Rob and then walked into the garage and found Vinnie. "What's up?"

"I wanted a chance to talk to you about the track one more time before you went out."

"I thought our strategy was for me to qualify on the pole so we wouldn't have to worry about getting up front," Dave said, grinning at Vinnie.

"Yeah, that's our strategy, but I wanted to talk about the tires. I think we should scuff at least two sets."

Scuffing was done during the practice laps. The team would mount sets of tires to be used during Sunday's race on his car and he'd run on them during the practice laps. That way the tires would be scuffed by the track's surface.

"Sounds good."

Dave went out on his first set of practice laps and liked the way the car was handling, but he heard something in the engine that concerned him. The team checked it out while he got a quick drink.

"Hey, Dave," Annie said, coming up behind him. She slung one arm around his shoulder, half-hugging him.

"Hey, yourself. What's up?" he asked.

The past few weeks Jared had been absent from the race track and his sister hadn't been herself. Her behavior wasn't as somber as it had been when she'd been going through her divorce, but she hadn't been as cheery as she usually was, either. And he was worried about her.

"Just wanted to see you before you hit your practice laps," she said.

"Why?" he asked.

"No special reason. Just hadn't seen you in a few days."

"You still with Jared?"

"Yes. He asked me to move in with him."

Dave was shocked. He hadn't realized things were moving so quickly. "What'd you say?"

"I told him to ask me again after Homestead."

There was confusion in his sister's eyes. The kind of confusion that came from wanting something, but being afraid to go after it.

"Is it because of me? I've been riding him hard about taking good care of you," Dave said.

"No, it's not that. I mean it does complicate things that you and Tucker are rivals, but that's not why I asked him to wait."

"Do you want to talk about it?" he asked. God knew he stunk at heart-to-hearts, relationships, but this was Annie, the one woman in the world that he'd do it for.

"Maybe later. I don't want to talk about it right before you race."

"Later then. I'm booked solid with interviews and stuff. I'll text you when I'm free…?"

He didn't want to think about Jared asking Annie to live with him. What if he asked her to marry him? He didn't want the guy for a brother-in-law when he still hadn't adjusted to him dating his sister.

"Okay, we'll talk later."

Dave watched her walk away. He glanced back at his crew where they were working to get the car ready. He should be over there with them getting his head in the game. The track here was different, comprised of mainly right turns instead of left ones. He knew that fans loved the race track because of the superb views it offered them, but to be honest, it wasn't one of his favorites.

He closed his eyes, envisioning the track and feeling the Gs his body would pull while he was going so fast and whipping around the track. But a loud crack of laughter drew him out of his head and the race he was running.

He glanced over to see Tucker talking to Annie and laughing. Dave's hands tightened into fists. He wanted Tucker out of both of their lives.

When he turned around he noticed Vinnie was watching the other garage as well. And the other man looked like he wasn't too pleased, either. Vinnie treated Annie like his younger sister.

"Vin, you got a minute to talk strategy?"

Vinnie turned his back on Annie and Tucker and walked over toward him. "I thought we already had."

"You look like you're going to go over there and say something you shouldn't."

"I just might. He's only being all buddy-buddy with her to annoy us."

"And it's working, isn't it?"

Vinnie grew still and stopped glaring over his shoulder.

"Let's just hope that Tucker's distracted by his goofing around with Annie. The Glen doesn't treat distracted drivers very well."

ANNIE SPENT THE DAY taking pictures of the track and her brother. But when evening fell and the parties and promotional gigs were well underway she found herself alone with Dave after an autographing session.

"Ready to talk?" he asked, as he they got on his golf cart and drove away from the crowds in the fan area and back to the motor home lot.

"Yes." She'd been trying all day to come up with a subtle way to ask Dave to stop being a jerk around Jared, but in the end, she hadn't been able to think of anything. "I want you to stop giving Jared such a hard time," she said.

Dave didn't respond.

"He's important to me, Dave. But I need my family if I'm going to have any chance at a real relationship with him."

Dave sighed that deep sound that meant he didn't like

what he was hearing, but knew that she was making sense.

"Hey, it's not just me. He hasn't been all friendly, either," Dave said at last.

"I know," Annie said. "Could I have picked a more difficult man to fall for?"

Dave braked the golf cart to a stop and turned to face her. There was something in his eyes that made her feel better. "You're serious about him?"

She took a deep breath. "Yes."

"Okay. I'll do better."

"You said that after Talladega," she reminded him.

"I mean it this time. I'll really give him a chance."

Annie breathed a sigh of relief. "Good. Now I can know if my instincts about him are right."

"What instincts?"

"The ones that have been telling me that he could be the one."

"You thought that about Malcolm," Dave reminded her.

"Yeah, I know. But the rest of you didn't."

"So we're going to be your litmus test?" Dave asked.

"Something like that. But even though you haven't really been too keen on him, I still am. Does that make sense?"

"I think you're saying, no matter what, you like this guy."

"Yeah, something like that."

Dave started driving again. "This has been one crazy year. Dad's heart attack, your love life, my racing."

"You okay?" she asked, knowing the timing of this stunk. She understood better than anyone the pressure that was put on Dave. He had to fill legendary racing shoes. It would have been different if Daddy had just been an okay driver, but he'd been a champion.

Dave gave her a glance that she couldn't read. "Yeah. I'd like to win this weekend but I feel like I'm getting a cold, which is making me a little fuzzy."

"Are you taking any medicine?"

"Yes. And mom sent over some soup."

"Are you going to be okay on Sunday?" she asked.

"Damn straight," Dave said.

Annie and her brother parted ways at the infield. She wasn't sure that her conversation with her brother would make the relationship between Jared and Dave any smoother, but she wanted it to. She wanted Jared to see what it felt like to be a part of a large family.

She knew it wouldn't replace the closeness he'd had with his own parents, but she hoped it would be another dimension in their relationship.

DAVE WON WATKINS GLEN, but Tucker got the better of him the following weekend in Michigan. This weekend they were in Bristol. Annie was staying with Jared in the motor home lot. She'd gone home to Orlando every

Monday for the last two weeks and he'd missed her during those three days.

He'd been sincere in wanting her to live with him full-time, and having her reject him had tightened his skin. Made him feel like…like he wanted her more than she wanted him.

To compensate he'd overscheduled his day, limiting the amount of time they had to spend together. But his plan had backfired because instead of insulating him from the sharp ache of missing her, the distance had intensified it.

The track was overrun with the Jenner clan when NASCAR arrived in Bristol. It was Brandon and Carol's hometown and everywhere he went Jared met another cousin of Annie's.

"Hey, Jared, come and join me for a cold one," Dave called as Jared walked toward his own motor home, just before dinnertime on Thursday.

"I don't have a lot of time."

"This won't take long," Dave assured him, handing him a cold beer.

Why didn't that reassure him?

He took the beer from Dave then leaned back against the side of the RV. Though he knew Dave to be laid-back most of the time, Jared was just beginning to see that side of the man.

"I heard you asked Annie to move in with you," Dave said.

"I'm not talking—"

"Hold up. I'm making a mess of this. I think you know how much the family tries to take care of our own," Dave stated.

"Yeah, I figured that out."

"Well, if you're with Annie then you're one of us."

"Thanks," he said, then changed the subject. "How's your dad?"

"Good. His doctor said he's progressing just as he should. I think winning a championship this year would make him recover quicker."

"Probably," Jared said, aware that this was the first time they'd ever talked racing.

"I'm still coming after Tucker with all I've got."

"He'll be ready."

Dave grinned a little ruefully at Jared. "I can't believe my sister is dating a guy on another team. It's odd."

"I know the feeling."

Dave glanced over his shoulder one time and then turned back to Jared, and started talking about football and the chances that the Panthers had of going all the way to the Super Bowl this year. Since Jared was a Cowboys fan from childhood he told him they had little chance.

His cell phone twittered and he pulled it out of his pocket to see a text message from Annie.

Where are you?

With Dave.

Dinner's ready.

"I've got to go."

"Later, man," Dave said.

Jared walked away and had a feeling of anticipation in his gut. He stepped into his motor home and froze realizing this was the dream he'd always wanted, but had been afraid to reach for.

The scents of roasting chicken and potatocs filled the air. There were two places set at the small kitchen table, a candlestick lit between them. Annie's iPod was plugged into the speaker system and the Cure was blasting from the speakers.

Annie came out of the back, stopping in the hallway. She had on a pair of jeans and a lacy shirt with ruffled sleeves and no shoes. Her hair hung in thick curls to her shoulders and she had no makeup on.

"Do you like chicken?" she asked.

Chicken, lamb, tofu, he didn't care what she made. The smells, the woman and this setting were more than he'd anticipated. Why wouldn't she move in with him? This felt settled to him.

He nodded.

"Well, good."

"What's that?" he asked pointing to the package, sitting on the table next to his spot.

"A present," she said, putting the food on the table and pouring them both a glass of white wine. "I'm not much of a cook, so this is kind of simple. Open your present."

He took a sip of his wine and removed the wrapping paper to find a small metal sign that read Home Is Where Your Story Begins.

She was watching him carefully and he realized that once again she'd surprised him. He'd always thought that life was happening outside of him. "Thanks."

"I thought we could hang it on the wall here. So you'd see it every week."

"I like it. But why did you choose this?"

She shrugged and glanced down at her plate. "I thought that maybe you forgot that your story—and your life—stem from the home you carry around within you."

"Is that why you won't move in with me?" he asked.

"Maybe part of it. Most of it's on me, because I don't want to rush, but another part is the fact that you don't let any roots form around you."

Her insight humbled him and made him feel a bit unworthy of her. Because he had no great truth or secret inside of him and he knew it.

CHAPTER SIXTEEN

DAVE QUALIFIED in the pole position in New Hampshire; Annie was so proud of her brother. She celebrated with his team. They were all talking about how they'd lowered the motor mount for his car and how it had made all the difference. It was still within legal standards, according to Vinnie and one of the other guys that Annie heard talking to an official. She went to look for Jared. Tucker had qualified in fourth but as she approached his garage she heard him talking with a reporter.

"Fourth suits me just fine today. I know that I'm going to be in first on Sunday."

Annie shook her head as he winked over at her.

"What about those carly-season rumors that your team was treating your tires?"

"I hope they've been laid to rest. We've endured every kind of testing available on our tires and still there's been no proof of wrongdoing."

"That's got to be a relief. Anything else you'd like to add?" the reporter asked.

"It has been an exciting season for us and we're just hoping to enjoy the ride all the way to Homestead," Tucker said, concluding the interview. Annie drifted behind the crowd and into the garage. She spotted Jared in the back talking to Reilly O'Connor, the general manager of Tucker's team.

Jared looked up at her, gesturing her over to his side. He wrapped an arm around her shoulder, pulling her up against him. He did it often and she liked it. Liked the way he immediately drew her close whenever they were together. She hoped it meant that he didn't like being apart any more than she did.

"Hi, Reilly," she said, greeting the other man whom she knew from years ago. His dad had been the general manager on her father's team. Teams on the NASCAR circuit liked to hire people whom they knew.

"Annie. How are your folks doing?"

"Good. Dad had a doctor's visit early this week and they are pleased with the progress he's making. Mom's got him on a strict diet and exercise routine."

"Your mom's the only one that man listens to," Reilly said.

"How true," she said. Reilly left a few minutes later and she was alone with Jared.

"Busy morning?" she asked.

"Just the usual. I have one of my dad's old partners and his family coming to the race this weekend. I thought Hal was going to show up in time for qualifying."

"It was pretty exciting today, wasn't it?" she said. There'd been a couple of minor wrecks during the practice lap; luckily they hadn't involved Dave or Tucker. "I got some spectacular pictures of Dave as he pulled through the smoke of that last wreck. I can't wait to pull up the photo and see if it's as good as I think it is."

"I'm sure it is," Jared said. "Dave's car was hot out there today."

"I think they did something different with the engine mount. Vinnie said it made all the difference."

Jared stared at her for a second before she realized what she'd just done—shared information from her brother's garage with one of his rival drivers.

"Oh, man, can you please ignore that?"

He shrugged. "Was it legal?"

"Yes. They mentioned they'd stayed within legal limits." She felt bad that she'd said anything to Jared. The way he was looking at her made her realize he wasn't just thinking about Dave, but wondering if she'd said anything about what she'd seen in Tucker's garage.

"It was totally unintentional. I don't think of you as part of Tucker's team all the time. Sometimes I just think of you as my boyfriend."

"I know," he said. "Don't worry about it anymore."

His cell phone rang and he answered it. She turned away from him to give him some privacy, all the while cursing herself. How could she be so lax? She knew that Dave hadn't done anything illegal, but teams guarded their strategies closely. They didn't want other drivers or crew chiefs to know what they were doing in their own garage.

"That was Hal and his family. Want to come and meet them?"

"Ah, sure," she said, wondering if it was simply because he didn't want to leave her alone in Tucker's garage.

Doubt was insidious and she could remember how it built during her marriage. She stopped walking and Jared glanced down at her. "Do you still trust me?"

"Of course. I think you'll like Hal. He's always been larger than life to me. When I was growing up he'd always tell me tales that sounded like they were too fantastical to be true."

She was very aware that he'd changed the subject but she let him. "What kind of stories?"

"Just his travels throughout Egypt and all of Africa."

"What does he do?" she asked, interested in spite of the fact that she wanted to make sure that they'd resolved the issue between them.

"He was a banker, like my dad. But he didn't like to stay in the office."

"Your family is so different than mine," she said. Her family was all about racing and she loved that.

"I know that. You have no idea how hard it was to find a place in NASCAR, coming from the outside the way Tucker and I did," he said, starting to walk toward the garage entrance.

"I bet. But you've found your place now," she said. "Jared?"

"Yes?"

"I know I'm being paranoid, but please tell me that you don't think I'm telling Dave what Tucker's doing in his garage."

"Honey, I don't think you're spying on us. If you were you wouldn't have slipped up just now and told me what Dave was doing. Okay?"

"Sorry if it seems like I'm overreacting."

He leaned down, brushing his lips over her forehead. "I'm just hoping you don't remember that I accused you of sabotaging Tucker's car."

"That's part of what my concern stems from," she admitted, deciding right then and there that she was going to stay out of both men's garages until the Chase was completed.

"Well, I don't think you're up to anything nefarious at the track."

And that was enough for now.

DAVE WON IN New Hampshire but was fined because his engine mount was too low. Jared hadn't said anything to Tucker or the officials about what Annie had said. He was a little concerned that she might think he had. But she never brought the subject up.

The fine moved Dave to the bottom of the points in the top ten cup contenders. But he was back on his game in Dover, finishing second behind Tucker, and then beating Tucker in Kansas and Talladega. In Talladega, Tucker was in a wreck near the end of the race and was a DNF—did not finish.

Tucker and Dave were very close in the points and most of the forecasters were predicting one or the other of them would win the NASCAR NEXTEL Cup Championship. But this week they were in Charlotte. Charlotte was the heart of NASCAR and where many drivers called home.

Jared brought Annie to his home, which was just down the mountain from Tucker's. They went out on ATVs, driving through the woods, and then he invited her to join him at a prerace bonfire Tuesday night at Tucker's house.

The autumn night was crisp and Annie looked cute in her tight jeans and the red fleece he'd given her for the chilly evening. She didn't mix or mingle with many of the other women at the event but instead hung out with the guys, which was something he'd noticed about her from the first. She was more comfortable in the pit or the garage talking to the men about cars than she was with a group of women.

"Dave would flip if he saw her over there talking with my team," Tucker said.

"You think?" Jared replied. "Her brother knows

her pretty well. He'd know she's not doing anything but chatting."

"Is that all she's doing?"

"What else would she be doing?"

"I don't know. But someone has been leaking details of what Billy and I have been doing to the car. Stuff that only someone who has been in my garage would know."

"Annie hasn't been in your garage lately," Jared said. He knew it for a fact because he'd made it a point to stay away from the garages and had noticed Annie doing the same.

"Yeah, I'd noticed that. So, do you think we have a spy?"

"I have no idea. Most of the guys on your team are new this year. But they are all aware that strategy is top secret."

"Billy doesn't think it's one of our guys but he did admit there are a couple he wasn't sure of."

"How are you going to find out who the leak is?"

Tucker shrugged and took a drink of his beer. "I don't know that we can. We're just playing things even closer to the vest than before."

Jared took a sip of his own beer as the sound of Annie's laughter carried over to him. He glanced at her and felt his gut tighten. She was his.

"You spend a lot of time together with her—is she getting to you yet?" Tucker asked, reminding Jared that he wasn't alone.

"I like it. I haven't thought of moving on," Jared said

almost absently. "She's unlike anyone I've ever met before…Annie has some interesting ideas about what a home should be. She's always cooking for me."

"Can she cook?"

"Ah, not really. But that doesn't seem to matter. It's that she's in there cooking."

Annie came over to join the two men, her cheeks rosy from the fire. "What are you two talking about? You look so intense, not like you're at a party."

"Just guy stuff."

"Oh, guy stuff. That either means women or cars."

"As if I'd have trouble with women," Tucker said. "And Jared has you."

"Are you dating someone, Tucker? I thought Heidi was just a friend."

"She is, Annie. And I'm not dating one special person."

She tipped her head to the side and glanced at him. Jared stared back. "Were you talking about me?"

"I was telling Tucker about your cooking. Just saying what a unique experience it was to eat meals you prepared."

"Ha. That's not what you said this morning when I made that frittata and it wouldn't come out of the frying pan."

"What did you say, Jared?" Tucker asked, really not helping the situation.

Annie came to his rescue, looping her arm through his and leaning against him. "Nothing, he just laughed."

"You shouldn't feel bad—he's had some of the best chefs in the world working for him over the years."

"I think I feel worse now," she said, with a fake pout.

Jared leaned down to kiss her, tasting the wine she'd been drinking all evening on her breath.

"I'll leave you two alone."

Tucker left them and Annie took another sip of her wine, smiling up at him. She was a little tipsy and he liked seeing this side of her. She was relaxed without the constraints she normally kept on herself.

He had the feeling she'd tell him anything when she was in this mood. "Are you having fun?"

"Yes. Are you?"

"I am. Tucker throws a good party."

"He does. Have you been to a lot of his parties?"

"Yeah, I think I've been to most of them. at least since I started traveling with him on the NASCAR circuit."

"What did you do before? Leave all the team owner stuff to someone else? That doesn't sound like you."

"I was hands-on away from the track. Still trying to manage the JM's corporation. But after about five years of that I had a change of heart."

"Really, what changed?"

"I finally figured out I hate being in an office all day."

"But you thrive on pressure and, don't take this the wrong way, but you are bossy."

"Is there a right way to take that?"

"Yes, as a compliment. So, why'd you stop?"

How could he explain to her what he'd never really understood himself. He'd woke up one morning and realized his corporation was going to be his entire life if he didn't get out of the office. One of the main reasons he'd been alone was his single-minded focus on work. No woman wanted to play second fiddle to a man who cared more about a coffeehouse than her.

He pulled her into his arms and leaned down to whisper in her ear. "I think I left so I could meet you."

She melted against him. "I'm glad you did."

DAVE WAS SECOND in the points going to Fort Worth in early November, which meant he had three more races to get to number one. He should have been on top of the world but he didn't want to finish second again. Unless he was mistaken, his family was all in the suite of his main rival. For Annie's sake he'd tried to let go of the animosity he felt toward Tucker.

For his own sake he knew he had to let it go. Those feelings were like poison on the track, distracting him from his A-game when he let himself dwell on them.

"Want to go to a party?" Dave asked, as he and Vinnie left the garage.

"Where?" Vinnie said.

"Ah, Jared is throwing one for the Aldridge team over at the Speedway Club."

Vinnie raised one eyebrow at him. "Why are you going?"

"Annie invited me and I told her I'd make Jared feel like part of the family."

"Yeah, we'll go."

Vinnie moved away to call his wife and Dave stepped away to give his friend some privacy.

"Hey, man. You got a second?" Rob asked, walking up to him.

"I've got a few minutes."

Rob glanced behind him to Vinnie. "I wanted to touch base with you about the job we talked about a few weeks ago."

Rob was a nice guy, but after meeting him for a beer a few times, Dave noticed that Rob was not really focused on doing any job and was certainly not suited for the Jenner team. Besides Dave had no openings. "We still don't have any openings right now. Give Mel you're contact info and she'll let you know if anything comes up."

"I already did," Rob said.

"I'll keep you in mind if something comes up."

"Is there anything I can do to stand out from the competition?"

Dave couldn't think of anything off the top of his head. "You're a good guy, Rob. It's just that we won't be reevaluating our team until after Homestead. I don't want to break up the winning combination we've got going."

"I can understand that," Rob said. "You know I've got the mechanical skills to be a part of a top team, but is there anything in particular you need from a team member...you know, personality-wise."

"Loyalty and a winning attitude," Dave said.

"Thanks, man."

"You ready to go? Darla is already over at the party. Annie invited her," Vinnie said, interrupting.

"Yeah, I'm ready. Vinnie, this is Rob Mandelay, he's a catch can man for Aldridge's team. Rob, this is Vinnie Festa, my crew chief."

"Nice to meet you, Rob," Vinnie said, offering his hand to the other man.

"You, too. Later Dave."

Rob left and Vinnie turned to him. "Why are you talking to someone on Aldridge's team?"

"We went to school together...he wants to switch teams."

"Is he good?"

"I don't know. I asked Mel to get his qualifications and stuff."

"I'll follow up with him, but I think you should keep your distance until after Homestead. Ready for this party?"

"Not really. Thanks for coming along."

"You and Annie are family and if she's serious about Jared MacNeil...well, then we'd better give him a chance."

"I know."

CHAPTER SEVENTEEN

ANNIE WAS SURPRISED to see Dave when he arrived at the party. She wasn't surprised to see Vinnie though because Darla had insisted she'd get her husband there.

Annie worked her way through the crowd to her brother's side. The two men were talking to Reilly, Tucker's general manager.

For this one moment it seemed as if all the rivalry stuff was being left at the door. Jared had hired a band and there was a small dance floor that was crowded with couples dancing.

She smoothed her hand down the blue cocktail dress she was wearing. The low neckline showcased the sapphire-and-diamond choker that Jared had given her. It was her first time wearing it and she kept reaching up to touch it.

She took a sip of her sparkling water, waiting until Dave was finished talking to Reilly before she joined him and Vinnie. Her life had changed a lot since the first race this season in Daytona.

Who would have thought one wreck would have such a deep impact on her life?

"I thought you couldn't make it."

"My other plans fell through," he said.

"I'm glad," she said, meaning it.

"You look nice."

"Thanks," she replied. She fingered the necklace again.

"Daddy and Mom are here, too."

Dave nodded toward a table where her parents were seated. Her father had his head bent toward Tucker, who was telling the older man something. Annie watched as her father put a hand on Tucker's shoulder and then she glanced at Dave and saw his features tighten.

"Are you hungry?" she asked. "There's a buffet toward the back."

"I'm fine."

Annie felt a hand on her back as Jared joined them. He reached around her to shake Dave's hand. The two men talked shop but Annie wasn't paying attention to the conversation. She couldn't take her eyes off of Dave, who had yet to really look away from the table where her parents and Tucker were sitting.

She felt his tension, or maybe just imagined it, but it was so strong that she knew it was real. She wanted to pull Dave into her arms and hug him like she used to do when they were little. Dave spent most of the time showing the world that he was a good sportsman and the gentleman that his nickname claimed him to be.

But she knew there were times when that mantle was a heavy one and she guessed this was one of them. There was a lull in the conversation.

"Annie?"

"Huh?"

"Is everything okay?" Jared asked.

She pulled her gaze away from her brother. "Yes, sorry about that. I was thinking about something else."

"What?" he asked.

She shook her head, positive that Dave would never forgive her if she said she was worried about him. Then Dave looked at her and she hoped he didn't know what she'd been thinking.

"It was nothing."

"Thanks for coming tonight," Jared said to Dave.

"No problem. Looks like you're becoming part of the family," Dave said.

Jared rubbed his hand down Annie's back, then wrapped his arm around the curve of her waist and puled her into his side. She took comfort from his presence next to her. It didn't relieve the worry she had for her brother but just having Jared with her made her not feel so alone.

"I guess so," Jared said, but there was an odd note in his voice. She wished Dave wouldn't say anything about family, but her brother had never really been one to listen to her.

"Dave, leave it be."

Jared tucked her closer to his side. She felt like she had someone who would be worrying over Dave with her, which was really silly. Jared didn't care that much about her family. Did he?

Someone bumped into them from behind, jarring Annie's drink. It splashed down her arm and onto Darla's jacket, who had just walked up and joined them.

"I'm sorry about that. Come on, let's go get you cleaned up," Annie said. "Will you excuse us?"

"Sure," Jared answered.

Annie took Darla's arm in hers and led her through the crowd toward the bathrooms. She set her drink down on the tray tucked next to the bar.

"What was going on over there?" Darla asked, as she pushed open the door to the ladies room.

"Dave's trying to be a nice guy, but I think he's struggling," Annie said as she washed the soda off her arm.

Darla dabbed at her jacket with a paper towel. "Vinnie's worried about him."

"Worried that he won't be able to win?" Annie asked.

"No, not that. Dave has this way of channeling everything into winning."

"Yes, he does."

"I'm not sure why he is worrying."

The women exited the restroom and Annie saw her

brother still standing across the room. She didn't think that Dave was going to be able to keep ignoring Tucker and Jared—and the fact that she brought his enemy into their family for much longer.

JARED WATCHED the women leave, unsure what to say to Dave now that they were alone. Despite their conversation a few weeks ago, Dave still didn't seem too welcoming. Aside from her parents, Jared thought Dave was the most important one to gain approval from.

"Nice run out there today," Jared said.

"Thanks. I like this track, even though I'm usually faster on the shorter tracks."

"I noticed. I don't envy guys like you and Tucker who drive like that every week."

"I think it's either in your blood or not. Most people don't understand the rush. You know, the drive to get out there."

Jared did know because Tucker had tried to explain it to him a time or two. "You sound like Tucker."

Dave's features tightened. And Jared had the feeling that Dave was never going to be able to let go of his rivalry with Tucker.

"I guess I must. After all, Tucker's a driver like I am. How long have you known him?"

"Since college."

"You two are tight?"

"He's like a brother to me," Jared said.

"Then I'm going to have to be especially gracious when I beat him in the points so you and Annie won't have any problems."

He had to smile at the cocky way Dave talked. They chatted about the upcoming race and then the conversation lagged.

"Thanks for coming to the party tonight. I don't know if Tucker would have done it."

"Well, he's not known for being a gentleman like I am," Dave said wryly.

"Are you really that nice all the time?" Jared asked.

"That's a deep, dark family secret and I'm not sure you qualify yet."

The door slammed shut once again. "Why not?"

"Annie's still not sure about your relationship," Dave said.

A part of Jared knew the other man was right. "She doesn't want to rush things."

"Like she did with Malcolm. Man, that guy was some piece of work."

"Did you like him?" Jared asked.

"No."

"Why not?"

"He never wanted to do anything with our family," Dave said. "He drove a wedge between Annie and the rest of us. I don't think she'd be happy with a man who did that again."

Jared felt the warning go through him. How hard was

he willing to try to make the Jenners like him? If he failed would Annie walk away from him?

"Thanks for the warning."

"No problem. I like you, Jared. That's the reason why I'm telling you this."

He wasn't too sure about Dave liking him. But he believed Dave loved his sister and was looking out for her. That made him want to listen to whatever advice the other man had to offer. "Anything else?"

"Nah."

Dave saw a buddy of his and moved on to talk to him. Jared watched the Jenner family, wondering at the dynamic that kept them so close. Was he doing the wrong thing by trying to fit into Annie's family?

"Want to dance?" Annie asked, coming up behind him.

"Yes. I'd love that."

He led her out onto the dance floor. The band leader looked over at them as Jared pulled Annie into his arms. The song they were playing ended.

"This next song is for Jared."

Jared glanced at Annie as the band started to play "Come Away With Me." He drew her closer. It had been an eternity since he'd last held her in his arms.

He couldn't resist kissing her. Her mouth opened under his and he told himself to take it slow, but slow wasn't part of the program with this woman. She was pure feminine temptation and he had her in his arms.

He slid his hands down her back, wishing they were alone.

Her fingers drifted over his shoulders and then slid down his back. He growled deep in his throat when she leaned forward against him.

She took control of the kiss, then she pulled back, resting her head on his shoulder as he danced her around the floor. The worry that he'd felt at Dave's words increased as he realized that he had no real idea how to keep her.

He'd hoped somehow that gifts would be an asset to wooing her, but they weren't. She liked them, but she was just as happy when he didn't give her jewelry. He'd hoped that maybe winning over her family would be a bonus, but according to Dave that wasn't going to do it.

He'd hoped that their lovemaking and the closeness that was growing between them would be enough. But now he was very afraid that it wouldn't be.

And he wasn't ready for the NASCAR season to end. He wasn't ready for her to go back to her life and send him back to his. Though he had no indication that she was leaning toward ending their relationship after the race at Homestead.

When the song ended he didn't let her go. He knew he should be circulating, working the room and making sure that his guests were enjoying themselves. But he needed this time with her for himself.

He held her in his arms as the band played romantic covers of songs made popular by Dean Martin and Ella Fitzgerald, classics that spoke of heartbreak and love.

He tried to push the conversation he'd had with Dave out of his mind but it wouldn't budge. All he could think was that every time he thought he was getting closer to Annie he was really drifting from her.

When the evening ended he accepted an invitation from the Jenner men to join them in the morning for an early round of golf. Annie didn't say anything but he hoped that it was the right thing to do. He would integrate himself into her family and maybe that would somehow make her see how much he wanted her.

DAVE WON IN Fort Worth and then they all traveled to Phoenix for the second to last race of the season. Annie was tired of the traveling, but at the same time she'd miss all the moving around they did. And she had no idea what was going to happen between her and Jared after the race in Homestead.

Though they'd decided to revisit living together in Florida at the end of the NASCAR season, he'd said little else about it and had in fact been more reserved since the race in Fort Worth. She'd done everything she could to show him that she was interested in a relationship with him that would last beyond November.

Annie wondered if that was part of the problem. She

honestly tried not to filter everything that happened between her and Jared through the lens of what had happened with Malcolm. But it was really hard. Especially when she felt like she was holding on too tightly to Jared. She was too afraid to let loose in case he left her and didn't come back.

Annie spent a lot of time photographing Dave and his team near Dave's garage because she didn't want to unintentionally pass along anything she saw in Tucker's garage or vice versa. She still couldn't believe she'd done that.

There was a major gathering of officials around Tucker's car after the qualifying laps were run and they were inspecting the cars. Annie drifted over that way but couldn't get close enough to see what was going on.

She saw Donovan Allen come out of Dave's hauler. "What's going on over there?"

"I don't know. The squawk on the radio was just that they'd found something they shouldn't have."

"Not with his tires, right? Didn't they send them off to be analyzed and find nothing wrong with them?"

"Yes. It's not the tires. Those were fine."

"Have you seen Jared?"

"No. But I bet he'll be in over there in that knot of spectators."

When Jared came out of the garage she'd never seen him look so angry before. She was actually a little afraid to approach him, not knowing what had happened with the officials. But as soon as he noticed her, he walked over to her.

"What happened?" she asked.

"I can't talk about it out here," he said, taking her arm and leading her over to one of the conference trailers. He rapped on the door and found it empty. "Let's go in here."

She climbed inside the small conference room and took a seat on one of the leather chairs. Jared followed her in, closing the door behind him. He opened the door that led into a second conference area and made sure that it was empty before he turned to her.

There were two televisions mounted on the walls. Two separate network reporters were live and speculating on what was going on with Tucker and his Number 186 car.

"This looks pretty serious. What's going on?"

"He was running with an illegal carburetor. That's why he broke the track record."

Annie was shocked. This was way more serious than just changing tire pressure or possibly treating tires with some kind of substance. "Are you sure? What did Tucker say?"

"He's denying the entire thing. Billy says that the carburetor they removed isn't the one he and his team installed before the qualifying laps."

She didn't know what to say. She had as many questions as Jared did. A big part of her wanted to find some way to calm him down. But she didn't understand cheating.

It was something that Malcolm had done, too. Thinking that if he did something unobserved he could just deny it and no one would be wiser.

The Tucker she'd come to know wasn't the kind of man who'd cheat.

"Well, of course, he'd deny it. And with all the scrutiny that was on his team earlier this year I can't see Billy or Tucker taking a chance on doing something illegal," Annie said, wishing now that she'd gone to Tucker's garage and maybe she could have prevented this. He would never have done anything illegal if she'd been in there with her camera.

Jared rubbed the back of his neck, reaching over to turn off the television sets. "I can't figure this out."

"Jared, you sound really ticked off. If Tucker misses a race will it cost you a lot of money?"

"No. Money means nothing to me. I can't believe this has happened with the car. Even the officials were shocked. This totally compromises Tucker's run for the NASCAR NEXTEL Cup Championship."

"That doesn't sound like Tucker. He might not have been part of the group who did this," she said. Tucker valued his friendship with Jared. She knew from the time she'd spent with both men.

"We have absolutely no idea what happened. We're so close to winning the championship."

Something about this entire setup didn't seem right to Annie. She understood wanting to win, but Tucker was fast enough to do it without cheating. And his standing in the points was still good. All he had to do was finish top five this week and next week and he'd win.

"How are they going to punish him? A fine?"

"I don't know. He's over in the 'bad boy' trailer right now. Billy's with him."

The "bad boy" trailer was the one place that no driver wanted to be. It was the trailer where the NASCAR bigwigs took drivers, crew chiefs and really anyone who did anything wrong to "talk" to them. To give them the kind of dressing-down that couldn't be delivered in public.

"You know Billy's been around a long time and there's never been a hint of him doing anything like this before. I can't imagine that he'd jeopardize his potential winnings from the championship to finish this way."

"Of course you can't imagine this kind of thing, Annie. You come from a family with a legacy of integrity and winning."

He left the trailer before she could respond. But she really had no idea what she'd have said to him because he hadn't sounded all too happy with her or her family.

CHAPTER EIGHTEEN

TUCKER CAME OUT of the "bad boy" trailer looking every inch the maverick he'd been labeled by NASCAR fans. In fact he looked ready for a fight.

Could someone have sabotaged his car?

"We need to talk," Tucker said as he stalked by Jared toward his own hauler.

Jared easily caught up with Tucker. "What about?"

"I'll tell you when we're alone."

The garage had been cleared of everyone with cold passes and those with hot passes had been around long enough to stay away from Tucker. His entire team looked ready to rumble. Jared followed Tucker up the stairs and into his hauler.

Billy was already inside, seated at the table near the back going over some kind of paperwork.

"What did you want to talk to me about?" Jared asked when they were all seated.

"I think someone from Dave's team sabotaged my car."

"Why? That makes no sense."

"But it's supposed to be believable that I'd throw away a chance at the championship?"

"No, that doesn't makes sense, either. Even the officials can't believe you'd deliberately do something this stupid," Jared said.

"I've never broken the rules. I've pushed and tried to see how far I could get an official to go for certain things but I'd never do something like this," Billy said.

"What do you mean?" Jared asked. He hadn't been to see the car yet.

"It was very obvious when we took the car apart—it's like we were trying to get caught. The carburetor is totally illegal, not even close to the one I installed."

Jared nodded. "Who would do something like this?"

"I already told you. *Dave Jenner*. He wants me totally out of the race."

Jared had a hard time imagining "Gentleman Dave" sneaking around Tucker's garage and planting an illegal piece of equipment in his car. It just didn't seem like the kind of thing that he'd do.

"Was there any mention of one of his guys in your garage? I think the officials would have noticed if someone from his team was messing with your car."

Tucker stood up. "No. No one saw anything."

"Well…" Without proof it was going to be hard to prove that anyone did anything to the car.

"Well, what? All that proves is that they were sneaky. And don't you think it's a little suspicious that Annie wasn't in my garage today. Every week she stops by, but not this week. What's up with that?"

Jared realized where Tucker was going with this. "I don't think that's why she stayed away. She hasn't been around for *several* weeks."

"There's no other person," Tucker said.

"You've got to admit it makes no sense. She was seen in every other garage area except ours," Billy said.

"You asked?"

Billy shrugged. "Yes. Don't get defensive. That's odd behavior."

"Ah, hell. She wasn't avoiding your garage so that one of Dave's guys could plant an illegal part in your car."

"How do you know?" Tucker asked. "Why else would she stay away?"

"Because a few weeks ago she told me something about what Dave's team was doing to his car. I think she decided to stay out of your garage so she didn't accidentally pick up some information and give it to Dave."

Tucker crossed his arms over his chest and leaned forward. "See, this is what I'm talking about. Cheating. The Jenners all feel safe doing whatever they want because they are part of a legacy. Even if I had photos of Dave doing this no one would want to believe it."

"Annie didn't cheat. As I just said, she told me something about Dave's car. And you have your own legacy, Tucker. You are just as much a part of NASCAR as Dave is."

"Not if Annie and Dave get their way." Tucker paced around the small room like he was going to explode. Jared had never seen him like this before.

No matter what Tucker believed or what had happened to his car he knew that Annie had nothing to do with it. As much as she loved her family he'd seen the love she had for NASCAR and the family of people who worked here.

"Maybe, Dave, but Annie's not like that."

"She is. You're just too blinded by her to see the truth. She's not going to accept you into the Jenner fold because they don't accept outsiders."

"Brandon Jenner didn't seem to be treating you like an outsider at the party the other night."

"That's just another reason for Dave to do this. He doesn't like me."

"You sound paranoid," Billy stated.

"See?" Jared said.

"Both of you," Billy said. "We need to stop arguing and figure this out."

"I have figured it out. Your girlfriend and her family have set me up," Tucker said, getting up in Jared's face.

Jared pushed Tucker away from him. "I don't appreciate your accusations."

Billy went back to studying the papers in front of him as Tucker continued. "I don't care what you appreciate. What kind of team owner spends more time with his driver's number-one rival than his own driver?"

"That's crap and you know it. I've been very careful to make sure that I don't do too much with Dave or any of the Jenners."

Tucker shook his head. "Hell, I know you have. I'm just mad and looking for someone to take it out on."

"I can understand that. If you're positive that you didn't put that carburetor in, then how can we find the real culprit?"

"I don't know. We'd need someone who had access to all the areas and all the teams."

"Annie does. I'll ask her if she saw anything," Jared said.

Tucker shook his head. "Listen, I know you think she's trustworthy and maybe she is when it comes to your relationship with her. But I don't think she's loyal to me. If she did uncover something that pointed to Dave or one of the other drivers who drives for her father, I'm not sure she'd tell us."

Jared didn't agree but knew there was no way he was going to change Tucker's mind. But as he left the hauler he saw Annie in a knot of Dave's men, chatting and talking. And he wondered if Tucker wasn't right about loyalty.

JARED didn't come back to his motor home until close to midnight and Annie wondered if she should go find a hotel room of her own to stay in. She'd heard that Tucker's team had filed a grievance with the officials stating that they believed that someone outside Tucker's team had tampered with his car.

"Who do they suspect tampered with the car?" she asked as she mixed Jared a drink.

"Thanks," he said when she handed him the scotch and soda. "Tucker is looking hard at Dave and his team."

"I don't think they'd do anything like that. I've known most of them for a good ten years at least. Some of them I've known my entire life."

"It's hard to believe someone you know is capable of doing something illegal, but it is possible."

She wasn't naive. "I understand that. Don't talk to me like I'm an idiot."

He held his hand up. "I wasn't. Honest, it's just been one hell of a long day."

She sat next to him on the couch. He put his arm around her shoulders and drew her closer to his side. The silence built between them as he continued to sip his drink. But she knew he wasn't relaxing. If anything he kept getting more tense. She knew he was going over the entire situation in his head.

"Other than Dave's team who else does Tucker think could do it?"

"No one. He's pretty focused on Dave and I can't say I blame him."

"I can," she said. No matter the rivalry between them, she couldn't see her brother tampering with another driver's car. It went totally against everything that Dave stood for.

"Of course, you can. Dave's your brother."

"And Tucker's your best friend," she said. "I don't think either of us is objective where they are concerned."

"True. But the two of them have been going at it since February and it's logical to look to each other's camps when something like this happens."

"Did he suspect me?" she asked.

Jared leaned his head against the back of the leather sofa and closed his eyes. She knew the answer before he uttered it out loud.

"Yes, he did."

"What reasons did he use? Just the fact that I was related to Dave?"

Jared turned his head without lifting it. "No, the fact that you'd stayed out of his garage today."

"But I've been staying away for weeks. I only did that because I know his team now and they talk to me because I'm your girlfriend. I didn't want to accidentally let something slip to Dave like I did to you a few weeks ago."

He lifted his free hand and caught one of her curls around his finger. "That's what I figured."

"And he listened to you?"

"After a fashion."

"Maybe you can get him to stop suspecting Dave. I'm sure my brother—"

"That'd be impossible. Someone is going to have to find concrete proof that Dave had no knowledge of what happened for Tucker to even come close to believing it."

"That's ridiculous. Everyone knows that Dave's a Jenner and we don't cheat. You know if Tucker wasn't such a maverick, he wouldn't have this problem."

She knew her words weren't fair but she didn't like the tone of accusation in Jared's voice. It was like he believed Dave might have had something to do with Tucker's problems.

"You know when you accuse Tucker of being a rebel you're condemning his entire team."

"So? You just did the same thing with me and Dave."

"Are you saying you think I'm a wild card, too?"

"I think you don't care what Tucker does as long as he wins and gets you owner points and makes you more money."

Jared sat up, drawing his arm from behind her back. "Don't hold back, Annie, tell me what's really on your mind."

"You're accusing the Jenner Racing team of spying and sabotage. That's something we would never do."

"And I guess now I know where you fall in all of this. Somehow I thought you'd see it differently."

She shook her head, shades of Malcolm coloring this entire situation. Was she supposed to look the other way and keep her mouth shut so that their relationship could continue? She couldn't do it. Couldn't pretend not to see the obstacles in their path.

"Why? Because we're sleeping together?"

"No. I'd think you'd be the first to defend Tucker because you know how it feels to be accused of something you didn't do."

She blanched. She did know exactly what that felt like. Clearly she recalled that moment when Jared had accused her of sabotaging Tucker's car, which should have warned her where he'd fall in any kind of conflict. "That was a totally different situation."

"Why? Because you're a Jenner and above reproach?" he asked, pushing to his feet. He stood there towering over her.

She shook her head. She should have expected this to happen sooner or later. She was grateful that it had happened now before she'd made a deeper commitment to Jared. Yeah, right, she thought, as if she could get any more deeply committed to this man than she already was.

"Somehow I knew this was going to come back to my family."

"It's hard to separate you from your family," he said. "Especially since they are always in my face."

"What are you saying?"

He shrugged at her.

"I knew that you didn't really trust me and this proves it."

Jared shook his head. "All this proves is that you'd choose blind loyalty to your family over anyone else."

"Don't act like you're the injured party here," she said.

"No, I'd never do that. I guess this is where the ride ends for you and I, right?"

She wrapped her arms around her waist, wondering how this had gotten so out of control. He just stared down at her and she knew she needed to find some words. Any words, something to say that would make him stay, but in the end she just shrugged her shoulders and watched him walk away.

DAVE WAS BEGINNING to believe some of the rumors he was hearing out of Tucker's camp about someone messing with his car. The other driver had been such a fierce competitor all year long it made no sense that he'd cheat in such an obvious way and get himself kicked out of the race.

NASCAR had decided not to let Tucker race today in Phoenix. Though a part of him was relieved he wouldn't be racing against Tucker another part knew that victory wouldn't be as sweet unless he got it honestly.

With the race a couple of hours away everyone was tense. Dave took a few minutes to himself in his hauler.

What a difference a few weeks made. His father had been at the last two races looking more like his old self than he had in years. This morning Annie looked miserable and Jared looked the same. He tried to get Annie to talk about it but she wouldn't.

And his team was really doing well. They had the car in the best shape it could be in.

When Dave came out of his hauler he saw Rob Mandelay walking toward him. "Do you have a minute?"

"Not really. I'm getting ready to race."

"This won't take long."

Dave smiled genially and led the way back toward his hauler, but didn't go inside. He needed to keep this short. Rob was becoming nothing short of a pain in his butt. He'd liked the man but just had no room for him right now.

"I wanted to talk to you about a job."

"We still don't have anything open, Rob. I'm aware that you want a job with my team but we're fully staffed," he said, offering the man his hand. "As I mentioned we'll probably need some new guys in January. I'll call you then."

"But I've already proven my loyalty to you," Rob stated.

"Ah, what are you talking about?" Dave asked, afraid to guess what Rob had done.

"When you guys got fined for lowering the motor mount, I told everyone that clearly that was Vinnie's idea," Rob said.

"Thanks, Rob. But we're a team. We all work

together. I appreciate the support though. Listen I've got to get going. We'll talk again later."

"There's one more thing," Rob added.

"What?" he asked, glancing around the garage area for Mel. He was going to have a long talk with her about staying close by so she could rescue him from people like Rob who didn't know when to move on.

"I fixed it so you could win the championship. Tucker's completely out of the way now. I think that deserves some kind of thanks."

Dave glanced at the other man, afraid to believe what he heard. He took Rob's arm and drew him farther away from the people milling just a few feet away.

"Why would you do that?"

"I figured if I helped you win then…well, you have to give me a job."

Rob must have been half-crazy to think that idea would work. All that he'd done was place the blame squarely in his court. Oh, hell, how was Dave going to fix this?

"Don't say anything about this to anyone else. We'll talk as soon as the race is over."

Dave left his hauler area and walked to the garage, not sure what to do. He should say something to the officials but he didn't want to be implicated in Rob's scheme. And the race countdown had already begun. He couldn't afford to get his head out of the game at this point.

But how could he compete knowing that someone had sabotaged Tucker's car for him? How could he hold his head up as a man and not say anything?

"Dave, we need to talk," Annie said, coming up next to him. She looped her arm through his and drew him to a stop in the middle of the garage area.

"I can't now. Let me run this race and then we can talk."

"I heard what Rob just said to you."

Dave glanced down at his sister, into eyes that were like his own. "Don't judge, Annie. I didn't ask him to do anything crazy."

"I know that. But we have to tell the officials so that Tucker can have a chance to race."

"It's too late for today."

"It's never too late for the truth."

"It is today. I'll go to them after this race is in the bag."

She shook her head and gave him a look that would have melted a lesser man on the spot. "I can't believe this. That's one step above cheating."

People were starting to notice them and he didn't want their conversation overheard so he led her back across the pavement to the hauler and opened the door. She climbed inside and he followed her.

"I know you didn't just call me a cheater. I had nothing to do with Tucker's problems."

"Yes, you did. Rob thinks that you're going to give him a job now."

"Well, I'm not. I never promised him a job or told him to do anything crazy like this."

"Dave…"

"Listen, let me run this race, win the championship for Daddy, and then I'll go and straighten this entire thing out."

"Win the championship for Daddy?"

"Yes. It's what I've wanted since February."

"I think that you aren't going to feel like the real winner unless the field is full of *all* of the competitors. Not just the ones you think you can beat."

"That's not fair, Annie."

"Life's not fair, Dave. And I expected better of you. If you're not going to the officials, then I will."

"I can't believe you're going to turn your back on your family," Dave said, grasping at straws.

"I don't think I am."

She walked out of the hauler and he lowered his head into his hands, letting her words echo in his head. What the hell was he thinking? Of course he had to take the steps necessary to clean up this mess. He'd never be able to live with himself if he didn't.

CHAPTER NINETEEN

THE FIRST PERSON that Annie saw when she left Dave's hauler was Tucker.

She went over to him. "Can we talk?"

"Sure."

"I…I'm sorry I didn't believe you or Jared when you said something about sabotage."

Tucker gave her a weird look and she realized she was making no sense at all. But she wanted to give Dave time to do the right thing.

"A lot of people still don't believe me so don't sweat it," he said. "I think I owe you an apology. I was pretty rough on you when I first suspected someone of tampering with my car. Jared put me in my place though."

"He did?"

"Yes. In no uncertain terms, he told me he trusted you," Tucker said.

And she'd told Jared he wasn't worthy of her trust. She'd chosen her family and loyalty to them over taking a chance on him. Because she felt safer with her family, they'd always been there for her. And she was afraid to give Jared the same trust. She was afraid to trust him not to just let her walk away.

"Listen, I just learned something that I think we need to take to the officials."

"Annie, you shouldn't be involved in this," Dave said, coming up behind her.

"Dave, I've made my choice."

"So have I. Tucker, let's talk in my hauler," Dave said in a no-nonsense voice.

She knew immediately that her brother was going to do the right thing. Tears stung her eyes and she turned around to hug him.

"What about?" Tucker said.

"I know who messed with your car," Dave said, dropping his arm from around her.

"Who?"

"Not out here," Dave replied. Tucker walked to Dave's hauler and opened the door.

The two men climbed into the hauler and Annie followed them.

"Okay, who was it?"

"A guy on your team," Dave said. "Rob Mandelay."

"My catch can guy?" Tucker asked. Tucker's fists tightened at his sides and he glared at Dave. "Kind of convenient that it's one of my guys."

"I know it sounds far-fetched, but trust me on this."

"Why would he do that?" Tucker demanded.

Dave looked sheepish but Annie felt proud of him.

He was doing the right thing, just like she knew he would. She knew she was going to have to do the same thing with Jared. Go and find him and try to make up for the things she said last night.

"He wanted a job with my team and thought that proving he was loyal to me would help his chances."

Tucker cursed. "Billy thought it had to be someone on our team because he didn't remember seeing anyone in another uniform in the garage. But we couldn't figure out who would do something this stupid. The crew gets financially rewarded if we win the championship."

"I'm sorry," Dave said.

"Why? Did you ask him to do it?" Tucker asked.

"No," Dave answered. "But I was glad that you were out of the race."

"Heck, if something like this happened to you I'd be happy to."

"Want me to go get an official?" Annie asked.

"No. I think Dave and I will handle this."

Dave and Tucker left together to find the officials. Annie wanted to find Jared, but suspected that just because everything was hopefully going to be settled between Dave and Tucker, that didn't mean their problems were solved, especially since the one thing that had become a wedge between them was her family. And she had no idea how to take them out of the equation.

She pulled out her phone and dialed Jared's cell

number but he didn't answer. She didn't blame him; he was probably still mad at her. She was mad at herself for letting the behavior she'd learned from her marriage mess up her relationship with Jared.

She'd found a man she wanted to spend the rest of her life with. Yes, she thought, she did want to spend the rest of her life with him. No matter that he couldn't become chummy with her family. She already knew she loved him and she needed to let him know that.

But he was going to be busy with the officials and Tucker. And she should…

She didn't want to think about it anymore. She loved Jared and wanted to spend the rest of her life with him. She couldn't wait to tell him. If he couldn't forgive her, then…well, then she'd convince him.

She left Jared a message that they needed to talk and to call when he could. Then she sat in one of Dave's chairs and stared at her phone as if that would somehow make it ring.

"LET'S GO, JARED. Tucker has some new information on the car," Billy said.

Jared pushed to his feet and followed the other man out of Tucker's hauler. They went to one of the NASCAR trailers. An official waited for them.

"Everyone's up there. We're waiting on one other guy."

"Who?"

"Rob Mandelay."

"Who's that?"

"Our catch can man," Billy said as he climbed into the trailer conference room. There were five people already in the room. Tucker, Dave, Vinnie, a NASCAR representative and an official—Marvin.

"What's going on?" Jared asked as he took a seat at the conference table.

"Dave had a confession from Mandelay that he messed with the carburetor," Tucker said.

"Damn, I hate that I was right and it was one of my guys," Billy said.

"Me, too."

"We don't know that anyone's right, yet," Marvin, the official said. "We need to talk to Mandelay and see what he says."

Jared understood but he wasn't too sure that this confession would clear Tucker. "Did he say why?"

"Something about proving his loyalty to me," Dave said.

The door opened and Mandelay walked in, accompanied by a second official.

"What's going on?" Rob asked, as he looked at all the faces around the table.

"We need to talk," Marvin said.

Rob glanced at Dave and then at Tucker. Jared thought the other man was running through his options.

"About?"

"Don't, Rob. We know you're the one who messed with the carburetor," Billy said.

"Because he said so," Rob said, pointing to Dave.

"Hey, man, I've got nothing to gain from saying that it was sabotage," Dave said. "Aldridge is my number one competition so if he stays out of the race I'm a shoe-in to win. But that's not what NASCAR is about and it's not what I'm about. Tell these men what you told me earlier."

Jared found a new respect for Dave. Rob shrugged then pushed to his feet. "Yeah, I did it. I changed it out so that Aldridge would be fined and possibly suspended."

"Did anyone ask you to do it?" Marvin asked.

Rob shook his head. "Not directly, but I thought if I could help Dave win the championship, he'd be more apt to hire me."

"Did he hint that if you somehow sabotaged Tucker's car he'd hire you?" Marvin asked.

"No. But we go way back and I know that loyalty is something that all the Jenners reward."

"Not blind loyalty. You should have been true to your driver. That's what we reward."

Jared realized that Annie was the same way. That she was looking for loyalty to her, not blind, just steady. That she wanted a man she knew would stand by her side and not leave her stranded.

After the NASCAR officials put their heads together,

they announced their decision. "Aldridge, your crew should work on readying your car for today's race. Marvin will go with you for an inspection."

"You'll have to start in the back," the NASCAR official added.

Jared knew that was because Tucker had no official qualifying time as he'd been disqualified. It didn't matter. He was relieved that Tucker was starting.

There was an official announcement thirty minutes later that the race would be delayed an hour and that Aldridge would be racing today. No more was said officially. The press and media people were swarming around the pits and the garages trying to get more information on what had happened, but word had come down that they wouldn't answer any questions until after the race.

Jared checked his voice mail and listened to the message from Annie. He wasn't sure what to say to her. He knew he owed her an apology. He'd gotten angry and let their conversation get out of control. And last night had been too long and too lonely.

He walked through the garage area looking for that familiar dark-haired woman. But he didn't see her at first. Then he found her, sitting in a chair outside of Dave's hauler watching her cell phone like it was some kind of holy relic.

He walked over to her and cleared his throat, unsure what to say now that he was here with her.

She glanced up at him. "Hey."

"Hey," he said. He always knew what to say, but right now he didn't. "I—"

"Wait, before you say anything I want you to know that I'm sorry for the way I acted. Dave's not better than Tucker and being a Jenner doesn't make me better than anyone else."

"Actually, I'm not sure about that. Dave has a lot of integrity. I hadn't really let myself see that side of him until today."

"I'm pretty sure he wasn't showing you his best side," Annie said. "But that doesn't excuse what I said."

"I think we both said things we regret," he replied. "I know I did."

Annie got to her feet. "Me, too. I…I don't want to fight with you, Jared. I realized today that I use my family as a shield."

"I have barriers, too."

"Yes, but you were willing to lower them for me, but I was…I was afraid to trust that you were the real thing," she said.

"What changed?" he asked, aching to draw her into his arms.

"Two things. The first is that I realized that I was trying so hard to keep you away because you are more important to me than anyone else."

"You're important to me, too, Annie. I've really tried to show you that," he said, drawing her into his arms.

He hugged her close. "What was the other thing?"

"I love you."

"I love you, too," he whispered into her ear. "More than I'd ever expected to. I always feared that love was the one thing that would be out of reach for me."

"Not anymore," she said, hugging him tightly to her. "You made me realize that home could be a person instead of a place."

"You made me realize that home is something I can carry around with me. I found the home I've been searching for in you."

They held each other for a long time. "I know you said to wait until Homestead to talk about our relationship, but... I want you in my life permanently."

"I'd like that."

The engines started firing up on pit road and the noise filled the air. "I have to go photograph the race."

"I have some things to take care of, too," he said, kissing her hard on the lips one more time.

As soon as she left, Jared went to find Alan Jenner. "I need to talk to Brandon. Do you know where he is?"

"Up in his owner's suite."

Jared had no jewelry and nothing prepared but he knew that today was the day he wanted to ask Annie to marry him and he couldn't do it without her father's permission.

TUCKER CAME FROM BEHIND to win the race and Annie and Dave both joined the other man in Victory lane.

Annie took photos of her brother and saw the mark of the man he was.

"That was a tough race today," Annie said. "I know you wanted to win for Daddy."

"Yeah, I did. I've been dealing with some weird emotional stuff about living up to his legacy and today… Well, today I realized that the real legacy isn't necessarily about the points I rack up and the races I win. I think Dad's legacy is the way he conducted himself."

"So you don't care that if you win next weekend and the NASCAR NEXTEL Cup Championship is yours?" she asked.

"Oh, I care. In fact, Vinnie and I are going to be talking strategy from now until the race is over next week. I really like your man, Annie. I think you've got a keeper this time," Dave said.

"Me, too," Annie replied.

Dave left to go to his after-race party and Annie followed along. Her parents were waiting in the garage area with a good number of her relatives.

"What's up?" she asked her mom as she joined the group. Everyone was standing in a loose circle and not really talking.

"Nothing. We all wanted to be down here together," her mother said.

"What for?"

"Just to support Dave," Alan said. "Where is he?"

"He was talking to some reporters a few minutes ago. Why?" Annie asked.

"I just need to talk to him," Alan said.

Annie dropped back to take photos of her family. She got the majestic Sierra Estrella Mountains in the background and hoped she captured the energy of the moment. There was excitement in her family's faces. And as her finger clicked on the shutter she realized that she'd been looking too hard in all the pictures she'd taken for some kind of truth. Some kind of proof from her family of what they'd meant to her.

"Annie, put that camera down and come over here," her father said.

She snapped one more of him, grateful that he looked fitter than he had in months. She dropped the Nikon, letting it hang around her neck by the strap. She noticed that Tucker, Vinnie and Billy had joined her family. Then she saw Jared standing in the middle of the loose circle of her family.

"What's up?"

"Ah…I need to ask you something," he said.

She swallowed hard. "Okay."

Jared got down on one knee in the middle of her family and friends and took her hand in his. "Will you marry me?"

Her eyes widened, and tears stung the back of them. "Yes."

Her family cheered and Jared got to his feet, pulling her into his arms. He kissed her long and hard.

"Congratulations," Dave said, clapping Jared on the back. "Welcome to the family."

"Thanks," Jared said.

Annie stared up into the eyes of the man she loved as someone broke out bottles of chilled champagne. "I can't believe this is happening."

"Believe it, Annie."

"This is going to be complicated," she said, thinking that Dave and Tucker were always going to be competing against each other, as were the other drivers on both of their teams.

"We can handle that," Jared said. "What matters most is the love we've found together."

For more thrill-a-minute romances set against the exciting backdrop of the NASCAR world, don't miss:

OLD FLAME, NEW SPARKS by Day Leclaire
ALMOST FAMOUS by Gina Wilkins
Available in August

THE ROOKIE by Jennifer LaBrecque
LEGENDS AND LIES by Katherine Garbera
Available in September

A CHANCE WORTH TAKING—by Carrie Weaver
TURN TWO—by Nancy Warren
Available in November

And for a sneak preview of TURN TWO, featuring a cameo by real-life NASCAR driver Carl Edwards, just turn the page....

SUNDAY WAS A PERFECT DAY for racing. Sunny but not too hot, the sky so clear and blue there was no danger of rain, and the air shifted with only a slight breeze. Taylor hoped that a perfect day was a good omen for Hank's first NASCAR NEXTEL Cup Series race.

She was so nervous she could barely stand still. She felt as proud of Hank as if he was her brother or son, and so nervous she thought she might throw up.

Her driver was fortunately made of sterner stuff. If he was nervous it didn't show. He stood proudly in his brand-new fire suit with the name of the chain of hardware stores sponsoring him prominently identified.

"How are you feeling?" she asked him.

He grinned at her, and she could see the excitement shining in his eyes. "I feel good," he said. "Real good." He glanced around as though he couldn't believe that he was here. "Today is going to be a great day."

They made their way to the staging area where

drivers were milling around, each with his P.R. manager. Fans watched from the perimeter.

Carl Edwards caught sight of Hank and immediately walked over.

"How you doing?" he asked Hank.

"I'm doing fine. Not too nervous." He stood there for a second and asked, "Do you have any advice for the rookie?"

"Yeah. Drive fast. But not faster than me."

They laughed and even that little release helped dim Taylor's stress level. She took a quick glance around and thought that most of the P.R. managers looked more tense than their drivers.

"Really, what I would say is just, you know, enjoy the moment. I'm guessing you've dreamed of this day since you were a little kid."

Hank nodded. She could picture him hanging around cars as a little guy, watching races, finally getting a chance to try a cart and falling in love with the sport.

"There's a lot more guys who dream of going out there than will ever get the chance. You have to drive like you mean it. Drive with your heart and your guts and all your dreams right out there. Keep your focus and—" he shrugged, looked up at the sky as though for inspiration "—do what has to be done."

"Okay."

"What we do is amazing, right?" He looked like

he'd pumped himself up with his pep talk. "This is so cool."

"It sure is. I've been practicing my backflips, in case I win."

Carl treated him to his toothy grin. "Stick to something you can handle. Like a cartwheel."

The picture of Hank in his blue-and-yellow suit, turning cartwheels was so ridiculous she had to laugh.

He appeared to take the suggestion seriously. "Think that's too flashy? Maybe I should stick to one of them... what do you call them? Somersaults."

Carl gave him a mock punch. "You're going to be okay."

Then the drivers were being introduced. She heard Hank's name called and felt another swell of pride. This was it. While he made his introductory lap, she walked back to the garage.

The air was buzzing with excitement. She took a moment to look up at the stands and enjoy the spectacle of one hundred and sixty-eight thousand or so fans all set for one of racing's premier events. The stands were a sea of color. Fans sported racing gear, most of which was in bold, primary colors. It was a rainbow of caps, jackets, T-shirts, coolers.

Hank arrived, looking pretty colorful himself in his brightly hued fire suit. He stood by his car, chatting with his crew chief. Photographers were everywhere, snapping photos from every conceivable angle. Hank, like most of the drivers, did his best to pretend he didn't notice.

As drivers walked by, they'd give him a good-natured shove or mumble something that she assumed meant good luck in some incomprehensible sports-guy speak.

As he continued talking to his crew chief, Taylor was thrilled to see a broadcaster walk by for a quick interview.

"How do you think you're going to do out there today?" Hank was asked. A no-brainer question and one she'd prepared him for.

"I'm going to do my best. I've got a great team behind me, a company I'm proud to race for and sponsors and fans who believe in me." He broke into his infectious grin. "I have to tell you and everybody out there who's rooting for me today that I feel ready for this."

Taylor stood by while he climbed into his car, put in earplugs, pulled on his helmet and plugged it in. She watched him strapping in, putting the steering wheel on—getting ready to go.

When she heard the words *Gentlemen, start your engines,* she though she might hyperventilate. This was it. Not only Hank's rookie race, but hers, too.

* * * * *

Available November 2007,
wherever books are sold.

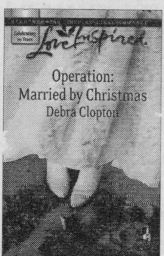

Love Inspired®

Celebrate Love Inspired's 10th anniversary with top authors and great stories all year long!

UNMARRIED MEN OF MULE HOLLOW: RUN FOR YOUR LIVES!

The famous runaway bride, Haley Bell Thornton, has returned home and come face-to-face with Will Sutton, the first of her many ditched fiancés. Can their determination to stay single defeat the town's tireless matchmakers, eager to hear decade-overdue wedding bells by Christmas?

Look for

Operation: Married by Christmas
by Debra Clopton

Available October wherever you buy books.

www.SteepleHill.com

Steeple Hill®

REQUEST YOUR FREE BOOKS!
2 FREE NOVELS PLUS 2 FREE GIFTS!

SPECIAL EDITION®
Life, Love and Family!

YES! Please send me 2 FREE Silhouette Special Edition® novels and my 2 FREE gifts. After receiving them, if I don't wish to receive any more books, I can return the shipping statement marked "cancel." If I don't cancel, I will receive 6 brand-new novels every month and be billed just $4.24 per book in the U.S., or $4.99 per book in Canada, plus 25¢ shipping and handling per book and applicable taxes, if any*. That's a savings of at least 15% off the cover price! I understand that accepting the 2 free books and gifts places me under no obligation to buy anything. I can always return a shipment and cancel at any time. Even if I never buy another book from Silhouette, the two free books and gifts are mine to keep forever.   235 SDN EEYU 335 SDN EEY6

Name	(PLEASE PRINT)	
Address		Apt.
City	State/Prov.	Zip/Postal Code

Signature (if under 18, a parent or guardian must sign)

Mail to the **Silhouette Reader Service**™:
IN U.S.A.: P.O. Box 1867, Buffalo, NY 14240-1867
IN CANADA: P.O. Box 609, Fort Erie, Ontario L2A 5X3

Not valid to current Silhouette Special Edition subscribers.

Want to try two free books from another line?
Call 1-800-873-8635 or visit www.morefreebooks.com.

* Terms and prices subject to change without notice. NY residents add applicable sales tax. Canadian residents will be charged applicable provincial taxes and GST. This offer is limited to one order per household. All orders subject to approval. Credit or debit balances in a customer's account(s) may be offset by any other outstanding balance owed by or to the customer. Please allow 4 to 6 weeks for delivery.

Your Privacy: Silhouette is committed to protecting your privacy. Our Privacy Policy is available online at www.eHarlequin.com or upon request from the Reader Service. From time to time we make our lists of customers available to reputable firms who may have a product or service of interest to you. If you would prefer we not share your name and address, please check here. ☐

SSE07

HARLEQUIN®

EVERLASTING LOVE™

Every great love has a story to tell™

An uplifting story of love and survival that spans generations.

Hayden MacNulty and Brian Conway both lived on Briar Hill Road their whole lives. As children they were destined to meet, but as a couple Hayden and Brian have much to overcome before romance ultimately flourishes.

Look for

The House on

Briar Hill Road

by award-winning author
Holly Jacobs

Available October wherever you buy books.

Love Inspired SUSPENSE

RIVETING INSPIRATIONAL ROMANCE

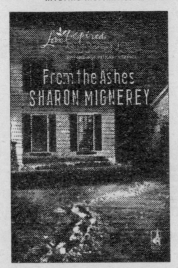

SHE COULDN'T HIDE FOREVER

As Christmas approaches, a vengeful enemy, bent on destroying her newfound happiness, targets Angela London and her new client, a retired athlete. Now she must thwart a dangerous threat—with her handsome client's help—or risk losing a love that promises to redeem them both.

Look for
FROM THE ASHES
BY SHARON MIGNEREY

Available October wherever you buy books.

Steeple Hill®

LIS44263

Love Inspired®

Celebrate Love Inspired's 10th anniversary with top authors and great stories all year long!

A Tiny Blessings Tale

Loving families and needy children continue to come together to fulfill God's greatest plans!

Look for these six new *Tiny Blessings* stories!

FOR HER SON'S LOVE BY KATHRYN SPRINGER
July 2007

MISSIONARY DADDY BY LINDA GOODNIGHT
August 2007

A MOMMY IN MIND BY ARLENE JAMES
September 2007

LITTLE MISS MATCHMAKER BY DANA CORBIT
October 2007

GIVING THANKS FOR BABY BY TERRI REED
November 2007

**A HOLIDAY TO REMEMBER
BY JILLIAN HART**
December 2007

Steeple
Hill®

Available wherever you buy books.

www.SteepleHill.com   LITBLIST

Author's Note

Not that it matters, but a great deal of the background to this story is accurate.

SMERSH, a contraction of Smiert Spionam—Death to Spies—exists and remains today the most secret department of the Soviet government.

At the beginning of 1956, when this book was written, the strength of SMERSH at home and abroad was about 40,000 and General Grubozaboyschikov was its chief. My description of his appearance is correct.

Today, the headquarters of SMERSH are where, in Chapter 4, I have placed them—at No. 13 Sretenka Ulitsa, Moscow. The Conference Room is faithfully described and the Intelligence chiefs who meet round the table are real officials who are frequently summoned to that room for purposes similar to those I have recounted.

I.F.
March 1956

PART 1
THE PLAN

CHAPTER 1

Roseland

The naked man who lay splayed out on his face beside the swimming pool might have been dead.

He might have been drowned and fished out of the pool and laid out on the grass to dry while the police or the next-of-kin were summoned. Even the little pile of objects in the grass beside his head might have been his personal effects, meticulously assembled in full view so that no one should think that something had been stolen by his rescuers.

To judge by the glittering pile, this had been, or was, a rich man. It contained the typical membership badges of the rich man's club—a money clip, made of a Mexican fifty-dollar piece and holding a substantial wad of banknotes, a well-used gold Dunhill lighter, an oval gold cigarette case with the wavy ridges and discreet turquoise button that means Fabergé, and the sort of novel a rich man pulls out of the bookcase to take into the garden—*The Little Nugget*—an old P. G. Wodehouse. There was also a bulky gold wrist-watch on a well-used brown crocodile strap. It was a Girard-

Perregaux model designed for people who like gadgets, and it had a sweep second-hand and two little windows in the face to tell the day of the month, and the month, and the phase of the moon. The story it now told was 2.30 on June 10th with the moon three-quarters full.

A blue and green dragon-fly flashed out from among the rose bushes at the end of the garden and hovered in mid-air a few inches above the base of the man's spine. It had been attracted by the golden shimmer of the June sunshine on the ridge of fine blond hairs above the coccyx. A puff of breeze came off the sea. The tiny field of hairs bent gently. The dragon-fly darted nervously sideways and hung above the man's left shoulder, looking down. The young grass below the man's open mouth stirred. A large drop of sweat rolled down the side of the fleshy nose and dropped glittering into the grass. That was enough. The dragon-fly flashed away through the roses and over the jagged glass on top of the high garden wall. It might be good food, but it moved.

The garden in which the man lay was about an acre of well-kept lawn surrounded on three sides by thickly banked rose bushes from which came the steady murmur of bees. Behind the drowsy noise of the bees the sea boomed softly at the bottom of the cliff at the end of the garden.

There was no view of the sea from the garden—no view of anything except of the sky and the clouds above the twelve-foot wall. In fact you could only see out of the property from the two upstairs bedrooms of the villa that formed the fourth side of this very private enclosure. From them you could see a great expanse of blue water in front of you and, on either side, the upper windows of neighbouring villas and the tops of the trees in their gardens—Mediterranean-type evergreen oaks, stone pines, casuarinas and an occasional palm tree.

The villa was modern—a squat elongated box without ornament. On the garden side the flat pink-washed facade was pierced by four iron-framed windows and by a central glass door leading on to a small square of pale green glazed tiles. The tiles merged into the lawn. The

other side of the villa, standing back a few yards from a
dusty road, was almost identical. But on this side the
four windows were barred, and the central door was of
oak.

The villa had two medium-sized bedrooms on the
upper floor and on the ground floor a sitting-room and
a kitchen, part of which was walled off into a lavatory.
There was no bathroom.

The drowsy luxurious silence of early afternoon was
broken by the sound of a car coming down the road. It
stopped in front of the villa. There was the tinny clang
of a car door being slammed and the car drove on. The
door bell rang twice. The naked man beside the swimming pool did not move, but, at the noise of the bell and
of the departing car, his eyes had for an instant opened
very wide. It was as if the eyelids had pricked up like an
animal's ears. The man immediately remembered where
he was and the day of the week and the time of the day.
The noises were identified. The eyelids with their fringe
of short sandy eyelashes drooped drowsily back over the
very pale blue, opaque, inward-looking eyes. The small
cruel lips opened in a wide jaw-breaking yawn which
brought saliva into the mouth. The man spat the saliva
into the grass and waited.

A young woman carrying a small string bag and
dressed in a white cotton shirt and a short, unalluring
blue skirt came through the glass door and strode man-
nishly across the glazed tiles and the stretch of lawn
towards the naked man. A few yards away from him,
she dropped her string bag on the grass and sat down
and took off her cheap and rather dusty shoes. Then she
stood up and unbuttoned her shirt and took it off and
put it, neatly folded, beside the string bag.

The girl had nothing on under the shirt. Her skin was
pleasantly sunburned and her shoulders and fine breasts
shone with health. When she bent her arms to undo the
side-buttons of her skirt, small tufts of fair hair showed
in her armpits. The impression of a healthy animal
peasant girl was heightened by the chunky hips in faded
blue stockinet bathing trunks and the thick short thighs

and legs that were revealed when she had stripped.

The girl put the skirt neatly beside her shirt, opened the string bag, took out an old soda-water bottle containing some heavy colourless liquid and went over to the man and knelt on the grass beside him. She poured some of the liquid, a light olive oil, scented, as was everything in that part of the world, with roses, between his shoulder blades and, after flexing her fingers like a pianist, began massaging the sternomastoid and the trapezius muscles at the back of the man's neck.

It was hard work. The man was immensely strong and the bulging muscles at the base of the neck hardly yielded to the girl's thumbs even when the downward weight of her shoulders was behind them. By the time she was finished with the man she would be soaked in perspiration and so utterly exhausted that she would fall into the swimming pool and then lie down in the shade and sleep until the car came for her. But that wasn't what she minded as her hands worked automatically on across the man's back. It was her instinctive horror for the finest body she had ever seen.

None of this horror showed in the flat, impassive face of the masseuse, and the upward-slanting black eyes under the fringe of short coarse black hair were as empty as oil slicks, but inside her the animal whimpered and cringed and her pulse-rate, if it had occurred to her to take it, would have been high.

Once again, as so often over the past two years, she wondered why she loathed this splendid body, and once again she vaguely tried to analyse her revulsion. Perhaps this time she would get rid of feelings which she felt guiltily certain were much more unprofessional than the sexual desire some of her patients awoke in her.

To take the small things first: his hair. She looked down at the round, smallish head on the sinewy neck. It was covered with tight red-gold curls that should have reminded her pleasantly of the formalized hair in the pictures she had seen of classical statues. But the curls were somehow too tight, too thickly pressed against each other and against the skull. They set her teeth on edge like finger-nails against pile carpet. And the golden curls came down so low into the back of the neck—almost (she thought in professional terms) to the fifth cervical vertebra. And there they stopped abruptly in a straight line of small stiff golden hairs.

The girl paused to give her hands a rest and sat back on her haunches. The beautiful upper half of her body was already shining with sweat. She wiped the back of her forearm across her forehead and reached for the bottle of oil. She poured about a tablespoonful on to the small furry plateau at the base of the man's spine, flexed her fingers and bent forward again.

This embryo tail of golden down above the cleft of the buttocks—in a lover it would have been gay, exciting, but on this man it was somehow bestial. No, reptilian. But snakes had no hair. Well, she couldn't help that. It seemed reptilian to her. She shifted her hands on down to the two mounds of the gluteal muscles. Now was the time when many of her patients, particularly the young ones on the football team, would start joking with her. Then, if she was not very careful, the suggestions would come. Sometimes she could silence these by digging sharply down towards the sciatic nerve. At other times, and particularly if she found the man attractive, there would be giggling arguments, a brief wrestling-match and a quick, delicious surrender.

With this man it was different, almost uncannily different. From the very first he had been like a lump of inanimate meat. In two years he had never said a word to her. When she had done his back and it was time for him to turn over, neither his eyes nor his body had once shown the smallest interest in her. When she tapped his shoulder, he would just roll over and gaze at the sky through half-closed lids and occasionally let out one of the long shuddering yawns that were the only sign that he had human reactions at all.

The girl shifted her position and slowly worked down the right leg towards the Achilles tendon. When she came to it, she looked back up the fine body. Was her revulsion *only* physical? Was it the reddish colour of the sunburn on the naturally milk-white skin, the sort of roast meat look? Was it the texture of the skin itself, the deep, widely spaced pores in the satiny surface? The thickly scattered orange freckles on the shoulders? Or was it the asexuality of the man? The indifference of these splendid, insolently bulging muscles? Or was it spiritual—an animal instinct telling her that inside this wonderful body there was an evil person?

The masseuse got to her feet and stood, twisting her head slowly from side to side and flexing her shoulders. She stretched her arms out sideways and then upwards and held them for a moment to get the blood down out of them. She went to her string bag and took out a hand-towel and wiped the perspiration off her face and body.

When she turned back to the man, he had already rolled over and now lay, his head resting on one open hand, gazing blankly at the sky. The disengaged arm was flung out on the grass, waiting for her. She walked over and knelt on the grass behind his head. She rubbed some oil into her palms, picked up the limp half-open hand and started kneading the short thick fingers.

The girl glanced nervously sideways at the red-brown face below the crown of tight golden curls. Superficially it was all right—handsome in a butcher's-boyish way, with its full pink cheeks, upturned nose and rounded chin. But, looked at closer, there was something cruel about the thin-lipped rather pursed mouth, a pigginess about the wide nostrils in the upturned nose, and the blankness that veiled the very pale blue eyes communicated itself over the whole face and made it look drowned and morgue-like. It was, she reflected, as if someone had taken a china doll and painted its face to frighten.

The masseuse worked up the arm to the huge biceps. Where had the man got these fantastic muscles from? Was he a boxer? What did he do with his formidable body? Rumour said this was a police villa. The two men-servants were obviously guards of some sort, although they did the cooking and the housework.

Regularly every month the man went away for a few days and she would be told not to come. And from time to time she would be told to stay away for a week, or two weeks, or a month. Once, after one of these absences, the man's neck and upper part of his body had been a mass of bruises. On another occasion the red corner of a half-healed wound had shown under a foot of surgical plaster down the ribs over his heart. She had never dared to ask about him at the hospital or in the town. When she had first been sent to the house, one of the men-servants had told her that if she spoke about what she saw she would go to prison. Back at the hospital, the Chief Superintendent, who had never recognized her existence before, had sent for her and had said the same thing. She would go to prison. The girl's strong fingers gouged nervously into the big deltoid muscle on the point of the shoulder. She had always known it was a matter of State Security. Perhaps that was what revolted her about this splendid body. Perhaps it was just fear of the organization that had the body in custody. She squeezed her eyes shut at the thought of who he might be, of what he could order to be done to her. Quickly she opened them again. He might have noticed. But the eyes gazed blankly up at the sky.

Now—she reached for the oil—to do the face.

The girl's thumbs had scarcely pressed into the sockets of the man's closed eyes when the telephone in the house started ringing. The sound reached impatiently out into the garden. At once the man was up on one knee like a runner waiting for the gun. But he didn't move forward. The ringing stopped. There was the mutter of a voice. The girl could not hear what it was saying, but it sounded humble, noting instructions. The voice stopped and one of the men-servants showed briefly at the door, made a gesture of summons, and went back into the house. Half way through the gesture, the naked man was already running. She watched the brown back flash through the open glass door. Better not let him find her there when he came out again—doing nothing, perhaps listening. She got to her feet, took two steps to the concrete edge of the pool and dived gracefully in.

Although it would have explained her instincts about the man whose body she massaged, it was as well for the girl's peace of mind that she did not know who he was.

His real name was Donovan Grant, or 'Red' Grant. But, for the past ten years, it had been Krassno Granitsky, with the code-name of 'Granit'.

He was the Chief Executioner of SMERSH, the murder *apparat* of the M.G.B., and at this moment he was receiving his instructions on the M.G.B. direct line with Moscow.

CHAPTER 2

The Slaughterer

Grant put the telephone softly back on its cradle and sat looking at it.

The bullet-headed guard standing over him said, 'You had better start moving.'

'Did they give you any idea of the task?' Grant spoke Russian excellently but with a thick accent. He could have passed for a national of any of the Soviet Baltic provinces. The voice was high and flat as if it were reciting something dull from a book.

'No. Only that you are wanted in Moscow. The plane is on its way. It will be here in about an hour. Half an hour for refuelling and then three or four hours, depending on whether you come down at Kharkov. You will be in Moscow by midnight. You had better pack. I will order the car.'

Grant got nervously to his feet. 'Yes. You are right. But they didn't even say if it was an operation? One likes to know. It was a secure line. They could have given a hint. They generally do.'

'This time they didn't.'

Grant walked slowly out through the glass door on to the lawn. If he noticed the girl sitting on the far edge of the pool he made no sign. He bent and picked up his book, and the golden trophies of his profession, and walked back into the house and up the few stairs to his bedroom.

The room was bleak and furnished only with an iron bedstead, from which the rumpled sheets hung down on one side to the floor, a cane chair, an unpainted clothes cupboard and a cheap washstand with a basin. The floor was strewn with English and American magazines. Garish paper-backs and hard-cover thrillers were stacked against the wall below the window.

Grant bent down and pulled a battered Italian fibre suitcase from under the bed. He packed into it a selection of well-laundered cheap respectable clothes from the cupboard. Then he washed his body hurriedly with cold water, and the inevitably rose-scented soap, and dried himself on one of the sheets from the bed.

There was the noise of a car outside. Grant hastily dressed in clothes as drab and nondescript as those he had packed, put on his wristwatch, pocketed his other belongings and picked up his suitcase and went down the stairs.

The front door was open. He could see his two guards talking to the driver of a battered ZIS saloon. 'Bloody fools,' he thought. (He still did most of his thinking in English.) 'Probably telling him to see I get on the plane all right. Probably can't imagine that a foreigner would want to live in their blasted country.' The cold eyes sneered as Grant put down his suitcase on the doorstep and hunted among the bunch of coats that hung from pegs on the kitchen door. He found his 'uniform', the drab raincoat and black cloth cap of Soviet officialdom, put them on, picked up his suitcase and went out and climbed in beside the plain-clothes driver, roughly shouldering aside one of the guards as he did so.

The two men stood back, saying nothing, but looking at him with hard eyes. The driver took his foot off the clutch, and the car, already in gear, accelerated fast away down the dusty road.

The villa was on the south-eastern coast of the Crimea, about half way between Feodosiya and Yalta. It was one of many official holiday *datchas* along the favourite stretch of mountainous coastline that is part of the Russian Riviera. Red Grant knew that he was immensely privileged to be housed there instead of in some dreary villa on the outskirts of Moscow. As the car climbed up into the mountains, he thought that they certainly treated him as well as they knew how, even if their concern for his welfare had two faces.

The forty-mile drive to the airport at Simferopol took an hour. There were no other cars on the road and the occasional cart from the vineyards quickly pulled into the ditch at the sound of their horn. As everywhere in Russia, a car meant an official, and an official could only mean danger.

There were roses all the way, fields of them alternating with the vineyards, hedges of them along the road and, at the approach to the airport, a vast circular bed planted with red and white varieties to make a red star against a white background. Grant was sick of them and he longed to get to Moscow and away from their sweet stench.

They drove past the entrance to the Civil Airport and followed a high wall for about a mile the military side of the aerodrome. At a tall wire gate the driver showed his pass to two tommy-gunned sentries and drove through on to the tarmac. Several planes stood about, big camouflaged military transports, small twin-engined trainers and two Navy helicopters. The driver stopped to ask a man in overalls where to find Grant's plane. At once a metallic twanging came from the observant control tower and a loudspeaker barked at them: 'To the left. Far down to the left. Number V-BO.'

The driver was obediently motoring on across the tarmac when the iron voice barked again. 'Stop!'

As the driver jammed on his brakes, there sounded a

deafening scream above their heads. Both men instinctively ducked as a flight of four MIG 17s came out of the setting sun and skimmed over them, their squat wind-brakes right down for the landing. The planes hit the huge runway one after the other, puffs of blue smoke spurting from their nose-tyres, and, with jets howling, taxied to the distant boundary line and turned to come back to the control tower and the hangars.

'Proceed!'

A hundred yards farther on they came to a plane with the recognition letters V-BO. It was a two-engined Ilyushin 12. A small aluminum ladder hung down from the cabin door and the car stopped beside it. One of the crew appeared at the door. He came down the ladder and carefully examined the driver's pass and Grant's identity papers and then waved the driver away and gestured Grant to follow him up the ladder. He didn't offer to help with the suitcase, but Grant carried it up the ladder as if it had been no heavier than a book. The crewman pulled the ladder up after him, banged the wide hatch shut and went forward to the cockpit.

There were twenty empty seats to choose from. Grant settled into the one nearest the hatch and fastened his seat-belt. A short crackle of talk with the control tower came through the open door to the cockpit, the two engines whined and coughed and fired and the plane turned quickly as if it had been a motor car, rolled out to the start of the north-south runway, and, without any further preliminaries, hurtled down it and up into the air.

Grant unbuckled his seat-belt, lit a gold-tipped Troika cigarette and settled back to reflect comfortably on his past career and to consider the immediate future.

Donovan Grant was the result of a midnight union between a German professional weight-lifter and a Southern Irish waitress. The union lasted for a quarter of an hour on the damp grass behind a circus tent outside Belfast. Afterwards the father gave the mother half-a-crown and the mother walked happily home to her bed in the kitchen of a café near the railway station.

When the baby was expected, she went to live with an aunt in the small village of Aughmacloy that straddles the border, and there, six months later, she died of puerperal fever shortly after giving birth to a twelve-pound boy. Before she died, she said that the boy was to be called Donovan (the weight-lifter had styled himself 'The Mighty O' Donovan) and Grant, which was her own name.

The boy was reluctantly cared for by the aunt and grew up healthy and extremely strong, but very quiet. He had no friends. He refused to communicate with other children and when he wanted anything from them he took it with his fists. In the local school he continued to be feared and disliked, but he made a name for himself boxing and wrestling at local fairs where the blood-thirsty fury of his attack, combined with guile, gave him victory over much older and bigger boys.

It was through his fighting that he came to the notice of the Sinn-Feiners who used Aughmacloy as a principal pipeline for their comings and goings with the north, and also of the local smugglers who used the village for the same purpose. When he left school he became a strong-arm for both these groups. They paid him well for his work but saw as little of him as they could.

It was about this time that his body began to feel strange and violent compulsions around the time of the full moon. When, in October of his sixteenth year, he first got 'The Feelings' as he called them to himself, he went out and strangled a cat. This made him 'feel better' for a whole month. In November, it was a big sheepdog, and, for Christmas, he slit the throat of a cow, at midnight in a neighbour's shed. These actions made him 'feel good'. He had enough sense to see that the village would soon start wondering about the mysterious deaths, so he bought a bicycle and on one night every month he rode off into the countryside. Often he had to go very far to find what he wanted and, after two months of having to satisfy himself with geese and chickens, he took a chance and cut the throat of a sleeping tramp.

There were so few people abroad at night that soon he took to the roads earlier, bicycling far and wide so that he came to distant villages in the dusk when solitary people were coming home from the fields and girls were going out to their trysts.

When he killed the occasional girl he did not 'interfere' with her in any way. That side of things, which he had heard talked about, was quite incomprehensible to him. It was only the wonderful act of killing that made him 'feel better'. Nothing else.

By the end of his seventeenth year, ghastly rumours were spreading round the whole of Fermanagh, Tyrone and Armagh. When a woman was killed in broad daylight, strangled and thrust carelessly into a haystack, the rumours flared into panic. Groups of vigilantes were formed in the villages, police reinforcements were brought in with police dogs, and stories about the 'Moon Killer' brought journalists to the area. Several times Grant on his bicycle was stopped and questioned, but he had powerful protection in Aughmacloy and his story of training-spins to keep him fit for his boxing were always backed up, for he was now the pride of the village and contender for the North of Ireland light-heavyweight championship.

Again, before it was too late, instinct saved him from discovery and he left Aughmacloy and went to Belfast and put himself in the hands of a broken-down boxing promoter who wanted him to turn professional. Discipline in the sleazy gymnasium was strict. It was almost a prison and, when the blood first boiled again in Grant's veins, there was nothing for it but to half kill one of his sparring partners. After twice having to be pulled off a man in the ring, it was only by winning the championship that he was saved from being thrown out by the promoter.

Grant won the championship in 1945, on his eighteenth birthday, and they took him for National Service and he became a driver in the Royal Corps of Signals. The training period in England sobered him, or at least made him more careful when he had 'The Feelings'.

Now, at the full moon, he took to drink instead. He would take a bottle of whisky into the woods round Aldershot and drink it all down as he watched his sensations, coldly, until unconsciousness came. Then, in the early hours of the morning, he would stagger back to camp, only half satisfied, but not dangerous any more. If a sentry caught him, it was only a day's C.B., because his commanding officer wanted to keep him happy for the Army championships.

But Grant's transport section was rushed to Berlin about the time of the Corridor trouble with the Russians and he missed the championships. In Berlin, the constant smell of danger intrigued him and made him even more careful and cunning. He still got dead drunk at the full moon, but all the rest of the time he was watching and plotting. He liked all he heard about the Russians, their brutality, their carelessness of human life, and their guile, and he decided to go over to them. But how? What could he bring them as a gift? What did they want?

It was the B.A.O.R. championships that finally told him to go over. By chance they took place on a night of the full moon. Grant, fighting for the Royal Corps, was warned for holding and hitting low and was disqualified in the third round for persistent foul fighting. The whole stadium hissed him as he left the ring—the loudest demonstration came from his own regiment—and the next morning the commanding officer sent for him and coldly said he was a disgrace to the Royal Corps and would be sent home with the next draft. His fellow drivers sent him to Coventry and, since no one would drive transport with him, he had to be transferred to the coveted motor cycle dispatch service.

The transfer could not have suited Grant better. He waited a few days and then, one evening when he had collected the day's outgoing mail from the Military Intelligence Headquarters on the Reichskanzlerplatz, he made straight for the Russian Sector, waited with his engine running until the British control gate was opened to allow a taxi through, and then tore through the closing gate at forty and skidded to a stop beside the concrete pillbox of the Russian Frontier post.

They hauled him roughly into the guardroom. A wooden-faced officer behind a desk asked him what he wanted.

'I want the Soviet Secret Service,' said Grant flatly. 'The Head of it.'

The officer stared coldly at him. He said something in Russian. The soldiers who had brought Grant in started to drag him out again. Grant easily shook them off. One of them lifted his tommy-gun.

Grant said, speaking patiently and distinctly, 'I have a lot of secret papers. Outside. In the leather bags on the motor cycle.' He had a brainwave. 'You will get into bad trouble if they don't get to your Secret Service.'

The officer said something to the soldiers and they stood back. 'We have no Secret Service,' he said in stilted English. 'Sit down and complete this form.'

Grant sat down at the desk and filled in a long form which asked questions about anyone who wanted to visit the Eastern zone—name, address, nature of business and so forth. Meanwhile the officer spoke softly and briefly into a telephone.

By the time Grant had finished, two more soldiers, noncommissioned officers wearing drab green forage caps and with green badges of rank on their khaki uniforms, had come into the room. The frontier officer handed the form, without looking at it, to one of them and they took Grant out and put him and his motor cycle into the back of a closed van and locked the door on him. After a fast drive lasting a quarter of an hour the van stopped, and when Grant got out he found himself in the courtyard behind a large new building. He was taken into the building and up in a lift and left alone in a cell without windows. It contained nothing but one iron bench. After an hour, during which, he supposed, they went through the secret papers, he was led into a comfortable office in which an officer with three rows of decorations and the gold tabs of a full colonel was sitting behind a desk.

The desk was bare except for a bowl of roses.

Ten years later, Grant, looking out of the window of the plane at a wide cluster of lights twenty thousand feet below, which he guessed was Kharkov, grinned mirthlessly at his reflection in the Perspex window.

Roses. From that moment his life had been nothing but roses. Roses, roses, all the way.

CHAPTER 3

Post-Graduate Studies

'So you would like to work in the Soviet Union, Mister Grant?'

It was half an hour later and the M.G.B. colonel was bored with the interview. He thought that he had extracted from this rather unpleasant British soldier every military detail that could possibly be of interest. A few polite phrases to repay the man for the rich haul of secrets his dispatch bags had yielded, and then the man could go down to the cells and in due course be shipped off to Vorkuta or some other labour camp.

'Yes, I would like to work for you.'

'And what work could you do, Mister Grant? We have plenty of unskilled labour. We do not need truck-drivers and,' the colonel smiled fleetingly, 'if there is any boxing to be done we have plenty of men who can box. Two possible Olympic champions amongst them, incidentally.'

'I am an expert at killing people. I do it very well. I like it.'

The colonel saw the red flame that flickered for an instant behind the very pale blue eyes under the sandy lashes. He thought, the man means it. He's mad as well as unpleasant. He looked coldly at Grant, wondering if it was worth while wasting food on him at Vorkuta. Better perhaps have him shot. Or throw him back into the British Sector and let his own people worry about him.

'You don't believe me,' said Grant impatiently. This was the wrong man, the wrong department. 'Who does the rough stuff for you here?' He was certain the Russians had some sort of a murder squad. Everybody said so. 'Let me talk to them. I'll kill somebody for them. Anybody they like. Now.'

The colonel looked at him sourly. Perhaps he had better report the matter. 'Wait here.' He got up and went out of the room, leaving the door open. A guard came and stood in the doorway and watched Grant's back, his hand on his pistol.

The colonel went into the next room. It was empty. There were three telephones on the desk. He picked up the receiver of the M.G.B. direct line to Moscow. When the military operator answered he said, 'SMERSH.' When SMERSH answered he asked for the Chief of Operations.

Ten minutes later he put the receiver back. What luck! A simple, constructive solution. Whichever way it went it would turn out well. If the Englishman succeeded, it would be splendid. If he failed, it would still cause a lot of trouble in the Western Sector—trouble for the British because Grant was their man, trouble with the Germans because the attempt would frighten a lot of their spies, trouble with the Americans because they were supplying most of the funds for the Baumgarten ring and would now think Baumgarten's security was no good. Pleased with himself, the colonel walked back into his office and sat down again opposite Grant.

'You mean what you say?'

'Of course I do.'

'Have you a good memory?'

'Yes.'

'In the British Sector there is a German called Dr.

Baumgarten. He lives in Flat 5 at No. 22 Kurfür-
stendamm. Do you know where that is?'

'Yes.'

'Tonight, with your motor cycle, you will be put back
into the British Sector. Your number plates will be
changed. Your people will be on the lookout for you.
You will take an envelope to Dr. Baumgarten. It will be
marked to be delivered by hand. In your uniform, and
with this envelope, you will have no difficulty. You will
say that the message is so private that you must see Dr.
Baumgarten alone. Then you will kill him.' The colonel
paused. His eyebrows lifted. 'Yes?'

'Yes,' said Grant stolidly. 'And if I do, will you give
me more of this work?'

'It is possible,' said the colonel indifferently. 'First
you must show what you can do. When you have completed your task and returned to the Soviet Sector, you
may ask for Colonel Boris.' He rang a bell and a man in
plain clothes came in. The colonel gestured towards
him. 'This man will give you food. Later he will give
you the envelope and a sharp knife of American
manufacture. It is an excellent weapon. Good luck.'

The colonel reached and picked a rose out of the bowl
and sniffed it luxuriously.

Grant got to his feet. 'Thank you, sir,' he said
warmly.

The colonel did not answer or look up from the rose.
Grant followed the man in plain clothes out of the
room.

The plane roared on across the Heartland of Russia.
They had left behind them the blast furnaces flaming far
away to the east around Stalino and, to the west, the
silver thread of the Dnieper branching away at
Dnepropetrovsk. The splash of light around Kharkov
had marked the frontier of the Ukraine, and the smaller
blaze of the phosphate town of Kursk had come and
gone. Now Grant knew that the solid unbroken
blackness below hid the great central Steppe where the
billions of tons of Russia's grain were whispering and

ripening in the darkness. There would be no more oases of light until, in another hour, they would have covered the last three hundred miles to Moscow.

For by now Grant knew a lot about Russia. After the quick, neat, sensational murder of a vital West German spy, Grant had no sooner slipped back over the frontier and somehow fumbled his way to 'Colonel Boris' than he was put into plain clothes, with a flying helmet to cover his hair, hustled into an empty M.G.B. plane and flown straight to Moscow.

Then began a year of semi-prison which Grant had devoted to keeping fit and to learning Russian while people came and went around him—interrogators, stool-pigeons, doctors. Meanwhile, Soviet spies in England and Northern Ireland had painstakingly investigated his past.

At the end of the year Grant was given as clean a bill of political health as any foreigner can get in Russia. The spies had confirmed his story. The English and American stool-pigeons reported that he was totally uninterested in the politics or social customs of any country in the world, and the doctors and psychologists agreed that he was an advanced manic depressive whose periods coincided with the full moon. They added that Grant was also a narcissist and asexual and that his tolerance of pain was high. These peculiarities apart, his physical health was superb and, though his educational standards were hopelessly low, he was as naturally cunning as a fox. Everyone agreed that Grant was an exceedingly dangerous member of society and that he should be put away.

When the dossier came before the Head of Personnel of the M.G.B., he was about to write 'Kill him' in the margin when he had second thoughts.

A great deal of killing has to be done in the U.S.S.R., not because the average Russian is a cruel man, although some of their races are among the cruellest peoples in the world, but as an instrument of policy. People who act against the State are enemies of the State, and the State has no room for enemies. There is too much to do for precious time to be allotted to them, and, if they are a persistent nuisance, they get killed. In a country with a population of 200,000,000, you can kill many thousands a year without missing them. If, as happened in the two biggest purges, a million people have to be killed in one year, that is also not a grave loss. The serious problem is the shortage of executioners. Executioners have a short 'life'. They get tired of the work. The soul sickens of it. After ten, twenty, a hundred death-rattles, the human being, however subhuman he may be, acquires, perhaps by a process of osmosis with death itself, a germ of death which enters his body and eats into him like a canker. Melancholy and drink take him, and a dreadful lassitude which brings a glaze to his eyes and slows up the movements and destroys accuracy. When the employer sees these signs he has no alternative but to execute the executioner and find another one.

The Head of Personnel of the M.G.B. was aware of the problem and of the constant search not only for the refined assassin, but also for the common butcher. And here at last was a man who appeared to be expert at both forms of killing, dedicated to his craft and indeed, if the doctors were to be believed, destined for it.

Head of Personnel wrote a short, pungent minute on Grant's papers, marked them 'SMERSH Otdyel II' and tossed them into his OUT tray.

Department 2 of SMERSH, in charge of Operations and Executions, took over the body of Donovan Grant, changed his name to Granitsky and put him on their books.

The next two years were hard for Grant. He had to go back to school, and to a school that made him long for the chipped deal desks in the corrugated iron shed, full of the smell of little boys and the hum of drowsy blue-bottles, that had been his only conception of what a school was like. Now, in the Intelligence School for Foreigners outside Leningrad, squashed tightly among the ranks of Germans, Czechs, Poles, Balts, Chinese and Negroes, all with serious dedicated faces and pens that raced across their notebooks, he struggled with subjects that were pure double-dutch to him.

There were courses in 'General Political Knowledge,' which included the history of Labour movements, of the Communist Party and the Industrial Forces of the world, and the teachings of Marx, Lenin and Stalin, all dotted with foreign names which he could barely spell. There were lessons on 'The Class-enemy we are fighting', with lectures on Capitalism and Fascism; weeks spent on 'Tactics, Agitation and Propaganda' and more weeks on the problems of minority peoples, Colonial races, the Negroes, the Jews. Every month ended with examinations during which Grant sat and wrote illiterate nonsense, interspersed with scraps of half-forgotten English history and mis-spelled Communist slogans, and inevitably had his papers torn up, on one occasion, in front of the whole class.

But he stuck it out, and when they came to 'Technical Subjects' he did better. He was quick to understand the rudiments of Codes and Ciphers, because he wanted to understand them. He was good at Communications, and immediately grasped the maze of contacts, cut-outs, couriers and post-boxes, and he got excellent marks for Fieldwork in which each student had to plan and operate dummy assignments in the suburbs and countryside around Leningrad. Finally, when it came to tests of Vigilance, Discretion, 'Safety First', Presence of Mind, Courage and Coolness, he got top marks out of the whole school.

At the end of the year, the report that went back to SMERSH concluded 'Political value Nil. Operational value Excellent'—which was just what Otdyel II wanted to hear.

The next year was spent, with only two other foreign students among several hundred Russsians, at the School for Terror and Diversion at Kuchino, outside Moscow. Here Grant went triumphantly through courses in judo, boxing, athletics, photography and radio under the general supervision of the famous Colonel Arkady Fotoyev, father of the modern Soviet spy, and completed his small-arms instruction at the hands of Lieutenant-Colonel Nikolai Godlovsky, the Soviet Rifle Champion.

Twice during this year, without warning, an M.G.B. car came for him on the night of the full moon and took him to one of the Moscow jails. There, with a black hood over his head, he was allowed to carry out executions with various weapons—the rope, the axe, the sub-machine gun. Electrocardiograms, blood-pressure and various other medical tests were applied to him before, during and after these occasions, but their purpose and findings were not revealed to him.

It was a good year and he felt, and rightly, that he was giving satisfaction.

In 1949 and '50 Grant was allowed to go on minor operations with Mobile Groups or *Avanposts*, in the satellite countries. These were beatings-up and simple assassinations of Russian spies and intelligence workers suspected of treachery or other aberrations. Grant carried out these duties neatly, exactly and inconspicuously, and though he was carefully and constantly watched he never showed the smallest deviation from the standards required of him, and no weakness of character or technical skill. It might have been different if he had been required to kill when doing a solo task at the full-moon period, but his superiors, realizing that at that period he would be outside their control, or his own, chose safe dates for his operations. The moon period was reserved exclusively for butchery in the prisons, and from time to time this was arranged for him as a reward for a successful operation in cold blood.

In 1951 and '52 Grant's usefulness became more fully and more officially recognized. As a result of excellent work, notably in the Eastern Sector of Berlin, he was granted Soviet citizenship and increases in pay which by 1953 amounted to a handsome 5000 roubles a month. In 1953 he was given the rank of Major, with pension rights back-dated to the day of his first contact with 'Colonel Boris', and the villa in the Crimea was allotted to him. Two bodyguards were attached to him, partly to protect him and partly to guard against the outside chance of his 'going private', as defection is called in M.G.B. jargon, and, once a month, he was transported to the nearest jail and allowed as many executions as there were candidates available.

Naturally Grant had no friends. He was hated or feared or envied by everyone who came in contact with him. He did not even have any of those professional acquaintanceships that pass for friendship in the discreet and careful world of Soviet officialdom. But, if he noticed the fact, he didn't care. The only individuals he was interested in were his victims. The rest of his life was inside him. And it was richly and excitingly populated with his thoughts.

Then, of course, he had SMERSH. No one in the Soviet Union who has SMERSH on his side need worry about friends, or indeed about anything whatever except keeping the black wings of SMERSH over his head.

Grant was still thinking vaguely of how he stood with his employers when the plane started to lose altitude as it picked up the radar beam of Tushino Airport just south of the red glow that was Moscow.

He was at the top of his tree, the chief executioner of SMERSH, and therefore of the whole of the Soviet Union. What could he aim for now? Further promotion? More money? More gold nicknacks? More important targets? Better techniques?

There really didn't seem to be anything more to go for. Or was there perhaps some other man whom he had never heard of, in some other country, who would have to be set aside before absolute supremacy was his?

CHAPTER 4

The Moguls of Death

SMERSH is the official murder organization of the Soviet government. It operates both at home and abroad and, in 1955, it employed a total of 40,000 men and women. SMERSH is a contraction of 'Smiert Spionam', which means 'Death to Spies'. It is a name used only among its staff and among Soviet officials. No sane member of the public would dream of allowing the word to pass his lips.

The headquarters of SMERSH is a very large and ugly modern building on the Sretenka Ulitsa. It is No. 13 on this wide, dull street, and pedestrians keep their eyes to the ground as they pass the two sentries with sub-machine guns who stand on either side of the broad steps leading up to the big iron double door. If they remember in time, or can do so inconspicuously, they cross the street and pass by on the other side.

The direction of SMERSH is carried out from the 2nd floor. The most important room on the 2nd floor is a very large light room painted in the pale olive green that is the common denominator of government offices all over the world. Opposite the sound-proofed door, two wide windows look over the courtyard at the back of the building. The floor is close-fitted with a colourful Caucasian carpet of the finest quality. Across the far left-hand corner of the room stands a massive oak desk. The top of the desk is covered with red velvet under a thick sheet of plate glass.

On the left side of the desk are IN and OUT baskets and on the right four telephones.

From the centre of the desk, to form a T with it, a conference table stretches diagonally out across the room. Eight straight-backed red leather chairs are drawn up to it. This table is also covered with red velvet, but without protective glass. Ash-trays are on the table, and two heavy carafes of water with glasses.

On the walls are four large pictures in gold frames. In 1955, these were a portrait of Stalin over the door, one of Lenin between the two windows and, facing each other on the other two walls, portraits of Bulganin and, where until January 13th, 1954, a portrait of Beria had hung, a portrait of Army General Ivan Aleksandrovitch Serov, Chief of the Committee of State Security.

On the left-hand wall, under the portrait of Bulganin, stands a large *Televisor,* or TV set, in a handsome polished oak cabinet. Concealed in this is a tape-recorder which can be switched on from the desk. The microphone for the recorder stretches under the whole area of the conference table and its leads are concealed in the legs of the table. Next to the *Televisor* is a small door leading into a personal lavatory and washroom and into a small projection room for showing secret films.

Under the portrait of General Serov is a bookcase containing, on the top shelves, the works of Marx, Engels, Lenin and Stalin, and more accessibly, books in all languages on espionage, counterespionage, police methods and criminology. Next to the bookcase, against the wall, stands a long narrow table on which are a dozen large leather-bound albums with dates stamped in gold on the covers. These contain photographs of Soviet

citizens and foreigners who have been assassinated by
SMERSH.

About the time Grant was coming in to land at
Tushino Airport, just before 11.30 at night, a tough-
looking, thick-set man of about fifty was standing at
this table leafing through the volume for 1954.

The Head of SMERSH, Colonel General Grubozaboyschikov, known in the building as 'G.', was
dressed in a neat khaki tunic with a high collar, and
dark blue cavalry trousers with two thin red stripes
down the sides. The trousers ended in riding boots of
soft, highly polished black leather. On the breast of the
tunic were three rows of medal ribbons—two Orders of
Lenin, Order of Suvorov, Order of Alexander Nevsky,
Order of the Red Banner, two Orders of the Red Star,
the Twenty Years Service medal and medals for the
Defence of Moscow and the Capture of Berlin. At
the tail of these came the rose-pink and grey ribbon of
the British C.B.E. and the claret and white ribbon of
the American Medal for Merit. Above the ribbons hung
the gold star of a Hero of the Soviet Union.

Above the high collar of the tunic the face was narrow
and sharp. There were flabby pouches under the eyes,
which were round and brown and protruded like
polished marbles below thick black brows. The skull
was shaven clean and the tight white skin glittered in the
light of the central chandelier. The mouth was broad
and grim above a deeply cleft chin. It was a hard,
unyielding face of formidable authority.

One of the telephones on the desk buzzed softly. The
man walked with tight and precise steps to his tall chair
behind the desk. He sat down and picked up the receiver
of the telephone marked in white with the letters V.Ch.
These letters are short for *Vysokochastoty* or High
Frequency. Only some fifty supreme officials are connected to the V.Ch. switchboard, and all are Ministers
of State or Heads of selected Departments. It is served
by a small exchange in the Kremlin operated by
professional security officers. Even they cannot

overhear conversations on it, but every word spoken over its lines is automatically recorded.

'Yes?'

'Serov speaking. What action has been taken since the meeting of the Praesidium this morning?'

'I have a meeting here in a few minutes' time, Comrade General—R.U.M.I.D., G.R.U. and of course M.G.B. After that, if action is agreed, I shall have a meeting with my Head of Operations and Head of Plans. In case liquidation is decided upon, I have taken the precaution of bringing the necessary operative to Moscow. This time I shall myself supervise the preparations. We do not want another Khoklov affair.'

'The devil knows we don't. Telephone me after the first meeting. I wish to report to the Praesidium tomorrow morning.'

'Certainly, Comrade General.'

General G. put back the receiver and pressed a bell under his desk. At the same time he switched on the wire-recorder. His A.D.C., an M.G.B. captain, came in.

'Have they arrived?'

'Yes, Comrade General.'

'Bring them in.'

In a few minutes six men, five of them in uniform, filed in through the door and, with hardly a glance at the man behind the desk, took their places at the conference table. They were three senior officers, heads of their departments, and each was accompanied by an A.D.C. In the Soviet Union, no man goes to a conference. For his own protection, and for the reassurance of his department, he invariably takes a witness so that his department can have independent versions of what went on at the conference and, above all, of what was said on its behalf. This is important in case there is a subsequent investigation. No notes are taken at the conference and decisions are passed back to departments by word of mouth.

On the far side of the table sat Lieutenant-General

Slavin, head of the G.R.U., the intelligence department of the General Staff of the Army, with a full colonel beside him. At the end of the table sat Lieutenant-General Vozdvishensky of R.U.M.I.D., the Intelligence Department of the Ministry of Foreign Affairs, with a middle-aged man in plain clothes. With his back to the door, sat Colonel of State Security Nikitin, Head of Intelligence for the M.G.B., the Soviet Secret Service, with a major at his side.

'Good evening, Comrades.'

A polite, careful murmur came from the three senior officers. Each one knew, and thought he was the only one to know, that the room was wired for sound, and each one, without telling his A.D.C., had decided to utter the bare minimum of words consonant with good discipline and the needs of the State.

'Let us smoke,' General G. took out a packet of Moskwa-Volga cigarettes and lit one with an American Zippo lighter. There was a clicking of lighters round the table. General G. pinched the long cardboard tube of his cigarette so that it was almost flat and put it between his teeth on the right side of his mouth. He stretched his lips back from his teeth and started talking in short clipped sentences that came out with something of a hiss from between the teeth and the uptilted cigarette.

'Comrades, we meet under instructions from Comrade General Serov. General Serov, on behalf of the Praesidium, has ordered me to make known to you certain matters of State Policy. We are then to confer and recommend a course of action which will be in line with this Policy and assist it. We have to reach our decision quickly. But our decision will be of supreme importance to the State. It will therefore have to be a correct decision.'

General G. paused to allow the significance of his words time to sink in. One by one, he slowly examined the faces of the three senior officers at the table. Their eyes looked stolidly back at him. Inside, these extremely important men were perturbed. They were about to look through the furnace door. They were about to learn a

State secret, the knowledge of which might one day have most dangerous consequences for them. Sitting in the quiet room, they felt bathed in the dreadful incandescence that shines out from the center of all power in the Soviet Union—the High Praesidium.

The final ash fell off the end of General G.'s cigarette on to his tunic. He brushed it off and threw the cardboard butt into the basket for secret waste beside his desk. He lit another cigarette and spoke through it.

'Our recommendation concerns a conspicuous act of terrorism to be carried out in enemy territory within three months.'

Six pairs of expressionless eyes stared at the head of SMERSH, waiting.

'Comrades,' General G. leant back in his chair and his voice became expository, 'the foreign policy of the U.S.S.R. has entered a new phase. Formerly, it was a "Hard" policy—a policy [he allowed himself the joke on Stalin's name] of steel. This policy, effective as it was, built up tensions in the West, notably in America, which were becoming dangerous. The Americans are unpredictable people. They are hysterical. The reports of our Intelligence began to indicate that we were pushing America to the brink of an undeclared atomic attack on the U.S.S.R. You have read these reports and you know what I say is true. We do not want such a war. If there is to be a war, it is we who will choose the time. Certain powerful Americans, notably the Pentagon Group led by Admiral Radford, were helped in their firebrand schemes by the very success of our "Hard" policy. So it was decided that the time had come to change our methods, while maintaining our aims. A new policy was created—the "Hard-Soft" policy. Geneva was the beginning of this policy. We were "soft". China threatens Quemoy and Matsu. We are "hard". We open our frontiers to a lot of newspaper men and actors and artists although we know many of them to be spies. Our leaders laugh and make jokes at receptions in Moscow. In the middle of the jokes we drop the biggest test bomb of all time. Comrades

Bulganin and Khrushchev and Comrade General Serov [General G. carefully included the names for the ears of the tape-recorder] visit India and the East and blackguard the English. When they get back, they have friendly discussions with the Britsh Ambassador about their forthcoming goodwill visit to London. And so it goes on—the stick and then the carrot, the smile and then the frown. And the West is confused. Tensions are relaxed before they have time to harden. The reactions of our enemies are clumsy, their strategy disorganized. Meanwhile the common people laugh at our jokes, cheer our football teams and slobber with delight when we release a few prisoners of war whom we wish to feed no longer!'

There were smiles of pleasure and pride round the table. What a brilliant policy! What fools we are making of them in the West!

'At the same time,' continued General G., himself smiling thinly at the pleasure he had caused, 'we continue to forge everywhere stealthily ahead—revolution in Morocco, arms to Egypt, friendship with Yugoslavia, trouble in Cyprus, riots in Turkey, strikes in England, great political gains in France—there is no front in the world on which we are not quietly advancing.'

General G. saw the eyes shining greedily round the table. The men were softened up. Now it was time to be hard. Now it was time for them to feel the new policy on themselves. The Intelligence services would also have to pull their weight in this great game that was being played on their behalf.

Smoothly, General G. leaned forward. He planted his right elbow on the desk and raised his fist in the air.

"But Comrades,' his voice was soft, 'where has there been failure in carrying out the State Policy of the U.S.S.R.? Who has all along been soft when we wished to be hard? Who has suffered defeats while victory was going to all other departments of the State? Who, with their stupid blunders, has made the Soviet Union look foolish and weak throughout the world? WHO?'

The voice had risen almost to a scream. General G.

thought how well he was delivering the denunciation demanded by the Praesidium. How splendid it would sound when the tape was played back to Serov!

He glared down the conference table at the pale, expectant faces. General G.'s fist crashed forward on to the desk.

'The whole Intelligence *apparat* of the Soviet Union, Comrades.' The voice was now a furious bellow. 'It is we who are the sluggards, the saboteurs, the traitors! It is we who are failing the Soviet Union in its great and glorious struggle! We!' His arm swept round the room. 'All of us!' The voice came back to normal, became more reasonable. 'Comrades, look at the record. *Sookin Sin* [he allowed himself the peasant obscenity], son-of-a-bitch, look at the record! First we lose Gouzenko and the whole of the Canadian *apparat* and the scientist Fuchs, then the American *apparat* is cleaned up, then we lose men like Tokaev, then comes the scandalous Khoklov affair which did great damage to our country, then Petrov and his wife in Australia—a bungled business if ever there was one! The list is endless—defeat after defeat, and the devil knows I have not mentioned the half of it.'

General G. paused. He continued in his softest voice. 'Comrades, I have to tell you that unless tonight we make a recommendation for a great Intelligence victory, and unless we act correctly on that recommendation, if it is approved, there will be trouble.'

General G. sought for a final phrase to convey the threat without defining it. He found it. 'There will be,' he paused and looked, with artificial mildness, down the table, 'displeasure.'

CHAPTER 5

Konspiratsia

The moujiks had received the knout. General G. gave them a few minutes to lick their wounds and recover from the shock of the official lashing that had been meted out.

No one said a word for the defence. No one spoke up for his department or mentioned the countless victories of Soviet Intelligence that could be set against the few mistakes. And no one questioned the right of the Head of SMERSH, who shared the guilt with them, to deliver this terrible denunciation. The Word had gone out from the Throne, and General G. had been chosen as the mouthpiece for the Word. It was a great compliment to General G. that he had been thus chosen, a sign of grace, a sign of coming preferment, and everyone present made a careful note of the fact that, in the Intelligence hierarchy, General G., with SMERSH behind him, had come to the top of the pile.

At the end of the table, the representative of the Foreign Ministry, Lieutenant-General Vozdvishensky of R.U.M.I.D., watched the smoke curl up from the tip of his long Kazbek cigarette and remembered how Molotov had privately told him, when Beria was dead, that General G. would go far. There had been no great foresight in this prophecy, reflected Vozdvishensky. Beria had disliked G. and had constantly hindered his advancement, side-tracking him away from the main ladder of power into one of the minor departments of the then Ministry of State Security, which, on the death of Stalin, Beria had quickly abolished as a Ministry. Until 1952, G. had been deputy to one of the heads of this Ministry. When the post was abolished, he devoted his energies to plotting the downfall of Beria, working under the secret orders of the formidable General Serov, whose record put him out of even Beria's reach.

Serov, a Hero of the Soviet Union and a veteran of the famous predecessors of the M.G.B.—the Cheka, the Ogpu, the N.K.V.D. and the M.V.D.—was in every respect a bigger man than Beria. He had been directly behind the mass executions of the 1930s when a million died, he had been *metteur en scène* of most of the great Moscow show trials, he had organized the bloody genocide in the Central Caucasus in February 1944, and it was he who had inspired the mass deportations from the Baltic States and the kidnapping of the German atom and other scientists who had given Russia her great technical leap forward after the war.

And Beria and all his court had gone to the gallows, while General G. had been given SMERSH as his reward. As for Army General Ivan Serov, he, with Bulganin and Khrushchev, now ruled Russia. One day, he might even stand on the peak, alone. But, guessed General Vozdvishensky, glancing up the table at the gleaming billiard-ball skull, probably with General G. not far behind him.

The skull lifted and the hard bulging brown eyes looked straight down the table into the eyes of General Vozdvishensky. General Vozdvishensky managed to look back calmly and even with a hint of appraisal.

That is a deep one, thought General G. Let us put the spotlight on him and see how he shows up on the sound-track.

'Comrades,' gold flashed from both corners of his mouth as he stretched his lips in a chairman's smile, 'let us not be too dismayed. Even the highest tree has an axe waiting at its foot. We have never thought that our departments were so successful as to be beyond criticism. What I have been instructed to say to you will not have come as a surprise to any of us. So let us take up the challenge with a good heart and get down to business.'

Round the table there was no answering smile to these platitudes. General G. had not expected that there would be. He lit a cigarette and continued.

'I said that we have at once to recommend an act of terrorism in the intelligence field, and one of our departments—no doubt my own—will be called upon to carry out this act.'

An inaudible sigh of relief went round the table. So at least SMERSH would be the responsible department! That was something.

'But the choice of a target will not be an easy matter, and our collective responsibility for the correct choice will be a heavy one.'

Soft-hard, hard-soft. The ball was now back with the conference.

'It is not just a question of blowing up a building or shooting a prime minister. Such bourgeois horseplay is not contemplated. Our operation must be delicate, refined and aimed at the heart of the Intelligence *apparat* of the West. It must do grave damage to the enemy *apparat*—hidden damage which the public will hear perhaps nothing of, but which will be the secret talk of government circles. But it must also cause a public scandal so devastating that the world will lick its lips and sneer at the shame and stupidity of our enemies. Naturally Governments will know that it is a Soviet *konspiratsia*. That is good. It will be a piece of "hard" policy. And the agents and spies of the West will know it, too, and they will marvel at our cleverness and they will tremble. Traitors and possible defectors will change their minds. Our own operatives will be stimulated.

They will be encouraged to greater efforts by our display of strength and genius. But of course we shall deny any knowledge of the deed, whatever it may be, and it is desirable that the common people of the Soviet Union should remain in complete ignorance of our complicity.'

General G. paused and looked down the table at the representative of R.U.M.I.D., who again held his gaze impassively.

'And now to choose the organization at which we will strike, and then to decide on the specific target within that organization. Comrade Lieutenant-General Vozdvishensky, since you observe the foreign intelligence scene from a neutral standpoint [this was a jibe at the notorious jealousies that exist between the military intelligence of the G.R.U. and the Secret Service of the M.G.B.], perhaps you would survey the field for us. We wish to have your opinion of the relative importance of the Western Intelligence Services. We will then choose the one which is the most dangerous and which we would most wish to damage.'

General G. sat back in his tall chair. He rested his elbows on the arms and supported his chin on the interlaced fingers of his joined hands, like a teacher preparing to listen to a long construe.

General Vozdvishensky was not dismayed by his task. He had been in intelligence, mostly abroad, for thirty years. He had served as a 'doorman' at the Soviet Embassy in London under Litvinoff. He had worked with the Tass Agency in New York and had then gone back to London, to Amtorg, the Soviet Trade Organization. For five years he had been Military Attaché under the brilliant Madame Kollontai in the Stockholm Embassy. He had helped train Sorge, the Soviet master spy, before Sorge went to Tokyo. During the war, he had been for a while Resident Director in Switzerland, or 'Schmidtland', as it had been known in the spy-jargon, and there he had helped sow the seeds of the sensationally successful but tragically misused 'Lucy' network. He had even gone several times into Germany as a courier to the 'Rote Kapelle', and had narrowly escaped being cleaned up with it. And after the war, on transfer to the Foreign Ministry, he had been on the inside of the Burgess and Maclean operation and on countless other plots to penetrate the Foreign Ministries of the West. He was a professional spy to his finger-tips and he was perfectly prepared to put on record his opinions of the rivals with whom he had been crossing swords all his life.

The A.D.C. at his side was less comfortable. He was nervous at R.U.M.I.D. being pinned down in this way, and without a full departmental briefing. He scoured his brain clear and sharpened his ears to catch every word.

'In this matter,' said General Vozdvishensky carefully, 'one must not confuse the man with the office. Every country has good spies and it is not always the biggest countries that have the most or the best. But Secret Services are expensive, and small countries cannot afford the co-ordinated effort which produces good intelligence—the forgery departments, the radio network, the record department, the digestive apparatus that evaluates and compares the reports of the agents. There are individual agents serving Norway, Holland, Belgium and even Portugal who could be a great nuisance to us if these countries knew the value of their reports or made good use of them. But they do not. Instead of passing their information on to the larger powers, they prefer to sit on it and feel important. So we need not worry with these smaller countries,' he paused, 'until we come to Sweden. There they have been spying on us for centuries. They have always had better information on the Baltic than even Finland or Germany. They are dangerous. I would like to put a stop to their activities.'

General G. interrupted. 'Comrade, they are always having spy scandals in Sweden. One more scandal would not make the world look up. Please continue.'

'Italy can be dismissed,' went on General Vozdvishensky, without appearing to notice the interruption. 'They are clever and active, but they do us no harm.

They are only interested in their own backyard, the Mediterranean. The same can be said of Spain, except that their counter-intelligence is a great hindrance to the Party. We have lost many good men to these Fascists. But to mount an operation against them would probably cost us more men. And little would be achieved. They are not yet ripe for revolution. In France, while we have penetrated most of their Services, the Deuxième Bureau is still clever and dangerous. There is a man called Mathis at the head of it. A Mendès-France appointment. He would be a tempting target and it would be easy to operate in France.'

'France is looking after herself,' commented General G.

'England is another matter altogether. I think we all have respect for her Intelligence Service,' General Vozdvishensky looked round the table. There were grudging nods from everyone present, including General G. 'Their Security Service is excellent. England, being an island, has great security advantages and their so-called M.I.5 employs men with good education and good brains. Their Secret Service is still better. They have notable successes. In certain types of operation, we are constantly finding that they have been there before us. Their agents are good. They pay them little money—only a thousand or two thousand roubles a month—but they serve with devotion. Yet these agents have no special privileges in England, no relief from taxation and no special shops such as we have, from which they can buy cheap goods. Their social standing abroad is not high, and their wives have to pass as the wives of secretaries. They are rarely awarded a decoration until they retire. And yet these men and women continue to do this dangerous work. It is curious. It is perhaps the Public School and University tradition. The love of adventure. But still it is odd that they play this game so well, for they are not natural conspirators.' General Vozdvishensky felt that his remarks might be taken as too laudatory. He hastily qualified them. 'Of course, most of their strength lies in the myth—in the myth of Scotland Yard, of Sherlock Holmes, of the Secret Service. We certainly have nothing to fear from these gentlemen. But this myth is a hindrance which it would be good to set aside.'

'And the Americans?' General G. wanted to put a stop to Vozdvishensky's attempts to qualify his praise of British Intelligence. One day that bit about the Public School and University tradition would sound well in court. Next, hoped General G., he will be saying that the Pentagon is stronger than the Kremlin.

'The Americans have the biggest and richest service among our enemies. Technically, in such matters as radio and weapons and equipment, they are the best. But they have no understanding for the work. They get enthusiastic about some Balkan spy who says he has a secret army in the Ukraine. They load him with money with which to buy boots for this army. Of course he goes at once to Paris and spends the money on women. Americans try to do everything with money. Good spies will not work for money alone—only bad ones, of which the Americans have several divisions.'

'They have successes, Comrade,' said General G. silkily. 'Perhaps you underestimate them.'

General Vozdvishensky shrugged. 'They must have successes, Comrade General. You cannot sow a million seeds without reaping one potato. Personally I do not think the Americans need engage the attention of this conference.' The head of R.U.M.I.D. sat back in his chair and stolidly took out his cigarette case.

'A very interesting exposition,' said General G. coldly. 'Comrade General Slavin?'

General Slavin of the G.R.U. had no intention of committing himself on behalf of the General Staff of the Army. 'I have listened with interest to the words of Comrade General Vozdvishensky. I have nothing to add.'

Colonel of State Security Nikitin of M.G.B. felt it would do no great harm to show up the G.R.U. as being too stupid to have any ideas at all, and at the same time to make a modest recommendation that would probably tally with the inner thoughts of those present—and that was certainly on the tip of General G.'s tongue. Colonel Nikitin also knew that, given the proposition that had been posed by the Praesidium, the Soviet Secret Service would back him up.

'I recommend the English Secret Service as the object of terrorist action,' he said decisively. 'The devil knows my department hardly finds them a worthy adversary, but they are the best of an indifferent lot.'

General G. was annoyed by the authority in the man's voice, and by having his thunder stolen, for he also had intended to sum up in favour of an operation against the British. He tapped his lighter softly on the desk to reimpose his chairmanship. 'Is it agreed then, Comrades? An act of terrorism against the British Secret Service?'

There were careful, slow nods all round the table.

'I agree. And now for the target within that organization. I remember Comrade General Vozdvishensky saying something about a myth upon which much of the alleged strength of this Secret Service depends. How can we help to destroy the myth and thus strike at the very motive force of this organization? Where does this myth reside? We cannot destroy all its personnel at one blow. Does it reside in the Head? Who is the Head of the British Secret Service?'

Colonel Nikitin's aide whispered in his ear. Colonel Nikitin decided that this was a question he could and perhaps should answer.

'He is an Admiral. He is known by the letter M. We have a *zapiska* on him, but it contains little. He does not drink very much. He is too old for women. The public does not know of his existence. It would be difficult to create a scandal round his death. And he would not be easy to kill. He rarely goes abroad. To shoot him in a London street would not be very refined.'

'There is much in what you say, Comrade,' said General G. 'But we are here to find a target who *will* fulfil our requirements. Have they no one who is a hero to the organization? Someone who is admired and whose ignominious destruction would cause dismay?

Myths are built on heroic deeds and heroic people. Have they no such men?'

There was silence round the table while everyone searched his memory. So many names to remember, so many dossiers, so many operations going on every day all over the world. Who was there in the British Secret Service? Who was that man who . . . ?

It was Colonel Nikitin of the M.G.B. who broke the embarrassed silence.

He said hesitantly, 'There is a man called Bond.'

CHAPTER 6

Death Warrant

'Y*b**nna mat!' The gross obscenity was a favourite with General G. His hand slapped down on the desk. 'Comrade, there certainly is "a man called Bond" as you put it.' His voice was sarcastic. 'James Bond. [He pronounced it 'Shems'.] And nobody, myself included, could think of this spy's name! We are indeed forgetful. No wonder the Intelligence *apparat* is under criticism.'

General Vozdvishensky felt he should defend himself and his department. 'There are countless enemies of the Soviet Union, Comrade General,' he protested. 'If I want their names, I send to the Central Index for them. Certainly I know the name of this Bond. He has been a great trouble to us at different times. But today my mind is full of other names—names of people who are causing us trouble today, this week. I am interested in football, but I cannot remember the names of every foreigner who has scored a goal against the Dynamos.'

'You are pleased to joke, Comrade,' said General G. to underline this out-of-place comment. 'This is a serious matter. I for one admit my fault in not remembering the name of this notorious agent. Comrade Colonel Nikitin will no doubt refresh our memories further, but I recall that this Bond has at least twice frustrated the operations of SMERSH. That is,' he added, 'before I assumed control of the department. There was this affair in France, at that Casino town. The man Le Chiffre. An excellent leader of the Party in France. He foolishly got into some money troubles. But he would have got out of them if this Bond had not interfered. I recall that the Department had to act quickly and liquidate the Frenchman. The executioner should have dealt with the Englishman at the same time, but he did not. Then there was this Negro of ours in Harlem. A great man—one of the greatest foreign agents we have ever employed, and with a vast network behind him. There was some business about a treasure in the Caribbean. I forget the details. This Englishman was sent out by the Secret Service and smashed the whole organization and killed our man. It was a great reverse. Once again my predecessor should have proceeded ruthlessly against this English spy.'

Colonel Nikitin broke in. 'We had a similar experience in the case of the German, Drax, and the rocket. You will recall the matter, Comrade General. A most important *konspiratsia*. The General Staff were deeply involved. It was a matter of High Policy which could have borne decisive fruit. But again it was this Bond who frustrated the operation. The German was killed. There were grave consequences for the State. There followed a period of serious embarrassment which was only solved with difficulty.'

General Slavin of G.R.U. felt that he should say something. The rocket had been an Army operation and its failure had been laid at the door of G.R.U. Nikitin knew this perfectly well. As usual M.G.B. was trying to make trouble for G.R.U.—raking up old history in this manner. 'We asked for this man to be dealt with by your department, Comrade Colonel,' he said icily. 'I cannot recall that any action followed our request. If it had, we should not now be having to bother with him.'

Colonel Nikitin's temples throbbed with rage. He controlled himself. 'With due respect, Comrade General,' he said in a loud, sarcastic voice, 'the request of G.R.U. was not confirmed by Higher Authority. Further embarrassment with England was not desired. Perhaps that detail has slipped your memory. In any case, if such a request had reached M.G.B., it would have been referred to SMERSH for action.'

'My department received no such request,' said General G. sharply. 'Or the execution of this man would have rapidly followed. However, this is no time for historical researches. The rocket affair was three years ago. Perhaps the M.G.B. could tell us of the more recent activities of this man.'

Colonel Nikitin whispered hurriedly with his aide. He turned back to the table. 'We have very little further information, Comrade General,' he said defensively. 'We believe that he was involved in some diamond smuggling affair. That was last year. Between Africa and America. The case did not concern us. Since then we have no further news of him. Perhaps there is more recent information on his file.'

General G. nodded. He picked up the receiver of the telephone nearest to him. This was the so-called *Kommandant Telefon* of the M.G.B. All lines were direct and there was no central switchboard. He dialled a number. 'Central Index? Here General Grubozaboyschikov. The *zapiska* of "Bond"—English spy. Emergency.' He listened for the immediate 'At once, Comrade General,' and put back the receiver. He looked down the table with authority. 'Comrades, from many points of view this spy sounds an appropriate target. He appears to be a dangerous enemy of the State. His liquidation will be of benefit to all departments of our Intelligence *apparat*. Is that so?'

The conference grunted.

'Also his loss will be felt by the Secret Service. But will it do more? Will it seriously wound them? Will it help to destroy this myth about which we have been speaking? Is this man a hero to his organization and his country?'

General Vozdvishensky decided that this question was intended for him. He spoke up. 'The English are not interested in heroes unless they are footballers or cricketers or jockeys. If a man climbs a mountain or runs very fast he also is a hero to some people, but not to the masses. The Queen of England is also a hero, and Churchill. But the English are not greatly interested in military heroes. This man Bond is unknown to the public. If he was known, he would still not be a hero. In England, neither open war nor secret war is a heroic matter. They do not like to think about war, and after a war the names of their war heroes are forgotten as quickly as possible. Within the Secret Service, this man may be a local hero or he may not. It will depend on his appearance and personal characteristics. Of these I know nothing. He may be fat and greasy and unpleasant. No one makes a hero out of such a man, however successful he is.'

Nikitin broke in. 'English spies we have captured speak highly of this man. He is certainly much admired in his Service. He is said to be a lone wolf, but a good looking one.'

The internal office telephone purred softly. General G. lifted the receiver, listened briefly and said, 'Bring it in.' There was a knock on the door. The A.D.C. came in carrying a bulky file in cardboard covers. He crossed the room and placed the file on the desk in front of the General and walked out, closing the door softly behind him.

The file had a shiny black cover. A thick white stripe ran diagonally across it from top right-hand corner to bottom left. In the top left-hand space there were the letters 'S.S.' in white, and under them 'SOVERSHENNOE SEKRETNO', the equivalent of 'Top Secret'. Across the centre was neatly painted in white letters 'JAMES BOND', and underneath 'Angliski Spion'.

General G. opened the file and took out a large envelope containing photographs which he emptied on to the glass surface of the desk. He picked them up one by one. He looked closely at them, sometimes through a magnifying glass which he took out of a drawer, and passed them across the desk to Nikitin who glanced at them and handed them on.

The first was dated 1946. It showed a dark young man sitting at a table outside a sunlit cafe. There was a tall glass beside him on the table and a soda-water siphon. The right forearm rested on the table and there was a cigarette between the fingers of the right hand that hung negligently down from the edge of the table. The legs were crossed in that attitude that only an Englishman adopts—with the right ankle resting on the left knee and the left hand grasping the ankle. It was a careless pose. The man didn't know that he was being photographed from a point about twenty feet away.

The next was dated 1950. It was a face and shoulders, blurred, but of the same man. It was a close-up and Bond was looking with careful, narrowed eyes at something, probably the photographer's face, just above the lens. A miniature button-hole camera, guessed General G.

The third was from 1951. Taken from the left flank, quite close, it showed the same man in a dark suit, without a hat, walking down a wide empty street. He was passing a shuttered shop whose sign said 'Charcuterie'. He looked as if he was going somewhere urgently. The clean-cut profile was pointing straight ahead and the crook of the right elbow suggested that his right hand was in the pocket of his coat. General G. reflected that it was probably taken from a car. He thought that the decisive look of the man, and the purposeful slant of his striding figure, looked dangerous, as if he was making quickly for something bad that was happening further down the street.

The fourth and last photograph was marked *Passe. 1953.* The corner of the Royal Seal and the letters '. . . REIGN OFFICE' in the segment of a circle showed in the bottom right-hand corner. The photograph, which had been blown up to cabinet size, must have been made at a frontier, or by the concierge of an hotel when Bond had surrendered his passport. General G. carefully went over the face with his magnifying glass.

It was a dark, clean-cut face, with a three-inch scar showing whitely down the sunburned skin of the right cheek. The eyes were wide and level under straight, rather long black brows. The hair was black, parted on the left, and carelessly brushed so that a thick black comma fell down over the right eyebrow. The longish straight nose ran down to a short upper lip below which was a wide and finely drawn but cruel mouth. The line of the jaw was straight and firm. A section of dark suit, white shirt and black knitted tie completed the picture.

General G. held the photograph out at arm's length. Decision, authority, ruthlessness—these qualities he could see. He didn't care what else went on inside the man. He passed the photograph down the table and turned to the file, glancing rapidly down each page and flipping brusquely on to the next.

The photographs came back to him. He kept his place with a finger and looked briefly up. 'He looks a nasty customer,' he said grimly. 'His story confirms it. I will read out some extracts. Then we must decide. It is getting late.' He turned back to the first page and began to rattle off the points that struck him.

'First name: JAMES. Height: 183 centimetres; weight: 76 kilograms; slim build; eyes: blue; hair: black; scar down right cheek and on left shoulder; signs of plastic surgery on back of right hand (see Appendix "A"); all-round athlete; expert pistol shot, boxer, knife-thrower; does not use disguises. Languages: French and German. Smokes heavily (N.B.: special cigarettes with three gold bands); vices: drink, but not to excess, and women. Not thought to accept bribes.'

General G. skipped a page and went on:

'This man is invariably armed with a .25 Beretta automatic carried in a holster under his left arm. Magazine holds eight rounds. Has been known to carry a knife strapped to his left forearm; has used steel-capped shoes; knows the basic holds of judo. In general, fights with tenacity and has a high tolerance of pain (see Appendix "B").'

General G. riffled through more pages giving extracts from agents' reports from which this data was drawn. He came to the last page before the Appendices which gave details of the cases on which Bond had been encountered. He ran his eye to the bottom and read out: 'Conclusion. This man is a dangerous professional terrorist and spy. He has worked for the British Secret Service since 1938 and now (see Highsmith file of December 1950) holds the secret number "007" in that Service. The double 0 numerals signify an agent who has killed and who is privileged to kill on active service. There are believed to be only two other British agents with this authority. The fact that this spy was decorated with the C.M.G. in 1953, an award usually given only on retirement from the Secret Service, is a measure of his worth. If encountered in the field, the fact and full details to be reported to headquarters (see SMERSH, M.G.B. and G.R.U. Standing Orders 1951 onwards).'

General G. shut the file and slapped his hand decisively on the cover. 'Well, Comrades. Are we agreed?'

'Yes,' said Colonel Nikitin, loudly.

'Yes,' said General Slavin in a bored voice.

General Vozdvishensky was looking down at his finger-nails. He was sick of murder. He had enjoyed his time in England. 'Yes,' he said. 'I suppose so.'

General G.'s hand went to the internal office telephone. He spoke to his A.D.C. 'Death Warrant,' he said harshly. 'Made out in the name of "James Bond".' He spelled the names out. 'Description: *Angliski Spion*. Crime: Enemy of the State.' He put the receiver back and leant forward in his chair. 'And now it will be a question of devising an appropriate *konspiratsia*. And one that cannot fail!' He smiled grimly. 'We cannot have another of those Khoklov affairs.'

The door opened and the A.D.C. came in carrying a bright yellow sheet of paper. He put it in front of General G. and went out. General G. ran his eyes down the paper and wrote the words 'To be killed. Grubozaboyschikov' at the head of the large empty space at the bottom. He passed the paper to the M.G.B. man who read it and wrote 'Kill him. Nikitin' and handed it across to the head of G.R.U. who wrote 'Kill him. Slavin'. One of the A.D.C.s passed the paper to the plainclothes man sitting beside the representative of R.U.M.I.D. The man put it in front of General Vozdvishensky and handed him a pen.

General Vozdvishensky read the paper carefully. He raised his eyes slowly to those of General G. who was watching him and, without looking down, scribbled the 'Kill him' more or less under the other signatures and scrawled his name after it. Then he took his hands away from the paper and got to his feet.

'If that is all, Comrade General?' He pushed his chair back.

General G. was pleased. His instincts about this man had been right. He would have to put a watch on him and pass on his suspicions to General Serov. 'One moment, Comrade General,' he said. 'I have something to add to the warrant.'

The paper was handed up to him. He took out his pen and scratched out what he had written. He wrote again, speaking the words slowly as he did so.

'To be killed with IGNOMINY. Grubozaboyschikov.'

He looked up and smiled pleasantly to the company. 'Thank you, Comrades. That is all. I shall advise you of the decision of the Praesidium on our recommendation. Good night.'

When the conference had filed out, General G. rose to his feet and stretched and gave a loud controlled yawn. He sat down again at his desk, switched off the wire-recorder and rang for his A.D.C. The man came in and stood beside his desk.

General G. handed him the yellow paper. 'Send this over to General Serov at once. Find out where Kronsteen is and have him fetched by car. I don't care if he's in bed. He will have to come. Otdyel II will know where to find him. And I will see Colonel Klebb in ten minutes.'

'Yes, Comrade General.' The man left the room.

General G. picked up the V.Ch. receiver and asked for General Serov. He spoke quietly for five minutes. At the end he concluded: 'And I am now about to give the task to Colonel Klebb and the Planner, Kronsteen. We will discuss the outlines of a suitable *konspiratsia* and they will give me detailed proposals tomorrow. Is that in order, Comrade General?'

'Yes,' came the quiet voice of General Serov of the High Praesidium. 'Kill him. But let it be excellently accomplished. The Praesidium will ratify the decision in the morning.'

The line went dead. The inter-office telephone rang. General G. said 'Yes' into the receiver and put it back.

A moment later the A.D.C. opened the big door and stood in the entrance. 'Comrade Colonel Klebb,' he announced.

A toad-like figure in an olive green uniform which bore the single red ribbon of the Order of Lenin came into the room and walked with quick short steps over to the desk.

General G. looked up and waved to the nearest chair at the conference table. 'Good evening, Comrade.'

The squat face split into a sugary smile. 'Good evening, Comrade General.'

The Head of Otdyel II, the department of SMERSH in charge of Operations and Executions, hitched up her skirts and sat down.

CHAPTER 7

The Wizard of Ice

The two faces of the double clock in the shiny, domed case looked out across the chess-board like the eyes of some huge sea monster that had peered over the edge of the table to watch the game.

The two faces of the chess clock showed different times. Kronsteen's showed twenty minutes to one. The long red pendulum that ticked off the seconds was moving in its staccato sweep across the bottom half of his clock's face, while the enemy clock was silent and its pendulum motionless down the face. But Makharov's clock said five minutes to one. He had wasted time in the middle of the game and he now had only five minutes to go. He was in bad 'time-trouble' and unless Kronsteen made some lunatic mistake, which was unthinkable, he was beaten.

Kronsteen sat motionless and erect, as malevolently inscrutable as a parrot. His elbows were on the table and his big head rested on clenched fists that pressed into his cheeks, squashing the pursed lips into a pout of hauteur and disdain. Under the wide, bulging brow the rather slanting black eyes looked down with deadly calm on his winning board. But, behind the mask, the blood was throbbing in the dynamo of his brain, and a thick worm-like vein in his right temple pulsed at a beat of over ninety. He had sweated away a pound of weight in the last two hours and ten minutes, and the spectre of a false move still had one hand at his throat. But to Makharov, and to the spectators, he was still 'The Wizard of Ice' whose game had been compared to a man eating fish. First he stripped off the skin, then he picked out the bones, then he ate the fish. Kronsteen had been Champion of Moscow two years running, was now in the final for the third time and, if he won this game, would be a contender for Grand Mastership.

In the pool of silence round the roped-off top table there was no sound except the loud tripping feet of Kronsteen's clock. The two umpires sat motionless in their raised chairs. They knew, as did Makharov, that this was certainly the kill. Kronsteen had introduced a brilliant twist into the Meran Variation of the Queen's Gambit Declined. Makharov had kept up with him until the 28th move. He had lost time on that move. Perhaps he had made a mistake there, and perhaps again on the 31st and 33rd moves. Who could say? It would be a game to be debated all over Russia for weeks to come.

There came a sigh from the crowded tiers opposite the Championship game. Kronsteen had slowly removed the right hand from his cheek and had stretched it across the board. Like the pincers of a pink crab, his thumb and forefinger had opened, then they had descended. The hand, holding a piece, moved up and sideways and down. Then the hand was slowly brought back to the face.

The spectators buzzed and whispered as they saw, on the great wall map, the 41st move duplicated with a shift of one of the three-foot placards. R-Kt8. That must be the kill!

Kronsteen reached deliberately over and pressed down the lever at the bottom of his clock. His red pendulum went dead. His clock showed a quarter to one. At the same instant, Makharov's pendulum came to life and started its loud, inexorable beat.

Kronsteen sat back. He placed his hands flat on the table and looked coldly across at the glistening, lowered face of the man whose guts he knew, for he too had suffered defeat in his time, would be writhing in agony like an eel pierced with a spear. Makharov, Champion of Georgia. Well, tomorrow Comrade Makharov could go back to Georgia and stay there. At any rate this year he would not be moving with his family up to Moscow.

A man in plain clothes slipped under the ropes and whispered to one of the umpires. He handed him a white envelope. The umpire shook his head, pointing at Makharov's clock, which now said three minutes to one. The man in plain clothes whispered one short sentence which made the umpire sullenly bow his head. He pinged a handbell.

'There is an urgent personal message for Comrade Kronsteen,' he announced into the microphone. 'There will be a three minutes' pause.'

A mutter went round the hall. Even though Makharov now courteously raised his eyes from the board and sat immobile, gazing up into the recesses of the high, vaulted ceiling, the spectators knew that the position of the game was engraved on his brain. A three minutes' pause simply meant three extra minutes for Makharov.

Kronsteen felt the same stab of annoyance, but his face was expressionless as the umpire stepped down from his chair and handed him a plain, unaddressed envelope. Kronsteen ripped it open with his thumb and extracted the anonymous sheet of paper. It said, in the large typewritten characters he knew so well, 'YOU ARE REQUIRED THIS INSTANT'. No signature and no address.

Kronsteen folded the paper and carefully placed it in his inside breast pocket. Later it would be recovered from him and destroyed. He looked up at the face of the plain-clothes man standing beside the umpire. The eyes were watching him impatiently, commandingly. To hell with these people, thought Kronsteen. He would *not* resign with only three minutes to go. It was unthinkable. It was an insult to the People's Sport. But, as he made a gesture to the umpire that the game could continue, he trembled inside, and he avoided the eyes of the plain-clothes man who remained standing, in coiled immobility, inside the ropes.

The bell pinged. 'The game proceeds.'

Makharov slowly bent down his head. The hand of his clock slipped past the hour and he was still alive.

Kronsteen continued to tremble inside. What he had done was unheard of in a employee of SMERSH, or of any other State agency. He would certainly be reported. Gross disobedience. Dereliction of duty. What might be the consequences? At the best a tongue-lashing from General G., and a black mark on his *zapiska*. And the worst? Kronsteen couldn't imagine. He didn't like to think. Whatever happened, the sweets of victory had turned bitter in his mouth.

But now it was the end. With five seconds to go on his clock, Makharov raised his whipped eyes no higher than the pouting lips of his opponent and bent his head in the brief, formal bow of surrender. At the double ping of the umpire's bell, the crowded hall rose to its feet with a thunder of applause.

Kronsteen stood up and bowed to his opponent, to the umpires, and finally, deeply, to the spectators. Then, with the plain-clothes man in his wake, he ducked under the ropes and fought his way coldly and rudely through the mass of his clamouring admirers towards the main exit.

Outside the Tournament Hall, in the middle of the wide Pushkin Ulitza, with its engine running, stood the usual anonymous black ZIK saloon. Kronsteen climbed into the back and shut the door. As the plain-clothes man jumped on to the running-board and squeezed into the front seat, the driver crashed his gears and the car tore off down the street.

Kronsteen knew it would be a waste of breath to apologize to the plain-clothes guard. It would also be contrary to discipline. After all, he was Head of the

Planning Department of SMERSH, with the honorary rank of full Colonel. And his brain was worth diamonds to the organization. Perhaps he could argue his way out of the mess. He gazed out of the window at the dark streets, already wet with the work of the night cleaning squad, and bent his mind to his defence. Then there came a straight street at the end of which the moon rode fast between the onion spires of the Kremlin, and they were there.

When the guard handed Kronsteen over to the A.D.C., he also handed the A.D.C. a slip of paper. The A.D.C. glanced at it and looked coldly up at Kronsteen with half-raised eyebrows. Kronsteen looked calmly back without saying anything. The A.D.C. shrugged his shoulders and picked up the office telephone and announced him.

When they went into the big room and Kronsteen had been waved to a chair and had nodded acknowledgment of the brief pursed smile of Colonel Klebb, the A.D.C. went up to General G. and handed him the piece of paper. The General read it and looked hard across at Kronsteen. While the A.D.C. walked to the door and went out, the General went on looking at Kronsteen. When the door was shut, General G. opened his mouth and said softly, 'Well, Comrade?'

Kronsteen was calm. He knew the story that would appeal. He spoke quietly and with authority. 'To the public, Comrade General, I am a professional chess player. Tonight I became Champion of Moscow for the third year in succession. If, with only three minutes to go, I had received a message that my wife was being murdered outside the door of the Tournament Hall, I would not have raised a finger to save her. My public knows that. They are dedicated to the game as myself. Tonight, if I had resigned the game and had come immediately on receipt of that message, five thousand people would have known that it could only be on the orders of such a department as this. There would have been a storm of gossip. My future goings and comings would have been watched for clues. It would have been the end of my cover. In the interests of State Security, I waited three minutes before obeying the order. Even so, my hurried departure will be the subject of much comment. I shall have to say that one of my children is gravely ill. I shall have to put a child into hospital for a week to support the story. I deeply apologize for the delay in carrying out the order. But the decision was a difficult one. I did what I thought best in the interests of the Department.'

General G. looked thoughtfully into the dark slanting eyes. The man was guilty, but the defence was good. He read the paper again as if weighing up the size of the offence, then he took out his lighter and burned it. He dropped the last burning corner on to the glass top of his desk and blew the ashes sideways on to the floor. He said nothing to reveal his thoughts, but the burning of the evidence was all that mattered to Kronsteen. Now nothing could go on his *zapiska*. He was deeply relieved and grateful. He would bend all his ingenuity to the matter on hand. The General had performed an act of great clemency. Kronsteen would repay him with the full coin of his mind.

'Pass over the photographs, Comrade Colonel,' said General G., as if the brief court-martial had not occurred. 'The matter is as follows. . . .'

So it is another death, thought Kronsteen, as the General talked and he examined the dark ruthless face that gazed levelly at him from the blown-up passport photograph. While Kronsteen listened with half his mind to what the General was saying, he picked out the salient facts—English spy. Great scandal desired. No Soviet involvement. Expert killer. Weakness for women (therefore not homosexual, thought Kronsteen). Drinks (but nothing is said about drugs). Unbribable (who knows? There is a price for every man). No expense would be spared. All equipment and personnel available from all intelligence departments. Success to be achieved within three months. Broad ideas required now. Details to be worked out later.

General G. fastened his sharp eyes on Colonel Klebb.

'What are your immediate reactions, Comrade Colonel?'

The square-cut rimless glass of the spectacles flashed in the light of the chandelier as the woman straightened from her position of bowed concentration and looked across the desk at the General. The pale moist lips below the sheen of nicotine-stained fur over the mouth parted and started moving rapidly up and down as the woman gave her views. To Kronsteen, watching the face across the table, the square, expressionless opening and shutting of the lips reminded him of the boxlike jabber of a puppet.

The voice was hoarse and flat and without emotion, '. . . resembles in some respects the case of Stolzenberg. If you remember, Comrade General, this also was a matter of destroying a reputation as well as a life. On that occasion the matter was simple. The spy was also a pervert. If you recall . . .'

Kronsteen stopped listening. He knew all these cases. He had handled the planning of most of them and they were filed away in his memory like so many chess gambits. Instead, with closed ears, he examined the face of this dreadful woman and wondered casually how much longer she would last in her job—how much longer he would have to work with her.

Dreadful? Kronsteen was not interested in human beings—not even in his own children. Nor did the categories of 'good' and 'bad' have a place in his vocabulary. To him all people were chess pieces. He was only interested in their reactions to the movements of other pieces. To foretell their reactions, which was the greater part of his job, one had to understand their individual characteristics. Their basic instincts were immutable. Self-preservation, sex and the instinct of the herd—in that order. Their temperaments could be sanguine, phlegmatic, choleric or melancholic. The temperament of an individual would largely decide the comparative strength of his emotions and his sentiments. Character would greatly depend on upbringing and, whatever Pavlov and the Behaviourists might say, to a certain extent on the character of the parents. And, of course, people's lives and behaviour would be partly conditioned by physical strengths and weaknesses.

It was with these basic classifications at the back of his mind that Kronsteen's cold brain considered the woman across the table. It was the hundredth time he had summed her up, but now they had weeks of joint work in front of them and it was as well to refresh the memory so that a sudden intrusion of the human element in their partnership should not come as a surprise.

Of course Rosa Klebb had a strong will to survive, or she would not have become one of the most powerful women in the State, and certainly the most feared. Her rise, Kronsteen remembered, had begun with the Spanish Civil War. Then, as a double agent inside P.O.U.M.—that is, working for the O.G.P.U. in Moscow as well as for Communist Intelligence in Spain—she had been the right hand, and some sort of a mistress, they said, of her chief, the famous Andreas Nin. She had worked with him from 1935-37. Then, on the orders of Moscow, he was murdered and, it was rumoured, murdered by her. Whether this was true or not, from then on she had progressed slowly but straight up the ladder of power, surviving setbacks, surviving wars, surviving, because she forged no allegiances and joined no factions, all the purges, until, in 1953 with the death of Beria, the bloodstained hands grasped the rung, so few from the very top, that was Head of the Operations Department of SMERSH.

And, reflected Kronsteen, much of her success was due to the peculiar nature of her next most important instinct, the Sex Instinct. For Rosa Klebb undoubtedly belonged to the rarest of all sexual types. She was a Neuter. Kronsteen was certain of it. The stories of men and, yes, of women, were too circumstantial to be doubted. She might enjoy the act physically, but the instrument was of no importance. For her, sex was nothing more than an itch. And this psychological and physiological neutrality of hers at once relieved her of so many human emotions and sentiments and desires. Sexual neutrality was the essence of coldness in an individual. It was a great and wonderful thing to be born with.

In her, the Herd instinct would also be dead. Her urge for power demanded that she should be a wolf and not a sheep. She was a lone operator, but never a lonely one, because the warmth of company was unnecessary to her. And, of course, temperamentally, she would be a phlegmatic—imperturbable, tolerant of pain, sluggish. Laziness would be her besetting vice, thought Kronsteen. She would be difficult to get out of her warm, hoggish bed in the morning. Her private habits would be slovenly, even dirty. It would not be pleasant, thought Kronsteen, to look into the intimate side of her life, when she relaxed, out of uniform. Kronsteen's pouting lips curled away from the thought and his mind hastened on, skipping her character, which was certainly cunning and strong, to her appearance.

Rosa Klebb would be in her late forties, he assumed, placing her by the date of the Spanish War. She was short, about five foot four, and squat, and her dumpy arms and short neck, and the calves of the thick legs in the drab khaki stockings, were very strong for a woman. The devil knows, thought Kronsteen, what her breasts were like, but the bulge of uniform that rested on the table-top looked like a badly packed sandbag, and in general her figure, with its big pear-shaped hips, could only be likened to a 'cello.

The *tricoteuses* of the French Revolution must have had faces like hers, decided Kronsteen, sitting back in his chair and tilting his head slightly to one side. The thinning orange hair scraped back to the tight, obscene bun; the shiny yellow-brown eyes that stared so coldly at General G. through the sharp-edged squares of glass, the wedge of thickly powdered, large-pored nose; the wet trap of a mouth, that went on opening and shutting as if it was operated by wires under the chin. Those French women, as they sat and knitted and chatted while the guillotine clanged down, must have had the same pale, thick chicken's skin that scragged in little folds under the eyes and at the corners of the mouth and below the jaws, the same big peasant's ears, the same tight, hard dimpled fists, like knobkerries, that, in the case of the Russian woman, now lay tightly clenched on the red velvet table-top on either side of the big bundle of bosom. And their faces must have conveyed the same impression, concluded Kronsteen, of coldness and cruelty and strength as this, yes, he had to allow himself the emotive word, *dreadful* woman of SMERSH.

'Thank you, Comrade Colonel. Your review of the position is of value. And now, Comrade Kronsteen, have you anything to add? Please be short. It is two o'clock and we all have a heavy day before us.' General G.'s eyes, bloodshot with strain and lack of sleep, stared fixedly across the desk into the fathomless brown pools below the bulging forehead. There had been no need to tell this man to be brief. Kronsteen never had much to say, but each of his words was worth speeches from the rest of the staff.

Kronsteen had already made up his mind, or he would not have allowed his thoughts to concentrate for so long on the woman.

He slowly tilted back his head and gazed into the nothingness of the ceiling. His voice was extremely mild, but it had the authority that commands close attention.

'Comrade General, it was a Frenchman, in some respects a predecessor of yours, Fouché, who observed that it is no good killing a man unless you also destroy his reputation. It will, of course, be easy to kill this man Bond. Any paid Bulgarian assassin would do it, if properly instructed. The second part of the operation, the destruction of this man's character, is more important and more difficult. At this stage it is only clear to me that the deed must be done away from England, and in a country over whose press and radio we have influence. If you ask me how the man is to be got there, I can only say that if the bait is important enough, and its capture is open to this man alone, he will be sent to seize it from wherever he may happen to be. To avoid the appearance of a trap, I would consider giving the bait a touch of eccentricity, of the unusual. The English pride themselves on their eccentricity. They treat the eccentric proposition as a challenge. I would rely partly on this reading of their psychology to have them send this important operator after the bait.'

Kronsteen paused. He lowered his head so that he was looking just over General G.'s shoulder.

'I shall proceed to devise such a trap,' he said indifferently. 'For the present, I can only say that if the bait is successful in attracting its prey, we are then likely to require an assassin with a perfect command of the English language.'

Kronsteen's eyes moved to the red velvet table-top in front of him. Thoughtfully, as if this was the kernel of the problem, he added: 'We shall also require a reliable and extremely beautiful girl.'

CHAPTER 8

The Beautiful Lure

Sitting by the window of her one room and looking out at the serene June evening, at the first pink of the sunset reflected in the windows across the street, at the distant onion spire of a church that flamed like a torch above the ragged horizon of Moscow roofs, Corporal of State Security Tatiana Romanova thought that she was happier than she had ever been before.

Her happiness was not romantic. It had nothing to do with the rapturous start to a love affair—those days and weeks before the first tiny tear-clouds appear on the horizon. It was quiet, settled happiness of security, of being able to look forward with confidence to the future, heightened by the immediate things, a word of praise she had had that afternoon from Professor Denikin, the smell of a good supper cooking on the electric stove, her favourite prelude to *Boris Goudonov* being played by the Moscow State Orchestra on the radio, and, over all, the beauty of the fact that the long winter and short spring were past and it was June.

The room was a tiny box in the huge modern apart-

ment building on the Sadovaya-Chernogriazskay Ulitza
that is the women's barracks of the State Security
Departments. Built by prison labour, and finished in
1939, the fine eight-storey building contains two
thousand rooms, some, like hers on the third floor,
nothing but square boxes with a telephone, hot and cold
water, a single electric light and a share of the central
bathrooms and lavatories, others, on the two top floors,
consisting of two- and three-room flats with bathrooms.
These were for high-ranking women. Graduation up the
building was strictly by rank, and Corporal Romanova
had to rise through Sergeant, Lieutenant, Captain,
Major and Lieutenant-Colonel before she would reach
the paradise of the eighth and Colonels' floor.

But heaven knew she was content enough with her
present lot. A salary of 1200 roubles a month (thirty per
cent more than she could have earned in any other
Ministry), a room to herself; cheap food and clothes
from the 'closed shops' on the ground floor of the
building; a monthly allocation of at least two Ministry
tickets to the Ballet or the Opera, a full two weeks' paid
holiday a year. And, above all, a steady job with good
prospects in Moscow—not in one of those dreary
provincial towns where nothing happened month after
month, and where the arrival of a new film or the visit
of a travelling circus was the only thing to keep one out
of bed in the evening.

Of course, you had to pay for being in the M.G.B.
The uniform put you apart from the world. People were
afraid, which didn't suit the nature of most girls, and
you were confined to the society of other M.G.B. girls
and men, one of whom, when the time came, you would
have to marry in order to stay with the Ministry. And
they worked like the devil—eight to six, five and a half
days a week, and only forty minutes off for lunch in the
canteen. But it was a good lunch, a real meal, and you
could do with little supper and save up for the sable coat
that would one day take the place of the well-worn
Siberian fox.

At the thought of her supper, Corporal Romanova

left the chair by the window and went to examine the pot of thick soup, with a few shreds of meat and some powdered mushroom, that was to be her supper. It was nearly done and smelled delicious. She turned off the electricity and let the pot simmer while she washed and tidied, as, years before, she had been taught to do before meals.

While she dried her hands, she examined herself in the big oval looking-glass over the washstand.

One of her early boy-friends had said she looked like the young Greta Garbo. What nonsense! And yet tonight she did look rather well. Fine dark brown silken hair brushed straight back from a tall brow and falling heavily down almost to the shoulders, there to curl slightly up at the ends (Garbo had once done her hair like that and Corporal Romanova admitted to herself that she had copied it), a good, soft pale skin with an ivory sheen at the cheekbones; wide apart, level eyes of the deepest blue under straight natural brows (she closed one eye after the other. Yes, her lashes were certainly long enough!) a straight, rather imperious nose—and then the mouth. What about the mouth? Was it too broad? It must look terribly wide when she smiled. She smiled at herself in the mirror. Yes, it was wide; but then so had Garbo's been. At least the lips were full and finely etched. There was the hint of a smile at the corners. No one could say it was a cold mouth! And the oval of her face. Was that too long? Was her chin a shade too sharp? She swung her head sideways to see it in profile. The heavy curtain of hair swung forward and across her right eye so that she had to brush it back. Well, the chin was pointed, but at least it wasn't sharp. She faced the mirror again and picked up a brush and started on the long, heavy hair. Greta Garbo! She was all right, or so many men wouldn't tell her that she was—let alone the girls who were always coming to her for advice about their faces. But a film star—a famous one! She made a face at herself in the glass and went to eat her supper.

In fact Corporal Tatiana Romanova was a very

beautiful girl indeed. Apart from her face, the tall, firm body moved particularly well. She had been a year in the ballet school in Leningrad and had abandoned dancing as a career only when she grew an inch over the prescribed limit of five feet six. The school had taught her to hold herself well and to walk well. And she looked wonderfully healthy, thanks to her passion for figure-skating, which she practised all through the year at the Dynamo ice-stadium and which had already earned her a place on the first Dynamo women's team. Her arms and breasts were faultless. A purist would have disapproved of her behind. Its muscles were so hardened with exercise that it had lost the smooth downward feminine sweep, and now, round at the back and flat and hard at the sides, it jutted like a man's.

Corporal Romanova was admired far beyond the confines of the English translation section of the M.G.B. Central Index. Everyone agreed that it would not be long before one of the senior officers came across her and peremptorily hauled her out of her modest section to make her his mistress, or if absolutely necessary, his wife.

The girl poured the thick soup into a small china bowl, decorated with wolves chasing a galloping sleigh round the rim, broke some black bread into it and went and sat in her chair by the window and ate it slowly with a nice shiny spoon she had slipped into her bag not many weeks before after a gay evening at the Hotel Moskwa.

When she had finished, she washed up and went back to her chair and lit the first cigarette of the day (no respectable girl in Russia smokes in public, except in a restaurant, and it would have meant instant dismissal if she had smoked at her work) and listened impatiently to the whimpering discords of an orchestra from Turkmenistan. This dreadful oriental stuff they were always putting on to please the kulaks of one of those barbaric outlying states! Why couldn't they play something *kulturny*? Some of that modern jazz music, or something classical. This stuff was hideous. Worse, it was old fashioned.

The telephone rang harshly. She walked over and turned down the radio and picked up the receiver.

'Corporal Romanova?'

It was the voice of her dear Professor Denikin. But out of office hours he always called her Tatiana or even Tania. What did this mean?

The girl was wide-eyed and tense. 'Yes, Comrade Professor.'

The voice at the other end sounded strange and cold. 'In fifteen minutes, at 8.30, you are required for interview by Comrade Colonel Klebb, of Otdyel II. You will call on her in her apartment, No. 1875, on the eighth floor of your building. Is that clear?'

'But, Comrade, why? What is . . . What is . . . ?'

The odd, strained voice of her beloved Professor cut her short.

'That is all, Comrade Corporal.'

The girl held the receiver away from her face. She stared at it with frenzied eyes as if she could wring more words out of the circles of little holes in the black earpiece. 'Hullo! Hullo!' The empty mouthpiece yawned at her. She realized that her hand and her forearm were aching with the strength of her grip. She bent slowly forward and put the receiver down on the cradle.

She stood for a moment, frozen, gazing blindly at the black machine. Should she call him back? No, that was out of the question. He had spoken as he had because he knew, and she knew, that every call, in and out of the building, was listened to or recorded. That was why he had not wasted a word. This was a State matter. With a message of this sort, you got rid of it as quickly as you could, in as few words as possible, and wiped your hands of it. You had got the dreadful card out of your hand. You had passed the Queen of Spades to someone else. Your hands were clean again.

The girl put her knuckles up to her open mouth and bit on them, staring at the telephone. What did they want her for? What had she done? Desperately she cast her mind back, scrabbling through the days, the months, the years. Had she made some terrible mistake in her work and they had just discovered it? Had she made some remark against the State, some joke that had been reported back? That was always possible. But which remark? When? If it had been a bad remark, she would have felt a twinge of guilt or fear at the time. Her conscience was clear. Or was it? Suddenly she remembered. What about the spoon she had stolen? Was it that? Government property! She would throw it out of the window, now, far to one side or the other. But no, it couldn't be that. That was too small. She shrugged her shoulders resignedly and her hand dropped to her side. She got up and moved towards the clothes cupboard to get out her best uniform, and her eyes were misty with the tears of fright and bewilderment of a child. It could be none of those things. SMERSH didn't send for one for that sort of thing. It must be something much, much worse.

The girl glanced through her wet eyes at the cheap watch on her wrist. Only seven minutes to go! A new panic seized her. She brushed her forearm across her eyes and grabbed down her parade uniform. On top of it all, whatever it was, to be late! She tore at the buttons on her white cotton blouse.

As she dressed and washed her face and brushed her hair, her mind went on probing at the evil mystery like an inquisitive child poking into a snake's hole with a stick. From whatever angle she explored the hole, there came an angry hiss.

Leaving out the nature of her guilt, contact with any tentacle of SMERSH was unspeakable. The very name of the organization was abhorred and avoided. SMERSH, 'Smiert Spionam', 'Death to Spies'. It was an obscene word, a word from the tomb, the very whisper of death, a word never mentioned even in secret office gossip among friends. Worst of all, within this horrible organization, Otdyel II, the Department of Torture and Death, was the central horror.

And the Head of Otdyel II, the woman, Rosa Klebb! Unbelievable things were whispered about this woman, things that came to Tatiana in her nightmares, things she forgot again during the day, but that she now paraded.

It was said that Rosa Klebb would let no torturing take place without her. There was a blood-spattered smock in her office, and a low camp-stool, and they said that when she was seen scurrying through the basement passages dressed in the smock and with the stool in her hand, the word would go round, and even the workers in SMERSH would hush their words and bend low over their papers—perhaps even cross their fingers in their pockets—until she was reported back in her room.

For, or so they whispered, she would take the camp-stool and draw it up close below the face of the man or woman that hung down over the edge of the interrogation table. Then she would squat down on the stool and look into the face and quietly say 'No. 1' or 'No. 10' or 'No. 25' and the inquisitors would know what she meant and they would begin. And she would watch the eyes in the face a few inches away from hers and breathe in the screams as if they were perfume. And, depending on the eyes, she would quietly change the torture, and say 'Now No. 36' or 'Now No. 64' and the inquisitors would do something else. As the courage and resistance seeped out of the eyes, and they began to weaken and beseech, she would start cooing softly. 'There, there my dove. Talk to me, my pretty one, and it will stop. It hurts. Ah me, it hurts so, my child. And one is so tired of the pain. One would like it to stop, and to be able to lie down in peace, and for it never to begin again. Your mother is here beside you, only waiting to stop the pain. She has a nice soft cosy bed all ready for you to sleep on and forget, forget, forget. Speak,' she would whisper lovingly. 'You have only to speak and you will have peace and no more pain.' If the eyes still resisted, the cooing would start again. 'But you are foolish, my pretty one. Oh so foolish. This pain is nothing. Nothing! You don't believe me, my little dove?

Well then, your mother must try a little, but only a very little, of No. 87.' And the interrogators would hear and change their instruments and their aim, and she would squat there and watch the life slowly ebbing from the eyes until she had to speak loudly into the ear of the person or the words would not reach the brain.

But it was seldom, so they said, that the person had the will to travel far along SMERSH'S road of pain, let alone to the end, and, when the soft voice promised peace, it nearly always won, for somehow Rosa Klebb knew from the eyes the moment when the adult had been broken down into a child crying for its mother. And she provided the image of the mother and melted the spirit where the harsh words of a man would have toughened it.

Then, after yet another suspect had been broken, Rosa Klebb would go back down the passage with her camp-stool and take off her newly soiled smock and get back to her work and the word would go round that all was over and normal activity would come back to the basement.

Tatiana, frozen by her thoughts, looked again at her watch. Four minutes to go. She ran her hands down her uniform and gazed once more at her white face in the glass. She turned and said farewell to the dear, familiar little room. Would she ever see it again?

She walked straight down the long corridor and rang for the lift.

When it came, she squared her shoulders and lifted her chin and walked into the lift as if it was the platform of the guillotine.

'Eighth,' she said to the girl operator. She stood facing the doors. Inside her, remembering a word she had not used since childhood, she repeated over and over 'My God—My God—My God.'

CHAPTER 9

A Labour of Love

Outside the anonymous, cream painted door, Tatiana already smelled the inside of the room. When the voice told her curtly to come in, and she opened the door, it was the smell that filled her mind while she stood and stared into the eyes of the woman who sat behind the round table under the centre light.

It was the smell of the Metro on a hot evening—cheap scent concealing animal odours. People in Russia soak themselves in scent, whether they have had a bath or not, but mostly when they have not, and healthy, clean girls like Tatiana always walk home from the office, unless the rain or the snow is too bad, so as to avoid the stench in the trains and the Metro.

Now Tatiana was in a bath of the smell. Her nostrils twitched with disgust.

It was her disgust and her contempt for a person who could live in the middle of such a smell that helped her to look down into the yellowish eyes that stared at her through the square glass panes. Nothing could be read in them. They were receiving eyes, not giving eyes. They slowly moved all over her, like camera lenses, taking her in.

Colonel Klebb spoke:

'You are a fine-looking girl, Comrade Corporal. Walk across the room and back.'

What were these honeyed words? Taut with a new fear, fear of the notorious personal habits of the woman, Tatiana did as she was told.

'Take your jacket off. Put it down on the chair. Raise your hands above your head. Higher. Now bend and touch your toes. Upright. Good. Sit down.' The woman spoke like a doctor. She gestured to the chair across the table from her. Her staring, probing eyes hooded themselves as they bent over the file on the table.

It must be my *zapiska,* thought Tatiana. How interesting to see the actual instrument that ordered the whole of one's life. How thick it was—nearly two inches thick. What could be on all those pages? She looked across at the open folder with wide, fascinated eyes.

Colonel Klebb riffled through the last pages and shut down the cover. The cover was orange with a diagonal black stripe. What did those colours signify?

The woman looked up. Somehow Tatiana managed to look bravely back.

'Comrade Corporal Romanova.' It was the voice of authority, of the senior officer. 'I have good reports of your work. Your record is excellent, both in your duties and in sport. The State is pleased with you.'

Tatiana could not believe her ears. She felt faint with reaction. She blushed to the roots of her hair and then turned pale. She put out a hand to the table edge. She stammered in a weak voice, 'I am g-grateful, Comrade Colonel.'

'Because of your excellent services you have been singled out for a most important assignment. This is a great honour for you. Do you understand?'

Whatever it was, it was better than what might have been. 'Yes, indeed, Comrade Colonel.'

'This assignment carries much responsibility. It bears a higher rank. I congratulate you on your promotion, Comrade Corporal, on completion of the assignment, to the rank of Captain of State Security.'

This was unheard of for a girl of twenty-four! Tatiana sensed danger. She stiffened like an animal who sees the steel jaws beneath the meat. 'I am deeply honoured, Comrade Colonel.' She was unable to keep the wariness out of her voice.

Rosa Klebb grunted non-committally. She knew exactly what the girl must have thought when she got the summons. The effect of her kindly reception, her shock of relief at the good news, her reawakening fears, had been transparent. This was a beautiful, guileless, innocent girl. Just what the *konspiratsia* demanded. Now she must be loosened up. 'My dear,' she said smoothly. 'How remiss of me. This promotion should be celebrated in a glass of wine. You must not think we senior officers are inhuman. We will drink together. It will be a good excuse to open a bottle of French champagne.'

Rosa Klebb got up and went over to the sideboard where her batman had laid out what she had ordered.

'Try one of these chocolates while I wrestle with the cork. It is never easy getting out champagne corks. We girls really need a man to help us with that sort of work, don't we?'

The ghastly prattle went on as she put a spectacular box of chocolates in front of Tatiana. She went back to the sideboard. 'They're from Switzerland. The very best. The soft centres are the round ones. The hard ones are square.'

Tatiana murmured her thanks. She reached out and chose a round one. It would be easier to swallow. Her mouth was dry with fear of the moment when she would finally see the trap and feel it snap round her neck. It must be something dreadful to need to be concealed under all this play-acting. The bite of chocolate stuck in her mouth like chewing-gum. Mercifully the glass of champagne was thrust into her hand.

Rosa Klebb stood over her. She lifted her glass merrily. *'Za vashe zdarovie,* Comrade Tatiana. And my warmest congratulations!'

Tatiana stitched a ghastly smile on her face. She

picked up her glass and gave a little bow. *'Za vashe zdarovie,* Comrade Colonel.' She drained the glass, as is the custom in Russian drinking, and put it down in front of her.

Rosa Klebb immediately filled it again, slopping some over the tabletop. 'And now to the health of your new department, Comrade.' She raised her glass. The sugary smile tightened as she watched the girl's reactions.

'TO SMERSH!'

Numbly, Tatiana got to her feet. She picked up the full glass. 'To SMERSH.' The word scarcely came out. She choked on the champagne and had to take two gulps. She sat heavily down.

Rosa Klebb gave her no time for reflection. She sat down opposite and laid her hands flat on the table. 'And now to business, Comrade.' Authority was back in the voice. 'There is much work to be done.' She leant forward. 'Have you ever wished to live abroad, Comrade? In a foreign country?'

The champagne was having its effect on Tatiana. Probably worse was to come, but now let it come quickly.

'No, Comrade. I am happy in Moscow.'

'You have never thought what it might be like living in the West—all those beautiful clothes, the jazz, the modern things?'

'No, Comrade.' She was truthful. She had never thought about it.

'And if the State required you to live in the West?'

'I would obey.'

'Willingly?'

Tatiana shrugged her shoulders with a hint of impatience. 'One does what one is told.'

The woman paused. There was girlish conspiracy in the next question.

'Are you a virgin, Comrade?'

Oh, my God, thought Tatiana. 'No, Comrade Colonel.'

The wet lips glinted in the light.

'How many men?'

Tatiana coloured to the roots of her hair. Russian

girls are reticent and prudish about sex. In Russia the sexual climate is mid-Victorian. These questions from the Klebb woman were all the more revolting for being asked in this cold inquisitorial tone by a State official she had never met before in her life. Tatiana screwed up her courage. She stared defensively into the yellow eyes. 'What is the purpose of these intimate questions please, Comrade Colonel?'

Rosa Klebb straightened. Her voice cut back like a whip. 'Remember yourself, Comrade. You are not here to ask questions. You forget to whom you are speaking. Answer me!'

Tatiana shrank back. 'Three men, Comrade Colonel.'

'When. How old were you?' The hard yellow eyes looked across the table into the hunted blue eyes of the girl and held them and commanded.

Tatiana was on the edge of tears. 'At school. When I was seventeen. Then at the Institute of Foreign Languages. I was twenty-two. Then last year. I was twenty-three. It was a friend I met skating.'

'Their names, please, Comrade.' Rosa Klebb picked up a pencil and pulled a scribbling pad towards her.

Tatiana covered her face with her hands and burst into tears. 'No,' she cried between her sobs. 'No, never, whatever you do to me. You have no right.'

'Stop that nonsense.' The voice was a hiss. 'In five minutes I could have those names from you, or anything else I wish to know. You are playing a dangerous game with me, Comrade. My patience will not last for ever.' Rosa Klebb paused. She was being too rough. 'For the moment we will pass on. Tomorrow you will give me the names. No harm will come to these men. They will be asked one or two questions about you—simple technical questions, that is all. Now sit up and dry your tears. We cannot have any more of this foolishness.'

Rosa Klebb got up and came round the table. She stood looking down at Tatiana. The voice became oily and smooth. 'Come, come, my dear. You must trust me. Your little secrets are safe with me. Here, drink some more champagne and forget this little unpleasantness. We must be friends. We have work to do together. You must learn, my dear Tania, to treat me as you would your mother. Here, drink this down.'

Tatiana pulled a handkerchief out of the waistband of her skirt and dabbed at her eyes. She reached out a trembling hand for the glass of champagne and sipped at it with bowed head.

'Drink it down, my dear.'

Rosa Klebb stood over the girl like some dreadful mother duck, clucking encouragement.

Obediently Tatiana emptied the glass. She felt drained of resistance, tired, willing to do anything to finish with this interview and get away somewhere and sleep. She thought, so this is what it is like on the interrogation table, and that is the voice the Klebb uses. Well, it was working. She was docile now. She would co-operate.

Rosa Klebb sat down. She observed the girl appraisingly from behind the motherly mask.

'And now, my dear, just one more intimate little question. As between girls. Do you enjoy making love? Does it give you pleasure? Much pleasure?'

Tatiana's hands came up again and covered her face. From behind them, in a muffled voice, she said, 'Well yes, Comrade Colonel. Naturally, when one is in love . . .' Her voice trailed away. What else could she say? What answer did this woman want?

'And supposing, my dear, you were not in love. Then would love-making with a man still give you pleasure?'

Tatiana shook her head indecisively. She took her hands down from her face and bowed her head. The hair fell down on either side in a heavy curtain. She was trying to think, to be helpful, but she couldn't imagine such a situation. She supposed . . . 'I suppose it would depend on the man, Comrade Colonel.'

'That is a sensible answer, my dear.' Rosa Klebb opened a drawer in the table. She took out a photograph and slipped it across to the girl. 'What about this man, for instance?'

Tatiana drew the photograph cautiously towards her as if it might catch fire. She looked down warily at the handsome, ruthless face. She tried to imagine . . . 'I cannot tell, Comrade Colonel. He is good-looking. Perhaps if he was gentle . . .' She pushed the photograph anxiously away from her.

'No, keep it, my dear. Put it up beside your bed and think of this man. You will learn more about him later in your new work. And now,' the eyes glittered behind the square panes of glass, 'would you like to know what your new work is to be? The task for which you have been chosen from all the girls in Russia?'

'Yes, indeed, Comrade Colonel.' Tatiana looked obediently across at the intent face that was now pointing at her like a gun-dog.

The wet, rubbery lips parted enticingly. 'It is a simple, delightful duty you have been chosen for, Comrade Corporal—a real labour of love, as we say. It is a matter of falling in love. That is all. Nothing else. Just falling in love with this man.'

'But who is he? I don't even know him.'

Rosa Klebb's mouth revelled. This would give the silly chit of a girl something to think about.

'He is an English spy.'

'Bogou moiou!' Tatiana clapped a hand over her mouth as much to stifle the use of God's name as from terror. She sat, tense with the shock, and gazed at Rosa Klebb through wide, slightly drunk eyes.

'Yes,' said Rosa Klebb, pleased with the effect of her words. 'He is an English spy. Perhaps the most famous of them all. And from now on you are in love with him. So you had better get used to the idea. And no silliness, Comrade. We must be serious. This is an important State matter for which you have been chosen as the instrument. So no nonsense, please. Now for some practical details.' Rosa Klebb stopped. She said sharply, 'And take your hand away from your silly face. And stop looking like a frightened cow. Sit up in your chair and pay attention. Or it will be the worse for you. Understood?'

'Yes, Comrade Colonel.' Tatiana quickly straightened her back and sat up with her hands in her lap as if she was back at the Security Officers' School. Her mind was in a ferment, but this was no time for personal things. Her whole training told her that this was an operation for the State. She was now working for her country. Somehow she had come to be chosen for an important *konspiratsia*. As an officer in the M.G.B., she must do her duty and do it well. She listened carefully and with her whole professional attention.

'For the moment,' Rosa Klebb put on her official voice, 'I will be brief. You will hear more later. For the next few weeks you will be most carefully trained for this operation until you know exactly what to do in all contingencies. You will be taught certain foreign customs. You will be equipped with beautiful clothes. You will be instructed in all the arts of allurement. Then you will be sent to a foreign country, somewhere in Europe. There you will meet this man. You will seduce him. In this matter you will have no silly compunctions. Your body belongs to the State. Since your birth, the State has nourished it. Now your body must work for the State. Is that understood?'

'Yes, Comrade Colonel.' The logic was inescapable.

'You will accompany this man to England. There, you will no doubt be questioned. The questioning will be easy. The English do not use harsh methods. You will give such answers as you can without endangering the State. We will supply you with certain answers which we would like to be given. You will probably be sent to Canada. That is where the English send a certain category of foreign prisoner. You will be rescued and brought back to Moscow.' Rosa Klebb peered at the girl. She seemed to be accepting all this without question. 'You see, it is a comparatively simple matter. Have you any questions at this stage?'

'What will happen to the man, Comrade Colonel?'

'That is a matter of indifference to us. We shall simply use him as a means to introduce you into England. The object of the operation is to give false information to the British. We shall, of course, Comrade, be very glad to have your own impressions of life in England. The reports of a highly trained and intelligent girl such as yourself will be of great value to the State.'

'Really, Comrade Colonel!' Tatiana felt important. Suddenly it all sounded exciting. If only she could do it well. She would assuredly do her very best. But supposing she could not make the English spy love her. She looked again at the photograph. She put her head on one side. It was an attractive face. What were these 'arts of allurement' that the woman had talked about? What could they be? Perhaps they would help.

Satisfied, Rosa Klebb got up from the table. 'And now we can relax, my dear. Work is over for the night. I will go and tidy up and we will have a friendly chat together. I shan't be a moment. Eat up those chocolates or they will go to waste.' Rosa Klebb made a vague gesture of the hand and disappeared with a preoccupied look into the next room.

Tatiana sat back in her chair. So that was what it was all about! It really wasn't so bad after all. What a relief! And what an honour to have been chosen. How silly to have been so frightened! Naturally the great leaders of the State would not allow harm to come to an innocent citizen who worked hard and had no black marks on her *zapiska*. Suddenly she felt immensely grateful to the father-figure that was the State, and proud that she would now have a chance to repay some of her debt. Even the Klebb woman wasn't really so bad after all.

Tatiana was still cheerfully reviewing the situation when the bedroom door opened and 'the Klebb woman' appeared in the opening. 'What do you think of this, my dear?' Colonel Klebb opened her dumpy arms and twirled on her toes like a mannequin. She struck a pose with one arm outstretched and the other arm crooked at her waist.

Tatiana's mouth had fallen open. She shut it quickly. She searched for something to say.

Colonel Klebb of SMERSH was wearing a semi-transparent nightgown in orange *crêpe de chine*. It had scallops of the same material round the low square neckline and scallops at the wrists of the broadly flounced sleeves. Underneath could be seen a brassière consisting of two large pink satin roses. Below, she wore old-fashioned knickers of pink satin with elastic above the knees. One dimpled knee, like a yellowish coconut, appeared thrust forward between the half open folds of the nightgown in the classic stance of the modeller. The feet were enclosed in pink satin slippers with pompoms of ostrich feathers. Rosa Klebb had taken off her spectacles and her naked face was now thick with mascara and rouge and lipstick.

She looked like the oldest and ugliest whore in the world.

Tatiana stammered, 'It is very pretty.'

'Isn't it,' twittered the woman. She went over to a broad couch in the corner of the room. It was covered with a garish piece of peasant tapestry. At the back, against the wall, were rather grimy satin cushions in pastel colours.

With a squeak of pleasure, Rosa Klebb threw herself down in the caricature of a Recamier pose. She reached up an arm and turned on a pink shaded table-lamp whose stem was a naked woman in sham Lalique glass. She patted the couch beside her.

'Turn out the top light, my dear. The switch is by the door. Then come and sit beside me. We must get to know each other better.'

Tatiana walked to the door. She switched off the top light. Her hand dropped decisively to the door knob. She turned it and opened the door and stepped coolly out into the corridor. Suddenly her nerve broke. She banged the door shut behind her and ran wildly off down the corridor with her hands over her ears against the pursuing scream that never came.

CHAPTER 10

The Fuse Burns

It was the morning of the next day.

Colonel Klebb sat at her desk in the roomy office that was her headquarters in the underground basement of SMERSH. It was more an operations room than an office. One wall was completely papered with a map of the Western Hemisphere. The opposite wall was covered with the Eastern Hemisphere. The opposite wall was covered with the Eastern Hemisphere. Behind her desk and within reach of her left hand, a Telekrypton occasionally chattered out a signal *en clair,* duplicating another machine in the Cipher Department under the tall radio masts on the roof of the building. From time to time, when Colonel Klebb thought of it, she tore off the lengthening strip of tape and read through the signals. This was a formality. If anything important happened, her telephone would ring. Every agent of SMERSH throughout the world was controlled from this room, and it was a vigilant and iron control.

The heavy face looked sullen and dissipated. The chicken-skin under the eyes was pouched and the whites of the eyes were veined with red.

One of the three telephones at her side purred softly. She picked up the receiver. 'Send him in.'

She turned to Kronsteen who sat, picking his teeth thoughtfully with an opened paper clip, in an armchair up against the left-hand wall, under the toe of Africa.

'Granitsky.'

Kronsteen slowly turned his head and looked at the door.

Red Grant came in and closed the door softly behind him. He walked up to the desk and stood looking down, obediently, almost hungrily, into the eyes of his Commanding Officer. Kronsteen thought that he looked like a powerful mastiff, waiting to be fed.

Rosa Klebb surveyed him coldly. 'Are you fit and ready for work?'

'Yes, Comrade Colonel.'

'Let's have a look at you. Take off your clothes.'

Red Grant showed no surprise. He took off his coat and, after looking around for somewhere to put it, dropped it on the floor. Then, unselfconsciously, he took off the rest of his clothes and kicked off his shoes. The great red-brown body with its golden hair lit up the drab room. Grant stood relaxed, his hands held loosely at his sides and one knee bent slightly forward, as if he was posing for an art class.

Rosa Klebb got to her feet and came round the desk. She studied the body minutely, prodding here, feeling there, as if she was buying a horse. She went behind the man and continued her minute inspection. Before she came back in front of him, Kronsteen saw her slip something out of her jacket pocket and fit it into her hand. There was a glint of metal.

The woman came round and stood close up to the man's gleaming stomach, her right arm behind her back. She held his eyes in hers.

Suddenly, with terrific speed and the whole weight of her shoulder behind the blow, she whipped her right fist, loaded with a heavy brass knuckle-duster, round and exactly into the solar plexus of the man.

Whuck!

Grant let out a snort of surprise and pain. His knees

gave slightly, and then straightened. For a flash the eyes closed tight with agony. Then they opened again and glared redly down into the cold yellow probing eyes behind the square glasses. Apart from an angry flush on the skin just below the breast bone, Grant showed no ill effects from a blow that would have sent any normal man writhing to the ground.

Rosa Klebb smiled grimly. She slipped the knuckle-duster back in her pocket and walked to her desk and sat down. She looked across at Kronsteen with a hint of pride. 'At least he is fit enough,' she said.

Kronsteen grunted.

The naked man grinned with sly satisfaction. He brought up one hand and rubbed his stomach.

Rosa Klebb sat back in her chair and watched him thoughtfully. Finally she said, 'Comrade Granitsky, there is work for you. An important task. More important than anything you have attempted. It is a task that will earn you a medal'—Grant's eyes gleamed—'for the target is a difficult and dangerous one. You will be in a foreign country, and alone. Is that clear?'

'Yes, Comrade Colonel.' Grant was excited. Here was a chance for that big step forward. What would the medal be? The Order of Lenin? He listened carefully.

'The target is an English spy. You would like to kill an English spy?'

'Very much indeed, Comrade Colonel.' Grant's enthusiasm was genuine. He asked nothing better than to kill an Englishman. He had accounts to settle with the bastards.

'You will need many weeks of training and preparation. On this assignment you will be operating in the guise of an English agent. Your manners and appearance are uncouth. You will have to learn at least some of the tricks,' the voice sneered, 'of a *chentleman.* You will be placed in the hands of a certain Englishman we have here. A former *chentleman* of the Foreign Office in London. It will be his task to make you pass as some sort of an English spy. They employ many different kinds of men. It should not be difficult. And you will have to learn many other things. The operation will be at the end of August, but you will start your training at once. There is much to be done. Put on your clothes and report back to the A.D.C. Understood?'

'Yes, Comrade Colonel.' Grant knew not to ask any questions. He scrambled into his clothes, indifferent to the woman's eyes on him, and walked over to the door, buttoning his jacket. He turned. 'Thank you, Comrade Colonel.'

Rosa Klebb was writing up her note of the interview. She didn't answer or look up and Grant went out and closed the door softly behind him.

The woman threw down her pen and sat back.

'And now, Comrade Kronsteen. Are there any points to discuss before we put the full machinery in motion? I should mention that the Praesidium has approved the target and ratified the death warrant. I have reported the broad lines of your plan to Comrade General Grubozaboyschikov. He is in agreement. The detailed execution has been left entirely in my hands. The combined planning and operations staff has been selected and is waiting to begin work. Have you any last minute thoughts, Comrade?'

Kronsteen sat looking up at the ceiling, the tips of his fingers joined in front of him. He was indifferent to the condescension in the woman's voice. The pulse of concentration beat in his temples.

'This man Granitsky. He is reliable? You can trust him in a foreign country? He will not go private?'

'He has been tested for nearly ten years. He has had many opportunities to escape. He has been watched for signs of itching feet. There has never been a breath of suspicion. The man is in the position of a drug addict. He would no more abandon the Soviet Union than a drugger would abandon the source of his cocaine. He is my top executioner. There is no one better.'

'And this girl, Romanova. She was satisfactory?'

The woman said grudgingly, 'She is very beautiful. She will serve our purpose. She is not a virgin, but she is prudish and sexually unawakened. She will receive instruction. Her English is excellent. I have given her a certain version of her task and its object. She is co-operative. If she should show signs of faltering, I have the addresses of certain relatives, including children. I shall also have the names of her previous lovers. If necessary, it would be explained to her that these people will be hostages until her task is completed. She has an affectionate nature. Such a hint would be sufficient. But I do not anticipate any trouble from her.'

'Romanova. That is the name of a *buivshi*—of one of the former people. It seems odd to be using a Romanov for such a delicate task.'

'Her grandparents were distantly related to the Imperial Family. But she does not frequent *buivshi* circles. Anyway, all our grandparents were former people. There is nothing one can do about it.'

'Our grandparents were not called Romanov,' said Kronsteen dryly. 'However, so long as you are satisfied.' He reflected a moment. 'And this man Bond. Have we discovered his whereabouts?'

'Yes. The M.G.B. English network reports him in London. During the day, he goes to his headquarters. At night he sleeps in his flat in a district of London called Chelsea.'

'That is good. Let us hope he stays there for the next few weeks. That will mean that he is not engaged on some operation. He will be available to go after our bait when they get the scent. Meanwhile,' Kronsteen's dark, pensive eyes continued to examine a particular point on the ceiling, 'I have been studying the suitability of centres abroad. I have decided on Istanbul for the first contact. We have a good *apparat* there. The Secret Service has only a small station. The head of the station is reported to be a good man. He will be liquidated. The centre is conveniently placed for us, with short lines of communication with Bulgaria and the Black Sea. It is relatively far from London. I am working out details of the point of assassination and the means of getting this Bond there, after he has contacted the girl. It will be either in France or very near it. We have excellent leverage on the French press. They will make the most of this kind of story, with its sensational disclosures of sex and espionage. It also remains to be decided when Granitsky shall enter the picture. These are minor details. We must choose the cameramen and the other operatives and move them quietly into Istanbul. There must be no crowding of our *apparat* there, no congestion, no unusual activity. We will warn all departments that wireless traffic with Turkey is to be kept absolutely normal before and during the operation. We don't want the British interceptors smelling a rat. The Cipher Department has agreed that there is no Security objection to handing over the outer case of a Spektor machine. That will be attractive. The machine will go to the Special Devices section. They will handle its preparation.'

Kronsteen stopped talking. His gaze slowly came down from the ceiling. He rose thoughtfully to his feet. He looked across and into the watchful, intent eyes of the woman.

'I can think of nothing else at the moment, Comrade,' he said. 'Many details will come up and have to be settled from day to day. But I think the operation can safely begin.'

'I agree, Comrade. The matter can now go forward. I will issue the necessary directives.' The harsh, authoritative voice unbent. 'I am grateful for your co-operation.'

Kronsteen lowered his head one inch in acknowledgement. He turned and walked softly out of the room.

In the silence, the Telekrypton gave a warning ping and started up its mechanical chatter. Rosa Klebb stirred in her chair and reached for one of the telephones. She dialled a number.

'Operations Room,' said a man's voice.

Rosa Klebb's pale eyes, gazing out across the room, lit on the pink shape on the wall-map that was England. Her wet lips parted.

'Colonel Klebb speaking. The *konspiratsia* against the English spy Bond. The operation will commence forthwith.'

PART **2**

THE EXECUTION

CHAPTER 11

The Soft Life

The blubbery arms of the soft life had Bond round the neck and they were slowly strangling him. He was a man of war and when, for a long period, there was no war, his spirit went into a decline.

In his particular line of business, peace had reigned for nearly a year. And peace was killing him.

At 7.30 on the morning of Thursday, August 12th, Bond awoke in his comfortable flat in the plane-tree'd square off the King's Road and was disgusted to find that he was thoroughly bored with the prospect of the day ahead. Just as, in at least one religion, *accidie* is the first of the cardinal sins, so boredom, and particularly the incredible circumstances of waking up bored, was the only vice Bond utterly condemned.

Bond reached out and gave two rings on the bell to show May, his treasured Scottish housekeeper, that he was ready for breakfast. Then he abruptly flung the single sheet off his naked body and swung his feet to the floor.

There was only one way to deal with boredom—kick

oneself out of it. Bond went down on his hands and did
twenty slow press-ups, lingering over each one so that
his muscles had no rest. When his arms could stand the
pain no longer, he rolled over on his back and, with his
hands at his sides, did the straight leg-lift until his
stomach muscles screamed. He got to his feet and, after
touching his toes twenty times, went over to arm and
chest exercises combined with deep breathing until he
was dizzy. Panting with the exertion, he went into the
big white-tiled bathroom and stood in the glass shower
cabinet under very hot and then cold hissing water for
five minutes.

At last, after shaving and putting on a sleeveless dark
blue Sea Island cotton shirt and navy blue tropical
worsted trousers, he slipped his bare feet into black
leather sandals and went through the bedroom into the
long big-windowed sitting-room with the satisfaction of
having sweated his boredom, at any rate for the time
being, out of his body.

May, an elderly Scotswoman with iron grey hair and a
handsome closed face, came in with the tray and put it
on the table in the bay window together with *The Times*,
the only paper Bond ever read.

Bond wished her good morning and sat down to
breakfast.

'Good morning-s.' (To Bond, one of May's endearing
qualities was that she would call no man 'sir' except—
Bond had teased her about it years before—English
kings and Winston Churchill. As a mark of exceptional
regard, she accorded Bond an occasional hint of an 's'
at the end of a word.)

She stood by the table while Bond folded his paper to
the centre news page.

'Yon man was here again last night about the
Televeesion.'

'What man was that?' Bond looked along the
headlines.

'Yon man that's always coming. Six times he's been
here pestering me since June. After what I said to him
the first time about the sinful thing, you'd think he'd

give up trying to sell us one. By hire purchase, too, if you please!'

'Persistent chaps these salesmen.' Bond put down his paper and reached for the coffee pot.

'I gave him a right piece of my mind last night. Disturbing folk at their supper. Asked him if he'd got any papers—anything to show who he was.'

'I expect that fixed him.' Bond filled his large coffee cup to the brim with black coffee.

'Not a bit of it. Flourished his union card. Said he had every right to earn his living. Electricians Union it was too. They're the Communist one, aren't they-s?'

'Yes, that's right,' said Bond vaguely. His mind sharpened. Was it possible *They* could be keeping an eye on him? He took a sip of the coffee and put the cup down. 'Exactly what did this man say, May?' he asked, keeping his voice indifferent, but looking up at her.

'He said he's selling Televeesion sets on commission in his spare time. And are we sure we don't want one. He says we're one of the only folk in the square that haven't got one. Sees there isn't one of those aerial things on the house, I dare say. He's always asking if you're at home so that he can have a word with you about it. Fancy his cheek! I'm surprised he hasn't thought to catch you coming in or going out. He's always asking if I'm expecting you home. Naturally I don't tell him anything about your movements. Respectable, quiet-spoken body, if he wasn't so persistent.'

Could be, thought Bond. There are many ways of checking up whether the owner's at home or away. A servant's appearance and reactions—a glance through the open door. 'Well, you're wasting your time because he's away,' would be the obvious reception if the flat was empty. Should he tell the Security Section? Bond shrugged his shoulders irritably. What the hell. There was probably nothing in it. Why would *They* be interested in him? And, if there was something in it, Security was quite capable of making him change his flat.

'I expect you've frightened him away this time.' Bond

smiled up at May. 'I should think you've heard the last of him.'

'Yes-s,' said May doubtfully. At any rate she had carried out her orders to tell him if she saw anyone 'hanging about the place'. She bustled off with a whisper of the old-fashioned black uniform she persisted in wearing even in the heat of August.

Bond went back to his breakfast. Normally it was little straws in the wind like this that would start a persistent intuitive ticking in his mind, and, on other days, he would not have been happy until he had solved the problem of the man from the Communist Union who kept on coming to the house. Now, from months of idleness and disuse, the sword was rusty in the scabbard and Bond's mental guard was down.

Breakfast was Bond's favourite meal of the day. When he was stationed in London it was always the same. It consisted of very strong coffee, from De Bry in New Oxford Street, brewed in an American *Chemex*, of which he drank two large cups, black and without sugar. The single egg, in the dark blue egg cup with a gold ring round the top, was boiled for three and a third minutes.

It was a very fresh, speckled brown egg from French *Marans* hens owned by some friend of May in the country. (Bond disliked white eggs and, faddish as he was in many small things, it amused him to maintain that there was such a thing as the perfect boiled egg.) Then there were two thick slices of wholewheat toast, a large pat of deep yellow Jersey butter and three squat glass jars containing Tiptree 'Little Scarlet' strawberry jam; Cooper's Vintage Oxford marmalade and Norwegian Heather Honey from Fortnum's. The coffee pot and the silver on the tray were Queen Anne, and the china was Minton, of the same dark blue and gold and white as the egg cup.

That morning, while Bond finished his breakfast with honey, he pin-pointed the immediate cause of his lethargy and of his low spirits. To begin with, Tiffany Case, his love for so many happy months, had left him and, after final painful weeks during which she had withdrawn to an hotel, had sailed for America at the end of July. He missed her badly and his mind still sheered away from the thought of her. And it was August, and London was hot and stale. He was due for leave, but he had not the energy or the desire to go off alone, or to try and find some temporary replacement for Tiffany to go with him. So he had stayed on in the half-empty headquarters of the Secret Service grinding away at the old routines, snapping at his secretary and rasping his colleagues.

Even M. had finally got impatient with the surly caged tiger on the floor below, and, on Monday of this particular week, he had sent Bond a sharp note appointing him to a Committee of Inquiry under Paymaster Captain Troop. The note said that it was time Bond, as a senior officer in the Service, took a hand in major administrative problems. Anyway, there was no one else available. Headquarters were shorthanded and the 00 Section was quiescent. Bond would pray report that afternoon, at 2.30, to Room 412.

It was Troop, reflected Bond, as he lit his first cigarette of the day, who was the most nagging and immediate cause of his discontent.

In every large business, there is one man who is the office tyrant and bugbear and who is cordially disliked by all the staff. This individual performs an unconsciously important role by acting as a kind of lightning conductor for the usual office hates and fears. In fact, he reduces their disruptive influence by providing them with a common target. The man is usually the general manager, or the Head of Admin. He is that indispensable man who is a watchdog over the small things—petty cash, heat and light, towels and soap in the lavatories, stationery supplies, the canteen, the holiday rota, the punctuality of the staff. He is the one man who has real impact on the office comforts and amenities and whose authority extends into the privacy and personal habits of the men and women of the organization. To want such a job, and to have the necessary qualifications for it, the man must have exactly those qualities which irritate and abrade. He must be parsimonious, observant, prying and meticulous. And he must be a strong disciplinarian and indifferent to opinion. He must be a little dictator. In all well-run businesses there is such a man. In the Secret Service, it is Paymaster Captain Troop, R.N. Retired, Head of Admin., whose job is, in his own words, 'to keep the place shipshape and Bristol fashion'.

It was inevitable that Captain Troop's duties would bring him into conflict with most of the organization, but it was particularly unfortunate that M. could think of no one but Troop to spare as Chairman for this particular Committee.

For this was yet one more of those Committees of Inquiry dealing with the delicate intricacies of the Burgess and Maclean case, and with the lessons that could be learned from it. M. had dreamed it up, five years after he had closed his own particular file on that case, purely as a sop to the Privy Council Inquiry into the Security Services which the Prime Minister had ordered in 1955.

At once Bond had got into a hopeless wrangle with Troop over the employment of 'intellectuals' in the Secret Service.

Perversely, and knowing it would annoy, Bond had put forward the proposition that, if M.I.5 and the Secret Service were to concern themselves seriously with the atom age 'intellectual spy', they must employ a certain number of intellectuals to counter them. 'Retired officers of the Indian Army,' Bond had pronounced, 'can't possibly understand the thought processes of a Burgess or a Maclean. They won't even know such people exist—let alone be in a position to frequent their cliques and get to know their friends and their secrets. Once Burgess and Maclean went to Russia, the only way to make contact with them again and, perhaps when they got tired of Russia, turn them into double agents against the Russians, would have been to send their closest friends to Moscow and Prague and Budapest with orders to wait until one of these chaps crept out of the masonry and made contact. And one of them, probably Burgess, would have been driven to make contact by his loneliness and by his ache to tell his story to someone.[1] But they certainly wouldn't take the risk of revealing themselves to some man with a trench-coat and a cavalry moustache and a beta minus mind.'

'Oh really,' Troop had said with icy calm. 'So you suggest we should staff the organization with long-haired perverts. That's quite an original notion. I thought we were all agreed that homosexuals were about the worst security risk there is. I can't see the Americans handing over many atom secrets to a lot of pansies soaked in scent.'

'All intellectuals aren't homosexual. And many of them are bald. I'm just saying that . . . ,' and so the argument had gone on intermittently through the hearings of the past three days, and the other committee members had ranged themselves more or less with Troop. Now, today, they had to draw up their recommendations and Bond was wondering whether to take the unpopular step of entering a minority report.

How seriously did he feel about the whole question, Bond wondered as, at nine o'clock, he walked out of his flat and down the steps to his car? Was he just being petty and obstinate? Had he constituted himself into a one-man opposition only to give his teeth something to bite into? Was he so bored that he could find nothing better to do than make a nuisance of himself inside his own organization? Bond couldn't make up his mind. He felt restless and indecisive, and, behind it all, there was a nagging disquiet he couldn't put his finger on.

As he pressed the self-starter and the twin exhausts of the Bentley woke to their fluttering growl, a curious bastard quotation slipped from nowhere into Bond's mind.

'Those whom the Gods wish to destroy, they first make bored.'

[1]Written in March 1956. I.F.

CHAPTER 12

A Piece of Cake

As it turned out, Bond never had to make a decision on the Committee's final report.

He had complimented his secretary on a new summer frock, and was half way through the file of signals that had come in during the night, when the red telephone that could only mean M. or his Chief-of-Staff gave its soft, peremptory burr.

Bond picked up the receiver. '007.'

'Can you come up?' It was the Chief-of-Staff.

'M.?'

'Yes. And it looks like a long session. I've told Troop you won't be able to make the Committee.'

'Any idea what it's about?'

The Chief-of-Staff chuckled. 'Well, I have as a matter of fact. But you'd better hear it from him. It'll make you sit up. There's quite a swerve on this one.'

As Bond put on his coat and went out into the corridor, banging the door behind him, he had a feeling of certainty that the starter's gun had fired and that the dog days had come to an end. Even the ride up to the top floor in the lift and the walk down the long quiet corridor to the door of M.'s staff office seemed to be charged with the significance of all those other occasions when the bell of the red telephone had been the signal that had fired him, like a loaded projectile, across the world towards some distant target of M.'s choosing. And the eyes of Miss Moneypenny, M.'s private secretary, had that old look of excitement and secret knowledge as she smiled up at him and pressed the switch on the intercom.

'007's here, sir.'

'Send him in,' said the metallic voice, and the red light of privacy went on above the door.

Bond went through the door and closed it softly behind him. The room was cool, or perhaps it was the venetian blinds that gave an impression of coolness. They threw bars of light and shadow across the dark green carpet up to the edge of the big central desk. There the sunshine stopped so that the quiet figure behind the desk sat in a pool of suffused greenish shade. In the ceiling directly above the desk, a big twin-bladed tropical fan, a recent addition to M.'s room, slowly revolved, shifting the thundery August air that, even high up above the Regent's Park, was heavy and stale after a week of heat-wave.

M. gestured to the chair opposite him across the red leather desk. Bond sat down and looked across into the tranquil, lined sailor's face that he loved, honoured and obeyed.

'Do you mind if I ask you a personal question, James?' M. never asked his staff personal questions and Bond couldn't imagine what was coming.

'No, sir.'

M. picked his pipe out of the big copper ash-tray and began to fill it, thoughtfully watching his fingers at work with the tobacco. He said harshly: 'You needn't answer, but it's to do with your, er, friend, Miss Case. As you know, I don't generally interest myself in these matters, but I did hear that you had been, er, seeing a lot of each other since that diamond business. Even some idea you might be going to get married.' M. glanced up at Bond and then down again. He put the loaded pipe into his mouth and set a match to it. Out of the corner of his mouth, as he drew at the jigging flame, he said: 'Care to tell me anything about it?'

Now what? wondered Bond. Damn these office gossips. He said gruffly, 'Well, sir, we did get on well. And there was some idea we might get married. But then she met some chap in the American Embassy. On the Military Attaché's staff. Marine Corps major. And I gather she's going to marry him. They've both gone back to the States, as a matter of fact. Probably better that way. Mixed marriages aren't often a success. I gather he's a nice enough fellow. Probably suit her better than living in London. She couldn't really settle down here. Fine girl, but she's a bit neurotic. We had too many rows. Probably my fault. Anyway it's over now.'

M. gave one of the brief smiles that lit up his eyes more than his mouth. 'I'm sorry if it went wrong, James,' he said. There was no sympathy in M.'s voice. He disapproved of Bond's 'womanizing', as he called it to himself, while recognizing that his prejudice was the relic of a Victorian upbringing. But, as Bond's chief, the last thing he wanted was for Bond to be permanently tied to one woman's skirts. 'Perhaps it's for the best. Doesn't do to get mixed with neurotic women in this business. They hang on your gun-arm, if you know what I mean. Forgive me for asking about it. Had to know the answer before I told you what's come up. It's a pretty odd business. Be difficult to get you involved if you were on the edge of marrying or anything of that sort.'

Bond shook his head, waiting for the story.

'All right then,' said M. There was a note of relief in his voice. He leant back in his chair and gave several quick pulls on his pipe to get it going. 'This is what's happened. Yesterday there was a long signal from Istanbul. Seems on Tuesday the Head of Station T got an anonymous typewritten message which told him to take a round ticket on the 8 p.m. ferry steamer from the Galata Bridge to the mouth of the Bosphorus and back. Nothing else. Head of T's an adventurous sort of chap, and of course he took the steamer. He stood up for'ard by the rail and waited. After about a quarter of an hour a girl came and stood beside him, a Russian girl, very good-looking, he says, and after they'd talked a bit about the view and so on, she suddenly switched and in the same sort of conversational voice she told him an extraordinary story.'

M. paused to put another match to his pipe. Bond interjected, 'Who is Head of T, sir? I've never worked in Turkey.'

'Man called Kerim, Darko Kerim. Turkish father and English mother. Remarkable fellow. Been Head of T since before the war. One of the best men we've got anywhere. Does a wonderful job. Loves it. Very intelligent and he knows all that part of the world like the back of his hand.' M. dismissed Kerim with a sideways jerk of his pipe. 'Anyway, the girl's story was that she was a Corporal in the M.G.B. Had been in the show since she left school and had just got transferred to the Istanbul centre as a cipher officer. She'd engineered the transfer because she wanted to get out of Russia and come over.'

'That's good,' said Bond. 'Might be useful to have one of their cipher girls. But why does she want to come over?'

M. looked across the table at Bond. 'Because she's in love.' He paused and added mildly, 'She says she's in love with you.'

'In love with *me*?'

'Yes, with you. That's what she says. Her name's Tatiana Romanova. Ever heard of her?'

'Good God, no! I mean, no, sir.' M. smiled at the mixture of expressions on Bond's face. 'But what the hell does she mean? Has she ever met me? How does she know I exist?'

'Well,' said M. 'The whole thing sounds absolutely ridiculous. But it's so crazy that it just might be true. This girl is twenty-four. Ever since she joined the M.G.B. she's been working in their Central Index, the same as our Records. And she's been working in the English section of it. She's been there six years. One of the files she had to deal with was yours.'

'I'd like to see that one,' commented Bond.

'Her story is that she first took a fancy to the photographs they've got of you. Admired your looks and so on.' M.'s mouth turned downwards at the corners as if he had just sucked at a lemon. 'She read up all your cases. Decided that you were the hell of a fellow.'

Bond looked down his nose. M.'s face was non-committal.

'She said you particularly appealed to her because you reminded her of the hero of a book by some Russian fellow called Lermontov. Apparently it was her favourite book. This hero chap liked gambling and spent his whole time getting in and out of scraps. Anyway, you reminded her of him. She says she came to think of nothing else, and one day the idea came to her that if only she could transfer to one of their foreign centres she could get in touch with you and you would come and rescue her.'

'I've never heard such a crazy story, sir. Surely Head of T didn't swallow it.'

'Now wait a moment,' M.'s voice was testy. 'Just don't be in too much of a hurry simply because something's turned up you've never come across before. Suppose you happened to be a film star instead of being in this particular trade. You'd get daft letters from girls all over the world stuffed with Heaven knows what sort of rot about not being able to live without you and so on. Here's a silly girl doing a secretary's job in Moscow. Probably the whole department is staffed by women, like our Records. Not a man in the room to look at, and here she is, faced with your, er, dashing features on a file that's constantly coming up for review. And she gets what I believe they call a 'crush' on these pictures just as secretaries all over the world get crushes on these dreadful faces in the magazines.' M. waved his pipe sideways to indicate his ignorance of these grisly female habits. 'The Lord knows I don't know much about these things, but you must admit that they happen.'

Bond smiled at the appeal for help. 'Well, as a matter of fact, sir, I'm beginning to see there is some sense in it.

There's no reason why a Russian girl shouldn't be just as silly as an English one. But she must have got guts to do what she did. Does Head of T say if she realized the consequences if she was found out?'

'He said she was frightened out of her wits,' said M. 'Spent the whole time on the boat looking round to see if anybody was watching her. But it seems they were the usual peasants and commuters that take these boats, and as it was a late boat there weren't many passengers anyway. But wait a minute. You haven't heard half the story.' M. took a long pull at his pipe and blew a cloud of smoke up towards the slowly turning fan above his head. Bond watched the smoke get caught up in the blades and whirled into nothingness. 'She told Kerim that this passion for you gradually developed into a phobia. She got to hate the sight of Russian men. In time this turned into a dislike of the régime and particularly of the work she was doing for them and, so to speak, against you. So she applied for a transfer abroad, and since her languages were very good— English and French—in due course she was offered Istanbul if she would join the Cipher Department, which meant a cut in pay. To cut a long story short, after six months' training, she got to Istanbul about three weeks ago. Then she sniffed about and soon got hold of the name of our man, Kerim. He's been there so long that everybody in Turkey knows what he does by now. He doesn't mind, and it takes people's eyes off the special men we send in from time to time. There's no harm in having a front man in some of these places. Quite a lot of customers would come to us if they knew where to go and who to talk to.'

Bond commented: 'The public agent often does better than the man who has to spend a lot of time and energy keeping under cover.'

'So she sent Kerim the note. Now she wants to know if he can help her.' M paused and sucked thoughtfully at his pipe. 'Of course Kerim's first reactions were exactly the same as yours, and he fished around looking for a trap. But he simply couldn't see what the Russians could gain from sending this girl over to us. All this time the steamer was getting further and further up the Bosphorus and soon it would be turning to come back to Istanbul. And the girl got more and more desperate as Kerim went on trying to break down her story. Then,' M.'s eyes glittered softly across at Bond, 'came the clincher.'

That glitter in M.'s eyes, thought Bond. How well he knew those moments when M.'s cold grey eyes betrayed their excitement and their greed.

'She had a last card to play. And she knew it was the ace of trumps. If she could come over to us, she would bring her cipher machine with her. It's the brand new Spektor machine. The thing we'd give our eyes to have.'

'God,' said Bond softly, his mind boggling at the immensity of the prize. The Spektor! The machine that would allow them to decipher the Top Scret traffic of all. To have that, even if its loss was immediately discovered and the settings changed, or the machine taken out of service in Russian embassies and spy centres all over the world, would be a priceless victory. Bond didn't know much about cryptography, and, for security's sake, in case he was ever captured, wished to know as little as possible about its secrets, but at least he knew that, in the Russian secret service, loss of the Spektor would be counted a major disaster.

Bond was sold. At once he accepted all M.'s faith in the girl's story, however crazy it might be. For a Russian to bring them this gift, and take the appalling risk of bringing it, could only mean an act of desperation—of desperate infatuation if you liked. Whether the girl's story was true or not, the stakes were too high to turn down the gamble.

'You see, 007?' said M. softly. It was not difficult to read Bond's mind from the excitement in his eyes. 'You see what I mean?'

Bond hedged. 'But did she say how she could do it?'

'Not exactly. But Kerim says she was absolutely definite. Some business about night duty. Apparently she's on duty alone certain nights of the week and sleeps on a camp bed in the office. She seemed to have no doubts about it, although she realized that she would be shot out of hand if anyone even dreamed of her plan. She was even worried about Kerim reporting all this back to me. Made him promise he would encode the signal himself and send it on a one-time-only pad and keep no copy. Naturally he did as she asked. Directly she mentioned the Spektor, Kerim knew he might be on to the most important coup that's come our way since the war.'

'What happened then, sir?'

'The steamer was coming up to a place called Orta-koy. She said she was going to get off there. Kerim promised to get a signal off that night. She refused to make any arrangements for staying in touch. Just said that she would keep her end of the bargain if we would keep ours. She said good night and mixed in the crowd going down the gangplank and that was the last Kerim saw of her.'

M. suddenly leant forward in his chair and looked hard at Bond. 'But of course he couldn't *guarantee* that we would make the bargain with her.'

Bond said nothing. He thought he could guess what was coming.

'This girl will only do these things on one condition.' M.'s eyes narrowed until they were fierce, significant slits. 'That you go out to Istanbul and bring her and the machine back to England.'

Bond shrugged his shoulders. That presented no difficulties. But . . . He looked candidly back at M. 'Should be a piece of cake, sir. As far as I can see there's only one snag. She's only seen photographs of me and read a lot of exciting stories. Suppose that when she sees me in the flesh, I don't come up to her expectations.'

'That's where the work comes in,' said M. grimly. 'That's why I asked those questions about Miss Case. It's up to you to see that you *do* come up to her expectations.'

CHAPTER 13

'B.E.A. Takes You There...'

The four small, square-ended propellers turned slowly, one by one, and became four whizzing pools. The low hum of the turbo-jets rose to a shrill smooth whine. The quality of the noise, and the complete absence of vibration, were different from the stuttering roar and straining horsepower of all other aircraft Bond had flown in. As the Viscount wheeled easily out to the shimmering east-west runway of London Airport, Bond felt as if he was sitting in an expensive mechanical toy.

There was a pause as the chief pilot gunned up the four turbo-jets into a banshee scream and then, with a jerk of released brakes, the 10.30 B.E.A. Flight 130 to Rome, Athens and Istanbul gathered speed and hurtled down the runway and up into a quick, easy climb.

In ten minutes they had reached 20,000 feet and were heading south along the wide air-channel that takes the Mediterranean traffic from England. The scream of the jets died to a low, drowsy whistle. Bond unfastened his seat-belt and lit a cigarette. He reached for the slim, expensive-looking attaché case on the floor beside him and took out *The Mask of Dimitrios* by Eric Ambler and put the case, which was very heavy in spite of its size, on the seat beside him. He thought how surprised the ticket clerk at London Airport would have been if she had weighed the case instead of letting it go unchecked as an 'overnight bag'. And if, in their turn, Customs had been intrigued by its weight, how interested they would have been when it was slipped under the Inspectoscope.

Q Branch had put together this smart-looking little bag, ripping out the careful handiwork of Swaine and Adeney to pack fifty rounds of .25 ammunition, in two flat rows, between the leather and the lining of the spine. In each of the innocent sides there was a flat throwing knife, built by Wilkinson's, the sword makers, and the tops of their handles were concealed cleverly by the stitching at the corners. Despite Bond's efforts to laugh them out of it, Q's craftsmen had insisted on building a hidden compartment into the handle of the case, which, by pressure at a certain point, would deliver a cyanide death-pill into the palm of his hand. (Directly he had taken delivery of the case, Bond had washed this pill down the lavatory.) More important was the thick tube of Palmolive shaving cream in the otherwise guileless spongebag. The whole top of this unscrewed to reveal the silencer for the Beretta, packed in cotton wool. In case hard cash was needed, the lid of the attaché case contained fifty golden sovereigns. These could be poured out by slipping sideways one ridge of welting.

The complicated bag of tricks amused Bond, but he also had to admit that, despite its eight-pound weight, the bag was a convenient way of carrying the tools of his trade, which otherwise would have to be concealed about his body.

Only a dozen miscellaneous passengers were on the plane. Bond smiled at the thought of Loelia Ponsonby's horror if she knew that that made the load thirteen. The day before, when he had left M. and had gone back to his office to arrange the details of his flight, his secretary had protested violently at the idea of his travelling on Friday the thirteenth.

'But it's always best to travel on the thirteenth,' Bond had explained patiently. 'There are practically no passengers and it's more comfortable and you get better service. I always choose the thirteenth when I can.'

'Well,' she had said resignedly, 'it's your funeral. But I shall spend the day worrying about you. And for heaven's sake don't go walking under ladders or anything silly this afternoon. You oughtn't to overplay your luck like this. I don't know what you're going to Turkey for, and I don't want to know. But I have a feeling in my bones.'

'Ah, those beautiful bones!' Bond had teased her. 'I'll take them out to dinner the night I get back.'

'You'll do nothing of the sort,' she had said coldly. Later she had kissed him goodbye with a sudden warmth, and for the hundredth time Bond had wondered why he bothered with other women when the most darling of them all was his secretary.

The plane sang steadily on above the endless sea of whipped-cream clouds that looked solid enough to land on if the engines failed. The clouds broke up and a distant blue haze, far away to their left, was Paris. For an hour they flew high over the burned-up fields of France until, after Dijon, the land turned from a pale to a darker green as it sloped up into the Juras.

Lunch came. Bond put aside his book and the thoughts that kept coming between him and the printed page, and, while he ate, he gazed down at the cool mirror of the Lake of Geneva. As the pine forests began to climb towards the snow patches between the beautifully scoured teeth of the Alps, he remembered early skiing holidays. The plane skirted the great eye-tooth of Mont Blanc, a few hundred yards to port, and Bond looked down at the dirty grey elephant's skin of the glaciers and saw himself again, a young man in his teens, with the leading end of the rope round his waist, bracing himself against the top of a rock-chimney on the Aiguilles Rouges as his two companions from the

University of Geneva inched up the smooth rock towards him.

And now? Bond smiled wryly at his reflection in the Perspex as the plane swung out of the mountains and over the grosgrained terazza of Lombardy. If that young James Bond came up to him in the street and talked to him, would he recognize the clean, eager youth that had been him at seventeen? And what would that youth think of him, the secret agent, the older James Bond? Would he recognize himself beneath the surface of this man who was tarnished with years of treachery and ruthlessness and fear—this man with the cold arrogant eyes and the scar down his cheek and the flat bulge beneath his left armpit? If the youth did not recognize him what would his judgement be? What would he think of Bond's present assignment? What would he think of the dashing secret agent who was off across the world in a new and most romantic role—to pimp for England?

Bond put the thought of his dead youth out of his mind. Never job backwards. What-might-have-been was a waste of time. Follow your fate, and be satisfied with it, and be glad not to be a second-hand motor salesman, or a yellow-press journalist, pickled in gin and nicotine, or a cripple—or dead.

Gazing down on the sun-baked sprawl of Genoa and the gentle blue waters of the Mediterranean, Bond closed his mind to the past and focused it on the immediate future—on this business, as he sourly described it to himself, of 'pimping for England'.

For that, however else one might like to describe it, was what he was on his way to do—to seduce, and seduce very quickly, a girl whom he had never seen before, whose name he had heard yesterday for the first time. And all the while, however attractive she was—and Head of T had described her as 'very beautiful'—Bond's whole mind would have to be not on what she was, but what she had—the dowry she was bringing with her. It would be like trying to marry a rich woman for her money. Would he be able to act the part? Perhaps he could make the right faces and say the right things, but would his body dissociate itself from his secret thoughts and effectively make the love he would declare? How did men behave credibly in bed when their whole minds were focused on a woman's bank balance? Perhaps there was an erotic stimulus in the notion that one was ravaging a sack of gold. But a cipher machine?

Elba passed below them and the plane slid into its fifty-mile glide towards Rome. Half an hour among the jabbering loudspeakers of Ciampino Airport, time to drink two excellent Americanos, and they were on their way again, flying steadily down towards the toe of Italy, and Bond's mind went back to sifting the minutest details of the rendezvous that was drawing closer at three hundred miles an hour.

Was it all a complicated M.G.B. plot of which he couldn't find the key? Was he walking into some trap that not even the tortuous mind of M. could fathom? God knew M. was worried about the possibility of such a trap. Every conceivable angle of the evidence, for and against, had been scrutinized—not only by M., but also by a full-dress operations meeting of Heads of Sections that had worked all through the afternoon and evening before. But, which ever way the case had been examined, no one had been able to suggest what the Russians might get out of it. They might want to kidnap Bond and interrogate him. But why Bond? He was an operating agent, unconcerned with the general working of the Service, carrying in his head nothing of use to the Russians except the details of his current duty and a certain amount of background information that could not possibly be vital. Or they might want to kill Bond, as an act of revenge. Yet he had not come up against them for two years. If they wanted to kill him, they had only to shoot him in the streets of London, or in his flat, or put a bomb in his car.

Bond's thoughts were interrupted by the stewardess. 'Fasten your seat-belts, please.' As she spoke the plane

dropped sickeningly and soared up again with an ugly
note of strain in the scream of the jets. The sky outside
was suddenly black. Rain hammered on the windows.
There came a blinding flash of blue and white light and
a crash as if an anti-aircraft shell had hit them, and the
plane heaved and bucketed in the belly of the electric
storm that had ambushed them out of the mouth of the
Adriatic.

Bond smelt the smell of danger. It is a real smell,
something like the mixture of sweat and electricity you
get in an amusement arcade. Again the lightning flung
its hands across the windows. Crash! It felt as if they
were the centre of the thunder clap. Suddenly the plane
seemed incredibly small and frail. Thirteen passengers!
Friday the Thirteenth! Bond thought of Loelia Ponsonby's words and his hands on the arms of his chair
felt wet. How old is this plane, he wondered? How
many flying hours has it done? Had the death-watch
beetle of metal fatigue got into the wings? How much of
their strength had it eaten away? Perhaps he wouldn't
get to Istanbul after all. Perhaps a plummeting crash
into the Gulf of Corinth was going to be the destiny he
had been scanning philosophically only an hour before.

In the centre of Bond was a hurricane-room, the kind
of citadel found in old-fashioned houses in the tropics.
These rooms are small, strongly built cells in the heart
of the house, in the middle of the ground floor and
sometimes dug down into its foundations. To this cell
the owner and his family retire if the storm threatens to
destroy the house, and they stay there until the danger is
past. Bond went to his hurricane-room only when the
situation was beyond his control and no other possible
action could be taken. Now he retired to this citadel,
closed his mind to the hell of noise and violent
movement, and focused on a single stitch in the back
of the seat in front of him, waiting with slackened
nerves for whatever fate had decided for B.E.A. Flight
No. 130.

Almost at once it got lighter in the cabin. The rain
stopped crashing on the Perspex window and the noise

of the jets settled back into their imperturbable whistle. Bond opened the door of his hurricane-room and stepped out. He slowly turned his head and looked curiously out of the window and watched the tiny shadow of the plane hastening far below across the quiet waters of the Gulf of Corinth. He heaved a deep sigh and reached into his hip-pocket for his gunmetal cigarette case. He was pleased to see his hands were dead steady as he took out his lighter and lit one of the Morland cigarettes with the three gold rings. Should he tell Lil that perhaps she had almost been right? He decided that if he could find a rude enough postcard in Istanbul he would.

The day outside faded through the colours of a dying dolphin and Mount Hymettus came at them, blue in the dusk. Down over the twinkling sprawl of Athens and then the Viscount was wheeling across the standard concrete air-strip with its drooping windsock and the notices in the strange dancing letters Bond had hardly seen since school.

Bond climbed out of the plane with the handful of pale, silent passengers and walked across to the transit lounge and up to the bar. He ordered a tumbler of Ouzo and drank it down and chased it with a mouthful of ice water. There was a strong bite under the sickly anisette taste and Bond felt the drink light a quick, small fire down his throat and in his stomach. He put down his glass and ordered another.

By the time the loudspeakers called him out again it was dusk and the half moon rode clear and high above the lights of the town. The air was soft with evening and the smell of flowers and there was the steady pulse-beat of the cicadas—zing-a-zing-a-zing—and the distant sound of a man singing. The voice was clear and sad and the song had a note of lament. Near the airport a dog barked excitedly at an unknown human smell. Bond suddenly realized that he had come into the East where the guard-dog howls all night. For some reason the realization sent a pang of pleasure and excitement into his heart.

They had only a ninety-minute flight to Istanbul, across the dark Aegean and the Sea of Marmara. An excellent dinner, with two dry Martinis and a half-bottle of Calvet claret, put Bond's reservations about flying on Friday the thirteenth, and his worries about his assignment, out of his mind and substituted a mood of pleased anticipation.

Then they were there and the plane's four propellers wheeled to a stop outside the fine modern airport of Yesilkoy, an hour's drive from Istanbul. Bond said goodbye and thank you for a good flight to the stewardess, carried the heavy little attaché case through the passport check into the customs, and waited for his suitcase to come off the plane.

So these dark, ugly, neat little officials were the modern Turks. He listened to their voices, full of broad vowels and quiet sibilants and modified u-sounds, and he watched the dark eyes that belied the soft, polite voices. They were bright, angry, cruel eyes that had only lately come down from the mountains. Bond thought he knew the history of those eyes. They were eyes that had been trained for centuries to watch over sheep and decipher small movements on far horizons. They were eyes that kept the knife-hand in sight without seeming to, that counted the grains of meal and the small fractions of coin and noted the flicker of the merchant's fingers. They were hard, untrusting, jealous eyes. Bond didn't take to them.

Outside the customs, a tall rangy man with drooping black moustaches stepped out of the shadows. He wore a smart dust-coat and a chauffeur's cap. He saluted and, without asking Bond his name, took his suitcase and led the way over to a gleaming aristocrat of a car—an old black basket-work Rolls-Royce coupé-deville that Bond guessed must have been built for some millionaire of the '20s.

When the car was gliding out of the airport, the man turned and said politely over his shoulder, in excellent English 'Kerim Bey thought you would prefer to rest tonight, sir. I am to call for you at nine tomorrow morning. What hotel are you staying at, sir?'

'The Kristal Palas.'

'Very good, sir.' The car sighed off down the wide modern road.

Behind them, in the dappled shadows of the airport parking place, Bond vaguely heard the crackle of a motor scooter starting up. The sound meant nothing to him and he settled back to enjoy the drive.

CHAPTER 14

Darko Kerim

James Bond awoke early in his dingy room at the Kristal Palas on the heights of Pera and absent-mindedly reached down a hand to explore a sharp tickle on the outside of his right thigh. Something had bitten him during the night. Irritably he scratched the spot. He might have expected it.

When he had arrived the night before, to be greeted by a surly night-concierge in trousers and a collarless shirt, and had briefly inspected the entrance hall with the fly-blown palms in copper pots, and the floor and walls of discoloured Moorish tiles, he had known what he was in for. He had half thought of going to another hotel. Inertia, and a perverse liking for the sleazy romance that clings to old-fashioned Continental hotels, had decided him to stay, and he had signed in and followed the man up to the third floor in the old rope-and-gravity lift.

His room, with its few sticks of aged furniture and an iron bedstead, was what he had expected. He only looked to see if there were the blood spots of squashed bugs on the wallpaper behind the bedhead before dismissing the concierge.

He had been premature. When he went into the bathroom and turned on the hot tap it gave a deep sigh, then a deprecating cough, and finally ejected a small centipede into the basin. Bond morosely washed the centipede away with the thin stream of brownish water from the cold tap. So much, he had reflected wryly, for choosing an hotel because its name had amused him and because he had wanted to get away from the soft life of big hotels.

But he had slept well, and now, with the reservation that he must buy some insecticide, he decided to forget about his comforts and get on with the day.

Bond got out of bed, drew back the heavy red plush curtains and leant on the iron balustrade and looked out over one of the most famous views in the world—on his right the still waters of the Golden Horn, on his left the dancing waves of the unsheltered Bosphorus, and, in between, the tumbling roofs, soaring minarets and crouching mosques of Pera. After all, his choice had been good. The view made up for many bedbugs and much discomfort.

For ten minutes Bond stood and gazed out across the sparkling water barrier between Europe and Asia, then he turned back into the room, now bright with sunshine, and telephoned for his breakfast. His English was not understood, but his French at last got through. He turned on a cold bath and shaved patiently with cold water and hoped that the exotic breakfast he had ordered would not be a fiasco.

He was not disappointed. The yoghourt, in a blue china bowl, was deep yellow and with the consistency of thick cream. The green figs, ready peeled, were bursting with ripeness, and the Turkish coffee was jet black and with the burned taste that showed it had been freshly ground. Bond ate the delicious meal on a table drawn up beside the open window. He watched the steamers and the caïques criss-crossing the two seas spread out before him and wondered about Kerim and what fresh news there might be.

Punctually at nine, the elegant Rolls came for him and took him through Taksim square and down the crowded Istiklal and out of Asia. The thick black smoke of the waiting steamers, badged with the graceful crossed anchors of the Merchant Marine, streamed across the first span of the Galata Bridge and hid the other shore towards which the Rolls nosed forward through the bicycles and trams, the well-bred snort of the ancient bulb horn just keeping the pedestrians from under its wheels. Then the way was clear and the old European section of Istanbul glittered at the end of the broad half-mile of bridge with the slim minarets lancing up into the sky and the domes of the mosques, crouching at their feet, looking like big firm breasts. It should have been the Arabian Nights, but to Bond, seeing it first above the tops of trams and above the great scars of modern advertising along the river frontage, it seemed a once beautiful theatre-set that modern Turkey had thrown aside in favour of the steel and concrete flat-iron of the Istanbul-Hilton Hotel, blankly glittering behind him on the heights of Pera.

Across the bridge, the car nosed to the right down a narrow cobbled street parallel with the waterfront and stopped outside a high wooden porte-cochère.

A tough-looking watchman with a chunky, smiling face, dressed in frayed khaki, came out of a porter's lodge and saluted. He opened the car door and gestured for Bond to follow him. He led the way back into his lodge and through a door into a small courtyard with a neatly raked gravel parterre. In the centre was a gnarled eucalyptus tree at whose foot two white ring-doves were pecking about. The noise of the town was a distant rumble and it was quiet and peaceful.

They walked across the gravel and through another small door and Bond found himself at one end of a great vaulted godown with high circular windows through which dusty bars of sunshine slanted across a vista of bundles and bales of merchandise. There was a cool, musty scent of spices and coffee and, as Bond followed the watchman down the central passage-way, a sudden strong wave of mint.

At the end of the long warehouse was a raised platform enclosed by a balustrade. On it half a dozen young men and girls sat on high stools and wrote busily in fat, old-fashioned ledgers. It was like a Dickensian counting-house and Bond noticed that each high desk had a battered abacus beside the inkpot. Not one of the clerks looked up as Bond walked between them, but a tall, swarthy man with a lean face and unexpected blue eyes came forward from the furthest desk and took delivery of him from the watchman. He smiled warmly at Bond, showing a set of extremely white teeth, and led him to the back of the platform. He knocked on a fine mahogany door with a Yale lock and, without waiting for an answer, opened it and let Bond in and closed the door softly behind him.

'Ah, my friend. Come in. Come in.' A very large man in a beautifully cut cream tussore suit got up from a mahogany desk and came to meet him, holding out his hand.

A hint of authority behind the loud friendly voice reminded Bond that this was the Head of Station T, and that Bond was in another man's territory and juridically under his command. It was no more than a point of etiquette, but a point to remember.

Darko Kerim had a wonderfully warm dry handclasp. It was a strong Western handful of operative fingers—not the banana skin handshake of the East that makes you want to wipe your fingers on your coat-tails. And the big hand had a coiled power that said it could easily squeeze your hand tighter and tighter until finally it cracked your bones.

Bond was six feet tall, but this man was at least two inches taller and he gave the impression of being twice as broad and twice as thick as Bond. Bond looked up into two wide apart, smiling blue eyes in a large smooth brown face with a broken nose. The eyes were watery and veined with red, like the eyes of a hound who lies too often too close to the fire. Bond recognized them as the eyes of furious dissipation.

The face was vaguely gipsy-like in its fierce pride and in the heavy curling black hair and crooked nose, and the effect of a vagabond soldier of fortune was heightened by the small gold ring Kerim wore in the lobe of his right ear. It was a startlingly dramatic face, vital, cruel and debauched, but what one noticed more than its drama was that it radiated life. Bond thought he had never seen so much vitality and warmth in a human face. It was like being close to the sun, and Bond let go the strong dry hand and smiled back at Kerim with a friendliness he rarely felt for a stranger.

'Thanks for sending the car to meet me last night.'

'Ha!' Kerim was delighted. 'You must thank our friends too. You were met by both sides. They always follow my car when it goes to the airport.'

'Was it a Vespa or a Lambretta?'

'You noticed? A Lambretta. They have a whole fleet of them for their little men, the men I call "The Faceless Ones". They look so alike, we have never managed to sort them out. Little gangsters, mostly stinking Bulgars, who do their dirty work for them. But I expect this one kept well back. They don't get up close to the Rolls any more since the day my chauffeur stopped suddenly and then reversed back as hard as he could. Messed up the paintwork and bloodied the bottom of the chassis but it taught the rest of them manners.'

Kerim went to his chair and waved to an identical one across the desk. He pushed over a flat white box of cigarettes and Bond sat down and took a cigarette and lit it. It was the most wonderful cigarette he had ever tasted—the mildest and sweetest of Turkish tobacco in a slim long oval tube with an elegant gold crescent.

While Kerim was fitting one into a long nicotine-stained ivory holder, Bond took the opportunity to glance round the room, which smelled strongly of paint and varnish as if it had just been redecorated.

It was big and square and panelled in polished mahogany, except behind Kerim's chair where a length of Oriental tapestry hung down from the ceiling and gently moved in the breeze as if there was an open window behind it. But this seemed unlikely as light came from three circular windows high up in the walls. Perhaps, behind the tapestry, was a balcony looking out over the Golden Horn, whose waves Bond could hear lapping at the walls below. In the centre of the right-hand wall hung a gold-framed reproduction of Annigoni's portrait of the Queen. Opposite, also imposingly framed, was Cecil Beaton's wartime photograph of Winston Churchill looking up from his desk in the Cabinet Offices like a contemptuous bulldog. A broad bookcase stood against one wall and, opposite, a comfortable padded leather settee. In the centre of the room the big desk winked with polished brass handles. On the littered desk were three silver photograph frames, and Bond caught a sideways view of the copperplate script of two Mentions in Dispatches and the Military Division of the O.B.E.

Kerim lit his cigarette. He jerked his head back at the piece of tapestry. 'Our friends paid me a visit yesterday,' he said casually. 'Fixed a limpet bomb on the wall outside. Timed the fuse to catch me at my desk. By good luck, I had taken a few minutes off to relax on the couch over there with a young Rumanian girl who still believes that a man will tell secrets in exchange for love. The bomb went off at a vital moment. I refused to be disturbed, but I fear the experience was too much for the girl. When I released her, she had hysterics. I'm afraid she had decided that my love-making is altogether too violent.' He waved his cigarette holder apologetically. 'But it was a rush to get the room put to rights in time for your visit. New glass for the windows and my pictures, and the place stinks of paint. However.' Kerim sat back in his chair. There was a slight frown on his face. 'What I cannot understand is this sudden breach of the peace. We live together very amicably in Istanbul. We all have our work to do. It is unheard of that my *chers collègues* should suddenly declare war in this way. It is quite worrying. It can only lead to trouble for our

Russian friends. I shall be forced to rebuke the man who did it when I have found out his name.' Kerim shook his head. 'It is most confusing. I am hoping it has nothing to do with this case of ours.'

'But was it necessary to make my arrival so public?' Bond asked mildly. 'The last thing I want is to get you involved in all this. Why send the Rolls to the airport? It only ties you in with me.'

Kerim's laugh was indulgent. 'My friend, I must explain something which you should know. We and the Russians and the Americans have a paid man in all the hotels. And we have all bribed an official of the Secret police at Headquarters and we receive a carbon copy of the list of all foreigners entering the country every day by air or train or sea. Given a few more days I could have smuggled you in through the Greek frontier. But for what purpose? Your existence here has to be known to the other side so that our friend can contact you. It is a condition she has laid down that she will make her own arrangements for the meeting. Perhaps she does not trust our security. Who knows? But she was definite about it and she said, as if I didn't know it, that her centre would immediately be advised of your arrival.' Kerim shrugged his broad shoulders. 'So why make things difficult for her? I am merely concerned with making things easy and comfortable for you so that you will at least enjoy your stay—even if it is fruitless.'

Bond laughed. 'I take it all back. I'd forgotten the Balkan formula. Anyway I'm under your orders here. You tell me what to do and I'll do it.'

Kerim waved the subject aside. 'And now, since we are talking of your comfort, how is your hotel? I was surprised you chose the Palas. It is little better than a disorderly house—what the French call a *baisodrome*. And it's quite a haunt of the Russians. Not that that matters.'

'It's not too bad. I just didn't want to stay at the Istanbul-Hilton or one of the other smart places.'

'Money?' Kerim reached into a drawer and took out a flat packet of new green notes. 'Here's a thousand

Turkish pounds. Their real value, and their rate on the black market, is about twenty to the pound. The official rate is seven. Tell me when you've finished them and I'll give you as many more as you want. We can do our accounts after the game. It's muck, anyway. Ever since Croesus, the first millionaire, invented gold coins, money has depreciated. And the face of the coin has been debased as fast as its value. First the faces of gods were on the coins. Then the faces of kings. Then of presidents. Now there's no face at all. Look at this stuff!' Kerim tossed the money over to Bond. 'Today it's only paper, with a picture of a public building and the signature of a cashier. Muck! The miracle is that you can still buy things with it. However. What else? Cigarettes? Smoke only these. I will have a few hundred sent up to your hotel. They're the best. *Diplomates*. They're not easy to get. Most of them go to the Ministries and the Embassies. Anything else before we get down to business? Don't worry about your meals and your leisure. I will look after both. I shall enjoy it and, if you will forgive me, I wish to stay close to you while you are here.'

'Nothing else,' said Bond. 'Except that you must come over to London one day.'

'Never,' said Kerim definitely. 'The weather and the women are far too cold. And I am proud to have you here. It reminds me of the war. Now,' he rang a bell on his desk. 'Do you like your coffee plain or sweet? In Turkey we cannot talk seriously without coffee or raki and it is too early for raki.'

'Plain.'

The door behind Bond opened. Kerim barked an order. When the door was shut, Kerim unlocked a drawer and took out a file and put it in front of him. He smacked his hand down on it.

'My friend,' he said grimly, 'I do not know what to say about this case.' He leant back in his chair and linked his hands behind his neck. 'Has it ever occurred to you that our kind of work is rather like shooting a film? So often I have got everybody on location and I think I can start turning the handle. Then it's the weather, and then it's the actors, and then it's the accidents. And there is something else that also happens in the making of a film. Love appears in some shape or form, at the very worst, as it is now, between the two stars. To me that is the most confusing factor in this case, and the most inscrutable one. Does this girl really love her idea of you? Will she love you when she sees you? Will you be able to love her enough to make her come over?'

Bond made no comment. There was a knock on the door and the head clerk put a china eggshell, enclosed in gold filigree, in front of each of them and went out. Bond sipped his coffee and put it down. It was good, but thick with grains. Kerim swallowed his at a gulp and fitted a cigarette into his holder and lit it.

'But there is nothing we can do about this love matter,' Kerim continued, speaking half to himself. 'We can only wait and see. In the meantime there are other things.' He leant forward against the desk and looked across at Bond, his eyes suddenly very hard and shrewd.

'There is something going on in the enemy camp, my friend. It is not only this attempt to get rid of me. There are comings and goings. I have few facts,' he reached up a big index finger and laid it alongside his nose, 'but I have this.' He tapped the side of his nose as if he was patting a dog. 'But this is a good friend of mine and I trust him.' He brought his hand slowly and significantly down on to the desk and added softly, 'And if the stakes were not so big, I would say to you, "Go home my friend. Go home. There is something here to get away from".'

Kerim sat back. The tension went out of his voice. He barked out a harsh laugh. 'But we are not old women. And this is our work. So let us forget my nose and get on with the job. First of all, is there anything I can tell you that you do not know? The girl has made no sign of life since my signal and I have no other information. But perhaps you would like to ask me some questions about the meeting.'

'There's only one thing I want to know,' said Bond flatly. 'What do you think of this girl? Do you believe her story or not? Her story about me? Nothing else matters. If she hasn't got some sort of a hysterical crush on me, the whole business falls to the ground and it's some complicated M.G.B. plot we can't understand. Now. Did you believe the girl?' Bond's voice was urgent and his eyes searched the other man's face.

'Ah, my friend,' Kerim shook his head. He spread his arms wide. 'That is what I asked myself then, and it is what I ask myself the whole time since. But who can tell if a woman is lying about these things? Her eyes were bright—those beautiful innocent eyes. Her lips were moist and parted in that heavenly mouth. Her voice was urgent and frightened at what she was doing and saying. Her knuckles were white on the guard rail of the ship. But what was in her heart?' Kerim raised his hands, 'God alone knows.' He brought his hands down resignedly. He placed them flat on the desk and looked straight at Bond. 'There is only one way of telling if a woman really loves you, and even that was can only be read by an expert.'

'Yes,' said Bond dubiously. 'I know what you mean. In bed.'

CHAPTER 15

Background to a Spy

Coffee came again, and then more coffee, and the big room grew thick with cigarette smoke as the two men took each shred of evidence, dissected it and put it aside. At the end of an hour they were back where they started. It was up to Bond to solve the problem of this girl and, if he was satisfied with her story, get her and the machine out of the country.

Kerim undertook to look after the administrative problems. As a first step he picked up the telephone and spoke to his travel agent and reserved two seats on every outgoing plane for the next week—by B.E.A., Air France, S.A.S. and Turkair.

'And now you must have a passport,' he said. 'One will be sufficient. She can travel as your wife. One of my men will take your photograph and he will find a photograph of some girl who looks more or less like her. As a matter of fact, an early picture of Garbo would serve. There is a certain resemblance. He can get one from the newspaper files. I will speak to the Consul General. He's an excellent fellow who likes my little cloak-and-dagger plots. The passport will be ready by this evening. What name would you like to have?'

'Take one out of a hat.'

'Somerset. My mother came from there. David Somerset. Profession, Company Director. That means nothing. And the girl? Let us say Caroline. She looks like a Caroline. A couple of clean-limbed young English people with a taste for travel. Finance Control Form? Leave that to me. It will show eighty pounds in travellers' cheques, let's say, and a receipt from the bank to show you changed fifty while you were in Turkey. Customs? They never look at anything. Only too glad if somebody has bought something in the country. You will declare some Turkish Delight—presents for your friends in London. If you have to get out quickly, leave your hotel bill and luggage to me. They know me well enough at the Palas. Anything else?'

'I can't think of anything.'

Kerim looked at his watch. 'Twelve o'clock. Just time for the car to take you back to your hotel. There might be a message. And have a good look at your things to see if anyone has been inquisitive.'

He rang the bell and fired instructions at the head clerk who stood with his sharp eyes on Kerim's and his lean head straining forward like a whippet's.

Kerim led Bond to the door. There came again the warm powerful handclasp. 'The car will bring you to lunch' he said. 'A little place in the Spice Bazaar.' His eyes looked happily into Bond's. 'And I am glad to be working with you. We will do well together.' He let go of Bond's hand. 'And now I have a lot of things to do very quickly. They may be the wrong things, but at any rate,' he grinned broadly, *'jouons mal, mais jouons vite!'*

The head clerk, who seemed to be some sort of chief-of-staff to Kerim, led Bond through another door in the wall of the raised platform. The heads were still bowed over the ledgers. There was a short passage with rooms on either side. The man led the way into one of these and Bond found himself in an extremely well-equipped darkroom and laboratory. In ten minutes he was out again on the street. The Rolls edged out of the narrow alley and back again on to the Galata Bridge.

A new concierge was on duty at the Kristal Palas, a small obsequious man with guilty eyes in a yellow face. He came out from behind the desk, his hands spread in apology. 'Effendi, I greatly regret. My colleague showed you to an inadequate room. It was not realized that you are a friend of Kerim Bey. Your things have been moved to No. 12. It is the best room in the hotel. In fact,' the concierge leered, 'it is the room reserved for honeymoon couples. Every comfort. My apologies, Effendi. The other room is not intended for visitors of distinction.' The man executed an oily bow, washing his hands.

If there was one thing Bond couldn't stand it was the sound of his boots being licked. He looked the concierge in the eyes and said, 'Oh.' The eyes slid away. 'Let me see this room. I may not like it. I was quite comfortable where I was.'

'Certainly, Effendi,' the man bowed Bond to the lift. 'But alas the plumbers are in your former room. The water supply . . .' the voice trailed away. The lift rose about ten feet and stopped at the first floor.

Well, the story of the plumbers makes sense, reflected Bond. And, after all, there was no harm in having the best room in the hotel.

The concierge unlocked a high door and stood back.

Bond had to approve. The sun streamed in through wide double windows that gave on to a small balcony. The motif was pink and grey and the style was mock French Empire, battered by the years, but still with all the elegance of the turn of the century. There were fine Bokhara rugs on the parquet floor. A glittering chandelier hung from the ornate ceiling. The bed against the right-hand wall was huge. A large mirror in a gold frame covered most of the wall behind it. (Bond was amused. The honeymoon room! Surely there should be a mirror on the ceiling as well.) The adjoining bathroom was tiled and fitted with everything, including a bidet and a shower. Bond's shaving things were neatly laid out.

The concierge followed Bond back into the bedroom, and when Bond said he would take the room, bowed himself gratefully out.

Why not? Bond again walked round the room. This time he carefully inspected the walls and the neighbourhood of the bed and the telephone. Why not take the room? Why would there be microphones or secret doors? What would be the point of them?

His suitcase was on a bench near the chest-of-drawers. He knelt down. No scratches round the lock. The bit of fluff he had trapped in the clasp was still there. He unlocked the suitcase and took out the little attaché case. Again no signs of interference. Bond locked the case and got to his feet.

He washed and went out of the room and down the stairs. No, there had been no messages for the Effendi. The concierge bowed as he opened the door of the Rolls. Was there a hint of conspiracy behind the permanent guilt in those eyes? Bond decided not to care if there was. The game, whatever it was, had to be played out. If the change of rooms had been the opening gambit, so much the better. The game had to begin somewhere.

As the car sped back down the hill, Bond's thoughts turned to Darko Kerim. What a man for Head of Station T! His size alone, in this country of furtive, stunted little men, would give him authority, and his giant vitality and love of life would make everyone his friend. Where had this exuberant shrewd pirate come from? And how had he come to work for the Service? He was the rare type of man that Bond loved, and Bond already felt prepared to add Kerim to the half-dozen of those real friends whom Bond, who had no 'acquaintances', would be ready to take to his heart.

The car went back over the Galata Bridge and drew up outside the vaulted arcades of the Spice Bazaar. The chauffeur led the way up the shallow worn steps and into the fog of exotic scents, shouting curses at the beggars and sack-laden porters. Inside the entrance the chauffeur turned left out of the stream of shuffling, jabbering humanity and showed Bond a small arch in the thick wall. Turretlike stone steps curled upwards.

'Effendi, you will find Kerim Bey in the far room on the left. You have only to ask. He is known to all.'

Bond climbed the cool stairs to a small ante-room where a waiter, without asking his name, took charge and led him through a maze of small, colourfully tiled, vaulted rooms to where Kerim was sitting at a corner table over the entrance to the bazaar. Kerim greeted him boisterously, waving a glass of milky liquid in which ice tinkled.

'Here you are my friend! Now, at once, some raki. You must be exhausted after your sight-seeing.' He fired orders at the waiter.

Bond sat down in a comfortable armed chair and took the small tumbler the waiter offered him. He lifted it towards Kerim and tasted it. It was identical with Ouzo. He drank it down. At once the waiter refilled his glass.

'And now to order your lunch. They eat nothing but offal cooked in rancid olive oil in Turkey. At least the offal at the Misir Carsarsi is the best.'

The grinning waiter made suggestions.

'He says the Doner Kebab is very good today. I don't believe him, but it can be. It is very young lamb broiled over charcoal with savoury rice. Lots of onions in it. Or is there anything you prefer? A pilaff or some of those damned stuffed peppers they eat here? All right then. And you must start with a few sardines grilled *en papillotte*. They are just edible.' Kerim harangued the waiter. He sat back, smiling at Bond. 'That is the only way to treat these damned people. They love to be cursed and kicked. It is all they understand. It is in the blood. All this pretence of democracy is killing them. They want some sultans and wars and rape and fun. Poor brutes, in their striped suits and bowler hats. They are miserable. You've only got to look at them. However, to hell with them all. Any news?'

Bond shook his head. He told Kerim about the

change of room and the untouched suitcase.

Kerim downed a glass of raki and wiped his mouth on the back of his hand. He echoed the thought Bond had had. 'Well, the game must begin sometime. I have made certain small moves. Now we can only wait and see. We will make a little foray into enemy territory after lunch. I think it will interest you. Oh, we shan't be seen. We shall move in the shadows, underground.' Kerim laughed delightedly at his cleverness. 'And now let us talk about other things. How do you like Turkey? No, I don't want to know. What else?'

They were interrupted by the arrival of their first course. Bond's sardines *en papillotte* tasted like any other fried sardines. Kerim set about a large plate of what appeared to be strips of raw fish. He saw Bond's look of interest. 'Raw fish,' he said. 'After this I shall have raw meat and lettuce and then I shall have a bowl of yoghourt. I am not a faddist, but I once trained to be a professional strong man. It is a good profession in Turkey. The public loves them. And my trainer insisted that I should eat only raw food. I got the habit. It is good for me, but,' he waved his fork, 'I do not pretend it is good for everyone. I don't care the hell what other people eat so long as they enjoy it. I can't stand sad eaters and sad drinkers.'

'Why did you decide not to be a strong man? How did you get into this racket?'

Kerim forked up a strip of fish and tore at it with his teeth. He drank down half a tumbler of raki. He lit a cigarette and sat back in his chair. 'Well,' he said with a sour grin, 'we might as well talk about me as about anything else. And you must be wondering "How did this big crazy man get into the Service?" I will tell you, but briefly, because it is a long story. You will stop me if you get bored. All right?'

'Fine.' Bond lit a *Diplomate*. He leant forward on his elbows.

'I come from Trebizond.' Kerim watched his cigarette smoke curl upwards. 'We were a huge family with many mothers. My father was the sort of man women can't resist. All women want to be swept off their feet. In their dreams they long to be slung over a man's shoulder and taken into a cave and raped. That was his way with them. My father was a great fisherman and his fame was spread all over the Black Sea. He went after the sword-fish. They are difficult to catch and hard to fight and he would always outdo all others after these fish. Women like their men to be heroes. He was a kind of hero in a corner of Turkey where it is a tradition for the men to be tough. He was a big, romantic sort of fellow. So he could have any woman he wanted. He wanted them all and sometimes killed other men to get them. Naturally he had many children. We all lived on top of each other in a great rambling old ruin of a house that our "aunts" made habitable. The aunts really amounted to a harem. One of them was an English governess from Istanbul my father had seen watching a circus. He took a fancy to her and she to him and that evening he put her on board his fishing boat and sailed up the Bosphorus and back to Trebizond. I don't think she ever regretted it. I think she forgot all the world except him. She died just after the war. She was sixty. The child before me had been an Italian girl and the girl had called him Bianco. He was fair. I was dark. I got to be called Darko. There were fifteen of us children and we had a wonderful childhood. Our aunts fought often and so did we. It was like a gipsy encampment. It was held together by my father who thrashed us, women or children, when we were a nuisance. But he was good to us when we were peaceful and obedient. You cannot understand such a family?'

'The way you describe it I can.'

'Anyway so it was. I grew up to be nearly as big a man as my father, but better educated. My mother saw to that. My father only taught us to be clean and to go to the lavatory once a day and never to feel shame about anything in the world. My mother also taught me a regard for England, but that is by the way. By the time I was twenty, I had a boat of my own and I was making money. But I was wild. I left the big house and went to live in two small rooms on the waterfront. I wanted to have my women where my mother would not know. There was a stroke of bad luck. I had a little Bessarabian hell-cat. I had won her in a fight with some gipsies, here in the hills behind Istanbul. They came after me, but I got her on board the boat. I had to knock her unconscious first. She was still trying to kill me when we got back to Trebizond, so I got her to my place and took away all her clothes and kept her chained naked under the table. When I ate, I used to throw scraps to her under the table, like a dog. She had to learn who was master. Before that could happen, my mother did an unheard of thing. She visited my place without warning. She came to tell me that my father wanted to see me immediately. She found the girl. My mother was really angry with me for the first time in my life. Angry? She was beside herself. I was a cruel ne'er-do-well and she was ashamed to call me son. The girl must immediately be taken back to her people. My mother brought her some of her own clothes from the house. The girl put them on, but when the time came, she refused to leave me.' Darko Kerim laughed hugely. 'An interesting lesson in female psychology, my dear friend. However, the problem of the girl is another story. While my mother was fussing over her and getting nothing but gipsy curses for her pains, I was having an interview with my father, who had heard nothing of all this and who never did hear. My mother was like that. There was another man with my father, a tall, quiet Englishman with a black patch over one eye. They were talking about the Russians. The Englishman wanted to know what they were doing along their frontier, about what was going on at Batoum, their big oil and naval base only fifty miles away from Trebizond. He would pay good money for information. I knew English and I knew Russian. I had good eyes and ears. I had a boat. My father had decided that I would work for the Englishman. And that Englishman, my dear friend, was Major Dansey, my predecessor as Head of this Station. And the rest,' Kerim made a wide gesture with his cigarette holder, 'you can imagine.'

'But what about this training to be a professional strong man?'

'Ah,' said Kerim slyly, 'that was only a sideline. Our travelling circuses were almost the only Turks allowed through the frontier. The Russians cannot live without circuses. It is as simple as that. I was the man who broke chains and lifted weights by a rope between the teeth. I wrestled against the local strong men in the Russian villages. And some of those Georgians are giants. Fortunately they are stupid giants and I nearly always won. Afterwards, at the drinking, there was always much talk and gossip. I would look foolish and pretend not to understand. Every now and then I would ask an innocent question and they would laugh at my stupidity and tell me the answer.'

The second course came, and with it a bottle of Kavaklidere, a rich coarse burgundy like any other Balkan wine. The Kebab was good and tasted of smoked bacon fat and onions. Kerim ate a kind of Steak Tartare—a large flat hamburger of finely minced raw meat laced with peppers and chives and bound together with yolk of egg. He made Bond try a forkful. It was delicious. Bond said so.

'You ought to eat it every day,' said Kerim earnestly. 'It is good for those who wish to make much love. There are certain exercises you should do for the same purpose. These things are important to men. Or at least they are to me. Like my father, I consume a large quantity of women. But, unlike him, I also drink and smoke too much, and these things do not go well with making love. Nor does this work I do. Too many tensions and too much thinking. It takes the blood to the head instead of to where it should be for making love. But I am greedy for life. I do too much of everything all the time. Suddenly one day my heart will fail. The Iron Crab will get me as it got my father. But I am not afraid of The Crab. At least I shall have died from an honourable disease. Perhaps they will put on my tombstone "This Man Died from Living Too Much".'

Bond laughed. 'Don't go too soon, Darko,' he said. 'M. would be very displeased. He thinks the world of you.'

'He does?' Kerim searched Bond's face to see if he was telling the truth. He laughed delightedly. 'In that case I will not let The Crab have my body yet.' He looked at his watch. 'Come, James,' he said. 'It is good that you remind me of my duty. We will have coffee in the office. There is not much time to waste. Every day at 2:30 the Russians have their council of war. Today you and I will do them the honour of being present at their deliberations.'

CHAPTER 16

The Tunnel of Rats

Back in the cool office, while they waited for the inevitable coffee, Kerim opened a cupboard in the wall and pulled out sets of engineers' blue overalls. Kerim stripped to his shorts and dressed himself in one of the suits and pulled on a pair of rubber boots. Bond picked out a suit and a pair of boots that more or less fitted him and put them on.

With the coffee, the head clerk brought in two powerful flashlights which he put on the desk.

When the clerk had left the room Kerim said, 'He is one of my sons—the eldest one. The others in there are all my children. The chauffeur and the watchman are uncles of mine. Common blood is the best security. And this spice business is good cover for us all. M. set me up in it. He spoke to friends of his in the City of London. I am now the leading spice merchant in Turkey. I have long ago repaid M. the money that was lent me. My children are shareholders in the business. They have a good life. When there is secret work to be done and I need help, I choose the child who will be most suitable. They all have training in different secret things. They are clever and brave. Some have already killed for me. They would all die for me—and for M. I have taught them he is just below God.' Kerim made a deprecating wave. 'But that is just to tell you that you are in good hands.'

'I hadn't imagined anything different.'

'Ha!' said Kerim non-committally. He picked up the torches and handed one to Bond. 'And now to work.'

Kerim walked over to the wide glass-fronted bookcase and put his hand behind it. There was a click and the bookcase rolled silently and easily along the wall to the left. Behind it was a small door, flush with the wall. Kerim pressed one side of the door and it swung inwards to reveal a dark tunnel with stone steps leading straight down. A dank smell, mixed with a faint zoo stench, came out into the room.

'You go first,' said Kerim. 'Go down the steps to the bottom and wait. I must fix the door.'

Bond switched on his torch and stepped through the opening and went carefully down the stairs. The light of the torch showed fresh masonry, and, twenty feet below, a glimmer of water. When Bond got to the bottom he found the the glimmer was a small stream running down a central gutter in the floor of an ancient stone-walled tunnel that sloped steeply up to the right. To the left, the tunnel went on downwards and would, he guessed, come out below the surface of the Golden Horn.

Out of range of Bond's light there was a steady, quiet, scuttling sound, and in the blackness hundreds of pinpoints of red light flickered and moved. It was the same uphill and downhill. Twenty yards away on either side, a thousand rats were looking at Bond. They were sniffing at his scent. Bond imagined the whiskers lifting slightly from their teeth. He had a quick moment of wondering what action they would take if his torch went out.

Kerim was suddenly beside him. 'It is a long climb. A quarter of an hour. I hope you love animals,' Kerim's laugh boomed hugely away up the tunnel. The rats scuffled and stirred. 'Unfortunately there is not much choice. Rats and bats. Squadrons of them, divisions—a whole air force and army. And we have to drive them in front of us. Towards the end of the climb it becomes quite congested. Let's get started. The air is good. It is dry underfoot on both sides of the stream. But in winter the floods come and then we have to use frogmen's suits. Keep your torch on my feet. If a bat gets in your hair, brush him off. It will not be often. Their radar is very good.'

They set off up the steep slope. The smell of the rats and of the droppings of bats was thick—a mixture of monkey house and chicken battery. It occurred to Bond that it would be days before he got rid of it.

Clusters of bats hung like bunches of withered grapes from the roof and when, from time to time, either Kerim's head or Bond's brushed against them, they exploded twittering into the darkness. Ahead of them as they climbed there was the forest of squeaking, scuffling red pin-points that grew denser on both sides of the central gutter. Occasionally Kerim flashed his torch forward and the light shone on a grey field sown with glittering teeth and glinting whiskers. When this happened, an extra frenzy seized the rats, and those nearest jumped on the backs of the others to get away. All the while, fighting tumbling grey bodies came sweeping down the central gutter and, as the pressure of the mass higher up the tunnel grew heavier, the frothing rear rank came closer.

The two men kept their torches levelled like guns on the rear ranks until, after a good quarter of an hour's climb, they reached their destination.

It was a deep alcove of newly faced brick in the side wall of the tunnel. There were two benches on each side of a thick tarpaulin-wrapped object that came down from the ceiling of the alcove.

They stepped inside. Another few yards' climb, Bond thought, and mass hysteria must have seized the distant thousands of rats further up the tunnel. The horde would have turned. Out of sheer pressure for space, the rats would have braved the lights and hurled themselves down on the two intruders, in spite of the two glaring eyes and the threatening scent.

'Watch,' said Kerim.

There was a moment of silence. Further up the tunnel the squeaking had stopped, as if at a word of command. Then suddenly the tunnel was a foot deep in a great wave of hurtling, scrambling grey bodies as, with a continuous high-pitched squeal, the rats turned and pelted back down the slope.

For minutes the sleek grey river foamed by outside the alcove until at last the numbers thinned and only a trickle of sick or wounded rats came limping and probing their way down the tunnel floor.

The scream of the horde slowly vanished down towards the river, until there was silence except for the occasional twitter of a fleeing bat.

Kerim gave a non-committal grunt. 'One of these days those rats will start dying. Then we shall have the plague in Istanbul again. Sometimes I feel guilty for not telling the authorities of this tunnel so that they can clean the place up. But I can't so long as the Russians are up here.' He jerked his head at the roof. He looked at his watch. 'Five minutes to go. They will be pulling up their chairs and fiddling with their papers. There will be the three permanent men—M.G.B., or one of them may be from army intelligence, G.R.U. And there will probably be three others. Two came in a fortnight ago, one through Greece and another through Persia. Another one arrived on Monday. God knows who they are, or what they are here for. And sometimes the girl, Tatiana, comes in with a signal and goes out again. Let us hope we will see her today. You will be impressed. She is something.'

Kerim reached up and untied the tarpaulin cover and pulled it downwards. Bond understood. The cover protected the shining butt of a submarine periscope, fully withdrawn. The moisture glistened on the thick grease of the exposed bottom joint. Bond chuckled. 'Where the hell did you get that from, Darko?'

'Turkish Navy. War surplus.' Kerim's voice did not invite further questions. 'Now Q Branch in London is trying to fix some way of wiring the damn thing for sound. It's not going to be easy. The lens at the top of this is no bigger than a cigarette-lighter, end on. When I raise it, it comes up to floor level in their room. In the corner of the room where it comes up, we cut a small mousehole. We did it well. Once when I came to have a look, the first thing I saw was a big mousetrap with a piece of cheese on it. At least it looked big through the lens.' Kerim laughed briefly. 'But there's not much room to fit a sensitive pick-up alongside the lens. And there's no hope of getting in again to do any more fiddling about with their architecture. The only way I managed to install this thing was to get my friends in the Public Works Ministry to turn the Russians out for a few days. The story was that the trams going up the hill were shaking the foundations of the houses. There had to be a survey. It cost me a few hundred pounds for the right pockets. The Public Works inspected half a dozen houses on either side of this one and declared the place safe. By that time, I and the family had finished our construction work. The Russians were suspicious as hell. I gather they went over the place with a toothcomb when they got back, looking for microphones and bombs and so on. But we can't work that trick twice. Unless Q Branch can think up something very clever, I shall have to be content with keeping an eye on them. One of these days they'll give away something useful. They'll be interrogating someone we're interested in or something of that sort.'

Alongside the matrix of the periscope in the roof of the alcove there was a pendulous blister of metal, twice the size of a football. 'What's that?' said Bond.

'Bottom half of a bomb—a big bomb. If anything happens to me, or if war breaks out with Russia, that bomb will be set off by radio-control from my office. It is sad [Kerim didn't look sad] but I fear that many innocent people will get killed besides the Russians. When the blood is on the boil, man is as unselective as nature.'

Kerim had been polishing away at the hooded eyepieces between the two handle-bars that stuck out on both sides of the base of the periscope. Now he glanced at his watch and bent down and gripped the two handles and slowly brought them up level with his chin. There was a hiss of hydraulics as the glistening stem of the periscope slid up into its steel sheath in the roof of the alcove. Kerim bent his head and gazed into the eyepieces and slowly inched up the handles until he could stand upright. He twisted gently. He centred the lens and beckoned to Bond. 'Just the six of them.'

Bond moved over and took the handles.

'Have a good look at them,' said Kerim. 'I know them, but you'd better get their faces in your mind. Head of the table is their Resident Director. On his left are his two staff. Opposite them are the three new ones. The latest, who looks quite an important chap, is on the Director's right. Tell me if they do anything except talk.'

Bond's first impulse was to tell Kerim not to make so much noise. It was as if he was in the room with the Russians, as if he was sitting in a chair in the corner, a secretary perhaps, taking shorthand of the conference.

The wide, all-round lens, designed for spotting air-craft as well as surface ships, gave him a curious pic-ture—a mouse's eye view of a forest of legs below the fore-edge of the table, and various aspects of the heads belonging to the legs. The Director and his two col-leagues were clear—serious dull Russian faces whose characteristics Bond filed away. There was the studious, professorial face of the Director—thick spectacles, lan-tern jaw, big forehead and thin hair brushed back. On his left was a square wooden face with deep clefts on either side of the nose, fair hair *en brosse* and a nick out of the left ear. The third member of the permanent staff had a shifty Armenian face with clever bright almond eyes. He was talking now. His face wore a falsely hum-ble look. Gold glinted in his mouth.

Bond could see less of the three visitors. Their backs were half towards him and only the profile of the nearest, and presumably most junior, showed clearly. This man's skin also was dark. He too would be from one of the southern republics. The jaw was badly shaved and the eye in profile was bovine and dull under a thick black brow. The nose was fleshy and porous. The upper lip was long over a sullen mouth and the beginning of a double chin. The tough black hair was cut very short so that most of the back of the neck looked blue to the level of the tips of the ears. It was a military haircut, done with mechanical clippers.

The only clues to the next man were an angry boil on the back of a fat bald neck, a shiny blue suit and rather bright brown shoes. The man was motionless during the whole period that Bond kept watch and apparently never spoke.

Now the senior visitor, on the right of the Resident Director, sat back and began talking. It was a strong, crag-like profile with big bones and a jutting chin under a heavy brown moustache of Stalin cut. Bond could see one cold grey eye under a bushy eyebrow and a low forehead topped by wiry grey-brown hair. This man was the only one who was smoking. He puffed busily at a tiny wooden pipe in the bowl of which stood half a cigarette. Every now and then he shook the pipe sideways so that the ash fell on the floor. His profile had more authority than any of the other faces and Bond guessed that he was a senior man sent down from Moscow.

Bond's eyes were getting tired. He twisted the handles gently and looked round the office as far as the blurring jagged edges of the mousehole would allow. He saw nothing of interest—two olive green filing cabinets, a hatstand by the door, on which he counted six more or less identical grey homburgs, and a sideboard with a heavy carafe of water and some glasses. Bond stood away from the eyepiece, rubbing his eyes.

'If only we could hear,' Kerim said, shaking his head sadly. 'It would be worth diamonds.'

'It would solve a lot of problems,' agreed Bond. Then, 'By the way Darko, how did you come on this tunnel? What was it built for?'

Kerim bent and gave a quick glance into the eyepieces and straightened up.

'It's a lost drain from the Hall of Pillars,' he said. 'The Hall of Pillars is now a thing for tourists. It's up above us on the heights of Istanbul, near St. Sophia. A

thousand years ago it was built as a reservoir in case of
siege. It's a huge underground palace, a hundred yards
long and about half as broad. It was made to hold
millions of gallons of water. It was discovered again
about four hundred years ago by a man called Gyllius.
One day I was reading his account of finding it. He said
it was filled in winter from *"a great pipe with a mighty
noise"*. It occurred to me that there might be another
"great pipe" to empty it quickly if the city fell to the
enemy. I went up to the Hall of Pillars and bribed the
watchman and rowed about among the pillars all one
night in a rubber dinghy with one of my boys. We went
over the walls with a hammer and an echo-sounder. At
one end, in the most likely spot, there was a hollow
sound. I handed out more money to the Minister of
Public Works and he closed the place for a week—"for
cleaning". My little team got busy.' Kerim ducked
down again for a look through the eyepieces and went
on. 'We dug into the wall above water-level and came
on the top of an arch. The arch was the beginning of a
tunnel. We got into the tunnel and went down it. Quite
exciting, not knowing where we were going to come out.
And, of course, it went straight down the hill—under
the Street of Books where the Russians have their place,
and out into the Golden Horn, by the Galata Bridge,
twenty yards away from my warehouse. So we filled in
our hole in the Hall of Pillars and started digging from
my end. That was two years ago. It took us a year and a
lot of survey work to get directly under the Russians.'
Kerim laughed. 'And now I suppose one of these days
the Russians will decide to change their offices. By then
I hope someone else will be Head of T.'

Kerim bent down to the rubber eyepieces. Bond saw
him stiffen. Kerim said urgently, 'The door's opening.
Quick. Take over. Here she comes.'

CHAPTER 17

Killing Time

It was seven o'clock on the same evening and James Bond was back in his hotel. He had had a hot bath and a cold shower. He thought that he had at last scoured the zoo smell out of his skin.

He was sitting, naked except for his shorts, at one of the windows of his room, sipping a vodka and tonic and looking out into the heart of the great tragic sunset over the Golden Horn. But his eyes didn't see the torn cloth of gold and blood that hung behind the minaretted stage beneath which he had caught his first glimpse of Tatiana Romanova.

He was thinking of the tall beautiful girl with the dancer's long gait who had walked through the drab door with a piece of paper in her hand. She had stood beside her Chief and handed him the paper. All the men had looked up at her. She had blushed and looked down. What had that expression on the men's faces meant? It was more than just the way some men look at a beautiful girl. They had shown curiosity. That was reasonable. They wanted to know what was in the signal, why they were being disturbed. But what else?

There had been slyness and contempt—the way people stare at prostitutes.

It had been an odd, enigmatic scene. This was part of a highly disciplined para-military organization. These were serving officers, each of whom would be wary of the others. And this girl was just one of the staff, with a Corporal's rank, who was now going through a normal routine. Why had they all unguardedly looked at her with this inquisitive contempt—almost as if she was a spy who had been caught and was going to be executed? Did they suspect her? Had she given herself away? But that seemed less likely as the scene played itself out. The Resident Director read the signal and the other men's eyes turned away from the girl and on to him. He said something, presumably repeating the text of the signal, and the men looked glumly back at him as if the matter did not interest them. Then the Resident Director looked up at the girl and the other eyes followed his. He said something with a friendly, inquiring expression. The girl shook her head and answered briefly. The other men now only looked interested. The Director said one word with a question mark on the end. The girl blushed deeply, and nodded, holding his eyes obediently. The other men smiled encouragement, slyly perhaps, but with approval. No suspicion there. No condemnation. The scene ended with a few sentences from the Director to which the girl seemed to say the equivalent of 'Yes, sir' and turned and walked out of the room. When she had gone, the Director said something with an expression of irony on his face and the men laughed heartily and the sly expression was back on their faces, as if what he had said had been obscene. Then they went back to their work.

Ever since, on their way back down the tunnel, and later in Kerim's office while they discussed what Bond had seen, Bond had racked his brains for a solution to this maddening bit of dumb crambo and now, looking without focus at the dying sun, he was still mystified.

Bond finished his drink and lit another cigarette. He put the problem away and turned his mind to the girl.

Tatiana Romanova. A Romanov. Well, she certainly

looked like a Russian princess, or the traditional idea of one. The tall, fine-boned body that moved so gracefully and stood so well. The thick sweep of hair down to the shoulders and the quiet authority of the profile. The wonderful Garbo-esque face with its curiously shy serenity. The contrast between the level innocence of the big, deep blue eyes and the passionate promise of the wide mouth. And the way she had blushed and the way the long eyelashes had come down over the lowered eyes. Had that been the prudery of a virgin? Bond thought not. There was the confidence of having been loved in the proud breasts and the insolently lilting behind—the assertion of a body that knows what it can be for.

On what Bond had seen, could he believe that she was the sort of girl to fall in love with a photograph and a file? How could one tell? Such a girl would have a deeply romantic nature. There were dreams in the eyes and the mouth. At that age, twenty-four, the Soviet machine would not yet have ground the sentiment out of her. The Romanov blood might well have given her a yearning for men other than the type of modern Russian officer she would meet—stern, cold, mechanical, basically hysterical and, because of their Party education, infernally dull.

It could be true. There was nothing to disprove her story in her looks. Bond wanted it to be true.

The telephone rang. It was Kerim. 'Nothing new?'

'No.'

'Then I will pick you up at eight.'

'I'll be ready.'

Bond laid down the receiver and slowly started to put on his clothes.

Kerim had been firm about the evening. Bond had wanted to stay in his hotel room and wait for the first contact to be made—a note, a telephone call, whatever it might be. But Kerim had said no. The girl had been adamant that she would choose her own time and place. It would be wrong for Bond to seem a slave to her convenience. 'That is bad psychology, my friend,' Kerim had insisted. 'No girl likes a man to run when she whistles. She would despise you if you made yourself too available. From your face and your dossier she would expect you to behave with indifference—even with insolence. She would want that. She wishes to court you, to buy a kiss,'—Kerim had winked—'from that cruel mouth. It is with an image she has fallen in love. Behave like the image. Act the part.'

Bond had shrugged his shoulders. 'All right, Darko. I daresay you're right. What do you suggest?'

'Live the life you would normally. Go home now and have a bath and a drink. The local vodka is all right if you drown it with tonic water. If nothing happens, I will pick you up at eight. We will have dinner at the place of a gipsy friend of mine. A man called Vavra. He is head of a tribe. I must anyway see him tonight. He is one of my best sources. He is finding out who tried to blow up my office. Some of his girls will dance for you. I will not suggest that they should entertain you more intimately. You must keep your sword sharp. There is a saying "Once a King, always a King. But once a Knight is enough!"'

Bond was smiling at the memory of Kerim's dictum when the telephone rang again. He picked up the receiver. It was only the car. As he went down the few stairs and out to Kerim in the waiting Rolls, Bond admitted to himself that he was disappointed.

They were climbing up the far hill through the poorer quarters above the Golden Horn when the chauffeur half turned his head and said something in a non-committal voice.

Kerim answered with a monosyllable. 'He says a Lambretta is on our tail. A Faceless One. It is of no importance. When I wish, I can make a secret of my movements. Often they have trailed this car for miles when there has been only a dummy in the back. A conspicuous car has its uses. They know this gipsy is a friend of mine, but I think they do not understand why. It will do no harm for them to know that we are having a night of relaxation. On a Saturday night, with a friend from England, anything else would be unusual.'

Bond looked back through the rear window and

watched the crowded streets. Fom behind a stopped tram a motor scooter showed for a minute and then was hidden by a taxi. Bond turned away. He reflected briefly on the way the Russians ran their centres—with all the money and equipment in the world, while the Secret Service put against them a handful of adventurous, underpaid men, like this one, with his second-hand Rolls and his children to help him. Yet Kerim had the run of Turkey. Perhaps, after all, the right man was better than the right machine.

At half-past eight they stopped half way up a long hill on the outskirts of Istanbul at a dingy-looking open-air café with a few empty tables on the pavement. Behind it were the tops of trees over a high stone wall. They got out and the car drove off. They waited for the Lambretta, but its wasplike buzz had stopped and at once it was on its way back down the hill. All they saw of the driver was a glimpse of a short squat man wearing goggles.

Kerim led the way through the tables and into the café. It seemed empty, but a man rose up quickly from behind the till. He kept one hand below the counter. When he saw who it was, he gave Kerim a nervous white smile. Something clanged to the floor. He stepped from behind the counter and led them out through the back and across a stretch of gravel to a door in the high wall and, after knocking once, unlocked it and waved them through.

There was an orchard with plant tables dotted about under the trees. In the centre was a circle of terrazza dancing floor. Round it were strung fairy lights, now dead, on poles planted in the ground. On the far side, at a long table, about twenty people of all ages had been sitting eating, but they had put down their knives and now looked towards the door. Some children had been playing in the grass behind the table. They also were now quiet and watching. The three-quarter moon showed everything up brightly and made pools of membraned shadow under the trees.

Kerim and Bond walked forward. The man at the head of the table said something to the others. He got up and came to meet them. The rest returned to their dinner and the children to their games.

The man greeted Kerim with reserve. He stood for a few moments making a long explanation to which Kerim listened attentively, occasionally asking a question.

The gipsy was an imposing, theatrical figure in Macedonian dress—white shirt with full sleeves, baggy trousers and laced soft leather topboots. His hair was a tangle of black snakes. A large downward-drooping black moustache almost hid the full red lips. The eyes were fierce and cruel on either side of a syphilitic nose. The moon glinted on the sharp line of the jaw and the high cheekbones. His right hand, which had a gold ring on the thumb, rested on the hilt of a short curved dagger in a leather scabbard tipped with filigree silver.

The gipsy finished talking. Kerim said a few words, forceful and apparently complimentary, about Bond, at the same time stretching his hand out in Bond's direction as if he was a compère in a night-club commending a new turn. The gipsy stepped up to Bond and scrutinized him. He bowed abruptly. Bond followed suit. The gipsy said a few words through a sardonic smile. Kerim laughed and turned to Bond. 'He says if you are ever out of work you should come to him. He will give you a job—taming his women and killing for him. That is a great compliment to a *gajo*—a foreigner. You should say something in reply.'

'Tell him that I can't imagine he needs any help in these matters.'

Kerim translated. The gipsy politely bared his teeth. He said something and walked back to the table, clapping his hands sharply. Two women got up and came towards him. He spoke to them curtly and they went back to the table and picked up a large earthenware dish and disappeared among the trees.

Kerim took Bond's arm and led him to one side.

'We have come on a bad night,' he said. 'The restaurant is closed. There are family troubles here which have to be solved—drastically, and in private. But I am an old friend and we are invited to share their supper. It will be disgusting but I have sent for raki. Then we may watch—but on condition that we do not interfere. I hope you understand, my friend.' Kerim gave Bond's arm an additional pressure. 'Whatever you see, you must not move or comment. A court has just been held and justice is to be done—their kind of justice. It is an affair of love and jealousy. Two girls of the tribe are in love with one of his sons. There is a lot of death in the air. They both threaten to kill the other to get him. If he chooses one, the unsuccessful one has sworn to kill him and the girl. It is an *impasse*. There is much argument in the tribe. So the son has been sent up into the hills and the two girls are to fight it out here tonight—to the death. The son has agreed to take the winner. The women are locked up in separate caravans. It will not be for the squeamish, but it will be a remarkable affair. It is a great privilege that we may be present. You understand? We are *gajos*. You will forget your sense of the proprieties? You will not interfere? They would kill you, and possibly me, if you did.'

'Darko,' said Bond, 'I have a French friend. A man called Mathis who is head of the Deuxième. He once said to me: *"J'aime les sensations fortes."* I am like him. I shall not disgrace you. Men fighting women is one thing. Women fighting women is another. But what about the bomb? The bomb that blew up your office. What did he say about that?'

'It was the leader of the Faceless Ones. He put it there himself. They came down the Golden Horn in a boat and he climbed up a ladder and fixed it to the wall. It was bad luck he didn't get me. The operation was well thought out. The man is a gangster. A Bulgarian "refugee" called Krilencu. I shall have to have a reckoning with him. God knows why they suddenly want to kill me, but I cannot allow such annoyances. I may decide to take action later tonight. I know where he lives. In case Vavra knew the answer, I told my chauffeur to come back with necessary equipment.'

A fiercely attractive young girl in a thick old-fashioned black frock, with strings of gold coins round her neck and about ten thin gold bracelets on each wrist,

came over from the table and swept a low jingling
curtsey in front of Kerim. She said something and
Kerim replied.

'We are bidden to the table,' said Kerim. 'I hope you
are good at eating with your fingers. I see they are all
wearing their smartest clothes tonight. That girl would
be worth marrying. She has a lot of gold on her. It is her
dowry.'

They walked over to the table. Two places had been
cleared on either side of the head gipsy. Kerim gave
what sounded like a polite greeting to the table. There
was a curt nod of acknowledgement. They sat down. In
front of each of them was a large plate of some sort of
ragout smelling strongly of garlic, a bottle of raki, a
pitcher of water and a cheap tumbler. More bottles of
raki, untouched, were on the table. When Kerim
reached for his and poured himself half a tumblerful,
everyone followed suit. Kerim added some water and
raised his glass. Bond did the same. Kerim made a short
and vehement speech and all raised their glasses and
drank. The atmosphere became easier. An old woman
next to Bond passed him a long loaf of bread and said
something. Bond smiled and said 'thank you'. He broke
off a piece and handed the loaf to Kerim who was
picking among his ragout with thumb and forefinger.
Kerim took the loaf with one hand and at the same time,
with the other, he put a large piece of meat in his mouth
and began to eat.

Bond was about to do the same when Kerim said
sharply and quietly, 'With the right hand, James. The
left hand is used for only one purpose among these
people.'

Bond halted his left hand in mid-air and moved it on
to grasp the nearest raki bottle. He poured himself
another half tumblerful and started to eat with his right
hand. The ragout was delicious but steaming hot. Bond
winced each time he dipped his fingers into it. Everyone
watched them eat and from time to time the old woman
dipped her fingers into Bond's stew and chose a piece
for him.

When they had scoured their plates, a silver bowl of

water, in which rose leaves floated, and a clean linen cloth, were put between Bond and Kerim. Bond washed his fingers and his greasy chin and turned to his host and dutifully made a short speech of thanks which Kerim translated. The table murmured its appreciation. The head gipsy bowed towards Bond and said, according to Kerim, that he hated all *gajos* except Bond, whom he was proud to call his friend. Then he clapped his hands sharply and everybody got up from the table and began pulling the benches away and arranging them round the dance floor.

Kerim came round the table to Bond. They walked off together. 'How do you feel? They've gone to get the two girls.'

Bond nodded. He was enjoying the evening. The scene was beautiful and thrilling—the white moon blazing down on the ring of figures now settling on the benches, the glint of gold or jewellery as somebody shifted his position, the glaring pool of terrazza and, all around, the quiet, sentinel trees standing guard in their black skirts of shadow.

Kerim led Bond to a bench where the chief gipsy sat alone. They took their places on his right.

A black cat with green eyes walked slowly across the terrazza and joined a group of children who were sitting quietly as if someone was about to come on to the dance floor and teach them a lesson. It sat down and began licking its chest.

Beyond the high wall, a horse neighed. Two of the gipsies looked over their shoulders towards the sound as if they were reading the cry of the horse. From the road came the silvery spray of a bicycle bell as someone sped down the hill.

The crouching silence was broken by the clang of a bolt being drawn. The door in the wall crashed back and two girls, spitting and fighting like angry cats, hurtled through and across the grass and into the ring.

CHAPTER 18

Strong Sensations

The head gipsy's voice cracked out. The girls separated reluctantly and stood facing him. The gipsy began to speak in a tone of harsh denunciation.

Kerim put his hand up to his mouth and whispered behind it. 'Vavra is telling them that this is a great tribe of gipsies and they have brought dissension among it. He says there is no room for hatred among themselves, only against those outside. The hatred they have created must be purged so that the tribe can live peacefully again. They are to fight. If the loser is not killed she will be banished for ever. That will be the same as death. These people wither and die outside the tribe. They cannot live in our world. It is like wild beasts forced to live in a cage.'

While Kerim spoke, Bond examined the two beautiful, taut, sullen animals in the centre of the ring.

They were both gipsy-dark, with coarse black hair to their shoulders, and they were both dressed in the collection of rags you associate with shanty-town Negroes —tattered brown shifts that were mostly darns and patches. One was bigger-boned than the other, and obviously stronger, but she looked sullen and slow-eyed and might not be quick on her feet. She was handsome in a rather leonine way, and there was a slow red glare in her heavy lidded eyes as she stood and listened impatiently to the head of the tribe. She ought to win, thought Bond. She is half an inch taller, and she is stronger.

Where this girl was a lioness, the other was a panther—lithe and quick and cunning sharp eyes that were not on the speaker but sliding sideways, measuring inches, and the hands at her sides were curled into claws. The muscles of her fine legs looked hard as a man's. The breasts were small, and, unlike the big breasts of the other girl, hardly swelled the rags of her shift. She looks a dangerous little bitch of a girl, thought Bond. She will certainly get in the first blow. She will be too quick for the other.

At once he was proved wrong. As Vavra spoke his last word, the big girl, who, Kerim whispered, was called Zora, kicked hard sideways, without taking aim, and caught the other girl square in the stomach and, as the smaller girl staggered, followed up with a swinging blow of the fist to the side of the head that knocked her sprawling on to the stone floor.

'Oi, Vida,' lamented a woman in the crowd. She needn't have worried. Even Bond could see that Vida was shamming as she lay on the ground, apparently winded. He could see her eyes glinting under her bent arm as Zora's foot came flashing at her ribs.

Vida's hands flickered out together. They grasped the ankle and her head struck into the instep like a snake's. Zora gave a scream of pain and wrenched furiously at her trapped foot. It was too late. The other girl was up on one knee, and then standing erect, the foot still in her hands. She heaved upwards and Zora's other foot left the ground and she crashed full length.

The thud of the big girl's fall shook the ground. For a moment she lay still. With an animal snarl, Vida dived on top of her, clawing and tearing.

My God, what a hell-cat, thought Bond. Beside him, Kerim's breath hissed tensely through his teeth.

But the big girl protected herself with her elbows and knees and at last she managed to kick Vida off. She staggered to her feet and backed away, her lips bared from her teeth and the shift hanging in tatters from her splendid body. At once she went in to the attack again, her arms groping forward for a hold and, as the smaller girl leapt aside, Zora's hand caught the neck of her shift and split it down to the hem. But immediately Vida twisted in close under the reaching arms and her fists and knees thudded into the attacker's body.

This in-fighting was a mistake. The strong arms clamped shut round the smaller girl, trapping Vida's hands low down so that they could not reach up for Zora's eyes. And, slowly, Zora began to squeeze, while Vida's legs and knees thrashed ineffectually below.

Bond thought that now the big girl must win. All Zora had to do was to fall on the other girl. Vida's head would crack down on the stone and then Zora could do as she liked. But all of a sudden it was the big girl who began to scream. Bond saw that Vida's head was buried deep in the other's breasts. Her teeth were at work. Zora's arms let go as she reached for Vida's hair to pull the head back and away from her. But now Vida's hands were free and they were scrabbling at the big girl's body.

The girls tore apart and backed away like cats, their shining bodies glinting through the last rags of their shifts and blood showing on the exposed breasts of the big girl.

They circled warily, both glad to have escaped, and as they circled they tore off the last of their rags and threw them into the audience.

Bond held his breath at the sight of the two glistening, naked bodies, and he could feel Kerim's body tense beside him. The ring of gipsies seemed to have come closer to the two fighters. The moon shone on glittering eyes and there was the whisper of hot, panting breath.

Still the two girls circled slowly, their teeth bared and

their breath coming harshly. The light glinted off their heaving breasts and stomachs and off their hard, boyish flanks. Their feet left dark sweat marks on the white stones.

Again it was the big girl, Zora, who made the first move with a sudden forward leap and arms held out like a wrestler's. But Vida stood her ground. Her right foot lashed out in a furious *coup de savate* that made a slap like a pistol shot. The big girl gave a wounded cry and clutched at herself. At once Vida's other foot kicked up to the stomach and she threw herself in after it.

There was a low growl from the crowd as Zora went down on her knees. Her hands went up to protect her face, but it was too late. The smaller girl was astride her, and her hands grasped Zora's wrists as she bore down on her with all her weight and bent her to the ground, her bared white teeth reaching towards the offered neck.

'BOOM!'

The explosion cracked the tension like a nut. A flash of flame lit the darkness behind the dance floor and a chunk of masonry sang past Bond's ear. Suddenly the orchard was full of running men and the head gipsy was slinking forward across the stone with his curved dagger held out in front of him. Kerim was going after him, a gun in his hand. As the gipsy passed the two girls, now standing wild-eyed and trembling, he shouted a word at them and they took to their heels and disappeared among the trees where the last of the women and children were already vanishing among the shadows.

Bond, the Beretta held uncertainly in his hand, followed slowly in the wake of Kerim towards the wide breach that had been blown out of the garden wall, and wondered what the hell was going on.

The stretch of grass between the hole in the wall and the dance floor was a turmoil of fighting, running figures. It was only as Bond came up with the fight that he distinguished the squat, conventionally dressed Bulgars from the swirling finery of the gipsies. There seemed to be more of the Faceless Ones than of the gipsies, almost two to one. As Bond peered into the struggling mass, a gipsy youth was ejected from it, clutching his stomach. He groped towards Bond, coughing terribly. Two small dark men came after him, their knives held low.

Instinctively Bond stepped to one side so that the crowd was not behind the two men. He aimed at their legs above the knees and the gun in his hand cracked twice. The two men fell, soundlessly, face downwards in the grass.

Two bullets gone. Only six left. Bond edged closer to the fight.

A knife hissed past his head and clanged on to the dance floor.

It had been aimed at Kerim, who came running out of the shadows with two men on his heels. The second man stopped and raised his knife to throw and Bond shot from the hip, blindly, and saw him fall. The other man turned and fled among the trees and Kerim dropped to one knee beside Bond, wrestling with his gun.

'Cover me,' he shouted. 'Jammed on the first shot. It's those bloody Bulgars. God knows what they think they're doing.'

A hand caught Bond round the mouth and yanked him backwards. On his way to the ground he smelled carbolic soap and nicotine. He felt a boot thud into the back of his neck. As he whirled over sideways in the grass he expected to feel the searing flame of a knife. But the men, and there were three of them, were after Kerim, and as Bond scrambled to one knee he saw the squat black figures pile down on the crouching man, who gave one lash upwards with his useless gun and then went down under them.

At the same moment as Bond leaped forward and brought his gun butt down on a round shaven head, something flashed past his eyes and the curved dagger of the head gipsy was growing out of a heaving back. Then Kerim was on his feet and the third man was running and a man was standing in the breach in the wall shouting one word, again and again, and one by one the attackers broke off their fights and doubled over to the man and past him and out on to the road.

'Shoot, James, shoot!' roared Kerim. 'That's Krilencu.' He started to run forward. Bond's gun spat once. But the man had dodged round the wall, and thirty yards is too far for night shooting with an automatic. As Bond lowered his hot gun, there came the staccato firing of a squadron of Lambrettas, and Bond stood and listened to the swarm of wasps flying down the hill.

There was silence except for the groans of the wounded. Bond listlessly watched Kerim and Vavra come back through the breach in the wall and walk among the bodies, occasionally turning one over with a foot. The other gipsies seeped back from the road and the older women came hurrying out of the shadows to tend their men.

Bond shook himself. What the hell had it all been about? Ten or a dozen men had been killed. What for? Whom had they been trying to get? Not him, Bond. When he was down and ready for the killing they had passed him by and made for Kerim. This was the second attempt on Kerim's life. Was it anything to do with the Romanova business? How could it possibly tie in?

Bond tensed. His gun spoke twice from the hip. The knife clattered harmlessly off Kerim's back. The figure that had risen from the dead twirled slowly round like a ballet dancer and toppled forward on his face. Bond ran forward. He had been just in time. The moon had caught the blade and he had had a clear field of fire. Kerim looked down at the twitching body. He turned to meet Bond.

Bond stopped in his tracks. 'You bloody fool,' he said angrily. 'Why the hell can't you take more care! You ought to have a nurse.' Most of Bond's anger came from knowing that it was he who had brought a cloud of death around Kerim.

Darko Kerim grinned shamefacedly. 'Now it is not good, James. You have saved my life too often. We might have been friends. Now the distance between us is too great. Forgive me, for I can never pay you back.' He held out his hand.   .

Bond brushed it aside. 'Don't be a damn fool, Darko,' he said roughly. 'My gun worked, that's all. Yours didn't. You'd better get one that does. For Christ's sake tell me what the hell this is all about. There's been too much blood splashing about tonight. I'm sick of it. I want a drink. Come and finish that raki.' He took the big man's arm.

As they reached the table, littered with the remains of the supper, a piercing, terrible scream came out of the depths of the orchard. Bond put his hand on his gun. Kerim shook his head. 'We shall soon know what the Faceless Ones were after,' he said gloomily. 'My friends are finding out. I can guess what they will discover. I think they will never forgive me for having been here tonight. Five of their men are dead.'

'There might have been a dead woman too,' said Bond unsympathetically. 'At least you've saved her life. Don't be stupid, Darko. These gipsies knew the risks when they started spying for you against the Bulgars. It was gang warfare.' He added a dash of water to two tumblers of raki.

They both emptied the glasses at one swallow. The head gipsy came up, wiping the tip of his curved dagger on a handful of grass. He sat down and accepted a glass of raki from Bond. He seemed quite cheerful. Bond had the impression that the fight had been too short for him. The gipsy said something, slyly.

Kerim chuckled. 'He said that his judgement was right. You killed well. Now he wants you to take on those two women.'

'Tell him even one of them would be too much for me. But tell him I think they are fine women. I would be glad if he would do me a favour and call the fight a draw. Enough of his people have been killed tonight. He will need these two girls to bear children for the tribe.'

Kerim translated. The gipsy looked sourly at Bond and said a few bitter words.

'He says that you should not have asked him such a difficult favour. He says that your heart is too soft for a good fighter. But he says he will do what you ask.'

The gipsy ignored Bond's smile of thanks. He started talking fast to Kerim, who listened attentively, occasionally interrupting the flow with a question. Krilencu's name was often mentioned. Kerim talked back. There was deep contrition in his voice and he refused to allow himself to be stopped by protests from the other. There came a last reference to Krilencu. Kerim turned to Bond.

'My friend,' he said drily. 'It is a curious affair. It seems the Bulgars were ordered to kill Vavra and as many of his men as possible. That is a simple matter. They knew the gipsy had been working for me. Perhaps, rather drastic. But in killing, the Russians have not much finesse. They like mass death. Vavra was a main target. I was another. The declaration of war against me personally I can also understand. But it seems that you were not to be harmed. You were exactly described so that there should be no mistake. That is odd. Perhaps it was desired that there should be no diplomatic repercussions. Who can tell? The attack was well planned. They came to the top of the hill by a roundabout route and free-wheeled down so that we should hear nothing. This is a lonely place and there is not a policeman for miles. I blame myself for having treated these people too lightly.' Kerim looked puzzled and unhappy. He seemed to make up his mind. He said, 'But now it is midnight. The Rolls will be here. There remains a small piece of work to be done before we go home to bed. And it is time we left these people. They have much to do before it is light. There are many bodies to go into the Bosphorus and there is the wall to be repaired. By daylight there must be no trace of these troubles. Our friend wishes you very well. He says you must return, and that Zora and Vida are yours until their breasts fall. He refuses to blame me for what has happened. He says that I am to continue sending him Bulgars. Ten were killed tonight. He would like some more. And now we will shake him by the hand and go. That is all he asks of

us. We are good friends, but we are also *gajos*. And I
expect he does not want us to see his women weeping
over their dead.'

Kerim stretched out his huge hand. Vavra took it and
held it and looked into Kerim's eyes. For a moment his
own fierce eyes seemed to go opaque. Then the gipsy let
the hand drop and turned to Bond. The hand was dry
and rough and padded like the paw of a big animal.
Again the eyes went opaque. He let go of Bond's hand.
He spoke rapidly and urgently to Kerim and turned his
back on them and walked away towards the trees.

Nobody looked up from his work as Kerim and Bond
climbed through the breach in the wall. The Rolls stood,
glittering in the moonlight, a few yards down the road
opposite the café entrance. A young man was sitting
beside the chauffeur. Kerim gestured with his hand.
'That is my tenth son. He is called Boris. I thought I
might need him. I shall.'

The youth turned and said, 'Good evening, sir.' Bond
recognized him as one of the clerks in the warehouse.
He was as dark and lean as the head clerk, and his eyes
also were blue.

The car moved down the hill. Kerim spoke to the
chauffeur in English. 'It is a small street off the Hippodrome Square. When we get there we will proceed
softly. I will tell you when to stop. Have you got the
uniforms and the equipment?'

'Yes, Kerim Bey.'

'All right. Make good speed. It is time we were all in
bed.'

Kerim sank back in his seat. He took out a cigarette.
They sat and smoked. Bond gazed out at the drab streets
and reflected that sparse street-lighting is the sure sign
of a poor town.

It was some time before Kerim spoke. Then he said,
'The gipsy said we both have the wings of death over us.
He said that I am to beware of a son of the snows and
you must beware of a man who is owned by the moon.'
He laughed harshly. 'That is the sort of rigmarole they

talk. But he says that Krilencu isn't either of these men. That is good.'

'Why?'

'Because I cannot sleep until I have killed that man. I do not know if what happened tonight has any connection with you and your assignment. I do not care. For some reason, war has been declared on me. If I do not kill Krilencu, at the third attempt he will certainly kill me. So we are now on our way to keep an appointment with him in Samarra.'

CHAPTER 19

The Mouth of Marilyn Monroe

The car sped through the deserted streets, past shadowy mosques from which dazzling minarets lanced up towards the three-quarter moon, under the ruined Aqueduct and across the Ataturk Boulevard and north of the barred entrances to the Grand Bazaar. At the Column of Constantine the car turned right, through mean twisting streets that smelled of garbage, and finally debouched into a long ornamental square in which three stone columns fired themselves like a battery of space-rockets into the spangled sky.

'Slow,' said Kerim softly. They crept round the square under the shadow of the lime trees. Down a street on the east side, the lighthouse below the Seraglio Palace gave them a great yellow wink.

'Stop.'

The car pulled up in the darkness under the limes. Kerim reached for the door handle. 'We shan't be long, James. You sit up front in the driver's seat and if a policeman comes along just say *"Ben Bey Kerim'in ortagiyim"*. Can you remember that? It means "I am

Kerim Bey's partner''. They'll leave you alone.'

Bond snorted. 'Thanks very much. But you'll be surprised to hear I'm coming with you. You're bound to get into trouble without me. Anyway I'm damned if I'm going to sit here trying to bluff policemen. The worst of learning one good phrase is that it sounds as if one knew the language. The policeman will come back with a barrage of Turkish and when I can't answer he'll smell a rat. Don't argue, Darko.'

'Well, don't blame me if you don't like this.' Kerim's voice was embarrassed. 'It's going to be a straight killing in cold blood. In my country you let sleeping dogs lie, but when they wake up and bite, you shoot them. You don't offer them a duel. All right?'

'Whatever you say,' said Bond. 'I've got one bullet left in case you miss.'

'Come on then,' said Kerim reluctantly. 'We've got quite a walk. The other two will be going another way.'

Kerim took a long walking-stick from the chauffeur, and a leather case. He slung them over his shoulder and they started off down the street into the yellow wink of the lighthouse. Their footsteps echoed hollowly back at them from the iron-shuttered shop frontages. There was not a soul in sight, not a cat, and Bond was glad he was not walking alone down this long street towards the distant baleful eye.

From the first, Istanbul had given him the impression of a town where, with the night, horror creeps out of the stones. It seemed to him a town the centuries had so drenched in blood and violence that, when daylight went out, the ghosts of its dead were its only population. His instinct told him, as it has told other travellers, that Istanbul was a town he would be glad to get out of alive.

They came to a narrow stinking alley that dived steeply down the hill to their right. Kerim turned into it and started gingerly down its cobbled surface. 'Watch your feet,' he said softly. 'Garbage is a polite word for what my charming people throw into their streets.'

The moon shone whitely down the moist river of cobbles. Bond kept his mouth shut and breathed through his nose. He put his feet down one after the other, flat-footedly, and with his knees bent, as if he was walking down a snowslope. He thought of his bed in the hotel and of the comfortable cushions of the car under the sweetly smelling lime trees, and he wondered how many more kinds of dreadful stench he was going to run into during his present assignment.

They stopped at the bottom of the alley. Kerim turned to him with a broad white grin. He pointed upwards at a towering block of black shadow. 'Mosque of Sultan Ahmet. Famous Byzantine frescoes. Sorry I haven't got time to show you more of the beauties of my country.' Without waiting for Bond's reply, he cut off to the right and along a dusty boulevard, lined with cheap shops, that sloped down towards the distant glint that was the Sea of Marmara. For ten minutes they walked in silence. Then Kerim slowed and beckoned Bond into the shadows.

'This will be a simple operation,' he said softly. 'Krilencu lives down there, beside the railway line.' He gestured vaguely towards a cluster of red and green lights at the end of the boulevard. 'He hides out in a shack behind a bill-boarding. There is a front door to the shack. Also a trapdoor to the street through the boarding. He thinks no one knows of this. My two men will go in at the front door. He will slip out through the hoarding. Then I shoot him. All right?'

'If you say so.'

They walked on down the boulevard, keeping close to the wall. After ten minutes, they came in sight of the twenty-foot-high boarding that formed a facing wall to the T intersection at the bottom of the street. The moon was behind the boarding and its face was in shadow. Now Kerim walked even more carefully, putting each foot softly in front of him. About a hundred yards from the boarding the shadows ended and the moon blazed whitely down on the intersection. Kerim stopped in the last dark doorway and stationed Bond in front of him, up against his chest. 'Now we must wait,' he whispered. Bond heard Kerim fiddling behind him. There came a soft plop as the lid of the leather case came off. A thin, heavy steel tube, about two feet long, with a bulge at each end, was pressed into Bond's hand. 'Sniperscope. German model,' whispered Kerim. 'Infra-red lens. Sees in the dark. Have a look at that big film advertisement over there. That face. Just below the nose. You'll see the outline of a trapdoor. In direct line down from the signal box.'

Bond rested his forearm against the door jamb and raised the tube to his right eye. He focused it on the patch of black shadow opposite. Slowly the black dissolved into grey. The outline of a huge woman's face and some lettering appeared. Now Bond could read the lettering. It said: 'NIYAGARA. MARILYN MONROE VE JOSEPH COTTEN' and underneath, the cartoon feature, 'BONZO FUTBOLOU'. Bond inched the glass down the vast pile of Marilyn Monroe's hair, and the cliff of forehead, and down the two feet of nose to the cavernous nostrils. A faint square showed in the poster. It ran from below the nose into the great alluring curve of the lips. It was about three feet deep. From it, there would be a longish drop to the ground.

Behind Bond there sounded a series of soft clicks. Kerim held forward his walking-stick. As Bond had supposed, it was a gun, a rifle, with a skeleton butt which was also a twist breech. The squat bulge of a silencer had taken the place of the rubber tip.

'Barrel from the new 88 Winchester,' whispered Kerim proudly. 'Put together for me by a man in Ankara. Takes the .308 cartridge. The short one. Three of them. Give me the glass. I want to get the trapdoor lined up before my men go in at the front. Mind if I use your shoulder as a rest?'

"All right.' Bond handed Kerim the Sniperscope. Kerim clipped it to the top of the barrel and slid the gun along Bond's shoulder.

'Got it,' whispered Kerim. 'Where Vavra said. He's a

good man that.' He lowered his gun just as two policemen appeared at the right-hand corner of the intersection. Bond stiffened.

'It's all right,' whispered Kerim. 'That's my boy and the chauffeur.' He put two fingers in his mouth. A very quick, very low-pitched whistle sounded for a fraction of a second. One of the policemen lifted his hand to the back of his neck. The two policemen turned and walked away, their boots ringing loudly on the paving stones.

'Few minutes more,' whispered Kerim. 'They've got to get round the back of that hoarding.' Bond felt the heavy barrel of the gun slip into place along his right shoulder.

The moonstruck silence was broken by a loud iron clang from the signal box behind the hoarding. One of the signal arms dropped. A green pinpoint of light showed among the cluster of reds. There was a soft slow rumble in the distance, away to the left by Seraglio Point. It came closer and sorted itself into the heavy pant of an engine and the grinding clangour of a string of badly coupled goods trucks. A faint yellow glimmer shone along the embankment to the left. The engine came labouring into view above the hoarding.

The train slowly clanked by on its hundred-mile journey to the Greek frontier, a broken black silhouette against the silver sea, and the heavy cloud of smoke from its cheap fuel drifted towards them on the still air. As the red light on the brake van glimmered briefly and disappeared, there came the deeper rumble as the engine entered a cutting, and then two harsh, mournful whoops as it whistled its approach to the little station of Buyuk, a mile farther down the line.

The rumble of the train died away. Bond felt the gun press deeper into his shoulder. He strained his eyes into the target of shadow. In the centre of it, a deeper square of blackness showed.

Bond cautiously lifted his left hand to shade his eyes from the moon. There came a hiss of breath from behind his right ear. 'He's coming.'

Out of the mouth of the huge, shadowed poster, between the great violet lips, half-open in ecstasy, the dark shape of a man emerged and hung down like a worm from the mouth of a corpse.

The man dropped. A ship going up towards the Bosphorus growled in the night like a sleepless animal in a zoo. Bond felt a prickle of sweat on his forehead. The barrel of the rifle depressed as the man stepped softly off the pavement towards them.

When he's at the edge of the shadow, he'll start to run, thought Bond. You damn fool, get the sights further down.

Now. The man bent for a quick sprint across the dazzling white street. He was coming out of the shadow. His right leg was bent forward and his shoulder was twisted to give him momentum.

At Bond's ear there was the clunk of an axe hitting into a tree-trunk. The man dived forward, his arms outstretched. There was a sharp 'tok' as his chin or his forehead hit the ground.

An empty cartridge tinkled down at Bond's feet. He heard the click of the next round going into the chamber.

The man's fingers scrabbled briefly at the cobbles. His shoes knocked on the road. Then he lay absolutely still.

Kerim grunted. The rifle came down off Bond's shoulder, Bond listened to the noises of Kerim folding up the gun and putting away the Sniperscope in its leather case.

Bond looked away from the sprawling figure in the road, the figure of the man who had been, but was no more. He had a moment of resentment against the life that made him witness these things. The resentment was not against Kerim. Kerim had twice been this man's target. In a way it had been a long duel, in which the man had fired twice to Kerim's once. But Kerim was the cleverer, cooler man, and the luckier, and that had been that. But Bond had never killed in cold blood, and he hadn't liked watching, and helping, someone else do it.

Kerim silently took his arm. They walked slowly away

from the scene and back the way they had come.

Kerim seemed to sense Bond's thoughts. 'Life is full of death, my friend' he said philosophically. 'And sometimes one is made the instrument of death. I do not regret killing that man. Nor would I regret killing any of those Russians we saw in that office today. They are hard people. With them, what you don't get from strength, you won't get from mercy. They are all the same, the Russians. I wish your government would realize it and be strong with them. Just an occasional little lesson in manners like I have taught them tonight.'

'In power politics, one doesn't often have the chance of being as quick and neat as you were tonight, Darko. And don't forget it's only one of their satellites you've punished, one of the men they always find to do their dirty work. Mark you,' said Bond, 'I quite agree about the Russians. They simply don't understand the carrot. Only the stick has any effect. Basically they're masochists. They love the knout. That's why they were so happy under Stalin. He gave it them. I'm not sure how they're going to react to the scraps of carrot they're being fed by Khrushchev and Co. As for England, the trouble today is that carrots for all are the fashion. At home and abroad. We don't show teeth any more—only gums.'

Kerim laughed harshly, but made no comment. They were climbing back up the stinking alley and there was no breath for talk. They rested at the top and then walked slowly towards the trees of the Hippodrome Square.

'So you forgive me for today?' It was odd to hear the longing for reassurance in the big man's usually boisterous voice.

'Forgive you? Forgive what? Don't be ridiculous.' There was affection in Bond's voice. 'You've got a job to do and you're doing it. I've been very impressed. You've got a wonderful set-up here. I'm the one who ought to apologize. I seem to have brought a great deal of trouble down on your head. And you've dealt with it. I've just tagged along behind. And I've got absolutely nowhere with my main job. M. will be getting pretty impatient. Perhaps there'll be some sort of message at the hotel.'

But when Kerim took Bond back to the hotel and went with him to the desk there was nothing for Bond. Kerim clapped him on the back. 'Don't worry, my friend,' he said cheerfully. 'Hope makes a good breakfast. Eat plenty of it. I will send the car in the morning and if nothing has happened I will think of some more little adventures to pass the time. Clean your gun and sleep on it. You both deserve a rest.'

Bond climbed the few stairs and unlocked his door and locked and bolted it behind him. Moonlight filtered through the curtains. He walked across and turned on the pink-shaded lights on the dressing-table. He stripped off his clothes and went into the bathroom and stood for a few minutes under the shower. He thought how much more eventful Saturday the fourteenth had been than Friday the thirteenth. He cleaned his teeth and gargled with a sharp mouthwash to get rid of the taste of the day and turned off the bathroom light and went back into the bedroom.

Bond drew aside one curtain and opened wide the tall windows and stood, holding the curtains open and looking out across the great boomerang curve of water under the riding moon. The night breeze felt wonderfully cool on his naked body. He looked at his watch. It said two o'clock.

Bond gave a shuddering yawn. He let the curtains drop back into place. He bent to switch off the lights on the dressing-table. Suddenly he stiffened and his heart missed a beat.

There had been a nervous giggle from the shadows at the back of the room. A girl's voice said, 'Poor Mister Bond. You must be tired. Come to bed.'

CHAPTER 20

Black on Pink

Bond whirled round. He looked over to the bed, but his eyes were blind from gazing at the moon. He crossed the room and turned on the pink-shaded light by the bed. There was a long body under the single sheet. Brown hair was spread out on the pillow. The tips of fingers showed, holding the sheet up over the face. Lower down the breasts stood up like hills under snow.

Bond laughed shortly. He leaned forward and gave the hair a soft tug. There was a squeak of protest from under the sheet. Bond sat down on the edge of the bed. After a moment's silence a corner of the sheet was cautiously lowered and one large blue eye inspected him.

'You look very improper.' The voice was muffled by the sheet.

'What about you! And how did you get here?'

'I walked down two floors. I live here too.' The voice was deep and provocative. There was very little accent.

'Well, I'm going to get into bed.'

The sheet came quickly down to the chin and the girl

pulled herself up on the pillows. She was blushing. 'Oh no. You mustn't.'

'But it's my bed. And anyway you told me to.' The face was incredibly beautiful. Bond examined it coolly. The blush deepened.

'That was only a phrase. To introduce myself.'

'Well I'm very glad to meet you. My name's James Bond.'

'Mine's Tatiana Romanova.' She sounded the second A of Tatiana and the first A of Romanova very long. 'My friends called me Tania.'

There was a pause while they looked at each other, the girl with curiosity, and with what might have been relief. Bond with cool surmise.

She was the first to break the silence. 'You look just like your photographs,' she blushed again. 'But you must put something on. It upsets me.'

'You upset me just as much. That's called sex. If I got into bed with you it wouldn't matter. Anyway, what have *you* got on?'

She pulled the sheet a fraction lower to show a quarter-inch black velvet ribbon round her neck. 'This.'

Bond looked down into the teasing blue eyes, now wide as if asking if the ribbon was inadequate. He felt his body getting out of control.

'Damn you, Tania. Where are the rest of your things? Or did you come down in the lift like that?'

'Oh no. That would not have been *kulturny*. They are under the bed.'

'Well, if you think you are going to get out of this room without . . .'

Bond left the sentence unfinished. He got up from the bed and went to put on one of the dark blue silk pyjama coats he wore instead of pyjamas.

'What you are suggesting is not *kulturny*.'

'Oh isn't it,' said Bond sarcastically. He came back to the bed and pulled up a chair beside it. He smiled down at her. 'Well I'll tell you something *kulturny*. You're one of the most beautiful women in the world.'

The girl blushed again. She looked at him seriously.

'Are you speaking the truth? I think my mouth is too big. Am I as beautiful as Western girls? I was once told I look like Greta Garbo. Is that so?'

'More beautiful,' said Bond. 'There is more light in your face. And your mouth isn't too big. It's just the right size. For me, anyway.'

'What is that—"light in the face"? What do you mean?'

Bond meant that she didn't look to him like a Russian spy. She seemed to show none of the reserve of a spy. None of the coldness, none of the calculation. She gave the impression of warmth of heart and gaiety. These things shone out through the eyes. He searched for a non-committal phrase. 'There is a lot of gaiety and fun in your eyes,' he said lamely.

Tatiana looked serious. 'That is curious,' she said. 'There is not much fun and gaiety in Russia. No one speaks of these things. I have never been told that before.'

Gaiety? She thought, after the last two months? How could she be looking gay? And yet, yes, there was a lightness in her heart. Was she a loose woman by nature? Or was it something to do with this man she had never seen before? Relief about him after the agony of thinking about what she had to do? It was certainly much easier than she had expected. He made it easy—made it fun, with a spice of danger. He was terribly handsome. And he looked very clean. Would he forgive her when they got to London and she told him? Told him that she had been sent to seduce him? Even the night on which she must do it and the number of the room? Surely he wouldn't mind very much. It was doing him no harm. It was only a way for her to get to England and make those reports. 'Gaiety and fun in her eyes.' Well, why not? It was possible. There was a wonderful sense of freedom being alone with a man like this and knowing that she would not be punished for it. It was really terribly exciting.

'You are very handsome,' she said. She searched for a

comparison that would give him pleasure. 'You are like an American film star.'

She was startled by his reaction. 'For God's sake! That's the worst insult you can pay a man!'

She hurried to make good her mistake. How curious that the compliment didn't please him. Didn't everyone in the West want to look like a film star? 'I was lying,' she said. 'I wanted to give you pleasure. In fact you are like my favourite hero. He's in a book by a Russian called Lermontov. I will tell you about him one day.'

One day? Bond thought it was time to get down to business.

'Now listen, Tania.' He tried not to look at the beautiful face on the pillow. He fixed his eyes on the point of her chin. 'We've got to stop fooling and be serious. What *is* all this about? Are you really going to come back to England with me?' He raised his eyes to hers. It was fatal. She had opened them wide again in that damnable guilelessness.

'But of course!'

'Oh!' Bond was taken aback by the directness of her answer. He looked at her suspiciously. 'You're sure?'

'Yes.' Her eyes were truthful now. She had stopped flirting.

'You're not afraid?'

He saw a shadow cross her eyes. But it was not what he thought. She had remembered that she had a part to play. She was to be frightened of what she was doing. Terrified. It had sounded so easy, this acting, but now it was difficult. How odd! She decided to compromise.

'Yes. I am afraid. But not so much now. You will protect me. I thought you would.'

'Well, yes, of course I will.' Bond thought of her relatives in Russia. He quickly put the thought out of his mind. What was he doing? Trying to dissuade her from coming? He closed his mind to the consequences he imagined for her. 'There's nothing to worry about. I'll look after you.' And now for the question he had been shirking. He felt a ridiculous embarrassment. This girl wasn't in the least what he had expected. It was spoiling everything to ask the question. It had to be done.

'What about the machine?'

Yes. It was as if he had cuffed her across the face. Pain showed in her eyes, and the edge of tears.

She pulled the sheet over her mouth and spoke from behind it. Her eyes above the sheet were cold.

'So that's what you want.'

'Now listen.' Bond put nonchalance in his voice. 'This machine's got nothing to do with you and me. But my people in London want it.' He remembered security. He added blandly. 'It's not all that important. They know all about the machine and they think it's a wonderful Russian invention. They just want one to copy. Like your people copy foreign cameras and things.' God, how lame it sounded!

'Now you're lying,' a big tear rolled out of one wide blue eye and down the soft cheek and on to the pillow. She pulled the sheet up over her eyes.

Bond reached out and put his hand on her arm under the sheet. The arm flinched angrily away.

'Damn the bloody machine,' he said impatiently. 'But for God's sake, Tania, you must know that I've got a job to do. Just say one way or the other and we'll forget about it. There are lots more things to talk about. We've got to arrange our journey and so on. Of course my people want it or they wouldn't have sent me out to bring you home with it.'

Tatiana dabbed her eyes with the sheet. Brusquely she pulled the sheet down to her shoulders again. She knew that she had been forgetting her job. It had just been that . . . Oh well. If only he had said that the machine didn't matter to him so long as she would come. But that was too much to hope for. He was right. He had a job to do. So had she.

She looked up at him calmly. 'I will bring it. Have no fear. But do not let us mention it again. And now listen.' She sat up straighter on the pillows. 'We must go tonight.' She remembered her lesson. 'It is the only chance. This evening I am on night duty from six o'clock. I shall be alone in the office and I will take the Spektor.'

Bond's eyes narrowed. His mind raced as he thought of the problems that would have to be faced. Where to hide her. How to get her out to the first plane after the loss had been discovered. It was going to be a risky business. They would stop at nothing to get her and the Spektor back. Roadblock on the way to the airport. Bomb in the plane. Anything.

'That's wonderful, Tania.' Bond's voice was casual. 'We'll keep you hidden and then we'll take the first plane tomorrow morning.'

'Don't be foolish.' Tatiana had been warned that here would be some difficult lines in her part. 'We will take the train. This Orient Express. It leaves at nine tonight. Do you think I haven't been thinking this thing out? I won't stay a minute longer in Istanbul than I have to. We will be over the frontier at dawn. You must get the tickets and a passport. I will travel with you as your wife.' She looked happily up at him. 'I shall like that. In one of those coupés I have read about. They must be very comfortable. Like a tiny house on wheels. During the day we will talk and read and at night you will stand in the corridor outside our house and guard it.'

'Like hell I will,' said Bond. 'But look here, Tania. That's crazy. They're bound to catch up with us somewhere. It's four days and five nights to London on that train. We've got to think of something else.'

'I won't,' said the girl flatly. 'That's the only way I'll go. If you are clever, how can they find out?'

Oh God, she thought. Why had they insisted on this train? But they had been definite. It was a good place for love, they had said. She would have four days to get him to love her. Then, when they got to London, life would be easy for her. He would protect her. Otherwise, if they flew to London, she would be put straight into prison. The four days were essential. And, they had warned her, we will have men on the train to see you don't get off. So be careful and obey your orders. Oh God. Oh God. Yet now she longed for those four days with him in the little house on wheels. How curious! It had been her duty to force him. Now it was her passionate desire.

She watched Bond's thoughtful face. She longed to stretch out a hand to him and reassure him that it would be all right; that this was a harmless *konspiratsia* to get her to England: that no harm could come to either of them, because that was not the object of the plot.

'Well, I still think it's crazy,' said Bond, wondering what M.'s reaction would be. 'But I suppose it may work. I've got the passport. It will need a Yugoslav visa,' he looked at her sternly. 'Don't think I'm going to take you on the part of the train that goes through Bulgaria, or I shall think you want to kidnap me.'

'I do.' Tatiana giggled. 'That's exactly what I want to do.'

'Now shut up, Tania. We've got to work this out. I'll get the tickets and I'll have one of our men come along. Just in case. He's a good man. You'll like him. Your name's Caroline Somerset. Don't forget it. How are you going to get to the train!'

'Karolin Siomerset,' the girl turned the name over in her mind. 'It is a pretty name. And you are Mister Siomerset.' She laughed happily. 'That is fun. Do not worry about me. I will come to the train just before it leaves. It is the Sirkeci Station. I know where it is. So that is all. And we do not worry any more. Yes?'

'Suppose you lose your nerve? Suppose they catch you?' Suddenly Bond was worried at the girl's confidence. How could she be so certain? A sharp tingle of suspicion ran down his spine.

'Before I saw you, I was frightened. Now I am not.' Tatiana tried to tell herself that this was the truth. Somehow it nearly was. 'Now I shall not lose my nerve, as you call it. And they cannot catch me. I shall leave my things in the hotel and take my usual bag to the office. I cannot leave my fur coat behind. I love it too dearly. But today is Sunday and that will be an excuse to come to the office in it. Tonight at half-past eight I shall walk out and take a taxi to the station. And now you must stop looking so worried.' Impulsively, because she had to, she stretched out a hand towards him. 'Say that you are pleased.'

Bond moved to the edge of the bed. He took her hand and looked down into her eyes. God, he thought. I hope it's all right. I hope this crazy plan will work. Is this wonderful girl a cheat? Is she true? Is she real? The eyes told him nothing except that the girl was happy, and that she wanted him to love her, and that she was surprised at what was happening to her. Tatiana's other hand came up and round his neck and pulled him fiercely down to her. At first the mouth trembled under his and then, as passion took her, the mouth yielded into a kiss without end.

Bond lifted his legs on to the bed. While his mouth went on kissing her, his hand went to her left breast and held it, feeling the peak hard with desire under his fingers. His hand strayed on down across her flat stomach. Her legs shifted languidly. She moaned softly and her mouth slid away from his. Below the closed eyes the long lashes quivered like humming birds' wings.

Bond reached up and took the edge of the sheet and pulled it right down and threw it off the end of the huge bed. She was wearing nothing but the black ribbon round her neck and black silk stockings rolled above her knees. Her arms groped up for him.

Above them, and unknown to both of them, behind the gold-framed false mirror on the wall over the bed, the two photographers from SMERSH sat close together in the cramped *cabinet de voyeur*, as, before them, so many friends of the proprietor had sat on a honeymoon night in a state room of the Kristal Palas.

And the view-finders gazed coldly down on the passionate arabesques the two bodies formed and broke and formed again, and the clockwork mechanism of the cine-cameras whirred softly on and on as the breath rasped out of the open mouths of the two men and the sweat of excitement trickled down their bulging faces into their cheap collars.

CHAPTER 21

Orient Express

The great trains are going out all over Europe, one by one, but still, three times a week, the Orient Express thunders superbly over the 1400 miles of glittering steel track between Istanbul and Paris.

Under the arc-lights, the long-chassied German locomotive panted quietly with the laboured breath of a dragon dying of asthma. Each heavy breath seemed certain to be the last. Then came another. Wisps of steam rose from the couplings between the carriages and died quickly in the warm August air. The Orient Express was the only live train in the ugly, cheaply architectured burrow that is Istanbul's main station. The trains on the other lines were engineless and unattended—wating for tomorrow. Only Track No. 3, and its platform, throbbed with the tragic poetry of departure.

The heavy bronze cipher on the side of the dark blue coach said, 'COMPAGNIE INTERNATIONALE DES WAGON-LITS ET DES GRANDS EXPRESS EUROPÉENS'. Above the cipher, fitted into metal slots, was a flat iron sign that announced, in black capitals on white, ORIENT EX-

PRESS, and underneath, in three lines:

ISTANBUL THESSALONIKI BEOGRAD
VENEZIA   MILAN
LAUSANNE   PARIS

James Bond gazed vaguely at one of the most romantic signs in the world. For the tenth time he looked at his
watch. 8.51. His eyes went back to the sign. All the
towns were spelled in the language of the country except
MILAN. Why not MILANO? Bond took out his handkerchief and wiped his face. Where the hell was the girl?
Had she been caught? Had she had second thoughts?
Had he been too rough with her last night, or rather this
morning, in the great bed?

8.55. The quiet pant of the engine had stopped. There
came an echoing whoosh as the automatic safety-valve
let off the excess steam. A hundred yards away, through
the milling crowd, Bond watched the station-master
raise a hand to the engine driver and fireman and start
walking slowly back down the train, banging the doors
of the third-class carriages up front. Passengers, mostly
peasants going back into Greece after a week-end with
their relatives in Turkey, hung out of the windows and
jabbered at the grinning crowd below.

Beyond, where the faded arc-lights stopped and the
dark blue night and the stars showed through the
crescent mouth of the station, Bond saw a red pinpoint
turn to green.

The station-master came nearer. The brown uni-
formed wagon-lit attendant tapped Bond on the arm.
'En voiture, s'il vous plaît.' The two rich-looking Turks
kissed their mistresses—they were too pretty to be
wives—and, with a barrage of laughing injunctions,
stepped on to the little iron pedestal and up the two tall
steps into the carriage. There were no other wagon-lit
travellers on the platform. The conductor, with an impatient glance at the tall Englishman, picked up the iron
pedestal and climbed with it into the train.

The station-master strode purposefully by. Two more
compartments, the first- and second-class carriages, and

then, when he reached the guard's van, he would lift the dirty green flag.

There was no hurrying figure coming up the platform from the *guichet*. High up above the *guichet,* near the ceiling of the station, the minute hand of the big illuminated clock jumped forward an inch and said 'Nine'.

A window banged down above Bond's head. Bond looked up. His immediate reaction was that the black veil was too wide-meshed. The intention to disguise the luxurious mouth and the excited blue eyes was amateurish.

'Quick.'

The train had begun to move. Bond reached for the passing handrail and swung up on to the step. The attendant was still holding open the door. Bond stepped unhurriedly through.

'Madam was late,' said the attendant. 'She came along the corridor. She must have entered by the last carriage.'

Bond went down the carpeted corridor to the centre coupé. A black 7 stood above a black 8 on the white metal lozenge. The door was ajar. Bond walked in and shut it behind him. The girl had taken off her veil and her black straw hat. She was sitting in the corner by the window. A long, sleek sable coat was thrown open to show a natural coloured shantung dress with a pleated skirt, honey-coloured nylons and a black crocodile belt and shoes. She looked composed.

'You have no faith, James.'

Bond sat down beside her. 'Tania,' he said, 'if there was a bit more room I'd put you across my knee and spank you. You nearly gave me heart failure. What happened?'

'Nothing,' said Tatiana innocently. 'What could happen? I said I would be here, and I am here. You have no faith. Since I am sure you are more interested in my dowry than in me, it is up there.'

Bond looked casually up. Two small cases were on the rack beside his suitcase. He took her hand. He said, 'Thank God you're safe.'

Something in his eyes, perhaps the flash of guilt, as he admitted to himself that he had been more interested in the girl than the machine, reassured her. She kept his hand in hers and sank contentedly back in her corner.

The train screeched slowly round Seraglio Point. The lighthouse lit up the roofs of the dreary shacks along the railway line. With his free hand Bond took out a cigarette and lit it. He reflected that they would soon be passing the back of the great bill-board where Krilencu had lived—until less than twenty-four hours ago. Bond saw again the scene in every detail. The white cross roads, the two men in the shadows, the doomed man slipping out through the purple lips.

The girl watched his face with tenderness. What was this man thinking? What was going on behind those cold level grey-blue eyes that sometimes turned soft and sometimes, as they had done last night before his passion had burned out in her arms, blazed like diamonds. Now they were veiled in thought. Was he worrying about them both? Worrying about their safety? If only she could tell him there was nothing to fear, that he was only her passport to England—him and the heavy case the Resident Director had given her that evening in the office. The Director had said the same thing. 'Here is your passport to England, Corporal,' he had said cheerfully. 'Look.' He had unzipped the bag: 'A brand new Spektor. Be certain not to open the bag again or let it out of your compartment until you get to the other end. Or this Englishman will take it away from you and throw you on the dust-heap. It is this machine they want. Do not let them take it from you, or you will have failed in your duty. Understood?'

A signal box loomed up in the blue dusk outside the window. Tatiana watched Bond get up and pull down the window and crane out into the darkness. His body was close to her. She moved her knee so that it touched him. How extraordinary, this passionate tenderness that had filled her ever since she had seen him last night standing naked at the window, his arms up to hold the curtains back, his profile, under the tousled black hair, intent and pale in the moonlight. And then the extraordinary fusing of their eyes and their bodies. The flame that had suddenly lit between them—between the two secret agents, thrown together from enemy camps a whole world apart, each involved in his own plot against the country of the other, antagonists by profession, yet turned, and by the orders of their governments, into lovers.

Tatiana stretched out a hand and caught hold of the edge of the coat and tugged at it. Bond pulled up the window and turned. He smiled down at her. He read her eyes. He bent and put his hands on the fur over her breasts and kissed her hard on the lips. Tatiana leant back, dragging him with her.

There came a soft double knock on the door. Bond stood up. He pulled out his handkerchief and brusquely scrubbed the rouge off his lips. 'That'll be my friend Kerim,' he said. 'I must talk to him. I will tell the conductor to make up the beds. Stay here while he does it. I won't be long. I shall be outside the door.' He leant forward and touched her hand and looked at her wide eyes and at her rueful, half-open lips. 'We shall have all the night to ourselves. First I must see that you are safe.' He unlocked the door and slipped out.

Darko Kerim's huge bulk was blocking the corridor. He was leaning on the brass guard-rail, smoking and gazing moodily out towards the Sea of Marmara that receded as the long train snaked away from the coast and turned inland and northwards. Bond leaned on the rail beside him. Kerim looked into the reflection of Bond's face in the dark window. He said softly, 'The news is not good. There are three of them on the train.'

'Ah!' An electric tingle ran up Bond's spine.

'It's the three strangers we saw in that room. Obviously they're on to you and the girl.' Kerim glanced sharply sideways. 'That makes her a double. Or doesn't it?'

Bond's mind was cool. So the girl had been bait. And yet, and yet. No, damn it. She couldn't be acting. It wasn't possible. The cipher machine? Perhaps after all it wasn't in that bag. 'Wait a minute,' he said. He turned and knocked softly on the door. He heard her unlock it and slip the chain. He went in and shut the door. She looked surprised. She had thought it was the conductor come to make up the beds.

She smiled radiantly. 'You have finished?'

'Sit down, Tatiana. I've got to talk to you.'

Now she saw the coldness in his face and her smile went out. She sat down obediently with her hands in her lap.

Bond stood over her. Was there guilt in her face, or fear? No, only surprise and coolness to match his own expression.

'Now listen, Tatiana,' Bond's voice was deadly. 'Something's come up. I must look into that bag and see if the machine is there.'

She said indifferently, 'Take it down and look.' She examined the hands in her lap. So now it was going to come. What the Director had said. They were going to take the machine and throw her aside, perhaps have her put off the train. Oh God! This man was going to do that to her.

Bond reached up and hauled down the heavy case and put it on the seat. He tore the zip sideways and looked in. Yes, a grey japanned metal case with three rows of squat keys, rather like a typewriter. He held the bag open towards her.

'Is that a Spektor?'

She glanced casually into the gaping bag. 'Yes.'

Bond zipped the bag shut and put it back on the rack. He sat down beside the girl. 'There are three M.G.B. men on the train. We know they are the ones who arrived at your centre on Monday. What are they doing here, Tatiana?' Bond's voice was soft. He watched her, searched her with all his senses.

She looked up. There were tears in her eyes. Were they the tears of a child found out? But there was no trace of guilt in her face. She only looked terrified of something.

She reached out a hand and then drew it back. 'You aren't going to throw me off the train now you've got the machine?'

'Of course not,' Bond said impatiently. 'Don't be

idiotic. But we must know what these men are doing. What's it all about? Did you know they were going to be on the train?' He tried to read some clue in her expression. He could only see a great relief. And what else? A look of calculation? Of reserve? Yes, she was hiding something. But what?

Tatiana seemed to make up her mind. Brusquely she wiped the back of her hand across her eyes. She reached forward and put the hand on his knee. The streak of tears showed on the back of the hand. She looked into Bond's eyes, forcing him to believe her.

'James,' she said. 'I did not know these men were on the train. I was told they were leaving today. For Germany. I assumed they would fly. That is all I can tell you. Until we arrive in England, out of reach of my people, you must not ask me more. I have done what I said I would. I am here with the machine. Have faith in me. Do not be afraid for us. I am certain these men do not mean us harm. Absolutely certain. Have faith.' (Was she so certain, wondered Tatiana? Had the Klebb woman told her all the truth? But she also must have faith —faith in the orders she had been given. These men must be the guards to see that she didn't get off the train. They would mean no harm. Later, when they got to London, this man would hide her away out of SMERSH and she would tell him everything he wanted to know. She had already decided this in the back of her mind. But God knew what would happen if she betrayed *Them* now. *They* would somehow get her, and him. She knew it. There were no secrets from these people. And *They* would have no mercy. So long as she played out her role, all would be well.) Tatiana watched Bond's face for a sign that he believed her.

Bond shrugged his shoulders. He stood up. 'I don't know what to think, Tatiana,' he said. 'You are keeping something from me, but I think it's something you don't know is important. And I believe you think we are safe. We may be. It may be a coincidence that these men are on the train. I must talk to Kerim and decide what to do. Don't worry. We will look after you. But we must be very careful.'

Bond looked round the compartment. He tried the communicating door with the next coupé. It was locked. He decided to wedge it when the conductor had gone. He would do the same for the door into the passage. And he would have to stay awake. So much for the honeymoon on wheels! Bond smiled grimly to himself and rang for the conductor. Tatiana was looking anxiously up at him. 'Don't worry, Tania,' he said again. 'Don't worry about anything. Go to bed when the man has gone. Don't open the door unless you know it's me. I will sit up tonight and watch. Perhaps tomorrow it will be easier. I will make a plan with Kerim. He is a good man.'

The conductor knocked. Bond let him in and went out into the corridor. Kerim was still there gazing out. The train had picked up speed and was hurtling through the night, its harsh melancholy whistle echoing back at them from the walls of a deep cutting against the sides of which the lighted carriage windows flickered and danced. Kerim didn't move, but his eyes in the mirror of the window were watchful.

Bond told him of the conversation. It was not easy to explain to Kerim why he trusted the girl as he did. He watched the mouth in the window curl ironically as he tried to describe what he had read in her eyes and what his intuition told him.

Kerim sighed resignedly. 'James,' he said, 'you are now in charge. This is your part of the operation. We have already argued most of this out today—the danger of the train, the possibility of getting the machine home in the diplomatic bag, the integrity, or otherwise, of this girl. It certainly appears that she has surrendered unconditionally to you. At the same time you admit that you have surrendered to her. Perhaps only partially. But you have decided to trust her. In this morning's telephone talk with M. he said that he would back your decision. He left it to you. So be it. But he didn't know we were to have an escort of three M.G.B. men. Nor did we. And I think that would have changed all our views. Yes?'

'Yes.'

'Then the only thing to do is eliminate these three men. Get them off the train. God knows what they're here for. I don't believe in coincidences any more than you. But one thing is certain. We are not going to share the train with these men. Right?'

'Of course.'

'Then leave it to me. At least for tonight. This is still my country and I have certain powers in it. And plenty of money. I cannot afford to kill them. The train would be delayed. You and the girl might get involved. But I shall arrange something. Two of them have sleeping berths. The senior man with the moustache and the little pipe is next door to you—here, in No. 6.' He gestured backwards with his head. 'He is travelling on a German passport under the name of "Melchior Benz, salesman". The dark one, the Armenian, is in No. 12. He, too, has a German passport—"Kurt Goldfarb, construction engineer". They have through tickets to Paris. I have seen their documents. I have a police card. The conductor made no trouble. He has all the tickets and passports in his cabin. The third man, the man with a boil on the back of his neck, turns out also to have boils on his face. A stupid, ugly looking brute. I have not seen his passport. He is travelling sitting up in the first-class, in the next compartment to me. He does not have to surrender his passport until the frontier. But he has surrendered his ticket.' Like a conjuror, Kerim flicked a yellow first-class ticket out of his coat pocket. He slipped it back. He grinned proudly at Bond.

'How the hell?'

Kerim chuckled. 'Before he settled down for the night, this dumb ox went to the lavatory. I was standing in the corridor and I suddenly remembered how we used to steal rides on the train when I was a boy. I gave him a minute. Then I walked up and rattled the lavatory door. I hung on to the handle very tight. "Ticket collector," I said in a loud voice. "Tickets please." I said it in French and again in German. There was a mumble from inside. I felt him try to open the door. I hung on tight so that he would think the door had stuck. "Do not derange yourself, *Monsieur*," I said politely. "Push the ticket under the door.'' There was more fiddling with the door handle and I could hear heavy breathing. Then there was a pause and rustle under the door. There was the ticket. I said *"Merci, Monsieur"* very politely. I picked up the ticket and stepped across the coupling into the next carriage.' Kerim airily waved a hand. 'The stupid oaf will be sleeping peacefully by now. He will think that his ticket will be given back to him at the frontier. He is mistaken. The ticket will be in ashes and the ashes will be on the four winds,' Kerim gestured towards the darkness outside. 'I will see that the man is put off the train, however much money he has got. He will be told that the circumstances must be investigated, his statements corroborated with the ticket agency. He will be allowed to proceed on a later train.'

Bond smiled at the picture of Kerim playing his private school trick. 'You're a card, Darko. What about the other two?'

Darko Kerim shrugged his massive shoulders. 'Something will occur to me,' he said confidently. 'The way to catch Russians is to make them look foolish. Embarrass them. Laugh at them. They can't stand it. We will somehow make these men sweat. Then we will leave it to the M.G.B. to punish them for failing in their duty. Doubtless they will be shot by their own people.'

While they were talking, the conductor had come out of No. 7. Kerim turned to Bond and put a hand on his shoulder. 'Have no fear, James,' he said cheerfully. 'We will defeat these people. Go to your girl. We will meet again in the morning. We shall not sleep much tonight, but that cannot be helped. Every day is different. Perhaps we shall sleep tomorrow.'

Bond watched the big man move off easily down the swaying corridor. He noticed that, despite the movement of the train, Kerim's shoulders never touched the walls of the corridor. Bond felt a wave of affection for the tough, cheerful professional spy.

Kerim disappeared into the conductor's cabin. Bond turned and knocked softly on the door of No. 7.

CHAPTER 22

Out of Turkey

The train howled on through the night. Bond sat
and watched the hurrying moonlit landscape and con-
centrated on keeping awake.

Everything conspired to make him sleep—the hasty
metal gallop of the wheels, the hypnotic swoop of the
silver telegraph wires, the occasional melancholy,
reassuring moan of the steam whistle clearing their way,
the drowsy metallic chatter of the couplings at each end
of the corridor, the lullaby creak of the woodwork in
the little room. Even the deep violet glimmer of the
night-light above the door seemed to say, 'I will watch
for you. Nothing can happen while I am burning. Close
your eyes and sleep, sleep.'

The girl's head was warm and heavy on his lap. There
was so obviously just room for him to slip under the
single sheet and fit close up against her, the front of his
thighs against the back of hers, his head in the spread
curtain of her hair on the pillow.

Bond screwed up his eyes and opened them again. He
cautiously lifted his wrist. Four o'clock. Only one more

hour to the Turkish frontier. Perhaps he would be able to sleep during the day. He would give her the gun and wedge the doors again and she could watch.

He looked down at the beautiful sleeping profile. How innocent she looked, this girl from the Russian Secret Service—the lashes fringing the soft swell of the cheek, the lips parted and unaware, the long strand of hair that had strayed untidily across her forehead and that he wanted to brush back neatly to join the rest, the steady slow throb of the pulse in the offered neck. He felt a surge of tenderness and the impulse to gather her up in his arms and strain her tight against him. He wanted her to wake, from a dream perhaps, so that he could kiss her and tell her that everything was all right, and see her settle happily back to sleep.

The girl had insisted on sleeping like this. 'I won't go to sleep unless you hold me,' she had said. 'I must know you're there all the time. It would be terrible to wake up and not be touching you. Please, James. Please, *duschka.*'

Bond had taken off his coat and tie and had arranged himself in the corner with his feet up on his suitcase and the Beretta under the pillow within reach of his hand. She had made no comment about the gun. She had taken off all her clothes, except the black ribbon round her throat, and had pretended not to be provocative as she scrambled impudically into bed and wriggled herself into a comfortable position. She had held up her arms to him. Bond had pulled her head back by her hair and had kissed her once, long and cruelly. Then he had told her to go to sleep and had leant back and waited icily for his body to leave him alone. Grumbling sleepily, she had settled herself, with one arm flung across his thighs. At first she had held him tightly, but her arm had gradually relaxed and then she was asleep.

Brusquely Bond closed his mind to the thought of her and focused on the journey ahead.

Soon they would be out of Turkey. But would Greece be any easier? No love lost between Greece and England. And Yugoslavia? Whose side was Tito on?

Probably both. Whatever the orders of the three M.G.B. men, either they already knew Bond and Tatiana were on the train or they would soon find out. He and the girl couldn't sit for four days in this coupé with the blinds drawn. Their presence would be reported back to Istanbul, telephoned from some station, and by the morning the loss of the Spektor would have been discovered. Then what? A hasty démarche through the Russian embassy in Athens or Belgrade? Have the girl taken off the train as a thief? Or was that all too simple? And if it was more complicated—if all this was part of some mysterious plot, some tortuous Russian conspiracy—should he dodge it? Should he and the girl leave the train at a wayside station, on the wrong side of the track, and hire a car and somehow get a plane to London?

Outside, the luminous dawn had begun to edge the racing trees and rocks with blue. Bond looked at his watch. Five o'clock. They would soon be at Uzunkopru. What was going on down the train behind him? What had Kerim achieved?

Bond sat back, relaxed. After all there was a simple, common sense answer to his problem. If, between them, they could quickly get rid of the three M.G.B. agents, they would stick to the train and to their original plan. If not, Bond would get the girl and the machine off the train, somewhere in Greece, and take another route home. But, if the odds improved, Bond was for going on. He and Kerim were resourceful men. Kerim had an agent in Belgrade who was going to meet the train. There was always the Embassy.

Bond's mind raced on, adding up the pros, dismissing the cons. Behind his reasoning, Bond calmly admitted to himself that he had an insane desire to play the game out and see what it was all about. He wanted to take these people on and solve the mystery and, if it was some sort of a plot, defeat it. M. had left him in charge. He had the girl and the machine under his hand. Why panic? What was there to panic about? It would be mad to run away and perhaps only escape one trap in order to fall into another one.

The train gave a long whistle and began to slacken speed.

Now for the first round. If Kerim failed. If the three men stayed on the train. . . .

Some goods-trucks, led by a straining engine, filed by. The silhouette of sheds showed briefly. With a jolt and a screech of couplings, the Orient Express took the points and swerved away from the through line. Four sets of rails with grass growing between them showed outside the window, and the empty length of the down platform. A cock crowed. The express slowed to walking speed and finally, with a sigh of vacuum brakes and a noisy whoosh of let-off steam, ground to a stop. The girl stirred in her sleep. Bond softly shifted her head on the pillow and got up and slipped out of the door.

It was a typical Balkan wayside station—a facade of dour buildings in over-pointed stone, a dusty expanse of platform, not raised, but level with the ground so that there was a long step down from the train, some chickens pecking about and a few drab officials standing idly, unshaven, not even trying to look important. Up towards the cheap half of the train, a chattering horde of peasants with bundles and wicker baskets waited for the customs and passport control so that they could clamber abroad and join the swarm inside.

Across the platform from Bond was a closed door with a sign over it which said POLIS. Through the dirty window beside the door Bond thought he caught a glimpse of the head and shoulders of Kerim.

'Passeports. Douanes!'

A plain-clothes man and two policemen in dark green uniform with pistol holsters at their black belts entered the corridor. The wagon-lit conductor preceded them, knocking on the doors.

At the door of No. 12 the conductor made an indignant speech in Turkish, holding out the stack of tickets and passports and fanning through them as if they were a pack of cards. When he had finished, the plain-clothes man, beckoning forward the two policemen, knocked smartly on the door and, when it was opened, stepped inside. The two policemen stood guard behind him.

Bond edged down the corridor. He could hear a jumble of bad German. One voice was cold, the other was frightened and hot. The passport and ticket of Herr Kurt Goldfarb were missing. Had Herr Goldfarb removed them from the conductor's cabin? Certainly not. Had Herr Goldfarb in truth ever surrendered his papers to the conductor? Naturally. Then the matter was unfortunate. An inquiry would have to be held. No doubt the German Legation in Istanbul would put the matter right (Bond smiled at this suggestion). Meanwhile, it was regretted that Herr Goldfarb could not continue his journey. No doubt he would be able to proceed tomorrow. Herr Goldfarb would get dressed. His luggage would be transported to the waiting-room.

The M.G.B. man who erupted into the corridor was the dark Caucasian type man, the junior of the 'visitors'. His sallow face was grey with fear. His hair was awry and he was dressed only in the bottom half of his pyjamas. But there was nothing comical about his desperate flurry down the corridor. He brushed past Bond. At the door of No. 6 he paused and pulled himself together. He knocked with tense control. The door opened on the chain and Bond glimpsed a thick nose and part of a moustache. The chain was slipped and Goldfarb went in. There was silence, during which the plain-clothes man dealt with the papers of two elderly French women in 9 and 10, and then with Bond's.

The officer barely glanced at Bond's passport. He snapped it shut and handed it to the conductor. 'You are travelling with Kerim Bey?' he asked in French. His eyes were remote.

'Yes.'

'*Merci, Monsieur. Bon voyage.*' The man saluted. He turned and rapped sharply on the door of No. 6. The door opened and he went in.

Five minutes later the door was flung back. The plain-clothes man, now erect with authority, beckoned forward the policemen. He spoke to them harshly in Turkish. He turned back to the coupé. 'Consider yourself under arrest, Mein Herr. Attempted bribery of officials is a grave crime in Turkey.' There was an angry clamour in Goldfarb's bad German. It was cut short by one hard sentence in Russian. A different Goldfarb, a Goldfarb with madman's eyes, emerged and walked blindly down the corridor and went in No. 12. A policeman stood outside the door and waited.

'And *your* papers, Mein Herr. Please step forward. I must verify this photograph.' The plain-clothes man held the green-backed German passport up to the light. 'Forward, please.'

Reluctantly, his heavy face pale with anger, the M.G.B. man who called himself Benz stepped out into the corridor in a brilliant blue silk dressing-gown. The hard brown eyes looked straight into Bond's, ignoring him.

The plain-clothes man slapped the passport shut and handed it to the conductor. 'Your papers are in order, Mein Herr. And now, if you please, the baggage.' He went in, followed by the second policeman. The M.G.B. man turned his blue back on Bond and watched the search.

Bond noticed the bulge under the left arm of the dressing-gown, and the ridge of a belt round the waist. He wondered if he should tip off the plain-clothes man. He decided it would be better to keep quiet. He might be hauled in as a witness.

The search was over. The plain-clothes man saluted coldly and moved on down the corridor. The M.G.B. man went back into No. 6 and slammed the door behind him.

Pity, thought Bond. One had got away.

Bond turned back to the window. A bulky man, wearing a grey Homburg, and with an angry boil on the back of his neck, was being escorted through the door marked POLIS. Down the corridor a door slammed.

Goldfarb, escorted by the policeman, stepped down off the train. With bent head, he walked across the dusty platform and disappeared through the same door.

The engine whistled, a new kind of whistle, the brave shrill blast of a Greek engine-driver. The door of the wagon-lit carriage clanged shut. The plain-clothes man and the second policeman appeared walking over to the station. The guard at the back of the train looked at his watch and held out his flag. There was a jerk and a diminishing crescendo of explosive puffs from the engine and the front section of the Orient Express began to move. The section that would be taking the northern route through the Iron Curtain—through Dragoman on the Bulgarian frontier, only fifty miles away—was left beside the dusty platform, waiting.

Bond pulled down the window and took a last look back at the Turkish frontier, where two men would be sitting in a bare room under what amounted to sentence of death. Two birds down, he thought. Two out of three. The odds looked more respectable.

He watched the dead, dusty platform, with its chickens and the small black figure of the guard, until the long train took the points and jerked harshly on to the single main line. He looked away across the ugly, parched countryside towards the golden guinea sun climbing out of the Turkish plain. It was going to be a beautiful day.

Bond drew his head in out of the cool, sweet morning air. He pulled up the window with a bang.

He had made up his mind. He would stay on the train and see the thing through.

CHAPTER 23

Out of Greece

Hot coffee from the meagre little buffet at Pithion (there would be no restaurant car until midday), a painless visit from the Greek customs and passport control, and then the berths were folded away as the train hurried south towards the Gulf of Enez at the head of the Aegean. Outside, there was extra light and colour. The air was drier. The men at the little stations and in the fields were handsome. Sunflowers, maize, vines and racks of tobacco were ripening in the sun. It was, as Darko had said, another day.

Bond washed and shaved under the amused eyes of Tatiana. She approved of the fact that he put no oil on his hair. 'It is a dirty habit,' she said. 'I was told that many Europeans have it. We would not think of doing it in Russia. It dirties the pillows. But it is odd that you in the West do not use perfume. All our men do.'

'We wash,' said Bond dryly.

In the heat of her protests, there came a knock on the door. It was Kerim. Bond let him in. Kerim bowed towards the girl. 'What a charming domestic scene,' he commented cheerfully, lowering his bulk into the corner near the door. 'I have rarely seen a handsomer pair of spies.'

Tatiana glowered at him. 'I am not accustomed to Western jokes,' she said coldly.

Kerim's laugh was disarming. 'You'll learn, my dear. In England, they are great people for jokes. There it is considered proper to make a joke of everything. I also have learned to make jokes. They grease the wheels. I have been laughing a lot this morning. Those poor fellows at Uzunkopree. I wish I could be there when the police telephone the German Consulate in Istanbul. That is the worst of forged passports. They are not difficult to make, but it is almost impossible to forge also their birth certificate—the files of the country which is supposed to have issued them. I fear the careers of your two comrades have come to a sad end, Mrs. Somerset.'

'How did you do it?' Bond knotted his tie.

'Money and influence. Five hundred dollars to the conductor. Some big talk to the police. It was lucky our friend tried a bribe. A pity that crafty Benz next door,' he gestured at the wall, 'didn't get involved. I couldn't do the passport trick twice. We will have to get him some other way. The man with the boils was easy. He knew no German and travelling without a ticket is a serious matter. Ah well, the day has started favourably. We have won the first round, but our friend next door will now be very careful. He knows what he has to reckon with. Perhaps that is for the best. It would have been a nuisance having to keep you both under cover all day. Now we can move about—even have lunch together, as long as you bring the family jewels with you. We must watch to see if he makes a telephone call at one of the stations. But I doubt if he could tackle the Greek telephone exchange. He will probably wait until we are in Yugoslavia. But there I have my machine. We can get reinforcements if we need them. It should be a most interesting journey. There is always excitement on the Orient Express,' Kerim got to his feet. He opened the door, 'and romance.' He smiled across the compartment. 'I will call for you at lunchtime! Greek food is worse than Turkish, but even my stomach is in the service of the Queen.'

Bond got up and locked the door. Tatiana snapped, 'Your friend is not *kulturny!* It is disloyal to refer to your Queen in that manner.'

Bond sat down beside her. 'Tania,' he said patiently, 'that is a wonderful man. He is also a good friend. As far as I am concerned he can say anything he likes. He is jealous of me. He would like to have a girl like you. So he teases you. It is a form of flirting. You should take it as a compliment.'

'You think so?' she turned her large blue eyes on his. 'But what he said about his stomach and the head of your State. That was being rude to your Queen. It would be considered very bad manners to say such a thing in Russia.'

They were still arguing when the train ground to a halt in the sun-baked, fly-swarming station of Alexandropolis. Bond opened the door into the corridor and the sun poured in across a pale mirrored sea that married, almost without horizon, into a sky the colour of the Greek flag.

They had lunch, with the heavy bag under the table between Bond's feet. Kerim quickly made friends with the girl. The M.G.B. man called Benz avoided the restaurant car. They saw him on the platform buying sandwiches and beer from a buffet on wheels. Kerim suggested they ask him to make a four at bridge. Bond suddenly felt very tired and his tiredness made him feel that they were turning this dangerous journey into a picnic. Tatiana noticed his silence. She got up and said that she must rest. As they went out of the wagon-restaurant they heard Kerim calling gaily for brandy and cigars.

Back in the compartment, Tatiana said firmly, 'Now it is you who will sleep.' She drew down the blind and shut out the hard afternoon light and the endless baked fields of maize and tobacco and wilting sunflowers. The compartment became a dark green underground cavern. Bond wedged the doors and gave her his gun and stretched out with his head in her lap and was immediately asleep.

The long train snaked along the north of Greece below the foothills of the Rhodope Mountains. Xanthi came, and Drama, and Serrai, and then they were in the Macedonian highlands and the line swerved due south towards Salonica.

It was dusk when Bond woke in the soft cradle of her lap. At once, as if she had been waiting for the moment, Tatiana took his face between her hands and looked down into his eyes and said urgently, 'Dushka, how long shall we have this for?'

'For long.' Bond's thoughts were still luxurious with sleep.

'But for how long?'

Bond gazed up into the beautiful, worried eyes. He cleared the sleep out of his mind. It was impossible to see beyond the next three days on the train, beyond their arrival in London. One had to face the fact that this girl was an enemy agent. His feelings would be of no interest to the interrogators from his Service and from the Ministries. Other intelligence services would also want to know what this girl had to tell them about the machine she had worked for. Probably at Dover she would be taken away to 'The Cage', that well-sentried private house near Guildford, where she would be put in a comfortable, but oh so well-wired room. And the efficient men in plain clothes would come one by one and sit and talk with her, and the recorder would spin in the room below and the records would be transcribed and sifted for their grains of new fact—and, of course, for the contradictions they would trap her into. Perhaps they would introduce a stool-pigeon—a nice Russian girl who would commiserate with Tatiana over her treatment and suggest ways of escape, of turning double, of getting 'harmless' information back to her parents. This might go on for weeks or months. Meanwhile Bond would be tactfully kept away from her, unless the interrogators thought he could extract further secrets by using their feelings for each other. Then what? The changed name, the offer of a new life in Canada, the thousand pounds a year she would be given from the secret funds? And where would he be when she came out of it all? Perhaps the other side of the world. Or, if he was still in London, how much of her feeling for him would have survived the grinding of the interrogation machine? How much would she hate or despise the English after going through all this? And, for the matter of that, how much would have survived of his own hot flame?

'Dushka,' repeated Tatiana impatiently. 'How long?'

'As long as possible. It will depend on us. Many people will interfere. We shall be separated. It will not always be like this in a little room. In a few days we shall have to step out into the world. It will not be easy. It would be foolish to tell you anything else.'

Tatiana's face cleared. She smiled down at him. 'You are right. I will not ask any more foolish questions. But we must waste no more of these days.' She shifted his head and got up and lay down beside him.

An hour later, when Bond was standing in the corridor, Darko Kerim was suddenly beside him. He examined Bond's face. He said slyly, 'You should not sleep so long. You have been missing the historic landscape of northern Greece. And it is time for the *premier service.'*

'All you think about is food,' said Bond. He gestured back with his head. 'What about our friend?'

'He has not stirred. The conductor has been watching for me. That man will end up the richest conductor in the wagon-lit company. Five hundred dollars for Gold-farb's papers, and now a hundred dollars a day retainer until the end of the journey.' Kerim chuckled. 'I have told him he may even get a medal for his services to Turkey. He believes we are after a smuggling gang. They're always using this train for running Turkish opium to Paris. He is not surprised, only pleased that he is being paid so well. And now, have you found out anything more from this Russian princess you have in there? I still feel disquiet. Everything is too peaceful.

Those two men we left behind may have been quite innocently bound for Berlin as the girl says. This Benz may be keeping to his room because he is frightened of us. All is going well with our journey. And yet, and yet . . .' Kerim shook his head. 'These Russians are great chess players. When they wish to execute a plot, they execute it brilliantly. The game is planned minutely, the gambits of the enemy are provided for. They are foreseen and countered. At the back of my mind,' Kerim's face in the window was gloomy, 'I have a feeling that you and I and this girl are pawns on a very big board—that we are being allowed our moves because they do not interfere with the Russian game.'

'But what is the object of the plot?' Bond looked out into the darkness. He spoke to his reflection in the window. 'What can they want to achieve? We always get back to that. Of course we have all smelt a conspiracy of some sort. And the girl may not even know that she's involved in it. I know she's hiding something, but I think it's only some small secret she thinks is unimportant. She says she'll tell me everything when we get to London. Everything? What does she mean? She only says that I must have faith—that there is no danger. You must admit, Darko,' Bond looked up for confirmation into the slow crafty eyes, 'that she's lived up to her story.'

There was no enthusiasm in Kerim's eyes. He said nothing.

Bond shrugged. 'I admit I've fallen for her. But I'm not a fool, Darko. I've been watching for any clue, anything that would help. You know one can tell a lot when certain barriers are down. Well they are down, and I know she's telling the truth. At any rate ninety per cent of it. And I know she thinks the rest doesn't matter. If she's cheating, she's also being cheated herself. On your chess analogy, that is possible. But you still get back to the question of what it's all in aid of.' Bond's voice hardened. 'And, if you want to know, all I ask is to go on with the game until we find out.'

Kerim smiled at the obstinate look on Bond's face.

He laughed abruptly. 'If it was me, my friend, I would slip off the train at Salonica—with the machine, and, if you like, with the girl also, though that is not so important. I would take a hired car to Athens and get on the next plane for London. But I was not brought up "to be a sport".' Kerim put irony into the words. 'This is not a game to me. It is a business. For you it is different. You are a gambler. M. also is a gambler. He obviously is, or he would not have given you a free hand. He also wants to know the answer to this riddle. So be it. But I like to play safe, to make certain, to leave as little as possible to chance. You think the odds look right, that they are in your favour?' Darko Kerim turned and faced Bond. His voice became insistent. 'Listen, my friend,' he put a huge hand on Bond's shoulder. 'This is a billiard table. An easy, flat, green billiard table. And you have hit your white ball and it is travelling easily and quietly towards the red. The pocket is alongside. Fatally, inevitably, you are going to hit the red and the red is going into that pocket. It is the law of the billiard room, or a gas main is about to explode, or lightning is about to strike. And the building collapses on top of you and on top of the billiard table. Then what has happened to that white ball that could not miss the red ball, and to the red ball that could not miss the pocket? The white ball could not miss according to the laws of the billiard table. But the laws of the billiard table are not the only laws, and the laws governing the progress of this train, and of you to your destination, are also not the only laws in this particular game.'

Kerim paused. He dismissed his harangue with a shrug of the shoulders. 'You already know these things, my friend,' he said apologetically. 'And I have made myself thirsty talking platitudes. Hurry the girl up and we will go and eat. But watch for surprises, I beg of you.' He made a cross with his fingers over the centre of his coat. 'I do not cross my heart. That is being too serious. But I cross my stomach, which is an important oath for me. There are surprises on the way for both of us. The gipsy said to watch out. Now I say the same. We

can play the game on the billiard table, but we must
both be on guard against the world outside the billiard
room. My nose,' he tapped it, 'tells me so.'

Kerim's stomach made an indignant noise like a
forgotten telephone receiver with an angry caller on the
other end. 'There,' he said solicitously. 'What did I say?
We must go and eat.'

They finished their dinner as the train pulled into the
hideous modern junction of Thessaloniki. With Bond
carrying the heavy little bag, they went back down the
train and parted for the night. 'We shall soon be disturbed again,' warned Kerim. 'There is the frontier at
one o'clock. The Greeks will be no trouble, but those
Yugoslavs like waking up anyone who is travelling soft.
If they annoy you, send for me. Even in their country
there are some names I can mention. I am in the second
compartment in the next carriage. I have it to myself.
Tomorrow I will move into our friend Goldfarb's bed in
No. 12. For the time being, the first-class is an adequate
stable.'

Bond dozed wakefully as the train laboured up the
moonlit valley of the Vardar towards the instep of
Yugoslavia. Tatiana again slept with her head in his lap.
He thought of what Darko had said. He wondered if he
should not send the big man back to Istanbul when they
had got safely through Belgrade. It was not fair to drag
him across Europe on an adventure that was outside his
territory and with which he had little sympathy. Darko
obviously suspected that Bond had become infatuated
with the girl and wasn't seeing the operation straight
any more. Well, there was a grain of truth in that. It
would certainly be safer to get off the train and take
another route home. But, Bond admitted to himself, he
couldn't bear the idea of running away from the plot, if
it was a plot. If it wasn't, he equally couldn't bear the
idea of sacrificing the three more days with Tatiana.
And M. had left the decision to him. As Darko had said,
M. also was curious to see the game through. Perversely, M. too wanted to see what this whole rigmarole
was about. Bond dismissed the problem. The journey

was going well. Once again, why panic?

Ten minutes after they had arrived at the Greek frontier station of Idomeni there was a hasty knocking on the door. It woke the girl. Bond slipped from under her head. He put his ear to the door. 'Yes?'

'*Le conducteur, Monsieur.* There has been an accident. Your friend Kerim Bey.'

'Wait,' said Bond fiercely. He fitted the Beretta into its holster and put on his coat. He tore open the door.

'What is it?'

The conductor's face was yellow under the corridor light. 'Come.' He ran down the corridor towards the first-class.

Officials were clustered round the open door of the second compartment. They were standing, staring.

The conductor made a path for Bond. Bond reached the door and looked in.

The hair stirred softly on the head. Along the right-hand seat were two bodies. They were frozen in a ghastly death-struggle that might have been posed for a film.

Underneath was Kerim, his knees up in a last effort to rise. The taped hilt of a dagger protruded from his neck near the jugular vein. His head was thrust back and the empty blood-shot eyes stared up at the light. The mouth was contorted into a snarl. A thin trickle of blood ran down the chin.

Half on top of him sprawled the heavy body of the M.G.B. man called Benz, locked there by Kerim's left arm round his neck. Bond could see a corner of the Stalin moustache and the side of a blackened face. Kerim's right arm lay across the man's back, almost casually. The hand ended in a closed fist and the knob of a knife-hilt, and there was a wide stain on the coat under the hand.

Bond listened to his imagination. It was like watching a film. The sleeping Darko, the man slipping quietly through the door, the two steps forward and the swift stroke at the jugular. Then the last violent spasm of the dying man as he flung up an arm and clutched his murderer to him and plunged the knife down towards the fifth rib.

This wonderful man who had carried the sun with him. Now he was extinguished, totally dead.

Bond turned brusquely and walked out of sight of the man who had died for him.

He began, carefully, non-committally, to answer questions.

CHAPTER 24

Out of Danger?

The Orient Express steamed slowly into Belgrade at three o'clock in the afternoon, half an hour late. There would be an eight hours' delay while the other section of the train came in through the Iron Curtain from Bulgaria.

Bond looked out at the crowds and waited for the knock on the door that would be Kerim's man. Tatiana sat huddled in her sable coat beside the door, watching Bond, wondering if he would come back to her.

She had seen it all from the window—the long wicker baskets being brought to the train, the flash of the police photographer's bulbs, the gesticulating *chef de train* trying to hurry up the formalities, and the tall figure of James Bond, straight and hard and cold as a butcher's knife, coming and going.

Bond had come back and had sat looking at her. He had asked sharp, brutal questions. She had fought desperately back, sticking coldly to her story, knowing that now, if she told him everything, told him for in-

205

stance that SMERSH was involved, she would certainly lose him for ever.

Now she sat and was afraid, afraid of the web in which she was caught, afraid of what might have been behind the lies she had been told in Moscow—above all afraid that she might lose this man who had suddenly become the light in her life.

There was a knock on the door. Bond got up and opened it. A tough cheerful india-rubbery man, with Kerim's blue eyes and a mop of tangled fair hair above a brown face, exploded into the compartment.

'Stefan Trempo at your service,' the big smile embraced them both. 'They call me "Tempo". Where is the Chef?'

'Sit down,' said Bond. He thought to himself, I know it. This is another of Darko's sons.

The man looked sharply at them both. He sat down carefully between them. His face was extinguished. Now the bright eyes stared at Bond with a terrible intensity in which there was fear and suspicion. His right hand slipped casually into the pocket of his coat.

When Bond had finished, the man stood up. He didn't ask any questions. He said, 'Thank you, sir. Will you come, please. We will go to my apartment. There is much to be done.' He walked into the corridor and stood with his back to them, looking out across the rails. When the girl came out he walked down the corridor without looking back. Bond followed the girl, carrying the heavy bag and his little attaché case.

They walked down the platform and into the station square. It had started to drizzle. The scene, with its sprinkling of battered taxis and vista of dull modern buildings, was depressing. The man opened the rear door of a shabby Morris Oxford saloon. He got in front and took the wheel. They bumped their way over the cobbles and on to a slippery tarmac boulevard and drove for a quarter of an hour through wide, empty streets. They saw few pedestrians and not more than a handful of other cars.

They stopped half way down a cobbled side-street.

Tempo led them through a wide apartment-house door and up two flights of stairs that had the smell of the Balkans—the smell of very old sweat and cigarette smoke and cabbage. He unlocked a door and showed them into a two-roomed flat with nondescript furniture and heavy red plush curtains drawn back to show the blank windows on the other side of the street. On a sideboard stood a tray with several unopened bottles, glasses and plates of fruit and biscuits—the welcome to Darko and to Darko's friends.

Tempo waved vaguely towards the drinks. 'Please, sir, make yourself and Madam at home. There is a bathroom. No doubt you would both like to have a bath. If you will excuse me, I must telephone!' The hard façade of the face was about to crumble. The man went quickly into the bedroom and shut the door behind him.

There followed two empty hours during which Bond sat and looked out of the window at the wall opposite. From time to time he got up and paced to and fro and then sat down again. For the first hour, Tatiana sat and pretended to look through a pile of magazines. Then she abruptly went into the bathroom and Bond vaguely heard water gushing into the bath.

At about 6 o'clock, Tempo came out of the bedroom. He told Bond that he was going out. 'There is food in the kitchen. I will return at nine and take you to the train. Please treat my flat as your own.' Without waiting for Bond's reply, he walked out and softly shut the door. Bond heard his foot on the stairs and the click of the front door and the self-starter of the Morris.

Bond went into the bedroom and sat on the bed and picked up the telephone and talked in German to the long-distance exchange.

Half an hour later there was the quiet voice of M.

Bond spoke as a travelling salesman would speak to the managing director of Universal Export. He said that his partner had gone very sick. Were there any fresh instructions?

'Very sick?'

'Yes, sir, very.'

'How about the other firm?'

'There were three with us, sir. One of them caught the same thing. The other two didn't feel well on the way out of Turkey. They left us at Uzunkopru—that's the frontier.'

'So the other firm's packed up?'

Bond could see M.'s face as he sifted the information. He wondered if the fan was slowly revolving in the ceiling, if M. had a pipe in his hand, if the Chief of Staff was listening on the other wire.

'What are your ideas? Would you and your wife like to take another way home?'

'I'd rather you decided, sir. My wife's all right. The sample's in good condition. I don't see why it should deteriorate. I'm still keen to finish the trip. Otherwise it'll remain virgin territory. We shan't know what the possibilities are.'

'Would you like one of our other salesmen to give you a hand?'

'It shouldn't be necessary, sir. Just as you feel.'

'I'll think about it. So you really want to see this sales campaign through?'

Bond could see M.'s eyes glittering with the same perverse curiosity, the same rage to know, as he himself felt. 'Yes, sir. Now that I'm half way, it seems a pity not to cover the whole route.'

'All right then. I'll think about giving you another salesman to lend a hand.' There was a pause on the end of the line. 'Nothing else on your mind?'

'No, sir.'

'Goodbye, then.'

'Goodbye, sir.'

Bond put down the receiver. He sat and looked at it. He suddenly wished he had agreed with M.'s suggestion to give him reinforcements, just in case. He got up from the bed. At least they would soon be out of these damn Balkans and down into Italy. Then Switzerland, France —among friendly people, away from the furtive lands.

And the girl, what about her? Could he blame her for the death of Kerim? Bond went into the next room and stood by the window, looking out, wondering, going back over everything, every expression and every gesture she had made since he had first heard her voice on that night in the Kristal Palas. No, he knew he couldn't put the blame on her. If she was an agent, she was an unconscious agent. There wasn't a girl of her age in the world who could have played this role, if it was a role she was playing, without betraying herself. And he liked her. And he had faith in his instincts. Besides, with the death of Kerim, had not the plot, whatever it was, played itself out? One day he would find out what the plot had been. For the moment he was certain. Tatiana was not a conscious part of it.

His mind made up, Bond walked over to the bathroom door and knocked.

She came out and he took her in his arms and held her to him and kissed her. She clung to him. They stood and felt the animal warmth come back between them, feeling it push back the cold memory of Kerim's death.

Tatiana broke away. She looked up at Bond's face. She reached up and brushed the black comma of hair away from his forehead.

Her face was alive. 'I am glad you have come back, James,' she said. And then, matter-of-factly, 'And now we must eat and drink and start our lives again.'

Later, after Slivovic and smoked ham and peaches, Tempo came and took them to the station and to the waiting express under the hard lights of the arcs. He said goodbye, quickly and coldly, and vanished down the platform and back into his dark existence.

Punctually at nine the new engine gave its new kind of noise and took the long train out on its all-night run down the valley of the Sava. Bond went along to the conductor's cabin to give him money and look through the passports of the new passengers.

Bond knew most of the signs to look for in forged passports, the blurred writing, the too exact imprints of the rubber stamps, the trace of old gum round the edges of the photograph, the slight transparencies on the pages where the fibres of the paper had been tampered with to alter a letter or a number, but the five new passports—three American and two Swiss—seemed innocent. The Swiss papers, favourites with the Russian forgers, belonged to a husband and wife, both over seventy, and Bond finally passed them and went back to the compartment and prepared for another night with Tatiana's head on his lap.

Vincovci came and Brod and then, against a flaming dawn, the ugly sprawl of Zagreb. The train came to a stop between lines of rusting locomotives captured from the Germans and still standing forlornly amongst the grass and weeds on the sidings. Bond read the plate on one of them—BERLINER MASCHINENBAU GMBH—as they slid out through the iron cemetery. Its long black barrel had been raked with machine gun bullets. Bond heard the scream of the dive-bomber and saw the up-flung arms of the driver. For a moment he thought nostalgically and unreasonably of the excitement and turmoil of the hot war, compared with his own underground skirmishings since the war had turned cold.

They hammered into the mountains of Slovenia where the apple trees and the chalets were almost Austrian. The train laboured its way through Ljubliana. The girl awoke. They had breakfast of fried eggs and hard brown bread and coffee that was mostly chicory. The restaurant car was full of cheerful English and American tourists from the Adriatic coast, and Bond thought with a lift of the heart that by the afternoon they would be over the frontier into western Europe and that a third dangerous night was done.

He slept until Sezana. The hard-faced Yugoslav plainclothes men came on board. Then Yugoslavia was gone and Poggioreale came and the first smell of the soft life with the happy jabbering of Italian officials and the carefree upturned faces of the station crowd. The new diesel-electric engine gave a slap-happy whistle, the meadow of brown hands fluttered, and they were loping easily down into Venezia, towards the distant sparkle of Trieste and the gay blue of the Adriatic.

We've made it, thought Bond. I really think we've

made it. He thrust the memory of the last three days away from him. Tatiana saw the tense lines in his face relax. She reached over and took his hand. He moved and sat close beside her. They looked out at the gay villas on the Corniche and at the sailing-boats and the people water-skiing.

The train clanged across some points and slid quietly into the gleaming station of Trieste. Bond got up and pulled down the window and they stood side by side, looking out. Suddenly Bond felt happy. He put an arm around the girl's waist and held her hard against him.

They gazed down at the holiday crowd. The sun shone through the tall clean windows of the station in golden shafts. The sparkling scene emphasized the dark and dirt of the countries the train had come from, and Bond watched with an almost sensuous pleasure the gaily dressed people pass through the patches of sunshine towards the entrance, and the sunburned people, the ones who had had their holidays, hasten up the platform to get their seats on the train.

A shaft of sun lit up the head of one man who seemed typical of this happy, playtime world. The light flashed briefly on golden hair under a cap, and on a young golden moustache. There was plenty of time to catch the train. The man walked unhurriedly. It crossed Bond's mind that he was an Englishman. Perhaps it was the familiar shape of the dark green Kangol cap, or the beige, rather well-used macintosh, that badge of the English tourist, or it may have been the grey-flannelled legs, or the scuffed brown shoes. But Bond's eyes were drawn to him, as if it was someone he knew, as the man approached up the platform.

The man was carrying a battered Revelation suitcase and, under the other arm, a thick book and some newspapers. He looks like an athlete, thought Bond. He has the wide shoulders and the healthy, good-looking bronzed face of a professional tennis player going home after a round of foreign tournaments.

The man came nearer. Now he was looking straight at Bond. With recognition? Bond searched his mind. Did he know this man? No. He would have remembered those eyes that stared out so coldly under the pale lashes. They were opaque, almost dead. The eyes of a drowned man. But they had some message for him. What was it? Recognition? Warning? Or just the defensive reaction to Bond's own stare?

The man came up with the wagon-lit. His eyes were now gazing levelly up the train. He walked past, the crepe-soled shoes making no sound. Bond watched him reach for the rail and swing himself easily up the steps into the first-class carriage.

Suddenly Bond knew what the glance had meant, who the man was. Of course! This man was from the Service. After all M. had decided to send along an extra hand. That was the message of those queer eyes. Bond would bet anything that the man would soon be along to make contact.

How like M. to make absolutely sure!

CHAPTER 25

A Tie with a Windsor Knot

To make the contact easy, Bond went out and stood in the corridor. He ran over the details of the code of the day, the few harmless phrases, changed on the first of each month, that served as a simple recognition signal between English agents.

The train gave a jerk and moved slowly out into the sunshine. At the end of the corridor the communicating door slammed. There was no sound of steps, but suddenly the red and gold face was mirrored in the window.

'Excuse me. Could I borrow a match?'

'I use a lighter.' Bond produced his battered Ronson and handed it over.

'Better still.'

'Until they go wrong.'

Bond looked up into the man's face, expecting a smile at the completion of the childish 'Who goes there? Pass, Friend' ritual.

The thick lips writhed briefly. There was no light in the very pale blue eyes.

The man had taken off his macintosh. He was

wearing an old reddish-brown tweed coat with his flannel trousers, a pale yellow Viyella summer shirt, and the dark blue and maroon zig-zagged tie of the Royal Artillery. It was tied with a Windsor knot. Bond mistrusted anyone who tied his tie with a Windsor knot. It showed too much vanity. It was often the mark of a cad. Bond decided to forget his prejudice. A gold signet ring, with an indecipherable crest, glinted on the little finger of the right hand that gripped the guard rail. The corner of a red bandana handkerchief flopped out of the breast pocket of the man's coat. On his left wrist there was a battered silver wrist watch with an old leather strap.

Bond knew the type—a minor public school and then caught up by the war. Field Security perhaps. No idea what to do afterwards so he stayed with the occupation troops. At first he would have been with the military police, then, as the senior men drifted home, there came promotion into one of the security services. Moved to Trieste where he did well enough. Wanted to stay on and avoid the rigours of England. Probably had a girl friend, or had married an Italian. The Secret Service had needed a man for the small post that Trieste had become after the withdrawal. This man was available. They took him on. He would be doing routine jobs—have some low-grade sources in the Italian and Yugoslav police, and in their intelligence networks. A thousand a year. A good life, without much being expected from him. Then, out of the blue, this had come along. Must have been a shock getting one of those Most Immediate signals. He'd probably be a bit shy of Bond. Odd face. The eyes looked rather mad. But so they did in most of these men doing secret work abroad. One had to be a bit mad to take it on. Powerful chap, probably on the stupid side, but useful for this kind of guard work. M. had just taken the nearest man and told him to join the train.

All this went through Bond's mind as he photographed an impression of the man's clothes and general appearance. Now he said, 'Glad to see you. How did it happen?'

'Got a signal. Late last night. Personal from M. Shook me I can tell you, old man.'

Curious accent. What was it? A hint of brogue— cheap brogue. And something else Bond couldn't define. Probably came from living too long abroad and talking foreign languages all the time. And that dreadful 'old man' at the end. Shyness.

'Must have,' said Bond sympathetically. 'What did it say?'

'Just told me to get on the Orient this morning and contact a man and a girl in the through carriage. More or less described what you look like. Then I was to stick by you and see you both through to Gay Paree. That's all, old man.'

Was there defensiveness in the voice? Bond glanced sideways. The pale eyes swivelled to meet his. There was a quick red glare in them. It was as if the safety door of a furnace had swung open. The blaze died. The door to the inside of the man was banged shut. Now the eyes were opaque again—the eyes of an introvert, of a man who rarely looks out into the world but is for ever surveying the scene inside him.

There's madness there all right, thought Bond, startled by the sight of it. Shell-shock perhaps, or schizophrenia. Poor chap, with that magnificent body. One day he would certainly crack. The madness would take control. Bond had better have a word to Personnel. Check up on his medical. By the way, what was his name?

'Well I'm very glad to have you along. Probably not much for you to do. We started off with three Redland men on our tail. They've been got rid of, but there may be others on the train. Or some more may get on. And I've got to get this girl to London without trouble. If you'd just hang about. Tonight we'd better stay together and share watches. It's the last night and I don't want to take any chances. By the way, my name's

James Bond. Travelling as David Somerset. And that's Caroline Somerset in there.'

The man fished in his pocket and produced a battered notecase which seemed to contain plenty of money. He extracted a visiting card and handed it to Bond. It said 'Captain Norman Nash', and, in the left-hand bottom corner, 'Royal Automobile Club'.

As Bond put the card in his pocket he slipped his finger across it. It was engraved. 'Thanks,' he said. 'Well, Nash, come and meet Mrs. Somerset. No reason why we shouldn't travel more or less together.' He smiled encouragingly.

Again the red glare quickly extinguished. The lips writhed under the young golden moustache. 'Delighted, old man.'

Bond turned to the door and knocked softly and spoke his name.

The door opened. Bond beckoned Nash in and shut the door behind him.

The girl looked surprised.

'This is Captain Nash, Norman Nash. He's been told to keep an eye on us.'

'How do you do.' The hand came out hesitantly. The man touched it briefly. His stare was fixed. He said nothing. The girl gave an embarrassed little laugh, 'Won't you sit down?'

'Er, thank you.' Nash sat stiffly on the edge of the banquette. He seemed to remember something, something one did when one had nothing to say. He groped in the side pocket of his coat and produced a packet of Players. 'Will you have a, er, cigarette?' He prized open the top with a fairly clean thumbnail, stripped down the silver paper and pushed out the cigarettes. The girl took one. Nash's other hand flashed forward a lighter with the obsequious speed of a motor salesman.

Nash looked up. Bond was standing leaning against the door and wondering how to help this clumsy, embarrassed man. Nash held out the cigarettes and the

lighter as if he was offering glass beads to a native chief.
'What about you, old man?'

'Thanks,' said Bond. He hated Virginia tobacco, but
he was prepared to do anything to help put the man at
ease. He took a cigarette and lit it. They certainly had to
make do with some queer fish in the Service nowadays.
How the devil did this man manage to get along in the
semi-diplomatic society he would have to frequent in
Trieste?

Bond said lamely, 'You look very fit, Nash. Tennis?'

'Swimming.'

'Been long in Trieste?'

There came the brief red glare. 'About three years.'

'Interesting work?'

'Sometimes. You know how it is, old man.'

Bond wondered how he could stop Nash calling him
'old man'. He couldn't think of a way. Silence fell.

Nash obviously felt it was his turn again. He fished in
his pocket and produced a newspaper cutting. It was the
front page of the *Corriere de la Sera*. He handed it to
Bond. 'Seen this, old man?' The eyes blazed and died.

It was the front page lead. The thick black lettering
on the cheap newsprint was still wet. The headlines said:

TERRIBLE ESPLOSIONE IN ISTANBUL
UFFICIO SOVIETICO DISTRUTTO
TUTTI I PRESENTI UCCISI

Bond couldn't understand the rest. He folded the cutting and handed it back. How much did this man know?
Better treat him as a strong-arm man and nothing else.
'Bad show,' he said. 'Gas main I suppose.' Bond saw
again the obscene belly of the bomb hanging down from
the roof of the alcove in the tunnel, the wires that
started off down the damp wall on their way back to the
plunger in the drawer of Kerim's desk. Who had pressed
the plunger yesterday afternoon when Tempo had got
through? The 'Head Clerk'? Or had they drawn lots and
then stood round and watched as the hand went down

and the deep roar had gone up in the Street of Books on the hill above. They would all have been there in the cool room. With eyes that glittered with hate. The tears would be reserved for the night. Revenge would have come first. And the rats? How many thousand had been blasted down the tunnel? What time would it have been? About four o'clock. Had the daily meeting been on? Three dead in the room. How many more in the rest of the building? Friends of Tatiana, perhaps. He would have to keep the story from her. Had Darko been watching? From a window at Valhalla? Bond could hear the great laugh of triumph echoing round its walls. At any rate Kerim had taken plenty with him.

Nash was looking at him. 'Yes, I daresay it was a gas main,' he said without interest.

A hand-bell tinkled down the corridor, coming nearer. *'Deuxième Service. Deuxième Service. Prenez vos places, s'il vous plaît.'*

Bond looked across at Tatiana. Her face was pale. In her eyes there was an appeal to be saved from any more of this clumsy, non-*kulturny* man. Bond said, 'What about lunch?' She got up at once. 'What about you, Nash?'

Captain Nash was already on his feet. 'Had it, thanks, old man. And I'd like to have a look up and down the train. Is the conductor—you know . . .?' he made a gesture of fingering money.

'Oh yes, he'll co-operate all right,' said Bond. He reached up and pulled down the heavy little bag. He opened the door for Nash. 'See you later.'

Captain Nash stepped into the corridor. He said, 'Yes, I expect so, old man.' He turned left and strode off down the corridor, moving easily with the swaying of the train, his hands in his trouser pockets and the light blazing on the tight golden curls at the back of his head.

Bond followed Tatiana up the train. The carriages were crowded with holiday-makers going home. In the third-class corridors people sat on their bags chattering and munching at oranges and at hard-looking rolls with bits of Salami sticking out of them. The men carefully examined Tatiana as she squeezed by. The women looked appraisingly at Bond, wondering whether he made love to her well.

In the restaurant car, Bond ordered Americanos and a bottle of Chianti Broglio. The wonderful European hors d'oeuvres came. Tatiana began to look more cheerful.

'Funny sort of man,' Bond watched her pick about among the little dishes. 'But I'm glad he's come along. I'll have a chance to get some sleep. I'm going to sleep for a week when we get home.'

'I do not like him,' the girl said indifferently. 'He is not *kulturny*. I do not trust his eyes.'

Bond laughed. 'Nobody's *kulturny* enough for you.'

'Did you know him before?'

'No. But he belongs to my firm.'

'What did you say his name is?'

'Nash. Norman Nash.'

She spelled it out. 'N.A.S.H.? Like that?'

'Yes.'

The girl's eyes were puzzled. 'I suppose you know what that means in Russia. *Nash* means "ours". In our Services, a man is *nash* when he is one of "our" men. He is *svoi* when he is one of "theirs"—when he belongs to the enemy. And this man calls himself Nash. That is not pleasant.'

Bond laughed. 'Really, Tania. You do think of extraordinary reasons for not liking people. Nash is quite a common English name. He's perfectly harmless. At any rate he's tough enough for what we want him for.'

Tatiana made a face. She went on with her lunch.

Some *tagliatelli verdi* came, and the wine, and then a delicious escalope. 'Oh it is so good,' she said. 'Since I came out of Russia I am all stomach.' Her eyes widened. 'You won't let me get too fat, James. You won't let me get so fat that I am no use for making love? You will have to be careful, or I shall just eat all day long and sleep. You will beat me if I eat all day long and sleep. You will beat me if I eat too much?'

'Certainly I will beat you.'

Tatiana wrinkled her nose. He felt the soft caress of her ankles. The wide eyes looked at him hard. The lashes came down demurely. 'Please pay,' she said. 'I feel sleepy.'

The train was pulling into Maestre. There was the beginning of the canals. A cargo gondola full of vegetables was moving slowly along a straight sheet of water into the town.

'But we shall be coming into Venice in a minute,' protested Bond. 'Don't you want to see it?'

'It will be just another station. And I can see Venice another day. Now I want you to love me. Please, James.' Tatiana leaned forward. She put a hand over his. 'Give me what I want. There is so little time.'

Then it was the little room again and the smell of the sea coming through the half-open window and the drawn blind fluttering with the wind of the train. Again there were the two piles of clothes on the floor, and the two whispering bodies on the banquette, and the slow searching hands. And the love-knot formed, and, as the train jolted over the points into the echoing station of Venice, there came the final lost despairing cry.

Outside the vacuum of the tiny room there sounded a confusion of echoing calls and metallic clanging and shuffling footsteps that slowly faded into sleep.

Padua came, and Vicenza, and a fabulous sunset over Verona flickered gold and red through the cracks of the blind. Again the little bell came tinkling down the corridor. They woke. Bond dressed and went into the corridor and leant against the guard rail. He looked out at the fading pink light over the Lombardy Plain and thought of Tatiana and of the future.

Nash's face slid up alongside his in the dark glass. Nash came very close so that his elbow touched Bond's. 'I think I've spotted one of the oppo, old man,' he said softly.

Bond was not surprised. He had assumed that, if it came, it would come tonight. Almost indifferently he said, 'Who is he?'

'Don't know what his real name is, but he's been through Trieste once or twice. Something to do with Albania. May be the Resident Director there. Now he's on an American passport. "Wilbur Frank." Calls himself a banker. In No. 9, right next to you. I don't think I could be wrong about him, old man.'

Bond glanced at the eyes in the big brown face. Again the furnace door was ajar. The red glare shone out and was extinguished.

'Good thing you spotted him. This may be a tough night. You'd better stick by us from now on. We mustn't leave the girl alone.'

'That's what I thought, old man.'

They had dinner. It was a silent meal. Nash sat beside the girl and kept his eyes on his plate. He held his knife like a fountain pen and frequently wiped it on his fork. He was clumsy in his movements. Half way through the meal, he reached for the salt and knocked over Tatiana's glass of Chianti. He apologized profusely. He made a great show of calling for another glass and filling it.

Coffee came. Now it was Tatiana who was clumsy. She knocked over her cup. She had gone very pale and her breath was coming quickly.

'Tatiana!' Bond half rose to his feet. But it was Captain Nash who jumped up and took charge.

'Lady's come over queer,' he said shortly. 'Allow me.' He reached down and put an arm round the girl and lifted her to her feet. 'I'll take her back to the compartment. You'd better look after the bag. And there's the bill. I can take care of her till you come.'

'Is all right,' protested Tatiana with the slack lips of deepening unconsciousness. 'Don't worry, James, I lie down.' Her head lolled against Nash's shoulder. Nash put one thick arm round her waist and manoeuvred her quickly and efficiently down the crowded aisle and out of the restaurant car.

Bond impatiently snapped his fingers for the waiter. Poor darling. She must be dead beat. Why hadn't he thought of the strain she was going through? He cursed himself for his selfishness. Thank heavens for Nash. Efficient sort of chap, for all his uncouthness.

Bond paid the bill. He took up the heavy little bag and walked as quickly as he could down the crowded train.

He tapped softly on the door of No. 7. Nash opened the door. He came out with his finger on his lips. He closed the door behind him. 'Threw a bit of a faint,' he said. 'She's all right now. The beds were made up. She's gone to sleep in the top one. Been a bit much for the girl I expect, old man.'

Bond nodded briefly. He went into the compartment. A hand hung palely down from under the sable coat. Bond stood on the bottom bunk and gently tucked the hand under the corner of the coat. The hand felt very cold. The girl made no sound.

Bond stepped softly down. Better let her sleep. He went into the corridor.

Nash looked at him with empty eyes. 'Well, I suppose we'd better settle in for the night. I've got my book.' He held it up. *War and Peace.* Been trying to plough through it for years. You take the first sleep, old man. You look pretty flaked out yourself. I'll wake you up when I can't keep my eyes open any longer.' He gestured with his head at the door of No. 9. 'Hasn't shown yet. Don't suppose he will if he's up to any monkey tricks.' He paused. 'By the way, you got a gun, old man?'

'Yes. Why, haven't you?'

Nash looked apologetic. ' 'Fraid not. Got a Luger at home, but it's too bulky for this sort of job.'

'Oh, well, said Bond reluctantly. 'You'd better take mine. Come on in.'

They went in and Bond shut the door. He took out the Beretta and handed it over. 'Eight shots,' he said softly. 'Semi-automatic. It's on safe.'

Nash took the gun and weighed it professionally in his hand. He clicked the safe on and off.

Bond hated someone else touching his gun. He felt naked without it. He said gruffly, 'Bit on the light side, but it'll kill if you put the bullets in the right places.'

Nash nodded. He sat down near the window at the end of the bottom bunk. 'I'll take this end,' he whispered. 'Good field of fire.' He put his book down on his lap and settled himself.

Bond took off his coat and tie and laid them on the bunk beside him. He leant back against the pillows and propped his feet on the bag with the Spektor that stood on the floor beside his attaché case. He picked up his Ambler and found his place and tried to read. After a few pages he found that his concentration was going. He was too tired. He laid the book down on his lap and closed his eyes. Could he afford to sleep? Was there any other precaution they could take?

The wedges! Bond felt for them in the pocket of his coat. He slipped off the bunk and knelt and forced them hard under the two doors. Then he settled himself again and switched off the reading light behind his head.

The violet eye of the nightlight shone softly down.

'Thanks, old man,' said Captain Nash softly.

The train gave a moan and crashed into a tunnel.

CHAPTER 26

The Killing Bottle

The light nudge at his ankle woke Bond. He didn't move. His senses came to life like an animal's.

Nothing had changed. There were the noises of the train—the soft iron stride, pounding out the kilometres, the quiet creak of the woodwork, a tinkle from the cupboard over the washbasin where a toothglass was loose in its holder.

What had woken him? The spectral eye of the nightlight cast its deep velvet sheen over the little room. No sound came from the upper bunk. By the window, Captain Nash sat in his place, his book open on his lap, a flicker of moonlight from the edge of the blind showing white on the double page.

He was looking fixed at Bond. Bond registered the intentness of the violet eyes. The black lips parted. There was a glint of teeth.

'Sorry to disturb you, old man. I feel in the mood for a talk!'

What was there new in the voice? Bond put his feet softly down to the floor. He sat up straighter. Danger, like a third man, was standing in the room.

'Fine,' said Bond easily. What had there been in those few words that had set his spine tingling? Was it the note of authority in Nash's voice? The idea came to Bond that Nash might have gone mad. Perhaps it was madness in the room, and not danger, that Bond could smell. His instincts about this man had been right. It would be a question of somehow getting rid of him at the next station. Where had they got to? When would the frontier come?

Bond lifted his wrist to look at the time. The violet light defeated the phosphorus numerals. Bond tilted the face towards the strip of moonlight from the window.

From the direction of Nash there came a sharp click. Bond felt a violent blow on his wrist. Splinters of glass hit him in the face. His arm was flung back against the door. He wondered if his wrist had been broken. He let his arm hang and flexed his fingers. They all moved.

The book was still open on Nash's lap, but now a thin wisp of smoke was coming out of the hole at the top of its spine and there was a faint smell of fireworks in the room.

The saliva dried in Bond's mouth as if he had swallowed alum.

So there had been a trap all along. And the trap had closed. Captain Nash had been sent to him by Moscow. Not by M. And the M.G.B. agent in No. 9, the man with an American passport, was a myth. And Bond had given Nash his gun. He had even put wedges under the doors so that Nash would feel more secure.

Bond shivered. Not with fear. With disgust.

Nash spoke. His voice was no longer a whisper, no longer oily. It was loud and confident.

'That will save us a great deal of argument, old man. Just a little demonstration. They think I'm pretty good with this little bag of tricks. There are ten bullets in it—.25 dum-dum, fired by an electric battery. You must admit the Russians are wonderful chaps for dreaming these things up. Too bad that book of yours is only for reading, old man.'

'For God's sake stop calling me "old man".' When there was so much to know, so much to think about, this was Bond's first reaction to utter catastrophe. It was the reaction of someone in a burning house who picks up the most trivial object to save from the flames.

'Sorry, old man. It's got to be a habit. Part of trying to be a bloody gentleman. Like these clothes. All from the wardrobe department. They said I'd get by like this. And I did, didn't I, old man? But let's get down to business. I expect you'd like to know what this is all about. Be glad to tell you. We've got about half an hour before you're due to go. It'll give me an extra kick telling the famous Mister Bond of the Secret Service what a bloody fool he is. You see, old man, you're not so good as you think. You're just a stuffed dummy and I've been given the job of letting the sawdust out of you.' The voice was even and flat, the sentences trailing away on a dead note. It was as if Nash was bored by the act of speaking.

'Yes,' said Bond. 'I'd like to know what it's all about. I can spare you half an hour.' Desperately he wondered: was there any way of putting this man off his stride? Upsetting his balance?

'Don't kid yourself, old man,' the voice was uninterested in Bond, or in the threat of Bond. Bond didn't exist except as a target. 'You're going to die in half an hour. No mistake about it. I've never made a mistake or I wouldn't have my job.'

'What is your job?'

'Chief Executioner of SMERSH.' There was a hint of life in the voice, a hint of pride. The voice went flat again. 'You know the name I believe, old man.'

SMERSH. So that was the answer—the worst answer of all. And this was their chief killer. Bond remembered the red glare that flickered in the opaque eyes. A killer. A psychopath—manic depressive, probably. A man who really enjoyed it. What a useful man for SMERSH to have found! Bond suddenly remembered what Vavra had said. He tried a long shot. 'Does the moon have any effect on you, Nash?'

The black lips writhed. 'Clever aren't you, Mister Secret Service. Think I'm barmy. Don't worry. I wouldn't be where I am if I was barmy.'

The angry sneer in the man's voice told Bond that he had touched a nerve. But what could he achieve by getting the man out of control? Better humour him and gain some time. Perhaps Tatiana. . . .

'Where does the girl come into all this?'

'Part of the bait,' the voice was bored again. 'Don't worry. She won't butt in on our talk. Fed her a pinch of chloral hydrate when I poured her that glass of wine. She'll be out for the night. And then for every other night. She's to go with you.'

'Oh really.' Bond slowly lifted his aching hand on to his lap, flexing the fingers to get the blood moving. 'Well, let's hear the story.'

'Careful, old man. No tricks. No Bulldog Drummond stuff'll get you out of this one. If I don't like even the smell of a move, it'll be just one bullet through the heart. Nothing more. That's what you'll be getting in the end. One through the centre of the heart. If you move it'll come a bit quicker. And don't forget who I am. Remember your wrist watch? I don't miss. Not ever.'

'Good show,' said Bond carelessly. 'But don't be frightened. You've got my gun. Remember? Get on with your story.'

'All right, old man, only don't scratch your ear while I'm talking. Or I'll shoot it off. See? Well, SMERSH decided to kill you—at least I gather it was decided even higher up, right at the top. Seems they want to take one good hard poke at the Secret Service—bring them down a peg or two. Follow me?'

'Why choose *me*?'

'Don't ask me, old man. But they say you've got quite a reputation in your outfit. The way you're going to be killed is going to bust up the whole show. It's been three months cooking, this plan, and it's a beaut. Got to be. SMERSH has made one or two mistakes lately. That Khoklov business for one. Remember the explosive cigarette case and all that? Gave the job to the wrong man. Should have given it to me. I wouldn't have gone over to the Yanks. However, to get back. You see, old man, we've got quite a planner in SMERSH. Man called Kronsteen. Great chess player. He said vanity would get you and greed and a bit of craziness in the plot. He said you'd fall for the craziness in London. And you did, didn't you, old man?'

Had they? Bond remembered just how much the eccentric angles of the story had aroused their curiosity. And vanity? Yes, he had to admit that the idea of this Russian girl being in love with him had helped. And there had been the Spektor. That had decided the whole thing—plain greed for it. He said non-committally: 'We were interested.'

'Then came the operation. Our Head of Operations is quite a character. I'd say she's killed more people than anyone in the world—or arranged for them to be killed. Yes, it's a woman. Name of Klebb—Rosa Klebb. Real swine of a woman. But she certainly knows all the tricks.'

Rosa Klebb. So at the top of SMERSH there was a woman! If he could somehow survive this and get after her! The fingers of Bond's right hand curled softly.

The flat voice in the corner went on: 'Well, she found this Romanova girl. Trained her for the job. By the way, how was she in bed? Pretty good?'

No! Bond didn't believe it. That first night must have been staged. But afterwards? No. Afterwards had been real. He took the opportunity to shrug his shoulders. It was an exaggerated shrug. To get the man accustomed to movement.

'Oh, well. Not interested in that sort of thing myself. But they got some nice pictures of you two.' Nash tapped his coat pocket. 'Whole reel of 16 millimetre. That's going into her handbag. It'll look fine in the papers.' Nash laughed—a harsh, metallic laugh. 'They'll have to cut some of the juiciest bits, of course.'

The change of rooms at the hotel. The honeymoon suite. The big mirror behind the bed. How well it all fitted! Bond felt his hands wet with perspiration. He wiped them down his trousers.

'Steady, old man. You nearly got it then. I told you not to move, remember?'

Bond put his hands back on the book in his lap. How much could he develop these small movements? How far could he go? 'Get on with the story,' he said. 'Did the girl know these pictures were being taken? Did she know SMERSH was involved in all this?'

Nash snorted. 'Of course she didn't know about the pictures. Rosa didn't trust her a yard. Too emotional. But I don't know much about that side. We all worked in compartments. I'd never seen her until today. I only know what I picked up. Yes, of course the girl knew she was working for SMERSH. She was told she had to get to London and do a bit of spying there.'

The silly idiot, thought Bond. Why the hell hadn't she told him that SMERSH was involved? She must have been frightened even to speak the name. Thought he would have her locked up or something. She had always said she would tell him everything when she got to England. That he must have faith and not be afraid. Faith! When she hadn't the foggiest idea herself what was going on. Oh, well. Poor child. She had been as fooled as he had been. But any hint would have been enough—would have saved the life of Kerim, for instance. And what about hers and his own?

'Then this Turk of yours had to be got rid of. I gather that took a bit of doing. Tough nut. I suppose it was his gang that blew up our Centre in Istanbul yesterday afternoon. That's going to create a bit of panic.'

'Too bad.'

'Doesn't worry me, old man. My end of the job's going to be easy.' Nash took a quick glance at his wrist watch. 'In about twenty minutes we go into the Simplon tunnel. That's where they want it done. More drama for the papers. One bullet for you. As we go into the tunnel. Just one in the heart. The noise of the tunnel will help in case you're a noisy dier—rattle and so forth. Then one in the back of the neck for her—with your gun—and out of the window she goes. Then one more for you with your gun. With your fingers wrapped round it, of course. Plenty of powder on your shirt. Suicide. That's what it'll look like at first. But there'll be two bullets in your heart. That'll come out later. More mystery! Search the Simplon again. Who was the man with the fair hair? They'll find the film in her bag, and in your pocket there'll be a long love letter from her to you—a bit threatening. It's a good one, SMERSH wrote it. It says that she'll give the film to the newspapers unless you marry her. That you promised to marry her if she stole the Spektor . . .' Nash paused and added in parentheses, 'As a matter of fact, old man, the Spektor's booby-trapped. When your cipher experts start fiddling with it, it's going to blow them all to glory. Not a bad dividend on the side.' Nash chuckled dully. 'And then the letter says that all she's got to offer you is the machine and her body—and all about her body and what you did with it. Hot stuff, that part! Right? So what's the story in the papers—the Left Wing ones that will be tipped off to meet the train? Old man, the story's got everything. Orient Express. Beautiful Russian spy murdered in Simplon tunnel. Filthy pictures. Secret cipher machine. Handsome British spy with career ruined murders her and commits suicide. Sex, spies, luxury train, Mr. and Mrs. Somerset . . .! Old man, it'll run for months! Talk of the Khoklov case! This'll knock spote off it. And what a poke in the eye for the famous Intelligence Service! Their best man, the famous James Bond. What a shambles. Then bang goes the cipher machine! What's your chief going to think of you? What's the public going to think? And the Government. And the Americans? Talk about security! No more atom secrets from the Yanks.' Nash paused to let it all sink in. With a touch of pride he said, 'Old man, this is going to be the story of the century!'

Yes, thought Bond. Yes. He was certainly right about that. The French papers would give it such a send-off there'd be no stopping it. They wouldn't mind how far they went with the pictures or anything else. There wasn't a press in the world that wouldn't pick it up. And the Spektor! Would M.'s people or the Deuxième have the sense to guess it was booby-trapped? How many of the best cryptographers in the West would go up with it? God, he must get out of this jam! But how?

The top of Nash's *War and Peace* yawned at him. Let's see. There would be the roar as the train went into the tunnel. Then at once the muffled click and the bullet. Bond's eyes stared into the violet gloom, measuring the depth of the shadow in his corner under the roof of the top bunk, remembering exactly where his attaché case stood on the floor, guessing what Nash would do after he had fired.

Bond said: 'You took a bit of a gamble on my letting you team up at Trieste. And how did you know the code of the month?'

Nash said patiently, 'You don't seem to get the picture, old man. SMERSH is good—really good. There's nothing better. We know your code of the month for every year. If anyone in your show noticed these things, noticed the pattern of them, like my show does, you'd realize that every January you lose one of your small chaps somewhere—maybe Tokyo, maybe Timbuctoo. SMERSH just picks one and takes him. Then they screw the code for the year out of him. Anything else he knows, of course. But it's the code they're after. Then it's passed round to Centres. Simple as falling off a log, old man.'

Bond dug his nails into the palms of his hands.

'As for picking you up at Trieste, old man, I didn't. Rode down with you—in the front of the train. Got out as we stopped and walked back up the platform. You see, old man, we were waiting for you in Belgrade. Knew you'd call your Chief—or the Embassy or someone. Been listening in on that Yugoslav's telephone for weeks. Pity we didn't understand the codeword he shot through to Istanbul. Might have stopped the firework display, or anyway saved our chaps. But the main target was you, old man, and we certainly had you sewn up all right. You were in the killing bottle from the minute you got off that plane in Turkey. It was only a question of when to stuff the cork in.' Nash took another quick glance at his watch. He looked up. His grinning teeth glistened violet. 'Pretty soon now, old man. It's just cork-hour minus fifteen.'

Bond thought: we knew SMERSH was good, but we never knew they were as good as this. The knowledge was vital. Somehow he must get it back. He must. Bond's mind raced round the details of his pitifully thin, pitifully desperate plan.

He said: 'SMERSH seems to have thought things out pretty well. Must have taken a lot of trouble. There's only one thing . . .' Bond let his voice hang in the air.

'What's that, old man?' Nash, thinking of his report, was alert.

The train began to slow down. Domodossola. The Italian frontier. What about customs? But Bond remembered. There were no formalities for the through carriages until they got to France, to the frontier, Vallorbes. Even then not for the sleeping cars. These expresses cut straight across Switzerland. It was only people who got out at Brigue or Lausanne who had to go through customs in the stations.

'Well, come on, old man.' Nash sounded hooked.

'Not without a cigarette.'

'Okay. Go ahead. But if there's a move I don't like, you'll be dead.'

Bond slipped his right hand into his hip-pocket. He drew out his broad gunmetal cigarette case. Opened it. Took out a cigarette. Took his lighter out of his trouser pocket. Lit the cigarette and put the lighter back. He left the cigarette case on his lap beside the book. He put his left hand casually over the book and the cigarette case as if to prevent them slipping off his lap. He puffed away at his cigarette. If only it had been a trick one— magnesium flare, or anything he could throw in the man's face! If only his Service went in for those explosive toys! But at least he had achieved his objective and hadn't been shot in the process. That was a start.

'You see.' Bond described an airy circle with his

cigarette to distract Nash's attention. His left hand slipped the flat cigarette case between the pages of his book. 'You see, it looks all right, but what about you? What are you going to do after we come out of the Simplon? The conductor knows you're mixed up with us. They'll be after you in a flash.'

'Oh that,' Nash's voice was bored again. 'You don't seem to have hoisted in that the Russians think these things out. I get off at Dijon and take a car to Paris. I get lost there. A bit of "Third Man" stuff won't do the story any harm. Anyway it'll come out later when they dig the second bullet out of you and can't find the second gun. They won't catch up with me. Matter of fact, I've got a date at noon tomorrow—Room 204 at the Ritz Hotel, making my report to Rosa. She wants to get the kudos for this job. Then I turn into her chauffeur and we drive to Berlin. Come to think of it, old man,' the flat voice showed emotion, became greedy, 'I think she may have the Order of Lenin for me in her bag. Lovely grub, as they say.'

The train began to move. Bond tensed. In a few minutes it would come. What a way to die, if he was going to die. Through his own stupidity—blind, lethal stupidity. And lethal for Tatiana. Christ! At any moment he could have done something to dodge this shambles. There had been no lack of opportunity. But conceit and curiosity and four days of love had sucked him along on the easy stream down which it had been planned that he should drift. That was the damnable part of the whole business—the triumph for SMERSH, the one enemy he had always sworn to defeat wherever he met it. We will do this, and he will do that. 'Comrades,, it is easy with a vain fool like this Bond. Watch him take the bait. You will see. I tell you he's a fool. All Englishmen are fools.' And Tatiana, the lure—the darling lure. Bond thought of their first night. The black stockings and the velvet ribbon. And all the time SMERSH had been watching, watching him go through his conceited paces, as it had been planned that he would, so that the smear could be built up—the smear on the Service that lived on the myth of its name. God, what a mess! If only . . . if only his tiny grain of a plan might work!

Ahead, the rumble of the train became a deep boom.

A few more seconds. A few more yards.

The oval mouth between the white pages seemed to gape wider. In a second the dark tunnel would switch out the moonlight on the pages and the blue tongue would lick out for him.

'Sweet dreams, you English bastard.'

The rumble became a great swift clanging roar.

The spine of the book bloomed flame.

The bullet, homing on Bond's heart, flashed over its two quiet yards.

Bond pitched forward to the floor and lay sprawled under the funereal violet light.

CHAPTER 27

Ten Pints of Blood

It had all depended on the man's accuracy. Nash had said that Bond would get one bullet through the heart. Bond had taken the gamble that Nash's aim was as good as he said it was. And it had been.

Bond lay like a dead man lies. Before the bullet, he had recalled the corpses he had seen—how their bodies had looked in death. Now he lay totally collapsed, like a broken doll, his arms and legs carefully outflung.

He explored his sensations. Where the bullet had crashed into the book, his ribs were on fire. The bullet must have gone through the cigarette case and then through the other half of the book. He could feel the hot lead over his heart. It felt as if it was burning inside his ribs. It was only a sharp pain in his head where it had hit the woodwork, and the violet sheen on the scuffed toecaps against his nose, that said he wasn't dead.

Like an archaeologist, Bond explored the carefully planned ruin of his body. The position of the sprawled feet. The angle of the half-bent knee that would give purchase when it was needed. The right hand that seemed to be clawing at his pierced heart, was within inches, when he could release the book, of the little attaché case—within inches of the lateral stitching that held the flat-bladed throwing-knives, two edged and sharp as razors, that he had mocked when Q Branch had demonstrated the catch that held them. And his left hand, outflung in the surrender of death, rested on the floor and would provide upward leverage when the moment came.

Above him there sounded a long, cavernous yawn. The brown toecaps shifted. Bond watched the shoe-leather strain as Nash stood up. In a minute, with Bond's gun in his right hand, Nash would climb on to the bottom bunk and reach up and feel through the curtain of hair for the base of the girl's neck. Then the snout of the Beretta would nuzzle in after the probing fingers, Nash would press the trigger. The roar of the train would cover the muffled boom.

It would be a near thing. Bond desperately tried to remember simple anatomy. Where were the mortal places in the lower body of a man? Where did the main artery run? The Femoral. Down the inside of the thigh. And the External Iliac, or whatever it was called, that became the Femoral? Across the centre of the groin. If he missed both, it would be bad. Bond had no illusions about being able to beat this terrific man in unarmed combat. The first violent stab of his knife had to be decisive.

The brown toecaps moved. They pointed towards the bunk. What was the man doing? There was no sound except the hollow iron clang as the great train tore through the Simplon—through the heart of the Wasenhorn and Monte Leone. The toothglass tinkled. The woodwork creaked comfortably. For a hundred yards on both sides of the little death cell rows of people were sleeping, or lying awake, thinking of their lives and loves, making little plans, wondering who would meet them at the Gare de Lyon. And, all the while, just along the corridor, death was riding with them down the same dark hole, behind the same great Diesel, on the same hot rails.

One brown shoe left the floor. It would have stepped half across Bond. The vulnerable arch would be open above Bond's head.

Bond's muscles coiled like a snake's. His right hand flickered a few centimetres to the hard stitching on the edge of the case. Pressed sideways. Felt the narrow shaft of the knife. Drew it softly half way out without moving his arm.

The brown heel lifted off the ground. The toe bent and took the weight.

Now the second foot had gone.

Softly move the weight here, take the purchase there, grasp the knife hard so that it wouldn't turn on a bone, and then . . .

In one violent corkscrew of motion, Bond's body twisted up from the floor. The knife flashed.

The fist with the long steel finger, and all Bond's arm and shoulder behind it, lunged upwards. Bond's knuckles felt flannel. He held the knife in, forcing it further.

A ghastly wailing cry came down to him. The Beretta clattered to the floor. Then the knife was wrenched from Bond's hand as the man gave a convulsive twist and crashed down.

Bond had planned for the fall, but, as he sidestepped towards the window, a flailing hand caught him and sent him thudding on to the lower bunk. Before he could recover himself, up from the floor rose the terrible face, its eyes shining violet, the violet teeth bared. Slowly, agonizingly, the two huge hands groped for him.

Bond, half on his back, kicked out blindly. His shoe connected; but then his foot was held and twisted and he felt himself slipping downwards.

Bond's fingers scrabbled for a hold in the stuff of the bunk. Now the other hand had him by the thigh. Nails dug into him.

Bond's body was being twisted and pulled down. Soon the teeth would be at him. Bond hammered out with his free leg. It made no difference. He was going.

Suddenly Bond's scrabbling fingers felt something hard. The book! How did one work the thing? Which way up was it? Would it shoot him or Nash? Desperately Bond held it out towards the great sweating face. He pressed at the base of the cloth spine.

'Click!' Bond felt the recoil. 'Click-click-click-click.' Now Bond felt the heat under his fingers. The hands on his legs were going limp. The glistening face was drawing back. A noise came from the throat, a terrible gurgling noise. Then, with a slither and a crack, the body fell forward on to the floor and the head crashed back against the woodwork.

Bond lay and panted through clenched teeth. He stared up at the violet light above the door. He noticed that the loop of the filament waxed and waned. It crossed his mind that the dynamo under the carriage must be defective. He blinked his eyes to focus the light more closely. The sweat ran into them and stung. He lay still, doing nothing about it.

The galloping boom of the train began to change. It sounded hollower. With a final echoing roar, the Orient Express sped out into the moonlight and slackened speed.

Bond lazily reached up and pulled at the edge of the blind. He saw warehouses and sidings. Lights shone brightly, cleanly on the rails. Good, powerful lights. The lights of Switzerland.

The train slid quietly to a stop.

In the steady, singing silence, a small noise came from the floor. Bond cursed himself for not having made certain. He quickly bent down, listening. He held the book forward at the ready, just in case. No movement. Bond reached and felt for the jugular vein. No pulse. The man was quite dead. The corpse had been settling.

Bond sat back and waited impatiently for the train to move again. There was a lot to be done. Even before he could see to Tatiana, there would have to be the cleaning up.

With a jerk the long express started softly rolling. Soon the train would be slaloming fast down through the foothills of the Alps into the Canton Valais. Already there was a new sound in the wheels—a hurrying lilt, as if they were glad the tunnel was past.

Bond got to his feet and stepped over the sprawling legs of the dead man and turned on the top light.

What a shambles! The place looked like a butcher's shop. How much blood did a body contain? He remembered. Ten pints. Well, it would soon all be there. As long as it didn't spread into the passage! Bond stripped the bed-clothes off the bottom bunk and set to work.

At last the job was done—the walls swabbed down around the covered bulk on the floor, the suitcases piled ready for the getaway at Dijon.

Bond drank down a whole carafe of water. Then he stepped up and gently shook the shoulder of fur.

There was no response. Had the man lied? Had he killed her with the poison?

Bond thrust his hand in against her neck. It was warm. Bond felt for the lobe of an ear and pinched it hard. The girl stirred sluggishly and moaned. Again Bond pinched the ear, and again. At last a muffled voice said, 'Don't.'

Bond smiled. He shook her. He went on shaking until Tatiana slowly turned over on her side. Two doped blue eyes gazed into his and closed again. 'What is it?' The voice was sleepily angry.

Bond talked to her and bullied her and cursed her. He shook her more roughly. At last she sat up. She gazed vacantly at him. Bond pulled her legs out so that they hung down over the edge. Somehow he manhandled her down on to the bottom bunk.

Tatiana looked terrible—the slack mouth, the upturned, sleep-drunk eyes, the tangle of damp hair. Bond got to work with a wet towel and her comb.

Lausanne came and, an hour later, the French frontier at Vallorbes. Bond left Tatiana and went out and

stood in the corridor, just in case. But the customs and
passport men brushed past him to the conductor's
cabin, and, after five inscrutable minutes, went on
down the train.

Bond stepped back into the compartment. Tatiana
was asleep again. Bond looked at Nash's watch, which
was now on his own wrist. 4.30. Another hour to Dijon.
Bond set to work.

At last Tatiana's eyes opened wide. Her pupils were
more or less centred. She said, 'Stop it now, James.' She
closed her eyes again. Bond wiped the sweat off his face.
He took the bags, one by one, to the end of the corridor
and piled them against the exit. Then he went along to
the conductor and told him that Madame was not well
and that they would be leaving the train at Dijon.

Bond gave the conductor a final tip. 'Do not derange
yourself,' he said. 'I have taken the luggage out so as
not to disturb Madame. My friend, the one with fair
hair, is a doctor. He has been sitting up with us all night.
I have put him to sleep in my bunk. The man was
exhausted. It would be kind not to waken him until ten
minutes before Paris.'

'Certainement, Monsieur.' The conductor had not
been showered with money like this since the good days
of travelling millionaires. He handed over Bond's
passport and tickets. The train began to slacken speed.
'Voilà que nous y sommes.'

Bond went back to the compartment. He dragged
Tatiana to her feet and out into the corridor and shut
the door on the white pile of death beside the bunk.

At last they were down the steps and on to the hard,
wonderful, motionless platform. A blue-smocked
porter took their luggage.

The sun was beginning to rise. At that hour of the
morning there were very few passengers awake. Only a
handful in the third class, who had ridden 'hard'
through the night, saw a young man help a young girl
away from the dusty carriage with the romantic names
on its side towards the drab door that said 'SORTIE'.

CHAPTER 28

La Tricoteuse

The taxi drew up at the Rue Cambon entrance to the Ritz Hotel.

Bond looked at Nash's watch. 11.45. He must be dead punctual. He knew that if a Russian spy was even a few minutes early or late for a rendezvous the rendezvous was automatically cancelled. He paid off the taxi and went through the door on the left that leads into the Ritz bar.

Bond ordered a double vodka martini. He drank it half down. He felt wonderful. Suddenly the last four days, and particularly last night, were washed off the calendar. Now he was on his own, having his private adventure. All his duties had been taken care of. The girl was sleeping in a bedroom at the Embassy. The Spektor, still pregnant with explosive, had been taken away by the bomb-disposal squad of the Deuxième Bureau. He had spoken to his old friend René Mathis, now head of the Deuxième, and the concierge at the Cambon entrance to the Ritz had been told to give him a pass-key and to ask no questions.

René had been delighted to find himself again involved with Bond in *une affaire noire.* 'Have confidence, *cher* James,' he had said. 'I will execute your mysteries. You can tell me the story afterwards. Two laundry-men with a large laundry basket will come to Room 204 at 12.15. I shall accompany them dressed as the driver of their *camion.* We are to fill the laundry basket and take it to Orly and await an R.A.F. Canberra which will arrive at two o'clock. We hand over the basket. Some dirty washing which was in France will be in England. Yes?'

Head of Station F had spoken to M. on the scrambler. He had passed over a short written report from Bond. He had asked for the Canberra. No, he had no idea what it was for. Bond had only shown up to deliver the girl and the Spektor. He had eaten a huge breakfast and had left the Embassy saying he would be back after lunch.

Bond looked again at the time. He finished his martini. He paid for it and walked out of the bar and up the steps to the concierge's lodge.

The concierge looked sharply at him and handed over a key. Bond walked over to the lift and got in and went up to the third floor.

The lift door clanged behind him. Bond walked softly down the corridor, looking at the numbers.

204. Bond put his right hand inside his coat and on to the taped butt of the Beretta. It was tucked into the waistband of his trousers. He could feel the metal of the silencer warm across his stomach.

He knocked once with his left hand.

'Come in.'

It was a quavering voice. An old woman's voice.

Bond tried the handle of the door. It was unlocked. He slipped the pass-key into his coat-pocket. He pushed the door open with one swift motion and stepped in and shut it behind him.

It was a typical Ritz sitting-room, extremely elegant, with good Empire furniture. The walls were white and the curtains and chair covers were of a small patterned chintz of red roses on white. The carpet was wine-red and close-fitted.

In a pool of sunshine, in a low armed chair beside a Directoire writing desk, a little old woman sat knitting.

The tinkle of the steel needles continued. The eyes behind light-blue tinted bi-focals examined Bond with polite curiosity.

'Oui, Monsieur?' The voice was deep and hoarse. The thickly powdered, rather puffy face under the white hair showed nothing but well-bred interest.

Bond's hand on the gun under his coat was taut as a steel spring. His half-closed eyes flickered around the room and back to the little old woman in the chair.

Had he made a mistake? Was this the wrong room? Should he apologize and get out? Could this woman possibly belong to SMERSH? She looked so exactly like the sort of respectable rich widow one would expect to find sitting by herself in the Ritz, whiling the time away with her knitting. The sort of woman who would have her own table, and her favourite waiter, in a corner of the restaurant downstairs—not, of course, the grill room. The sort of woman who would doze after lunch and then be fetched by an elegant black limousine with white side-walled tyres and be driven to the tearoom in the rue de Berri to meet some other rich crone. The old-fashioned black dress with the touch of lace at the throat and wrists, the thin gold chain that hung down over the shapeless bosom and ended in a folding lorgnette, the neat little feet in the sensible black-buttoned boots that barely touched the floor. It couldn't be Klebb! Bond had got the number of the room wrong. He could feel the perspiration under his arms. But now he would have to play the scene through.

'My name is Bond, James Bond.'

'And I, Monsieur, am the Comtesse Metterstein. What can I do for you?' The French was rather thick. She might be German Swiss. The needles tinkled busily.

'I am afraid Captain Nash has met with an accident.

He won't be coming today. So I came instead.'

Did the eyes narrow a fraction behind the pale blue spectacles?

'I have not the pleasure of the Captain's acquaintance, Monsieur. Nor of yours. Please sit down and state your business.' The woman inclined her head an inch towards the high-backed chair beside the writing desk.

One couldn't fault her. The graciousness of it all was devastating. Bond walked across the room and sat down. Now he was about six feet away from her. The desk held nothing but a tall old-fashioned telephone with a receiver on a hook, and, within reach of her hand, an ivory-buttoned bellpush. The black mouth of the telephone yawned at Bond politely.

Bond stared rudely into the woman's face, examining it. It was an ugly face, toadlike, under the powder and under the tight cottage-loaf of white hair. The eyes were so light brown as to be almost yellow. The pale lips were wet and blubbery below the fringe of nicotine-stained moustache. Nicotine? Where were her cigarettes? There was no ashtray—no smell of smoke in the room.

Bond's hand tightened again on his gun. He glanced down at the bag of knitting, at the shapeless length of small-denier beige wool the woman was working on. The steel needles. What was there odd about them? The ends were discoloured as if they had been held in fire. Did knitting needles ever look like that?

'Eh bien, Monsieur?' Was there an edge to the voice? Had she read something in his face?

Bond smiled. His muscles were tense, wating for any movement, any trick. 'It's no use,' he said cheerfully, gambling. 'You are Rosa Klebb. And you are Head of Otdyel II of SMERSH. You are a torturer and a murderer. You wanted to kill me and the Romanov girl. I am very glad to meet you at last.'

The eyes had not changed. The harsh voice was patient and polite. The woman reached out her left hand towards the bellpush. 'Monsieur, I am afraid you are deranged. I must ring for the *valet de chambre* and have you shown to the door.'

Bond never knew what saved his life. Perhaps it was the flash of realization that no wires led from the bellpush to the wall or into the carpet. Perhaps it was the sudden memory of the English 'Come in' when the expected knock came on the door. But, as her finger reached the ivory knob, he hurled himself sideways out of the chair.

As Bond hit the ground there was a sharp noise of tearing calico. Splinters from the back of his chair sprayed around him. The chair crashed to the floor.

Bond twisted over, tugging at his gun. Out of the corner of his eye he noticed a curl of blue smoke coming from the mouth of the 'telephone'. Then the woman was on him, the knitting needles glinting in her clenched fists.

She stabbed downwards at his legs. Bond lashed out with his feet and hurled her sideways. She had aimed at his legs! As he got to one knee, Bond knew what the coloured tips of the needles meant. It was poison. Probably one of those German nerve poisons. All she had to do was scratch him, even through his clothes.

Bond was on his feet. She was coming at him again. He tugged furiously at his gun. The silencer had caught. There was a flash of light. Bond dodged. One of the needles rattled against the wall behind him and the dreadful chunk of woman, the white bun of wig askew on her head, the slimy lips drawn back from her teeth, was on top of him.

Bond, not daring to use his naked fists against the needles, vaulted sideways over the desk.

Panting and talking to herself in Russian, Rosa Klebb scuttled round the desk, the remaining needle held forward like a rapier. Bond backed away, working at the stuck gun. The back of his legs came against a small chair. He let go the gun and reached behind him and snatched it up. Holding it by the back, with its legs pointing like horns, he went round the desk to meet her.

But she was beside the bogus telephone. She swept it up and aimed it. Her hand went to the button. Bond leapt forward. He crashed the chair down. Bullets sprayed into the ceiling and plaster pattered down on his head.

Bond lunged again. The legs of the chair clutched the woman round the waist and over her shoulders. God she was strong! She gave way, but only to the wall. There she held her ground, spitting at Bond over the top of the chair, while the knitting needle quested towards him like a long scorpion's sting.

Bond stood back a little, holding the chair at arms' length. He took aim and high-kicked at the probing wrist. The needle sailed away into the room and pinged down behind him.

Bond came in closer. He examined the position. Yes, the woman was held firmly against the wall by the four legs of the chair. There was no way she could get out of the cage except by brute force. Her arms and legs and head were free, but the body was pinned to the wall.

The woman hissed something in Russia. She spat at him over the chair. Bond bent his head and wiped his face against his sleeve. He looked up and into the mottled face.

'That's all, Rosa,' he said. 'The Deuxième will be here in a minute. In an hour or so you'll be in London. You won't be seen leaving the hotel. You won't be seen going into England. In fact very few people will see you again. From now on you're just a number on a secret file. By the time we've finished with you you'll be ready for the lunatic asylum.

The face, a few feet away, was changing. Now the blood had drained out of it, and it was yellow. But not, thought Bond, with fear. The pale eyes looked levelly into his. They were not defeated.

The wet, shapeless mouth lengthened in a grin.

'And where will you be when I am in the asylum, Mister Bond?'

'Oh, getting on with my life.'

'I think not, *Angliski spion*.'

Bond hardly noticed the words. He had heard the

click of the door opening. A burst of laughter came from the room behind him.

'*Eh bien,*' it was the voice of delight that Bond remembered so well. 'The 70th position! Now, at last, I have seen everything. And invented by an Englishman! James, this really is an insult to my countrymen.'

'I don't recommend it,' said Bond over his shoulder. 'It's too strenuous. Anyway, you can take over now. I'll introduce you. Her name's Rosa. You'll like her. She's a big noise in SMERSH—she looks after the murdering, as a matter of fact.'

Mathis came up. There were two laundry-men with him. The three of them stood and looked respectfully into the dreadful face.

'Rosa,' said Mathis thoughtfully. 'But, this time, a Rosa Malheur. Well, well! But I am sure she is uncomfortable in that position. You two, bring along the *panier de fleurs*—she will be more comfortable lying down.'

The two men walked to the door. Bond heard the creak of the laundry basket.

The woman's eyes were still locked in Bond's. She moved a little, shifting her weight. Out of Bond's sight, and not noticed by Mathis, who was still examining her face, the toe of one shiny buttoned boot pressed under the instep of the other. From the point of its toe there slid forward half an inch of thin knife blade. Like the knitting needles, the steel had a dirty bluish tinge.

The two men came up and put the big square basket down beside Mathis.

'Take her,' said Mathis. He bowed slightly to the woman. 'It has been an honour.'

'*Au revoir*, Rosa,' said Bond.

The yellow eyes blazed briefly.

'Farewell, Mister Bond.'

The boot, with its tiny steel tongue, flashed out.

Bond felt a sharp pain in his right calf. It was only the sort of pain you would get from a kick. He flinched and stepped back. The two men seized Rosa Klebb by the arms.

Mathis laughed. 'My poor James,' he said. 'Count on SMERSH to have the last word.'

The tongue of dirty steel had withdrawn into the leather. Now it was only a harmless bundle of old woman that was being lifted into the basket.

Mathis watched the lid being secured. He turned to Bond. 'It is a good day's work you have done, my friend,' he said. 'But you look tired. Go back to the Embassy and have a rest because this evening we must have dinner together. The best dinner in Paris. And I will find the loveliest girl to go with it.'

Numbness was creeping up Bond's body. He felt very cold. He lifted his hand to brush back the comma of hair over his right eyebrow. There was no feeling in his fingers. They seemed as big as cucumbers. His hand fell heavily to his side.

Breathing became difficult. Bond sighed to the depth of his lungs. He clenched his jaws and half closed his eyes, as people do when they want to hide their drunkenness.

Through his eyelashes he watched the basket being carried to the door. He prized his eyes open. Desperately he focused Mathis.

'I shan't need a girl, René,' he said thickly.

Now he had to gasp for breath. Again his hand moved up towards his cold face. He had an impression of Mathis starting towards him.

Bond felt his knees begin to buckle.

He said, or thought he said, 'I've already got the loveliest . . .'

Bond pivoted slowly on his heel and crashed headlong to the wine-red floor.